THE IRON SHIP

First published 2015 by Solaris
an imprint of Rebellion Publishing Ltd,
Riverside House, Osney Mead,
Oxford, OX2 0ES, UK

www.solarisbooks.com

ISBN: 978 1 78108 350 5

10 9 8 7 6 5 4 3 2 1

A CIP catalogue record for this book is available
from the British Library.

Designed & typeset by Rebellion Publishing

Printed in the US

The
IRON
SHIP

*The **GATES** of the **WORLD** Book One*

K. M. McKINLEY

SOLARIS

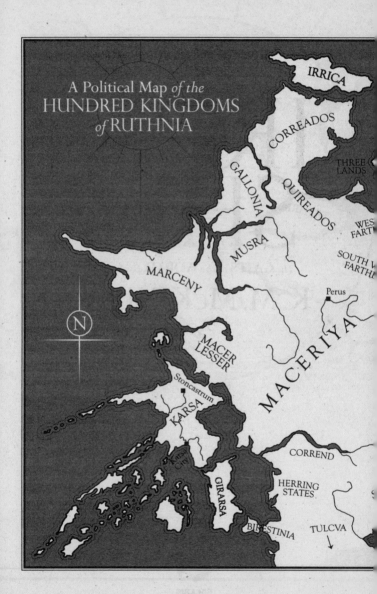

A Political Map *of the*
HUNDRED KINGDOMS
of RUTHNIA

IRRICA

CORREADOS

THREE
LANDS

GALLONIA

QUIREADOS

WES
FART

MUSRA

SOUTH W
FARTHI

MARCENY

Perus

MACER
LESSER

MACERIYA

Stoncastrum

KARSA

Katsa
City

CORREND

GIRARSA

HERRING
STATES

BIRESTINIA

TULCVA

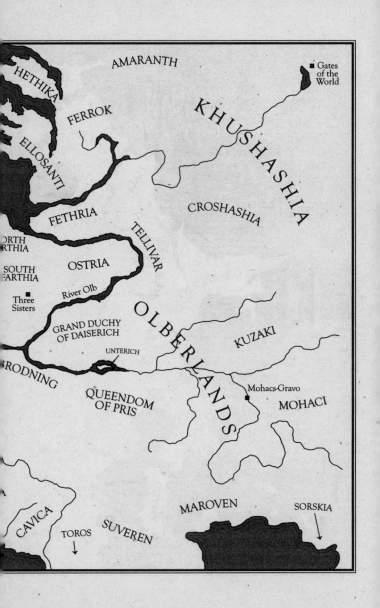

PROLOGUE

BETWEEN THE LANDS of the Hundred Kingdoms and the senescent empire of Ocerzerkiya lay the Red Expanse. A desert of convoluted stone and fine, shifting sand, it had proved insurmountable in all the long ages of men upon the world. Out on the brilliant sea, generations of sailors passed by on floatstone ships, but though they passed within bowshot of the cliffs, the interior remained a mystery to them. A place of death. The Skull Coast, the sailors called it.

To their wisdom they turned their backs, for the land's face deceived. On the clifftops plants grew in great abundance, flower fields telling lies of water, of which there was none, for the plants teased moisture from the sea mists with thorny fingers. There was not the meanest stream for a hundred leagues. The rare fruits of the bushes were poisonous. Rangy beasts hunted this maquis, and stranger things still clambered ashore with the fogs to gorge upon them. Besides, any fool could see from the landward edge—for only fools approached it—that the thickets gave out quickly. Within a mile of the cliff edge the verdant strip stopped. Beyond it sand grains whispered over each other with no root nor branch to constrain them for hundreds of miles.

On the ocean side a sea chasm fronted the Red Expanse, so deep that only the drying of the seas would reveal the cliffs' feet, whose red stone stretched from northern horizon to southern without break. Not a cove or a strand dented them. There was nowhere to land should any captain have been foolhardy enough to wish to do so. None were; the Red Expanse was a deadly land of harsh beauty and manifold dangers.

But it had not always been so.

Wind caressed worn stones that lay in lines of unnatural straightness, if only there were human eyes present to see. Sand ran into depressions that would have revealed themselves as stone lined channels if only they had been asked. Tussocks of razored grass grew upon tumbled masonry. The gridded remains of rooms hid beneath the thorns. Surfaces of roads, wider and finer than any in the Hundred, lay concealed beneath shrouds of gravel.

And there were other, stranger things. Obelisks of volcanic glass. Machine skeletons of rustless metal large enough to rival the Brodning Colossi. Riven temples of cyclopean scale and peculiar geometries tucked forgotten into dry canyons. Nothing there was whole. All was broken in times so incomprehensibly distant they had passed from myth.

In the gymnasia of Perus, philosophs, sophists, magi and magisters crawled toward an understanding of the history of the world, and yet they were in ignorance of this trove of relics upon the Hundred's northern border. There were a few bold visionaries, eccentric figures, that maintained that the Red Expanse was not as it appeared. But they were ridiculed, and those who ventured there to prove their case never returned. The greedy eyes of archaeologists remained intent on different soil.

So it was that the existence of the Iron Fane remained secret, along with all the other secrets jealously hoarded by the sand.

A LONE FIGURE, robed head to foot in heavy red cloth, trekked through ungentle fields. Her face was shrouded against biting flies. Her feet and legs were wrapped tightly. Even so, her robes and wrappings were cut through to the skin by thorn and grass. The heat was punishing, she was burdened; her robes were wet with her sweat. In her left hand she carried a tall staff of black wood that she did not require to walk. Under her right arm was a large book, onerously heavy, bound in cloth matching that of her costume. She had carried it a long way. The sun was at her back, merciless already this early in the morning. To her left a field of flowers bobbed in a hot wind, white petals blinking over yellow hearts. They climbed a slope that ended abruptly in cobalt blue sky. There was no slope on the far side. A sheer drop a thousand feet straight to the sea waited there. She could not hear the waves.

To the right of her path the flowers persisted for a dozen yards, giving way to a scant margin of wiry grass two yards wide. Past that, the sands of the interior took hold. The slope of the hill high over the path saw a rallying of vegetation, a band where the fogs curled back on themselves and reared defiantly, before they were defeated once and for all by the desert. On the other side the Red Expanse took on the aspect most assumed of it; trackless, sandy, gnarled with brooding crags. A red desert on one hand, a blue one on the other, a thin ribbon of green to divide them. At the centre of the ribbon, a path. At the end of the path, the Iron Fane.

She was the fane's lone pilgrim, and its only priestess. Adamanka Shrane was her name.

Close to her journey's end, Shrane walked quickly. Her legs bled from dozens of shallow cuts. Sand chafed the delicate spaces between her toes. There were blisters on her heels. She put her hurts from her mind and hurried. She was nearly there.

The path curved around a rock face worn into strange contortions by the wind. Her heart leapt at this familiar landmark. Past the crag the path sloped down toward a low bluff. From her vantage she could see in the stone the entrance to the fane, visible as a rectangle of absolute blackness. A natural cave, squared by inhuman hands at the dawn of time, or so the book told her. Shrane had faith, and believed everything that was written in the book.

She walked faster, barely restraining herself from breaking into a run. There was no one to see, but there is a proper form to all things and that included her approach. Her heart quickened. The cave offered more than comfort and renewal, although she would find both within. It was a home from which she was exiled.

Steps with perfect square edges led to the door. Coolness enveloped her as she passed under its lintel. She stopped a moment to enjoy the absence of the sun.

She went inside.

A deep and placid pool filled a third of the cave. Tangled bones crowded the pool's brim and shone dully on its bed, for the water was death to anything but the faithful, and that meant in these sad times Shrane and Shrane alone. More animal bones, these neatly stacked in piles, stretched back into the gloom. A path led through these bone piles to a second doorway closed by a slab of black metal. That Shrane would open soon, and enter. But not yet.

Stepping toward the pool, her reflection came tentatively to greet her. Glimmer lights twinkled in the water, filling her hair with stars. She stared at herself a long while, at the wrinkles and the grey twists in her hair. How old she had become.

She unwrapped herself without haste. Thirst tortured her, but she must maintain her dignity. Her leg wrappings came away first, then her head scarf. She shucked off her outer robe. Each piece's removal had an accompanying prayer. This was duly voiced as she removed her vest and underwear, revealing coppery skin that, away from her lined face and hands, was still smooth. The robes had not saved her entirely from the sun, and she was patched with sunburn at the throat, face, hands and feet. She glanced over her shoulder at an echo deeper in the cave. There was something inhuman in the balance of her features. Her skin had an uncommon sheen to it. Her eyes glinted too brightly. A briefly impressed unease to those who saw her. When they looked again, she was a woman in her middle years, tired and travelworn. No less and no more.

She shut her eyes, held her arms out wide, palms forward. Speaking prayers she had learned as a child, she stepped into the water. Circular ripples painted themselves in light on the ceiling as her body broke the surface.

A little gasp escaped her. The cold soothed her injured feet, killed the burn in her skin. The sensation brought a smile to her lips, but she did not cease her prayer. She continued down the steps until the water reached her chin, then ducked her head under it. The still surface of the pool slid closed over her head, and she was gone among the bones.

Seconds passed. She burst back through the surface. Her eyes snapped open in an unlined face. She opened her mouth wide and shouted, showing white, young teeth. She ran her hands over her hair newly dark, cupped firm breasts and shivered. She licked at the water running from her face, salty with her sweat. She took a deep breath, ducked and emerged again, then sucked at the water's surface directly. The cracks in her lips closed. The blisters on her feet shrank. The last wrinkles smoothed themselves from her skin.

The first ritual done, she laughed with pleasure and bathed leisurely in the pool.

When Shrane stepped out she was refreshed and cleansed and renewed. The scratches on her legs had closed. Her other wounds had likewise disappeared. All signs of hurt and exhaustion had departed her, for she had grown young. She gazed a long time at herself in pleasure. Moving more easily now, she chose a rib bone from the skeleton of a hyena on the edge of the pool and took it to the cairn nearest the water, her cairn. Carefully selecting a spot, she slid the rib home. In this way she honoured the creatures whose lives had been stolen so that she might restore hers. There were over one hundred bones in her cairn. She remembered placing every one. A few more visits to the pool and it would be as large and dense as those of her mothers', centuries dead. This troubled her. The pool's effects did not work forever, and every journey brought the possibility it would be her last.

Shrane washed her clothes, took them outside and left them to dry on rocks away from the cave mouth. The heat on her skin made her shudder, but her delight was born of higher emotion, the joy all religious feel upon experiencing the divine.

She returned to the cave still unclad. There she took up her staff and book, wrapped tightly in its cloth. She waited a moment for her eyes to readjust to the darkness before approaching the black door.

There was a small cavity in the stone in front of the door. Into this she slid the ferrule at the base of her staff. The near-silent click of it going home echoed through the cave. She twisted it in her hand and muttered certain ancient words no one understood. The plain wood warmed in her hand. Patterns of firelight turned around it. Firefly motes spun in the air.

The water of the pool rippled. The door drew back into the wall, a squealing groan of metal boomed through the cave. The air beyond was colder than that of the outer cave and smelled so strongly of iron it tasted of blood. Shrane's breath plumed, and she went forward unhesitatingly.

Stairs wound down into a grotto. The walls were rippled by rock formations laid down in wetter days, and beyond the carved steps the cave had been left as nature made it.

The glow of Shrane's staff sent the rock forms into flickering life. Once this had unnerved her. No longer.

She rounded the final curve in the stair, and the light of her staff fell upon an artefact alien to the stone; a statue, ten feet tall and massive across the shoulders. Anthropoid in shape, it depicted no man. The arms were too long, the legs too widely set, the head blocky and disproportionate. What features it once possessed were mysterious, scabbed over with flakes of rust, but there was a suggestion of a jutting jaw and brow. Orange oxides streaked the floor on which it stood. Four-fingered hands were clenched in fists. It stood in a half crouch, as if it had attempted to rise at great cost in effort only to fail, the head bowed in final defeat. She did not know how old the statue was. The contents of the book she carried were thirty centuries old, the statue and rituals it described were older. The book gave no date for the statue's creation.

Shrane slotted her staff into a hole in the floor. By the patterned light of its magic, she put the book before the statue, knelt, and bowed her head like the statue's. In this posture of obeisance, she unwrapped the book.

The original book was written in the waning days of Old Maceriya. Her predecessor, her mother, told her what she had was a copy of a copy of a copy of a copy of a copy. Pages of fine vellum bound in soft leather, each illuminated with designs that disturbed the eye, and dense with esoteric diagrams.

One day, she would choose her successor. Only she was permitted to read it until then. Some of the oldest passages told that the Iron Priestess had once been one of many, and that men had come here also. There was no portentous myth written in the book that told her, but there were many odd things gathered together between its covers. She had gleaned this impression from the prescriptions for rituals no longer observed, and from dry financial records of gifts to a church no one remembered. Whatever the truth of it, her creed had always been a secretive one. For generations there had only been a handful of adherents, then a few, then one. Adamanka Shrane was the last.

She whispered words awkward as pebbles in her mouth. She ran her fingertips over the seventy-four relevant pages in the book. Once done, she drew a small flint knife from the book's spine and cut her left forefinger tip with it. A perfect bead of dark blood welled there. Glints of yellow sparkled in it. Not all of it was light reflected from her staff.

"I am the iron wife. I await your return," she said as she stood, careful to keep her finger elevated in front of her. "As my mothers waited, so I wait. In my blood flows your blood. Blood calls to blood. I wait." She smeared blood on the statue as high as she could reach, below the sternum. "Lords of ancient ages, usurped masters, titans betrayed by gods, I honour you. I await you." A stain barely perceptible lingered a moment on the corroded surface. Was it gone into the metal, or did her eyes trick her and did the powdery oxide coating the statue simply suck the wetness from it? She had never decided. She brought her forefinger to her mouth, and licked off the mixture of blood and rust that stained it.

She concluded her rites and genuflected to the statue. She had performed the ritual one hundred times before, and its actions came to her automatically. She came here trembling with excitement, her eagerness building with every step she took north toward the Red Expanse, but once the ritual was begun her ardour dimmed. Long living in hope, she no longer believed it was her who would receive the sign. For years she had watched the statue for hours after the rite. Latterly she had concluded her task without conscious thought and gone from the fane quickly.

She flipped through the book to the pages toward the end. Hundreds of tally boxes filled the last third of the book, fifty to a page, each stamped with a bloody fingerprint. Ten pages from the end she found the next empty box and pressed her finger down hard onto it, leaving a smeared oval of blood. She blew upon it until it had dried, and shut the book. The hollows of the statue's eyes glowered down at her in silence. The sense of divine immanence that energised her upon her journey inevitably gave way to disappointment. Her god did not show himself. He never did.

She felt the cold of the cave now. The staff's light faded. She wondered how long this could go on. One of her successors would die unexpectedly, or give up. It was a certainty. A matter of time.

Eager to depart before her staff-glow went out, she hurried for the steps. The last light was dimming to an ember glow when a scrape troubled the cave. Metal upon metal, sly in the thickening dark.

Shrane spun on her heel. Her eyes narrowed as she peered into the rapidly dimming cave. She saw better than most in the dark, but the night under the earth cannot be pierced by mortal eyes no matter how keen. A slam of her staff on the floor made it flare brightly once more. To do so caused knots in her stomach and the grip of age to tighten on the bones within her youthful-seeming skin. Such power as hers was limited, and dearly paid for.

Her heart pounded. Her neck throbbed with the strength of her pulse. Her throat thickened. "Has the one arrived whom I await?" The ritual question; one she thought she would never ask.

The statue remained still. The flickering glow of her staff picked out hard lines and previously unseen details. She saw shapes in it she had not seen before. Did its form appear sharper? It had not moved.

Her long years of vigilance had not prepared her for this. Fear tainted her exultation.

"Have you come? Have you finally come?" she asked, abandoning the cant as she approached.

She looked up into its great and formless face. "Am I no longer alone?" she whispered. She held her breath. Nothing. Her shoulders slumped. She took a step backwards. Something crunched under her heel. She lifted her foot. A flake of rust as big as her hand lay in three pieces, broken by her tread. A sick feeling of sacrilege welled up in her. This could only have come from the statue. It had fallen, that was what caused the noise. Her disappointment redoubled.

A tremendous grinding hit her. She staggered back, ears ringing. A wash of heat boiled off the statue. Rust flakes exploded off it as it moved, singeing her skin. She screamed. The statue juddered into life, standing tall over her as it attained its full height. Coals burned deep in hollow sockets. The statue lifted its fist before its face, arms shaking with effort, shedding rust. The hand burst open, a violent flower, more rust pattering from it. The metal beneath gleamed. It stared at its fingers and worked them wonderingly, a creature given fingers which had never before had them, but somehow remembered their possession.

"You have come!" Shrane cried, and dropped to her knees.

The statue's head swivelled, predator-swift. To a screeching of metal it stepped forward off its plinth.

"Utelemek carramon ite delik!" It moved oddly, suddenly, without the smooth, careless delicacy of the human body, as if every movement were considered before being precisely actioned and abruptly halted when complete.

Old words, like those in the book. Shrane had never heard them spoken but for her own voice and that of her instructress. The statue spoke them differently, without her clumsy, laboured pronunciation.

"I, I do not understand. I..." said Shrane. She bowed low, frightened.

"Utelemek carramon ite delik!" The voice became insistent. Angry. Intense heat from the thing hit her like a blow. The skin cracked, uncovering untarnished metal that shone with a dull maroon glow.

"You have returned, now tell me what I must do!"

"Utelemek carramon ite delik!" It stretched out a hand to Shrane. The hand burned forge-hot, going from red to amber. Her staff flared as bright with magical sympathy. It seared her hand, and she dropped it with a scream.

The statue's hand came close to her face. If it touched her it would surely kill her. She wanted to run, but could not. Its forefinger uncurled. Her skin blistered as it drew close. She was screaming in agony before it touched her. When it did, she believed it to be the end. Pain drew itself as a steel band about her head, and tightened mercilessly.

"Know now," the statue said. "And go."

There was a bang. A smell of glimmer hit by iron. Shrane fell with great weight and heat atop her.

She awoke some time later. The thin light leaking into the cave from outside had taken on the grey of evening. The statue was over her, leaning in like a lover, supported on one hand. The fire in its eyes had gone. The metal was cold but clean, the form of god revealed.

She was burned all over. Her skin was a mess of blisters and sores. The worst pain came from the wound upon her forehead where it had touched her. It throbbed with a sickening warmth.

From the pain came knowledge. She knew what she had to do.

She kept the agony at bay with thoughts of the pool waiting at the top of the stairs. She prayed to her reawakened god that it still possessed the power to heal her. The journey to the pool was endless, but there was joy in her heart that grew with every agonising step.

After dozens of lifetimes of waiting, it had been her that had received the sign.

CHAPTER ONE
The Haunted Marsh

"'As you gaze on where I lie, have a care, you too shall die.'"

Aarin Kressind moved so that his good eye was better positioned, and reread the words. The grave marker was exiled from the burial grounds atop the cliffs, half hidden by the wooden stair of the Path of the Dead. A commemoration for a criminal, the inscription was worn by time and weather and barely legible. A stylised face of a man, described entirely by arcs and circles, gaped at the top of the stone, staring out to distant sea in dismay.

That was the resting place referred to; not the cliffside, but the ocean, the ultimate home of the dispossessed and the criminal. Aarin wondered who the marker had been raised for, and if their ghost still roamed the marshes.

Aarin looked back up the greyed wood of the Path. If he held his hands boxed so, either side of his face— hands that were smooth and inkstained yet strong—he could shut out the city. Karsa did not encroach on the Path of the Dead. Through his hands he was looking back a hundred years to a time before Karsa had swollen with self-importance and burst its guts all around the county. He saw the Path of the Dead as it had been for a thousand years. A notch in the cliff edge closed by black iron gates leading down from the plateau, turning the instant it crossed the edge to lead down smooth, treacherous rock to the top of the wooden stair. The land around the steps was free of the spires and roof ridges that crowded the sky both left and right. Once all the dead of Karsa City had been brought this way and on out to the Black Isle. No longer. That lone and dismal outpost of the cliffs in the marsh had become choked with bones two centuries ago. Cemeteries lined the route to the head of the path, a plot in one of those was the best a man could hope for.

Aarin's moment of reflection passed. His irritation overcame him.

"Pasquanty! Move yourself!" he yelled upwards.

His deacon's reply was reedy with distance and broken by the wind, but his fear was unmistakeable. "Coming, Guider Kressind!" The stairs vibrated quicker with his tread.

The ledge broke the precipitous descent in two. Black rock stretched down six hundred feet to the marshes. The stairs were rickety, grey wood pinned to the cliffs by rusty iron. Aarin would have to report their condition to the Order. This was not fitting. The living forgot the dead at their peril.

On both sides of the path, Karsa City spilled over the brinks of the cliffs as if pushed. A static avalanche of shacks teetered over the marsh. Wood and sheet metal huts held in place by braced diagonal beams and optimistic cantilevers, connected by bridges and walkways woven from equal parts rope and hope. The shanty extended eighteen fathoms down and stopped in an abrupt line. The high water mark was still some eight hundred feet below the bottommost shacks, but it was not the vagaries of the tides that discouraged people from building lower.

Ordure streaked black rock and wood. Privy holes opened in the underside of the buildings directly onto the roofs of their neighbours. Between the shanties the sewage of the upper city spewed from modern culverts piercing the cliffs. All part of Per Allian's plan to clean up the capital. No thought had been given to the marshes. It appeared neither Allian nor his sponsor Prince Alfra cared for them or their sanctity. Aarin seethed at it. The slums were a disgrace. Every time he came here it was worse.

The sewer's rank bounty supported its own indelicate web of life. Gulls screeched in wheeling formation, fighting the unpredictable gusts deflected from the cliff face to return to their roosts. By day they feasted on the crabs and worms and other things that gorged on Karsa's shit. Thousands—tens of thousands, some said—plagued the new cliff edge districts in aerial hordes, worse off to the north where the Slot climbed down to the sea. There the city proper tumbled eagerly about the locks, coming as far as the high watermark one hundred yards above the marsh. There were clouds over the tight streets of the Slot and the Locksides, dark and thick in resolute defiance of the wind. Hard to tell from that distance if it was smog or yet more of the blasted gulls.

There were no gulls over the Path of the Dead, their cries were always distant. There was a war on in cliff-edge Karsa, unofficial but earnest nonetheless, between the gulls and the people. Each side regarded the other as trespassers on their territory, but the stair was kept out of it. That was for the dead.

Aarin was one of a very few with a key to the gates, and therefore had little fear for the height, the path or the haunted marsh it crossed.

Aarin was a tall man, heavily built around the shoulders if gangly in the limbs. One eye was a milk-white orb crossed by a ragged scar. Despite this disfigurement he was handsome if seldom smiling. He wore robes of green and gold under his weather-beaten cleric's coat. His hair, a mix of his father's red and mother's sandy tresses, was in the stark Guider's style, shaved all over but for the front part of his skull. Further signifiers to his vocation were the rings he wore, and the chain about his neck of linked, stylised skulls. Anyone who set eyes upon him, living or dead, would be immediately aware of his calling as a minister to the deceased.

If that did not prove informative enough, then his companions surely were.

The twins were some three dozen yards back and upwards, between Aarin and Pasquanty. The chest they carried was heavy, but the twins, neither twins nor any longer alive, lacked the capacity to feel discomfort at bearing its weight or to complain about it. They marched onto the ledge, and stopped before the priest. One had been a pale-skinned Karsan, the other a darker northerner, though both had become somewhat grey in death. Their dead eyes rolled ceaselessly, seeing nothing, oblivious to the dread of the place.

Pasquanty came next. Aarin's deacon was a habitually anxious man, and so he was very afraid. He glanced at the sky fearfully as he stepped onto the ledge. Evening was coming. Light was draining from the sky surely as water runs from a tipped basin. The horizon blushed pink over the distant ocean. Above the cliffs the clouds were purple, and brooded sullenly at their bruising.

"You will not delay the coming of dark by checking its progress every half minute, deacon," said Aarin irritably. "I am not by nature a vicious man, Pasquanty, but your nervousness is testing me. Remember what you are!"

"I... I am sorry, Guider Kressind." Pasquanty's Karsarin had a slight accent, that of Corrend. His apology did not stop him from anxiously checking the sky once again.

"Do stop that! We have nothing to fear, you or I. We will pass unharmed."

"But the spectres, Guider Kressind. The roaming ones, the..."

"There is nothing to fear from them either, if you are wise. Be wise! And stop looking at the sky! It will be dark soon, do you need to know the exact moment that dusk comes? Take a care or you'll fall."

Pasquanty had a pair of large eyes whose soulfulness was somewhat undone by their watery nature and the mountain of a nose that divided them. Pasquanty's blink was unusually expressive, indeed, all his facial configurations were as melodramatic as those of a mime. No one was ever in any doubt as to how Pasquanty felt. At that moment, he broadcast misery. This endless play of emotion was one of the many factors that provoked Aarin's irritation.

"I am sure that you do it on purpose," said Aarin.

"What, Guider Kressind?" said Pasquanty.

"Being confused! Your face displays your innermost thoughts, plain as the words on a broadsheet. The appearance of this expression on you, Pasquanty, is not, alas, uncommon."

"I am sorry, Guider Kressind."

"As you said! Come on!" Aarin was habitually close-mouthed, and having to talk so much annoyed him further. The dark bulk of the Twin was heaving itself over the edge of the world. The first few stars were igniting. "The moons will be in position soon. We have nothing to fear from the dark, but we do risk running out of time."

The silent twins set into the lurching motion of the dead, and went first.

A perilous climb in day became more dangerous as daylight ebbed. The steps were provided with long rope handrails passed through iron loops driven into the rock. The rope could be grasped should one slip, but alas, like so much to do with the Order in those times, they were poorly maintained and untrustworthy. The wind grew stronger along with the dark, and so Aarin and Pasquanty breathed sighs of relief when they reached the place where the black rock of the cliffs met the mud and grasses of the marsh. The cliffs rose implacably over them, the shanties clinging to them mighty as barnacles. Refuse was heaped everywhere. There had been none of the greater tides to clear it all away for months, only lesser inundations, and these only gathered the trash into mounds fit to mock the mounds of barrow-kings. There would be wealth of a kind hidden in them, but the gleaners had departed no matter. No one was poor or desperate enough to chance the marshes at dusk when the Twin approached and both moons rose.

Ahead of them the Path of the Dead became a bleached boardwalk, meandering towards the Black Isle.

Pasquanty leaned out over the water-smoothed railings. "The grass, I hear voices..."

"Pay them no heed. Most are harmless. If we listen we will draw the ghosts out and will spend our night hearing their petitions. Pay them no heed!"

Pasquanty gulped, sending his oversized larynx bobbing up and down his skinny neck. Aarin gave him a despairing look. He set out at a brisk pace.

The boardwalk ran on pilings moated by dank pools. The marshes were bleak wastes that went on for miles. There were a few islets, topped by a fuzz of salt furze and dwarf sycamore hardy enough to withstand drowning by the tides. Between them were many smaller rocky protrusions mottled with grey limpets who waited with the patience of ages for the sea. Chains of bright orange iron were anchored to three of the largest sea rocks, grouped together within sight of the cliffs.

"The killing rocks?" said Pasquanty.

"What else?"

"Have you ever...?"

"Officiated? Of course. The deaths of the condemned are unpleasant. Drowning is the best they can hope for, the anguillons or the dead get them in the main. I don't like it, before you ask. To see death without being able to send souls on to peace goes against my inclination."

"They are criminals."

"Everybody deserves the chance of the hereafter, Pasquanty. But others greater than we deem it otherwise. I see it as part of our duties, and best borne with dignity. Be glad there are no executions scheduled."

Pasquanty had to strain to hear. The wind droned through the railings, rattling the grasses and snatching at Aarin's words. He dared not ask Aarin to speak up.

"They say their spirits are the ones that haunt the marshes."

At this Aarin did stop and turn, so unexpectedly it caused the twins to stumble.

"Their ghosts are the most common of the spirits one might meet on the marsh, but not the most dangerous. Cease thinking on them! You will draw them to us." He shook his head. "How many times must I tell you this?"

Pasquanty swallowed again. Aarin resisted the urge to push him into the mud eighteen feet below.

Their feet knocked hollowly on the wood. Silver water rippled in creeks. The evidence of the tides was visible in looped patterns of scummy brown foam. There was a lot the marsh could tell you, if you knew where to look. Aarin was not born to the place, but had had the sense to ask those who were. He was thinking on one of them, a gleaner whose back was stooped from carrying his coracle around with him perpetually like a species of human snail, when a curlew let out its haunting cry. Aarin stopped dead. A trio of oyster catchers burst from the the a reed bed half a mile away. He narrowed his eyes, scanning the horizon. The sun was finally slipping under the sea, the rising Twin taking an opportunistic bite from its rim. The last light was confusing, bouncing from wet sand and water in dazzling scintillations of bronze, silver, and gold. The flatness of the landscape made perspective a trickster, turning the trunks of driftwood trees into sticks, and stones into mysterious islands.

"What is it?" asked Pasquanty.

"We should proceed carefully," said Aarin.

"I thought that was the general plan, out here, you know, on the Paths of the Dead." Pasquanty made a pathetic attempt at a laugh. It came out shrill.

"*More* carefully. We have been noticed. Do not leave the boardwalk, Pasquanty."

"You know," grumbled the deacon, "none of this is making me feel any better."

Who would they meet? wondered Aarin. It could just be gleaners, of course. Whole clans of them roamed the marshes. But with the tide due tonight, they would have gone to higher ground or their floating villages. In any case, few of them would come this way at this hour. The area was treacherous with quicksand, and lousy with the dead. There was talk that bands of the Drowned King's reavers had been seen. This Aarin doubted; it was too close to the city. More likely they'd come across Rattling Jimkin, the Wailing Death, or Hollow Anika. Such colourful names, thought Aarin, but a shiver troubled him nonetheless. It was one thing to watch the ghostlights roaming the mud from the clifftop, another thing to be among them down here in the muck, Guider or not.

"Still, needs must," he said to himself. "Needs must."

He hoped it wasn't Hollow Anika.

Of course, it was.

There was a broad space of temporary dunes halfway out to the Black Isle. The marsh winds laboriously built them up for the next Great Tide to wash them flat again. After the flood the dunefields became places of sucking quicksands and sinister creeks along with everything else, then the mud dried and the dunes crept up again, gathering around whatever minor prominence that encourage their growth. They were at the apex of their height; twenty-three feet this close to the Great Tide, five over the height of the boardwalk. Aarin slowed as they approached. Sand banked over the edge of the rails. He halted Pasquanty with a touch to his arm. The Correndian stopped. "The boardwalk is buried for twenty yards or so," he whispered.

Pasquanty squinted. "Is it safe?"

"No. But if we keep our wits about us we should be pass unmolested." Aarin loosened his iron darts in their case at his belt all the same.

"I hear nothing," said Pasquanty.

"It is not a good sign, deacon. No bird or beast. The ghosts on the wind are gone. Something has scared them all away. We would be safe on the boardwalk." He tapped at a worn sigil carved into the rail. "But a covering of sand can render the wards inoperative. We must be extremely cautious."

"And when we are past?"

Aarin looked into the distance at the broken crags of the Black Isle. Past the dunes, the boardwalk curved across foetid pools choked with the city's outfall. He grumbled and pulled his brass spyglass from its leather tube and put it to his good eye. More delays. "I see nothing there, living or dead, and the walk is sound. We should be alright, once we are past the dunes."

Pasquanty opened his narrow mouth, but Aarin silenced him with a scowl. He held his finger to his lips in a savage gesture that pressed them white. Pasquanty warned, the Guiders proceeded.

They came nearer to the buried part of the walk. A desolate wailing froze them in their tracks.

"What was that?" said Pasquanty, his voice a squeak.

Aarin's eyes flashed in anger. "Shut up!"

The wailing stopped. When it began again it was closer to the boardwalk.

"You fool," hissed Aarin. "You have given us away!"

"To what, to who?" quailed Pasquanty.

"Hollow Anika, that is the cry of Hollow Anika! Come! We must hurry!"

They reached the buried part of the boardwalk, and struggled up onto the dune covering it. The sand was pocked with the impacts of a recent shower, and was damp and cloying. Pasquanty, wracked with fear, stumbled in it, leaving a splayed handprint in the sand. Aarin was indomitable, hitching up his Guider's robes and ploughing on. The twins were not troubled at all. They broke into a trot and stolidly barged Pasquanty out of the way.

"Guider Kressind, wait!" called the deacon.

The wailing loudened, dreadful keening that came from many throats singing out their pain as one. *"Where, where, where?"* the voices sang. *"Where are my children?"*

Pasquanty struggled up. He followed as quick as he could after the retreating figure of Aarin. Movement caught his eye, and there, standing on the dune crest above the boardwalk, was a woman. Stick thin, her pretty face emaciated so that her eyes appeared enormous in their sockets. Thin fingers plucked at a filthy dress.

"You! You, have you seen my children?"

Aarin's feet tocked on wood, safe again. He turned back to see Hollow Anika float down to the covered walkway, the toes of her bare feet trailing across the sand, and interpose herself directly between Aarin and Pasquanty, cutting off the deacon from his master.

"Lost gods damn him!" cursed Aarin. He strode back onto the sand, passing the twins. His dead servants dutifully trundled about to follow, and he was forced to pause and command them to proceed on to the isle. Hollow Anika was turning toward Pasquanty, revealing the space in her back to Aarin that gave her her name. She was as hollow as a rotten old tree, a pit from her shoulders to her buttocks that stretched away forever. Dull red light shone from somewhere very deep.

"Hello little priest," said the spectre to Pasquanty. The deacon fell to his knees and moaned. *"Have you seen them? Have you seen my children?"* She reached skeletally thin fingers out to him.

"Don't look in her eyes!" bellowed Aarin. He needn't have said so, for the deacon had wrapped himself into a ball, his arms about his head. "Stand away from him, departed one!"

"I am not departed," said Hollow Anika, swivelling on the spot to face Aarin. *"I am here. Can you not see?"* Her head lolled to one side and her mouth split in a wide, blacktoothed grin. *"Come with me. Such pretty singing we will make."* She rushed at him, arms outreached, eyes unblinking. That was always the worst, thought Aarin.

"I command you to hold!" he shouted. He withdrew five darts in a fan from their case. He threw them one at a time, long practice allowing him to work a fresh missile up his hand into position between forefinger and thumb after each cast. The first two went wide, but the third hit home, eliciting a piercing shriek from the spectre. She thrashed at her shoulder where the iron pierced her, but could not bear to touch the dart to pluck it out. She snarled and came on again.

Aarin set his feet wider and tossed his last two darts. He neatly hit her in each foot, pinning her in place not four paces from himself. Where the iron met her flesh, glowing smoke curled upward, bright in the evening. She screamed with her mouth closed, the sound emanating from the cavity in her back. She glared at him, dead eyes full of hate.

"Come on, Pasquanty! Get past her! Onto the wood once more!"

Pasquanty crawled past, as far from the revenant as he could get. His hands found part of the railing buried in the sand. The touch of the wood gave him strength and he scrambled past her with redoubled speed. She watched him go to his superior, whose sleeve he grabbed in a shocking lapse of etiquette.

"I saw, I saw..." Pasquanty gulped. For once, Aarin forgave the squirmings of his face. "I saw the dead, howling at me from the pit in her back. Like they were a long way down, though she stood upright..."

"The souls she has snared," said Aarin. He looked disdainfully at Pasquanty's hands clutching his arm. The Correndian muttered an apology and removed them.

Pasquanty looked back to where the spectre stood silently, still watching them. "Will she be waiting here when we return?"

"In all likelihood no, not even Hollow Anika enjoys the bite of iron." Aarin became brisk. "We should hurry. We have wasted enough time with this. We are fortunate, in a way. Hollow Anika will have scared away the other dead. We should find no more trouble on our way to the Black Isle."

"Are you certain?"

"No," said Aarin, "I am not. But whatever the marshes hide, you will see worse upon the isle. You should prepare yourself, Pasquanty."

"Guider..."

"You wanted to come. You wanted to *learn*. It is too late now to raise objections."

CHAPTER TWO
The Black Isle

NIGHT WAS SMOTHERING the marsh by the time Aarin and Pasquanty made the base of the Black Isle. The White Moon was rising, its pale face brightening by the second as it crossed the edge of the much larger Twin. The Red Moon would follow soon. Quicker, it ran always ahead, outpacing its brother to rise twice most nights.

Aarin's servants were named for the contrast between the lesser heavenly bodies, and in reference to the Twin. A joke he had had to explain to Pasquanty.

The island towered over the priests, almost as high as the cliffs of which it was a fragment. The walls of the Black Isle were too lofty to be overwhelmed by even the mightiest tide, and its summit was never covered by the sea.

Evening brought a sharp drop in temperature. Pasquanty, sweaty with fear, was chilled uncomfortably.

"We must be ready to begin the ritual before the moons have completed their transit of the Twin," said Aarin. "Conjunction is in an hour and a half."

"She will not come otherwise?" said Pasquanty.

"She will come whenever she is called," said Aarin. "But we are more likely to get something approaching the truth if she is brought out when the Twin is at its noon and encompasses both moons within its circle."

The night was at its darkest despite the early hour. The White Moon had yet to attain its full brilliance. All was a murky grey, the isle a forbidding slab smeared with pale patches. The Guiders mounted the steps carved up a fault in a rock. These were very steep, steeper even than those that came down from Karsa's cliffs, and Aarin and Pasquanty had to resort to the chains running alongside the stairs. This was iron, chill to the hands and slick in the way of cold metal, greasy as lead. The smell of it pervaded the narrow cut.

They passed the first white blemish, a cairn of bones carefully stacked by type on a shelf in the stone. Many more followed. Had it been light, they would have been able to see the tangle of remains around the shores of the isle. It was to Pasquanty's good fortune they could not.

The summit opened before them as both moons sailed high overhead, lighting the marshes in their combined, roseate glare. Piles of bones the height of several men were illuminated in pink monochrome, the harshness of the lunar light picking out their details. The Twin loomed over everything, twenty times the size of the larger White Moon and black as pitch, the bulk of it swallowing stars by the score.

"We are not too late," said Aarin. "The monolith is this way."

He led Pasquanty and the twins through the towers of stacked bones, in places so densely placed as to make a labyrinth. Pasquanty started at every shadow. The wind moaned through the spaces between the mounds, playing tunes on hollow bones.

"Calm down, deacon," said Aarin. "This place is holy, an area of proper passage. We will encounter none of the dead here, they have all gone, and those that have refused to go do not come here in case they are forced into the next life. The walls are very thin here, and we are safe."

"That can happen?"

"So many rites have been accomplished here, the presence of a Guider is not always necessary for even the most reluctant or most wounded of souls," said Aarin. He strode unerringly. They kept on going, and going, until the distance they had gone was further than the isle should allow.

"The Stone of Passage," said Aarin, holding up a hand. Pasquanty looked through the gap between two enormous piles of bones. He spied a wide, circular space. Aarin passed through, Pasquanty and the twins followed. Only when he was in the ceremonial space did he see the monolith.

Forty feet tall, irregularly shaped, black like the rocks of the cliffs and the island, but shot through with silvery veins of glimmer. There were shadowed hollows all over it that Pasquanty realised, after a moment, were sigils like those on the path.

"The holiest site of our order," said Aarin. "Here the Guiders of the dead performed the funeral rites for untold aeons. It is still a place of great power. You should really have been here before, Pasquanty."

"So much glimmer!" said Pasquanty.

Aarin made a face. "Yes. Do you know, the Glimmer Guild wanted to tear it down and smash it up? The aldermen said no. If only they had done the same for the rest of the island." He referred to the disused quarry on the far side of the Black Isle. "Nothing is sacred anymore, the glimmer pollutes the land, the money it brings pollutes men's souls. I sometimes wish I were born in simpler times, Pasquanty. When the powers were wilder and the gods still sat in their thrones."

He fell silent, staring at the stone, so Pasquanty respectfully did the same. Shortly, Aarin looked up at the Twin's great black circle, whose centre was coasting into position directly over the Stone of Passage. The Earth quaked at its presence, a far off rumble and a swaying beneath their feet. A fall of bones somewhere nearby clattered from their heap, then silence again.

"The Earth heralds the Twin's ascendancy. Now is the time. Remember what I told you, do not approach the stone. Do not address her. Do you understand?"

Pasquanty nodded.

"And just so we are absolutely clear, do not speak with anyone about what you witness here."

"Of course, Guider Kressind."

Aarin directed the twins to the base of the monolith. They placed the casket and withdrew. Pasquanty watched them nervously. They seemed more... alive in this place. There was a gleam in their eyes that was usually absent. They moved with greater purpose, with fewer of their ticks and gurning. Perhaps a glimmer of their former intelligence. Pasquanty fervently hoped their eyes reflected the moons' light and he imagined the rest.

The chest was three feet long, eighteen inches high and deep. The wood was covered in a pale, dirty leather whose origin Pasquanty didn't like to think on, but often found himself morbidly considering. Thick three thick iron bands ran around the chest vertically, two horizontally. A ridiculous amount of reinforcement for such a small chest. Silvered chains enwrapped it, closed in neat patterns by iron padlocks. Aarin knelt by the chest, and fumbled out a ring of keys from under his robe. He muttered irritably as he clicked his way around the ring. Pasquanty took a few halting steps forward, but Aarin held his hand up and shooed him back. Aarin undid the padlocks upon the chains, then the lock inset into the lid. There were no incantations or passes. The majority of Guiding did not require the pomp propriety demanded of it. Without an audience, Guiders were able to cut corners.

Aarin grasped the lid and glanced over his shoulder. "You want to see? Come and look then. She will not come forth until called. Quickly now." Aarin looked up. The moons moved toward the centre of the second planet. "We are approaching the most propitious moment."

Pasquanty looked within. A set of yellow bones filled the chest. The skull was on top, the jaw detached and placed in front of it. A coil of dark iron chain occupied a good portion of the space.

"Pasquanty, meet the mother."

"Mother..." began Pasquanty.

"Don't say her full name you idiot!" hissed Aarin. "Even an amateur like you will pull her out in a place like this. Now stand back, right back."

Pasquanty scurried back right to the edge of the bone cairns. Aarin stood, and took five backward steps.

"Mother Moude," he said. That was enough.

A sparkle of light travelled across the web of glimmer embedded into the rock. Weak phosphorescence played about the lip of the open chest. At the edge of hearing they heard a building shriek that became abruptly louder as if the screamer had burst through a door into the same room as they. The phosphorescence flared, becoming dazzling. The ghost of Mother Moude shot out from the chest, trailing the iron chain behind her.

"Perfidy! Perfidy!" she howled. "Trapped! Trapped! Damn you, damn you, priest! The banished gods take you and rend you!"

The ghost looped around Aarin's head until it reached such distance that it jerked on the end of the chain. She wailed and flew down and then rapidly ascended. The chain snapped taut, and the ghost was arrested. She tried several times, crying piteously and clawing at the air each time she reached the chain's fullest extent, before coming to a halt with her feet level with Aarin's eyes. The chain ended in a barbed hook that pierced the ghost's ankle. Spectral blood leaked from the wound, dissipating into glowing smoke on the wind.

"Curse you! Curse you a thousand times! Why do you not let me free?"

"You are my servant," said Aarin. "As is the law. You were convicted, Mother Moude. You pay the price for your crimes."

"A hanging, and this limbo? Caught in the brakes of the borderlands, and for what? What?" Mother Moude's form flickered, passing rapidly through all the forms of her life: infant, girl, young woman, middle-age, to rotting corpse and finally a glowing skeleton then back again. When executed she had been a handsome woman just past the prime of her life, and despite the horror of her decaying form Pasquanty could not take his eyes from her. "For what? For healing magic and midwife's cantrips! Ghost-talking those who could not stand a man's attention? I brought peace and comfort and for this I am damned? This is men's law! Men's law!" she shrieked. She lunged at Aarin, arms outstretched, the flesh melting from her and her jaw extending impossibly. Aarin stood his ground.

"It is *the* law," he said coldly.

"Fuck you priest! Fuck you! What do you know of proper power? Nothing, nothing!" her words broke into wailing.

"I am not a priest."

Mother Moude's hands went over her eyes. She stopped, and peeked through her fingers, one eye alight with unholy energy. "You've a peeping friend here I see! Has he come to see the downcast whore? I was no whore! Why did they call me so? Why? And what so if I were? Men make whores, not women! Men's law! Men's law!" she shouted. "If he'll see a whore, then a whore he'll get. I was well regarded in my time!"

She laughed deeply, it was a lusty sound in sickening juxtaposition to her wild state. Pasquanty looked up to see Mother Moude naked and in the full glory of early womanhood. His mouth went dry. He tore his eyes away and stared at the ground, his cheeks burning. In the glow of the ghost he saw the entire surface of the plateau was made of compacted bone.

"Stop tormenting my deacon, Mother Moude," said Aarin. The dead witch's head snapped back to regard him. She ran through all the forms that she knew to be most disturbing to men, but Aarin did not look away. "I bid you answer a question, as you must."

"You scrabble along the fences of death. I'll tell you nothing! Nothing! Let me go! Let me go! Wicked man! In life I was imprisoned by marriage, in death by your art. For my petty acts of freedom I was condemned. Let me go!"

"I cannot."

"What is it, when in this world and the next men can hold such as we in bondage!" She wailed and made another futile ascent. "You are lacking morals. You priest! No god set you so high."

"I am not a priest, their kind is gone from the Earth, because there are no gods," said Aarin. "Not any more. Now speak, Mother Moude. You know what I want to know."

"Speak it, if you would ask. Do not make me your slave to guess your every whim. Bastard! Fiend! Fucking priest!"

"Why is the Rite of Passage changing?" he said. "It becomes easier. There are rumours of Ocerzerkiyan magi who can talk the ghost from a living man. At the same time, the ghosts who will not go become harder to send on. Something is happening."

Mother Moude laughed, this time in a shrill, unpleasant manner.

"You will see, you will see! The layers in the Earth hold the answer. The lights in the sky know! Go ask them!"

"I am asking you."

"And I answered, now leave me be."

"What is causing it?"

"One question you get, priest, one question!" She screamed so loud it seemed the sky would split. Aarin stood his ground. She stopped, and smiled. She sank lower, the chain coiling on the ground beneath her. She became sly. "I'll grant you a second answer if you let me go. Have pity, it burns here in the marches. Let me free! Let me go into the blazing world, do not leave me to torment here in the shadowed edge. No matter how you judge my sins, you are not an unmerciful man. I know, I see!"

"I cannot, as well you know," Aarin said regretfully. "Back into your box, Mother."

"Then fuck you, and fuck your family, all you dirty Kressinds and your grasping hands! The world is changing around you; you push the mechanisms of its change as ignorant as dogs at the grain mill, thinking you control the way of change, but yoked always to a single point and forced round and round in circles. Fuck you and fuck you! As my soul chafes under the winds of limbo, I laugh, because you do not know what awaits you!"

"What awaits us?" said Aarin calmly.

Mother Moude smiled. There was a lunatic light in her eye that was not there when she had died. She beckoned. Aarin took a step closer. She bent her lips, now full and plump, now shrivelled back from grave-long teeth, to his ear.

"Lights in the sky! The bands in the Earth!"

She grabbed for him. Aarin held up his hand. The ghost collided with the iron amulet he held flat on his palm. She threw up her arms and recoiled, coming apart into streamers of shining smoke that disappeared on the wind, her shriek going with it.

Mother Moude's chain rattled to the floor. Aarin regarded it, letting the night sounds of the wind and distant spectres moaning out on the marshes blow away the memory of Moude's scream. He bent and picked up the chain. The cold of it burned his hand, but he did not flinch. It clinked softly as he placed it back into the chest. The bones were as they had been, neatly arrayed with the skull on top.

Pasquanty recovered himself. He had been present at many Rites of Passage, and had learned much of the art himself, but this necromancy was new to him. His legs were feeble and his bowels were watery. "She did not reveal much, Guider Kressind."

"She never does," said Aarin. He locked the chest carefully. "She never will. But we know more than we did."

"This art is too much for me."

"For me too, Pasquanty," said Aarin softly. He placed his hands on the lid of the chest. "I would let her go if I could, you know. I cannot. It is too dangerous, her soul is tormented. But I did not bind her, and would not have done so."

Pasquanty looked at him questioningly.

"I would not judge her, if I were you. Laws change. Customs change. Look at the world we live in now, Pasquanty, with its myriad wonders; *everything* changes. Is it right to damn someone forever for transgressing contemporary mores?"

"I... I had not thought, Guider," said Pasquanty. He had not. Nevertheless, his distaste at the witch did not leave his open features.

"Well perhaps you should. We are the Guiders of the Dead. It is our task to think on such things. What is life if fleeting, and death but eternal?"

"Ours is an onerous task."

Aarin gave him a sharp look. "Don't quote the code at me. A fool lives his life by rote. *Think*." He looked at the chest. "One day, I am sure I will try to lay her to rest. Until then—"

"She is too useful to you." Pasquanty interrupted. He dare not do this ordinarily, but this was no ordinary night. Aarin was not so clean of sin.

Aarin's expression, part guilt and part sorrow, told the truth of Pasquanty's statement.

"We must stay here. It is too dangerous to go back in the dark, just the two of us. There is a bothy on the far side of the island. It is stocked with food and wine. We are not the only visitants to the isle. There will be ample to sustain us for two days, until the Great Tide is done."

"I wish to be away. I am uneasy, I confess Guider Kressind," said Pasquanty. "This is forbidden."

"Is it? Then our entire order is guilty," said Aarin flatly. "You wanted to know how certain rites are performed, and so you do. You may count yourself a criminal among criminals. We must stay."

AT ONE OF the clock, three hours after the passage of the Twin over the Earth, the tide came in, dragged in the wake of the conjoined moons and second world.

The tides came in many forms. The greatest of all tides came in one unstoppable rush, but this, born of the second order of conjunction, came in two: the minor swell and the major. The minor was steady, creeping up the land inch by inch, covering it by degree, filling the creeks of the marshes and joining reeking pools into wide lagoons of cleaner water. A gentle wash coaxed in by the White Moon and the Red. The way prepared by this pelagic vanguard, the true force of the ocean was revealed.

The Great Tide came as a mountain. A tall slope of grey water two hundred feet high. Sweeping over the flats it was surprisingly silent, stealthy as the ghosts that roamed the marsh at low tide. Creek, sandbank, dune and all were engulfed by the whisper of water. The tide slopped against the isle of the dead, send a sluggish spume up the seaward side, nearly as high as the bothy in which Aarin and Pasquanty passed the night. The Black Isle was then true to its name, an island isolate in the dark sea.

The tide moved over the marsh between the Black Isle and the west cliffs, covering in seconds what took men a half hour or more to traverse on foot. Where the water met the cliffs, again it slapped with disguised force against the rock. A sheet of lacy foam rushed up to within a few hundred feet of the lowest cliff shanty, and slipped back. The lower three locks at the end of the Slot were engulfed. The floatstone ships clustered around them rose up on the sea to become level with the Bottomhouses, buoyant as corks.

For a few minutes the brown sea churned at itself, spreading patterns of white upon its surface. Marsh became ocean. The sea quieted.

Such was the power of the Great Tide.

The bothy was a conical stone construction, well hidden from the curious, not that anyone but the Guiders and their servants came to the island. There Aarin and Pasquanty spent the night in passable comfort. They were warm, at least, and fed. Pasquanty drank a good deal of wine, but he did not sleep much, and when he did his dreams were terrifying. He spent much of the night staring at the black crack of the door in the hut, waiting for the sky to turn silver, then blue.

The morning came draped in fog, chill and sharp.

Pasquanty spent the first hours of the day wandering the island while Aarin went about business of his own. He had no stomach for further instruction. If he were truthful, the events of the last night had placed a distance between he and his master. Shudders came with the memory of the witch's shrieks.

Beside an ancient cairn of bones he stopped to watch the sea. The outpourings of ten thousand chimneys dirtied the fog clinging to the mainland, and there was little to see in what should have been a grand view. Pasquanty was drawn instead to the miniature geographies of the bone pile, described in skulls and femurs, pelvises and vertebrae. The bones were grey with age, the outer layers of many flaked away. Where they were not covered by beards of moss, the brittle lattice at the centre was clearly visible.

Pasquanty stared at this, his mind arrested by glum thoughts, his own mortality chief among them. He had only become a Guider's deacon because his father insisted he do so, painting a glowing picture of his sure and certain advancement. The priesthood was the fate of many fourth sons, Aarin and himself included. For reasons unknown but for those described in conflicting myths, such boys possessed enough of the mage talent to Guide the dead, not enough for ought else. The Dead God's Quarter, they were named. Pasquanty had learned to view much in life with suspicion at an early age, and predictably, the Order of Guiders was not so grand as his father promised; fusty with age, bitter with suspicion. The older masters were as terrifying as the dead. He followed Aarin around like a puppy, clinging at the one opportunity he saw for a sinecure. The warm arms of living women, the comfortable house of a Guider, a regular stipend. That was what he craved, not the empty stares of the dead.

He had never wanted to follow the path he had set his feet upon. Now he was on it, he could not get off.

To dwell on such matters was inadvisable. He made a warding sign and tore his attention away from the bones, and shuffled a half pace away.

In the late morning the mists and smokes of the far shore lifted, and Karsa City was revealed. Rank after rank of buildings stretching up and down the coast. Ships of floatstone laboured up to the Slot to gather at the feet of the Locks while the Great Tide lasted. They jockeyed for position, fighting their way, it seemed to him, to the gates. Each lock carried a toll, the lowermost were covered over. Now was the cheapest time for a captain to bring his goods to the heart of the city and thence by train on into the heart of the hilly kingdom. The larger ships anchored instead at the Bottomhouses, the wharf of the high water mark. Pasquanty fancied he could hear the cries of the stevedores. At the docks cargoes from all over the One Hundred Lands were stored, or dragged up Lockside's wooden funiculars into the city. Their laden trucks crawled up the cliffside like ants, spilling water from their ballast tanks as they rose, empty trucks descending on parallel tracks.

However, the white of the floatstone boats reminded him too much of the bones, and he turned his attention away from this also and sent it out over the water. The marshes were as if they had never been. The debris of the city mingled with driftwood on the filthy waters. Nearer to the shore, by those districts where the outlying factories of Karsa were situated, multicoloured plumes tainted the surface. Waves kissed the stone of the Black Isle thirty feet below Pasquanty's feet. Strange roilings disturbed the oily surface.

He found he didn't care to look at the water either.

The deacon went away, keeping his eyes downcast so he wouldn't see the sea. The view he found was not much better; the bones of the dead made up the isle's summit in mosaic. The thin soil covering them he was sure was nothing but flesh all dried and gone to dust. Eyeless sockets mocked him. The mocking caws of ravens grated on his hearing.

It was a long time until nightfall.

Pasquanty awoke at the dead of night to a rumbling shush, quiet but powerful under Aarin's snores. With relief he realised it was the tide going out, and fell into less troubled sleep.

The next day, the marsh was returned. With the water gone, the drop from the top of the Isle looked unbelievably far, as if giants had lifted them up in the dark.

There were people here and there, figures like seeds dropped on the mud, gleaning for fresh treasures dragged in by the sea or digging for the shellfish making their slow retreat from the surface. Potmen went about, retrieving their wicker cages and the treasures within. The long carcass of an emperor anguillon lay stinking in the sun. The day was the realm of men, and they laboured free of the harassment of ghosts.

On the way back Aarin paused to retrieve his darts from the boardwalk where Hollow Anika had come to them. The dunes had been rinsed away, but incredibly three of the five darts he had thrown sat upon the planks as neatly as if placed there.

Of Anika there was no sign.

Aarin weighed the darts carefully in his hand before slotting them back into their case. Pasquanty asked a few questions then, but Aarin did not answer. The darts were expensive to produce, and he was in poor humour. They passed the remainder of the return journey as silent as the twins.

At the base of the stairs they ignored gleaners' calls for benediction, fixing their minds upon their ascent.

CHAPTER THREE
The Hag of Mogawn

DRAYMEN WERE UNLOADING crates from their wagons when the tide hit the Citadel of Mogawn. The swell was higher than the island's cliffs, high enough to surge up to Mogawn's walls. Waves broke over the edges of the island, running briefly through the scrubby woodlands around the castle. Seawater hissing aggressively around the trees as waves broke up on the floatstone and fizzed down the holes. As it appeared they would be overwhelmed, the island lurched like a cow getting to its feet. The rattle of anchor chains on their drums clattered across the courtyard as the Great Tide picked up the whole of Mogawn and placed it upon its shoulder. The draymen were unused to the motion, and staggered, then laughed at themselves for staggering. The dray dogs shifted and bayed uneasily. Their handlers went to them and reached up to scratch between their ears.

Mansanio watched from the balcony upon the west tower. His fingers tapped the balustrade in exasperation. "They should have been done hours ago," he said. He inspected his nails with a frown. As seneschal to the countess he expected of himself a certain standard of presentation and tutted at the damage he had inflicted on his manicure, slight though it was.

Mogawn swayed gently from its floating, finding equilibrium upon the sea. Mansanio walked easily along the balcony; he had lived in the citadel for a long time. Accommodation would have to be arranged for the draymen. He had hoped they would be gone before the tide hit and had held off. There was no ducking it now, not at all. The castle was stuck with them.

"Astred, Hovernia! Find space for the draymen!" he called into the tower. "Astred!" he bellowed impatiently. A plump, middle-aged woman of obvious low birth came huffing out onto the balcony.

"I can only be in one place at a time, seneschal..."

He grimaced at her. "Don't come any closer, you're sweating."

She stopped and dropped an insolent curtsy. "As you wish, Lord Seneschal. Lodgings for the draymen is it? I don't know why you become so exercised by this, it's all in the doings of the day."

Back down in the courtyard the countess was striding among the crates and gesturing with a mixture of excitement and impatience. She was looking at every crate, pointing to ones that were on the flagstones. Mansanio could not hear what she was saying with those damn dogs all barking at once and the creak of the island as it settled, but she did not sound pleased. She never did. Her sharp tongue was part of his wages.

Their leader reassured her. He was better dressed than the rest, pretensions to nobility in his costume. A new money boy, wearing aristocrat's clothes. The world was all topsy turvy. Mansanio despaired at it. Nobody knew their place any more.

The drayman took the countess over to a crate, gently opened it to show her the inside. She chewed at her nails, and nodded. She ran back up the stairs into the donjon, yelling over her shoulder loud enough for him to hear.

"They had better not be, Goodfellow Gorwyn!"

Goodfellow Gorwyn. A noble's clothes and a noble's name and title. Nothing was sacred any more.

Mansanio's eyes narrowed, alert for any signs of derision. The men looked at her with amusement, at her mannish clothes and unfeminine manner. He tensed.

"She don't need you protecting her," Astred said, far too close to him.

"The world is cruel," he said. His hands clenched, scraping grains of sand from the salt-worn stone.

Astred laughed derisorily. "You're a stiff one, that's for sure. The world is cruel, aye, but she can look out for herself can our countess. Our Lucinia was beaten out of tough iron."

Mansanio gave a sour smile. "That's precisely what I am trying to protect *the countess* from. A lady should not be so openly disagreeable, even to them that give her offence. And I do not approve of your over-familiarity."

Astred snorted and wiped her hands on her pinafore. Such meaty hands, pasty and flabby, like those of a fat youth. Her arms were blotched, her face piggy. She smelled vinegary.

"Where are they to go then? The hall or the barracks?"

"Please," said Mansanio. "Put them in the barracks. Give them ale, but not too much. Anything to keep them away from the donjon and the hall. I do not want them bothering the lady."

"Yes, Master Mansanio," she said.

"Not the hall!" he called after her. He returned his attention to the courtyard.

The workmen had finally removed the loads from the wagons. Pairs of them were unsteadily carrying them on poles into the main part of Mogawn. They were landsmen through and through, unsure on their feet though the rocking was subsiding, and the bloody dogs would not stop barking.

Only the major swell of a Great Tide could perturb such a massive chunk of floatstone. Once afloat, it sat out all but the worst storms with implacable patience, its twenty-seven anchor chains keeping it from drifting. The citadel occupied three quarters of the island's surface, a single ward surrounded by a curtain wall that in these years served as protection from waves and anguillons, never men. A tall donjon was set into the wall atop the island's tallest point. The island had not moved for centuries, and so it stayed at the north. The west tower was the second greatest. Rickety workshops and barns jostled the hall and temple, crowding the ward.

Mogawn was more a village than a fortress. A lesser tower made the southern corner of the walls' bent diamond. To the east, facing the coast, was the gatehouse. Set in an outcurving of the curtain wall, it was half the height of the donjon, slightly lower than the west tower, and sported four round turrets of its own. Two sets of gates framed a lesser bailey, now little more than a subsidiary courtyard lined with junk. The outer gate opened onto a road that wound down through the innards of the island. The original fortifications had been adapted to comfort. Large windows had been knocked in the walls, crenellations removed or gone into disrepair. Chimneys sprouted from bedrooms that once housed only warriors and weapons. These conversions had been luxurious when completed; executed at the height of the Count of Mogawn's power. They had begun their slip into decay long before Mansanio's day.

Mansanio wondered how the garrison had kept their blades free of rust in less peaceful times. When most other foes had gone, the salt of the sea remained a relentless adversary.

And yet in its dotage Mogawn was still formidable. With the causeway to the mainland covered by even the lowest of tides, the sea had ever been the castle's most impregnable defence. There was no altering that for convenience. When Mansanio first saw Mogawn, he had thought it the most marvellous place in the world. Nearly thirty years later his opinion had not changed, and that was after becoming intimately acquainted with the many inconveniences of living upon an isolated, wind-blasted, freezing piece of buoyant rock that was surrounded by stinking marsh two thirds of the time and monster-choked ocean the rest. Occasionally, if it felt too much, he would climb to the topmost turret of the donjon where the lady had her glass, and with it spy out the fumes that hung on windless days over the twin valleys of distant Karsa City. Then he would be glad, and wish that the stews of the capital were more distant still.

These visits to the small observatory were one of his few vices, furtively indulged, and he never asked to use to the telescope. Of course the countess would not object, she probably would not care that he had not asked. He suspected she would mock him for his lack of knowledge, then teach him what she knew without complaint. But that would not do, a servant should not request to use the possessions of his mistress, nor aspire to her station in any way. Except...

No, there were no exceptions. None. Never.

The courtyard had emptied. Mansanio hurried off to watch over his countess. The banished gods alone knew how they were taunting her.

Mansanio picked his way across the muddy ward, holding his robes of office daintily out of the muck. The months of Gannever and Seventh had been very fine, bringing a belated summer to Karsa and the isles, but on balance the year had been a wet one, and the rains had returned halfway through Takcrop almost as soon as the harvest was over. Mud and sand were ever present in the yard, washed in by the highest tides, and blown in at the lowest. No matter that the courtyard was paved. The unspeakable slurry came back almost as fast as it was cleared. He sidestepped a wide puddle, keeping a wary eye on the dray dogs as he did. They looked back at him with brown eyes that contrived to be simultaneously intelligent and empty. One stretched its long neck out, arched its back and stretched from its back legs. It eyes were half closed, nose snuffling frantically at him. Mansanio was suspicious of its motives; he had never liked dogs.

The donjon's door was halfway up the side, narrow stairs leading to it with a tight turn at the top. A defensive feature turned huge inconvenience. The door banged wide, workmen emerged, laughing and joking. He heard the countess shouting in a friendly manner, one that quickened his pace. He entered in a cold fury, and faced the workmen down with an imperious stare. Their laughter choked off. They tugged their caps and cleared their throats.

The reception hall of the donjon was crowded with large wooden crates, some open and spilling straw and packing rags onto the floor. As he feared, the countess was attempting to curry favour with the lower orders, swapping bawdy, workman's wit with the last pair of stragglers, if wit was the appropriate word for such filthy badinage. It was imperative he got them away from her.

He clapped his hands as he entered. "Your quarters are prepared, goodmen. You are to be entertained in our barracks. Our guards will see to you. We have provided a barrel of beer in thanks for your labours."

The men looked from Mansanio to the countess. She winked. "Listen to my servant, goodfellows!"

Mansanio shuddered inwardly at the honorific's misapplication.

"I thank you for your efforts," she continued speaking to the men. "I've waited so long for this machine, you have made me very happy. Enjoy your stay, but be warned you will not spend it in idleness. You will be trapped here with me until the tide recedes, late Martday morning. I may call on you tomorrow, for my equipment is complicated, and heavy. It may require a man's touch," she said, with outrageous innuendo.

"Yes, yes!" said Mansanio letting his annoyance show. "Please, goodmen, to your quarters where all is waiting."

"Good night, my lady," said the remaining two men. They all looked the same to Mansanio in their draymen's work clothes, all equally dirty, all so terribly common. He supposed these two to be the underforemen. Gorwyn was nowhere to be seen. He didn't like the way one of them was looking at the countess. "And thank you for the additional funds. Most appreciated."

They bowed and doffed their caps all the way to the door. Additional funds? How much extra she had given them? He glared at them as if he would push them out of the donjon hall with his stare.

"If you had but waited two days, then we would not be suffering this minor inconvenience, my lady," Mansanio said when they had gone.

She looked at him in disbelief. "Wait for this? When I have waited for six months already?"

"Two extra nights does not seem excessive when you put it in those terms, my lady."

She went back to her crates. "A minor inconvenience. Minor," she said. "They're glad of the extra pay. Why put them in the barracks? They're not very comfortable. When was the last time anyone stayed there. Probably before Iapetus's time."

"You know that is not true, my lady. Guests are often quartered there. There are many of the draymen. We would not wish them to ruin the linens of the hall. There is an issue of status here, and your finances, my lady, are not infinite..."

"Unlike your patience, I suppose, eh, Mansanio? My finances are robust enough to withstand a little extra beer and ten silver thalers! Mansanio, I had to have it! Don't look like that! If you're worried about the money, get Holless to set up a shankey game. He'll fleece them blind."

"We will not have the money still," he pointed out.

"No, but Holless will, and he spends most of it when he goes ashore in the Mogawn-by-Land's taverns."

"Which are mainly owned by you. Of course, my lady."

"Oh, don't be so... so... unctuous about it! You bloody Ellosantins think you are so full of charm and understanding. And attractive too, no doubt, with your dusky skin and big brown eyes. Well it won't wash here in Karsa, do you hear? Oily, the lot of you. That's what I think. Put them in the hall!"

"As you have mentioned, my lady." Mansanio bore her prejudices without complaint. No matter that her father was his countryman, and had brought Mansanio to the isles with him.

"And you're going grey, and you're getting wrinkles. You're losing some of your filthy foreign allure."

Mansanio's even expression got a little stonier.

"Oh do stop standing around like an extra poker by the fire. Come and give me some help, damn you. And don't you pull a face at me! I'll make sure you don't get your precious hands too dirty." She gave him a fierce smile. She loved to bate him. He, for the love of her, allowed her to do so. Only her.

"And," she said, as he reluctantly rolled his sleeves up, "I do wish you'd stop referring to Ardwynion and his sons as the 'guard'. He's half blind and the boys, sweet as they are, are only slightly more fearsome than you. And another thing. You never responded to my telling you to put them in the hall. I know you well, you old devil. If you don't acknowledge my orders, you think it doesn't count."

"My ears are not so young, my lady."

"Put them in the bloody hall!"

"The barracks are the appropriate place for men of their station," said Mansanio.

"Really now? So you didn't put them there to keep them away from me, or should I say, me away from them." She had a most lubricious way of smiling that affected Mansanio in many conflicting ways.

"There are standards, my lady."

"Are there? In our brave new world?" she waved a hand. Mansanio noted with dismay that it was filthy, and her fingernails bitten down to the quick. "Rot etiquette, rot standards I say. If I want a tumble with a dog handler than I'll bloody well have one, do you hear? I don't give a shit for what should be or should not be done!" Her ears were colouring at the tips. Provided the flush stayed off her face, he should be able to salvage the situation.

"It is my duty to ensure standards are met, my lady, that is all."

She gave a crooked grin, her eyes blazing with malicious amusement. "You're jealous, aren't you? That's it, isn't it?"

Mansanio was mortified.

"Oh do stop being such the mother hen, Mansanio. I am teasing you. How many years have I been doing that? Twenty? Ever since I could talk. And still you get flustered. You really are quite inflexible. I scandalise you, but I can assure you that I am not yet in the habit of screwing the lower orders. It looks to me like you are starting to believe the rumours." She chuckled at that, but Mansanio could see the hurt. And she did not know the half of what was said about her. Nothing riled him more than when he heard her referred to by her nickname; nothing upset her more either, he was sure, although she went to great lengths to pretend she did not care. More, she went to great lengths to provoke it, so she could publicly display her lack of concern.

They called her the Hag of Mogawn. It was ludicrously unfair. Countess Lucinia was no Maceriyan ideal of beauty. She was, if he were entirely honest, plain, a state she did little to alleviate by the manner of her dress and behaviour. A heavy nose, weak chin, a brow that could kindly be described as strong but might better be said to be furious. She looked far too much like her father and not enough like any one of her female relatives. She was unkempt, dirty in habit and mind, foul-mouthed, libidinous. She smoked, and was prone to drink, but she was brilliant, truly, truly brilliant. What man could not love a mind like hers? That she remained alone pained him as much as if she had taken a husband. Mansanio could never rid himself of the hope that one day she might reciprocate his feelings.

She did not know how close she had come to the truth. Mansanio was jealous, and he was also guilty. In attempting to shield her from the rumours, he'd become to half believe them himself.

He was just as adept at hiding his feelings as she was, however.

"Gorwyn is a noble, of the Gorwyn family. Don't look so bloody surprised man! Times change. Some of us are having to work," she stressed the last word gleefully, with a wicked expression. "What does that do to your notions of status? By your own rules you should put him in the hall."

"The barracks—"

"Put him in the fucking hall, Mansanio!"

"As you wish." He looked at the crates dubiously. "What do I do to help?"

She looked at him in disbelief. "Get a crowbar, you outland fool! Then use it to prise the lids off! You do know how to use a crowbar, don't you?"

"Yes, mistress. Of course."

"Then get to it!"

He retrieved the tool. With delicate disinclination he fumbled at the first lid. The countess rebuked him and he tried harder. He was no stranger to manual work, no matter how hard he feigned incompetence. She always saw right through him, except in that one important regard.

"Come and look at this, Mansanio," she said.

He walked over to her as if it troubled him to be drawn from his work opening boxes, although that could not be further from the truth.

Standing by the countess was something Mansanio relished. Her body gave off a quick and lively heat more nourishing to him than the sun of his homeland. He relished the smell of her. She had a vigorous scent, and tonight the air buzzed around her intoxicatingly.

It was his privilege to be allowed so close. He forced his attention from her to the object she was uncovering in the box. The upper third of a sphere made of blacked bronze poked out of the straw. The Twin. Threaded holes waited for bolts to attach a curved rule about its vertical circumference. At about a yard and a half in diameter, it was huge. An incomplete topography was graven into its surface, her supposed map of the second world. Those lines had bought the countess much derision from those she desired as peers. Mansanio's heart sank to see them so brazenly displayed.

"You see this?" she said eagerly. "This is the Twin. Other planetary bodies await in the boxes. Once this is assembled..." She looked up into the rafters. She smiled. "We'll see then, won't we? We'll show them, you and I."

"Goodlady, you should take your dinner."

"Hmmm? Yes, yes. You are quite right."

"Goodlady." Mansanio stood, waiting to accompany her to the dining room.

"What are you doing?"

"Goodlady?"

"Bring it to me here! Can't you see I'm busy?"

Mansanio suppressed a sigh. "I will see to it immediately."

"Don't be like that." Most of her attention was on the boxes. All trace of her anger had gone. She patted Mansanio on the arm. "You are too good to me, Mansanio. A more loyal servant a lady never had. I'm sorry I tease you, it is but in jest."

"Of course, goodlady," he said. He left for the kitchen, his skin tingling where she had touched him.

The feeling of happiness quite deserted him when he returned from the kitchens bearing his mistress's dinner. Light blazed from the hall. Laughter echoed from the open windows. The countess had called the men back to help her unpack her precious equipment already.

His frown deepened at the sight of Bolth, the cook's lad, carrying a crate clinking with bottles up the steps to the donjon door.

It was going to be a long night.

DAWN WAS APPROACHING. The Twin was setting, the White Moon followed slowly, the Red Moon had already gone.

The countess was in her observatory. The turret provided only a modest platform for the her equipment. Her telescope and its turntable occupied the most of it, and so the circular walkway around the outer edge was crowded with every other bit of astronomical and astrological paraphernalia that would not fit in the middle (Mansanio could never remember the difference). But with the folding glass doors all around the wooden walls open and the dome cracked wide, the universe was let in, filling the room with endless space. The sea was dark in all directions, the sky blazed with stars. On the horizon, the lights of Karsa City made a poor attempt to outshine them. The chill of early autumn filled the room. Mansanio busied himself tending to the room's three braziers while the countess disgraced herself, smoking her pipe while entertaining the chief of the draymen. Both were slightly drunk. Learning that Gorwyn actually was lesser nobility did nothing to warm the seneschal to the man.

"I do not think your guardian likes me much," said Gorwyn. He lounged on the countess's couch as if he were the master of the place. Mansanio pretended not to hear the man's comment, as a good servant should not.

"Him?" said the countess. "Ha! Old Mother Hen. He is a relic of my past, a man out of my father's country. I am cruel to him sometimes, but he is honest as the day is long and his devotion is as deep as the seas. You will not say anything against him, do you hear...?" she stuck her head forward questioningly, searching for a name.

"Tuom, madam. I am sorry, I do not mean to slander your servant."

"Sorry, sorry. I am terrible for names," she waved a hand. "Too much other nonsense in here," she tapped her skull. "But I can't be calling you Master Gorwyn all night. The time is past for that." The countess removed the long stem of her pipe from her mouth. Clouds of blue smoke spilled out with her laughter. "What you said about my servant was no slander, sir, for he does not like you. You don't like him do you, Mansanio?"

"As you say, countess," muttered the seneschal.

"He doesn't think I should be having strange men up in my den," she said. Her eyes twinkled suggestively. "If you weren't the son of Houter Gorwyn, he'd have you defenestrated."

Tuom smirked. "Then I thank my father for being who he is."

"He also does not think the likes of you or I should demean ourselves with physical labour, or by concerning ourselves with anything but lording it over those born lower than we."

"He is welcome to his opinion, but he would be wrong. My father was quite insistent that I acquaint myself with our family's interests."

"That a family such as yours should have any trade at all is quite scandalous, as far as Mansanio sees it."

"Father believes the old families will survive only by following the new money's lead. They are not afraid to engage with the meaner things in life. Already, the richest among the new families are richer by far than the old lords. Land is no longer enough, countess. Industry is the key to wealth. Father says that our kind face a rapid decline into penury if we are not wise to it. I am sad to say I believe him. And so, here I am, third heir to a barony and a master of drays!"

They laughed.

"Well said!" she said. "This is an exciting era, Tuom."

"For some, perhaps. I would have preferred things the way they used to be," said Gorwyn. "But I'd rather be a rich drudge than an impoverished lord. As my father says, the aristocracy has had to change before, so we can change again. The world is not static, whatever the appearance of it. Those who think so forget our warlord forebears who bludgeoned their way to riches. It is fortunate our dilemma is less bloody."

"But I disagree!" said the countess. "If only this change were more like those in the past. From warrior to indolent landlord. I rather feel it is going the other way this time around."

"Then you are more sanguine in nature than I. I prefer the dogs to the dracon."

"They say that once my ancestors were pirates, wandering where they would upon the seas, until one of them fell in love with a kelpie girl and set down iron chains to snare her, blah blah blah. This, of course, is nonsense. What is true is that they were clever enough to get themselves granted the rights to the floatstone islands that once shoaled hereabouts. Carving them up made them, and by extension me, rich. We were new money once, so long ago that people forget. My ancestors did not disdain industry, nor will I."

"What is it that you do here now, countess?"

"Lucinella, please," she said. Mansanio's spine stiffened to hear her offering the familiar form of her name up like a penny.

"Lucinella." The man tried the name. Emboldened, he stood and went over to the countess. Mansanio risked directly watching. The man was ten years younger than his mistress. He had the look in his eyes; another young buck who would soon be bragging he was bold enough to have bedded the Hag of Mogawn. Mansanio's hands shook with anger.

"I am engaged on a quest for knowledge, and am rich enough to indulge my whim. Come here, look at this."

"More stargazing, Lucinella?"

"Oh now, I have saved the best for last." She put her drink and pipe down and walked to a set of wheels on iron stalks. She worked the handles of the crank to her telescope. "The entire structure is mounted on a turntable, masterfully geared. Clever fellow from Corrend. All mechanical, no assistance from glimmer machines. I spin a wheel here, and so! The centre of the room and the dome rotate around the periphery, which is fixed. That includes Mansanio there."

Tuom grinned, pacing to keep himself level with the countess. She giggled.

"One would almost think that you had been within such an observatory before, Goodfellow Tuom."

"Oh no, this is my first time." He said this with such licentious innuendo Mansanio's blood boiled.

"Is it now?" she said. She stopped the turning, glanced behind her to make sure the slot was lined up with the setting Twin, and hopped back onto the turntable. She declined the angle of the telescope, pressed her eye to the eyepiece, then beckoned to Tuom. He replaced her at the sight.

"What do you see?"

"Blackness. It's the Twin. It is, as they say, the kingdom of shadow."

They both sniggered, sharing the mirth of drunkards. Mansanio felt deliberately slighted.

"It is and it is not, Goodfellow Tuom. Look longer."

She rested a hand on his back. He accepted it. Mansanio seethed.

Tuom gave a sharp intake of breath, and stood up.

"You saw it?"

He looked at her in wonderment, then bent back to the telescope. "A fire on the Twin!"

"And how did it look?" she said.

"A bright spark... A yellow lightning. It is gone. There it is again!" He was fascinated, and shifted himself so that he might be more comfortable at the eyepiece.

"The Twin is retreating from the Earth for another month. The Great Tide will flow back. But it is getting closer. Mark my words. The orbit of the Twin and the White and Red Moons are not as Sastrin, Hessind and the others suggest, that is pure ellipses. There is variation in them, a grand cycle beyond that already described. Floster Hessind's mathematical model well established that there is an influence of mass from one body upon the other. Hence, I believe, the fire you saw, a result of flexion in the surface of that world that reveals the fires beneath."

Tuom stood and smiled apologetically. "Flexion? Fires within worlds?"

"And where do you think our own volcanoes spring from? The inferno? The throats of dragons, chained underground?"

"You are rather leaving me behind with all this."

"No matter. Just know, the device you have delivered to me today will help me prove this."

"How?"

"I am afraid you would not understand."

"What does it mean?"

The countess smiled. "I have my ideas, but I would not like to speculate. You will know the rumours concerning me. I am mad! I am dissolute! I am a man! I am a whore!" A touch of sadness entered her smile. "Only one of these things is true, and then only from a very narrow view. My true crime is to challenge the established orthodoxy of my discipline, and far worse it is that I am a woman. No, I must keep some secrets. I think you will have quite enough to gossip about when you return to the capital." She took a step closer to him, and placed her hands on his shoulders. He smiled back at her. "Here, I am sure you understand the mathematics of this kind of attraction better."

"Indeed I do," he said.

"Mansanio!" she called, not taking her eyes from Gorwyn. "I will be retiring for the night soon. Please close up the observatory shutters. Then you may go."

"Yes, goodlady," he said reflexively. "Shall I prepare your room for you?"

Her smile, lustful and teasing, quite transformed her features. "No, that will be all."

Mansanio closed the shutters, taking as long as he could. The countess's whispers and giggles set a fire burning in him. Shame for her, and terrible jealousy for Gorwyn. Had he a knife, he fumed, he would smite him down, then we would see who laughed last.

But there was no knife, there never was. He was weak as milk, and loathed himself for it.

Their laughter tormented him as he descended the stairs.

CHAPTER FOUR
The God of Wine and Drama

"DRINK! DRINK! DRINK!" The patrons of the Nelly Bold hammered their tankards down in time with their words.

Eliturion, god, in one aspect, of wine, indulged them. A full firkin of ale was to his lips, small as a dainty bucket in his giant grasp. Foaming beer cascaded from the sides of his mouth, running down his long red moustaches, in amber falls, over his beard, his ample belly, and thereafter the floor. As much as he spilt, he drank more, the gurgle audible in his gut.

"Drink drink drink!" the patrons chanted with glee. As often as they watched Eliturion's party piece, it still delighted them. "Drink drink drink!"

The god upended the barrel. The cries of the crowd became raucous. He stood, tipping the firkin right back. He held it away from him, slopping what little remained all over those nearest him. They shrieked with delight as he let out an almighty belch at the ceiling. Arms out, he turned slowly to let every handclap caress him. Then he cast the firkin toward the bar like a man at skittles, scattering drinkers. He sat down heavily. His ale throne creaked alarmingly.

The god was as big as gods were expected to be. In those years of the glimmer, that was larger than life. In recent centuries he had run to fat.

"Oi! Eli!" shouted the landlady. "Don't roll your bleeding ale barrels about in here. How many times?"

Eliturion gave a raffish grin and another belch. "Sorry Nell," he called back.

"Nell was my great-great-grandmother, you arse!" As the god was too large to admonish physically, she took her annoyance out on others, slapping customers out of the way, so that the barrel could be rolled out of the room and back to the cellars.

"Well, that should answer your question as to how many times I have been told that!" he crowed. The crowd laughed.

Nelly's great-great-granddaughter, whose name was in actual fact Ellany, shook her head and stalked off back behind the Nelly Bold's ornately carved bar. She had said it all before a hundred, a thousand times. As had her mother, and her father, and so on back to the beginning of the inn. Eliturion came and went, sometimes favouring some other drinking spot for a season or a decade, but he always came back to the Nelly Bold; crook-grinned and irrepressible as a pup. He was a fixture, part of her inheritance, so to speak, and damn good for business. So she left it at that. The crowd cheered her as she resumed her station.

"Give us a story, your divinity!" someone shouted.

"Yes, yes! A story!" someone else joined in. The request was taken up by many. Eliturion raised his mighty hands and smiled a smile, outwardly benevolent, forcefully demanding of calm.

"Really now?" he said indulgently.

"Yes!" the crowd shouted. "A story!"

Eliturion would give them a story, he always did. But even for a god as diminished as he the ritual question had to be asked, and ritual, minor objections raised, before he made a great show of giving in.

"Oh, I don't know," said Eliturion.

"A story!" they roared.

"Well," he said, signalling to Ellany for another drink. He scratched under his nose, a merchant's gesture. "Drama is my second domain, drinking being my first."

"Hooray!" the crowd shouted.

"Quieten down now," he said. Ellany wheeled his drink over on a barrow, a more modest one-gallon pot. He nodded gratefully, lifted it, and took a long pull. The crowd waited. And then he began.

"The question you've got to ask yourself is," he said, "where does a story start? I'm sure you have your ideas; with a great event, perhaps. A battle, or a catastrophe; with fiery rains and titanic waves, the gnashing of teeth and the end of an empire. Or if you are of gentler humour, something less dramatic: a conversation, or a conversion. Or a bet! Yes, a wager!" he said, his face lifting as if he had hit upon the very thing. But it fell again. "No, no. That will not do. Maybe you would consider the fundamentals of life. A marriage, a birth... A death, although that is more of an ending."

"Give us a battle!" shouted something.

"Tell us about Res Iapetus and the driving of the gods!" said another.

"Hush, hush now, I'm telling this, not you, and tales of old Res put me out of sorts. Where was I?" He hunkered down conspiratorially. The crowd's members drew in closer, many dragged their stools over as close as they could to Eliturion's table. Conversation tailed off to a murmur, then an attentive quiet, rich with belches and winy breath. "There have been those of my priests, when I still had priests, who maintained stories have a force of their own, that they are separate from what, for wont of a better term, I am forced to call by modern sophists, 'reality', although from my perspective it's all much the same. These priests had it that stories are dangerous things. Far more than a novelty or a moral message, they become something separate, a law to themselves, an artistic rather than objective truth that is as powerful as a stone cold fact. Not a lie, not at all. A subjective actuality, if you will, with a power all its own." He paused. "It's all shit, but a pretty idea."

"You're drunk!" shouted someone.

"And so are you," the god retorted, pointing a finger. "But I have wisdom enough to know what I am talking about, whereas you are a nincompoop. And tomorrow I'll still be drunk." The crowd laughed. "Stories catch people up in them, yes; in the wildest sense people and stories feed off each other—people push stories onto one another, and so stories inform the fate of nations. A mage pushes his will onto the world by telling himself lies so convincing they become true, and so all stories have their power. The fundamental of it is that without people there would be no stories at all. You people give the world form through stories, and that makes people the more important to me, you understand? The world sometimes looks like it works to the rules of every legend you ever read, but who's to say it isn't the other way round? Because it is; I should know.

"It's just that the 'world'—not that I like the exclusivity of that term either—is a damn sight more complicated than you people will ever understand. Your appreciation of what this"—he cast his eyes heavenward and gestured to the rafters. Three dozen pairs of eyes rolled up, and saw stars among the smoke there—"this bauble of a universe is, is defined by the stories you tell to explain it. And by that I mean your creeds, you sciences, your philosophies, your faulty, faulty memories and recollections..."

"Eh?" said somebody. Someone else farted. Acclaim and disgust were shouted equally at him.

"What? What do I mean?" he shouted at the man who said "eh?" "Why, you goodman are a collection of stories that you have told yourself, nothing more. On occasion, your stories embrace a greater part of the truth, but never yet has one contained the whole, and never will one do so. That is why you will never understand, no more than the inhabitants of an anthill will understand the world beyond their nest, not matter how mighty tall it may become, or how involuted the motions acted out within."

"Rubbish!" shouted someone. Such barracking was also part of the ritual of the Nelly Bold, hallowed by time since the inn had been built, when Eliturion, small and broken, had come in, draggled by rain and rejection for his first drink.

"People!" he declaimed, one fat finger in the air. "People tell stories. People are stories. People come first, and stories later. People are more important, that's my opinion. I'm the god of fucking stories, and I know best." He belched. The crowd cheered. "That's probably why I am still here when my brothers and sisters are not."

"Give us a story, you old windbag!" shouted someone. Others laughed. The more sober they were, the more nervous their laughter. Most laughed fearlessly.

Eliturion clapped. "You wanted a story, and then you shall have one. We are gods and are not affected in the same way as you mortals are by pernicious narrative. You should be wary what you ask of me, but now it is too late. So be it! Take your piece, and be wary of it."

He lowered his voice.

"This story is about six people, six siblings. They're at the heart of all this, so it's them we'll name as our principal dramatis personae, to use the Old Maceriyan term."

"Who? Who? Which brothers?"

"I said siblings, you arse! And if you do me the courtesy and wait, then you shall find out! That is the simplest precept of the story! Listen, and discover!" His eyes flashed, the questioner quailed. "So, where to start? We talked about births. So, do you start with their births? And if so, of which sibling? The first? She's a woman. Not to be discounted on that fact, although her father already has. Or the oldest son? He's mad, but not so much as he believes, so perhaps not. Or the fourth? He plays the major role, at least for a while. Or the sixth? Sweet Rel with the world about to smash down on his shoulders, perhaps we should start with *his* birth?"

One of the patrons, ensconced away from the racket in his own high-backed booth, empty but for him despite the press, pricked up his ears. He had five siblings. He regarded himself mad. He had a brother named Rel. Such was Eliturion's way to snare his listeners, often his stories concerned those who listened, though rarely did those whose lives were detailed dare reveal themselves.

There had been suicides over it. The god drew no sanction over this. He was, after all, a god. No prison could hold him.

Very well, tonight was his night. As a teller of tales himself, Guis Kressind grudgingly appreciated the attention. He leaned forward to better hear what slander Eliturion would offer his family. For had the god not already intimated, that all stories are by nature lies? A truth he held fast to. It allowed him to hate his own work and not despair.

"Do you go back, look at their father in his prime, all arrogant and ambitious and dangerous? Do you go back to his father, or his mother, to see what made him that way? Or further, to whenever poor, impoverished so-and-so of so-and-so saved a lord which won a favour which granted a licence which garnered some wealth and set these six up for their privileged lives, five generations later? Don't you think that would belittle the story of so-and-so, making his story only a backdrop on the stage for a story you happen to be more interested in? Unfair, goodmen and goodwomen! Unfair!" He sniffed thoughtfully. Eliturion never was one to allow a drama go unpaused. Guis thought him quite the worst actor in the Off Parade. "His story is quite a tale, actually. Who are you to weigh one life's worth against another? Nobody, that's who."

"And what's your qualification?"

"Shut up, idiot, he's a god!"

"He's a drunk more like!"

Eliturion smiled. "I am both. And the goodman there is correct. I am not qualified to judge, and that's also a truth. But you asked for a story, and I choose the story to tell, so be quiet."

He began again, and his voice boomed. "Do you go back to times when the Old Maceriyans ruled the Earth and there were a damn sight more gods around than there are now? Or back before, to the first men, of before that to the days of the Morfaan, or even before the gods were born, when dark titans subjugated the Earth and wild magic ran as quicksilver across burning skies?

"Yes yes, the gods were born. No, they didn't create the world. Some of them used to say they did, before old Res Iapetus drove them away, but that's not true. A god's as much a part of the world as a man, perhaps less so, because a god doesn't make stories, he's just *in* them, a god is *made* by stories. Even me."

"But you're telling it," said a youth at the god's table, flush with drink and enraptured.

Eliturion dropped his head level with the youth's own. "Marvellous! A finer level of idiot here this evening. Well done. See lad, I didn't make this story, I'm only *telling* it." He frowned and shouted at a man at the back. "Hey, you, yeah you. Are you paying attention?"

The man nodded quickly, eyes wide as a rabbit's before the hawk.

"Good." Eliturion sprawled back. His gut forced the table across the floor with a wooden groan. "We could of course take another path back, to whatever muddy little ball the ancestors of men first dragged themselves up onto two feet, or to when the ancestors of the ancestors of men swapped flippers for feet, gills for lungs. That happened, incredible though it may sound to you. Your lot will figure that our eventually, and I'll be long gone by the time you do. Go back. Back to the birth of the world. This one, or that one, doesn't matter. Or that time when the stars the worlds turn about first burst into light. Back, back, back, back, back, all the way to the one and only real beginning there is, when there was nothing. When there was only thought without will and all was formless and then light and fury and then... Oh! There was something. A whole lot of something." He gazed thoughtfully over the heads of the crowd. A gulp of beer brought him back. "That's not for the telling. It'd take as long as the universe is old, perhaps longer, what with a few embellishments and all."

Through the window, people bustled about the square and the narrow alleys of the Off Parade, intent on pleasure. Inside the Nelly Bold, all had fallen quiet. "You have to take a stand! You have to pin them down! Stories! They're not alive as such, but they have the seeming of it, and that's as dangerous as alive, if not more. Think on this, how do you kill something with the semblance of life, but which is not alive? Eh? Eh? Got you there, haven't I? I digress. You have to square up to your story. You have to say, 'This is where my story begins'—well, it's not my story, you understand..."

"You already said that!"

"Hush now, so I did. You don't have the patience for my story because it's longer to tell than the time you have. Do you have four lifetimes to hear it? No. I'm not sure I do any more either."

He drained his cup.

"So, not my story, but I do get to decide where it starts." He leaned forward, his face aglow with divine mischief and beer. "And it starts with a hanging."

CHAPTER FIVE
Eliturion's Story

THE MAN ON the gallows was trying to be brave, although he wasn't, and trying to be noble, which he once thought he was, but found himself, in dismay, to be a coward.

"I am not afraid to die," he shouted, which was a lie. "I have done nothing wrong," which was another. Nobody heard him. He had a reedy voice at the best of times, and now was the worst. Fear strangled it into a warble that failed him completely. He was the last to be hanged in a long line of men. The crowd's bloodlust had run out long before this man's last seconds ran out. They talked over him, not caring for his testimony, or for him, or his death.

The evening was drawing in. A poet would make some comparison there. The little extra life he had enjoyed during his wait was a concession to his former station. This station had not been exalted, but it was higher than the run of the herd of men, not quite a goodfellow, this man, but more than a goodman. And so he had breathed a few hours more. At the last, as the clocks prepared to chime the sixth bell and twilight approached, his breathing time was finally done. How quick time goes, more quickly even for gods than for men.

"I do not regret what I did," he said. Another lie, for he would not have been where he was had he not done what he did. He had been found guilty, quite rightly, and had no one to blame for his predicament but himself.

His mendacity mattered as little as his crime. The crowd paid little attention to this quivering man in his fine clothes soiled with the filth of the Drum, that most notorious of gaols. They were speaking over him, laughing at the jests of their friends, eating, arguing, pissing in corners, hawking goods, angrily forcing a path past one another because their errands were more important than anyone else's. All the bitter ingredients in the stew of human behaviour. A few stared at the condemned man, a couple shouted obscenities or threw dogshit at him, but their energy was low. There was an edge to the air as there often is in the autumn. It was nearly time to go home.

The man had spent the extra hours given him weeping and shaking and composing his last words, chiefly but not exclusively in that order. He started to speak, then stopped, his eyes bulging, his mouth working without sound. His face hardened. "Listen! I—" he shouted. The crowd heard that.

He did not finish.

The executioner deemed his time done, and so he was. With ill grace he yanked the lever. The trapdoor slammed downward with that awful, final noise the gallows make. The man dropped, the rope snapped taught and the man bounced. The gallowsman may have been impatient but he was good at his job. The condemned man's neck bones parted and severed that path of thought that runs the length of the body.

The man's feet twitched, one shoe fell off. A trickle of urine ran from his stockinged foot, his last statement on the sorry condition of mortality.

The crowd roused itself and gave a ragged cheer.

Who this man was, and what he did—these things are not important. He was gone from his life and so from our story. He will not be back, save but briefly.

Two well dressed gentlemen near the back of the crowd though, they *are* important. They were there to watch the hanging, but not to see the man die.

They hung back from the throng under the projecting upper storey of a shop, sipping hot wine from horn cups. Their clothes marked them out as men of a higher degree than the rabble around them.

They were at once within and apart from the crowd, as is always the way of the rich among the poor. This one's Garten, the other Trassan. A pair of brothers among the siblings I mentioned. Garten was shorter and slimmer than Trassan, who was taller and stouter. Garten wore the stiff formal clothes of a bureaucrat—a long tunic belted at the waist, capacious sleeves, a round collar, the cloth stiffened into wide pleats below his waist. He wore sober hose of black underneath, and shoes that still shone despite the ordure caking the cobbles of the square. His top hat took his height up over Trassan's, who had the bigger physique. His badges of office were silver and bright, declaring him to be an officer of the Admiralty under the patronage and protection of Duke Rommen Abing, and therefore in favour with Prince Alfra. Otherwise his clothes were sober grey of very fine cloth. He wore a fur coat cast over his shoulders and pinned at the throat, his arms out of the sleeves as is the fashion of the moment. This was not part of his guild clothing, but it was cold, and therefore excusable. Unusually for a bureaucrat he wore a gentlemen's sword at his side. Others in his vocation frowned at this. His carrying of the weapon was not technically incorrect. Garten was a goodfellow, albeit of the newer blood, and so entitled to wear the blade even if bureaucrats traditionally did not. No one spoke openly against it; Garten Kressind was uncommonly skilled with the weapon, as I see some of you know.

His brother Trassan was an engineer, a clever, quick-minded man when it came to mechanisms and power to output ratios and suchlike, a little duller of thought when it came to many other things, as is the way with focussed minds. He could rarely find his hammer, or his shoes, or his mistress, and therefore had many spares of each. But he was ambitious, and that was why he had met with his older brother the day before another brother's exile and a threeweek before their sister's second wedding. If their father had known of it, he would have approved of this subterfuge. Trassan wore clothes that once, several iterations back in their ancestry, would have been practical, but had bled out much of their utility under the scissors of fashion. The leather apron he wore was too flimsy for work, the heavy boots overly heeled, the hat too broad and too feathered, his goggles were a decorative hatband of brass and glass that would not have protected the eyes of a rat.

He had, of course, more practical versions of these garments, but on the street all men of means are expected to wear the costume of their profession, and he was no different.

"That was a bad death," said Trassan. "A very poor speech." His words rode clouds of steam from his mouth.

Despite the various trades they had undertaken and their individual ways of thinking, the Kressind siblings were more similar than different, and each enjoyed moving oratory in their own way. Both were disappointed. "Give him credit, it must be hard to speak out over a crowd like this, staring the end in the face," said Garten. This was the way between them. One spoke, the other disagreed, sometimes in jest, sometimes for devilment. Only rarely were their disagreements sincere enough that they came to blows. They were uncommonly close as a family. However, they as rarely agreed immediately.

"Other people manage it," Trassan said. "It's not like he's going to get another chance. That would spur me on to better efforts. This is not one of Guis's plays. There is no rehearsal."

"You're being harsh, brother. The man was about to die."

"And now he is dead. Proves my point don't you think?" Trassan shrugged. "Those gallows aren't up to much either."

He pointed out the various failings of the equipment, and suggested improvements. His brother was interested, although not as interested as Trassan. The crowd was breaking up, giving a clearer view of the corpse turning at the end of its rope. Only a handful of people were staying for the ghosting. There had been many ghosts that day, shrieking their way into the afterlife. Even marvels, alas, pall through familiarity.

The sun had already gone into the west, painting the smog in the sky mauve by way of farewell. The great round bulk of the Twin loomed large above the rooftops and factory chimneys, the spires and domes, the derricks and cranes and crenellations of the city beyond the square. The Twin was dark and unknowable, the Twin scowled at the proceedings as if it disapproved. The Twin blotted out half of the birthing stars. The White Moon ran before it, bright and terrified. The Red Moon trailed it, as if building the nerve to make its oblique dash across the Twin to the safety of the horizon. Bashful stars hid in the clouds.

Garten laid a hand on his brother's shoulder. "There! There he is!"

Aarin Kressind stepped onto the gallows, robed in green and gold. He had his hood up, and his hands were held deep into his trailing sleeves. A bareheaded acolyte, bearing the ceremonial chest and candlestick of the ghosting, shivered behind him. He had an uncommonly memorable face, all nose and eyes. Guider Kressind's more uncanny servants were kept out of sight. You know of what I speak.

"He doesn't seem cold, not like that deacon of his," said Garten.

"Pasquanty? That rat? Aarin told me he wears a fur vest under that get-up," said Trassan.

Garten gave a snort of laughter. Those immediately in front of him in the crowd turned and scowled. Levity was inappropriate at a ghosting. The living on the scaffold got little respect, but the dead were another matter.

Guider Kressind went through the eleven lines of release as the corpse of the man was brought down and laid upon a white sheet on the boards. Candles were lit and snuffed out in the proper order, the chest of souls opened and closed. The Guider went to the head of the man, and bent forward. He removed his hands from his sleeves with a flourish, revealing many rings of no small value. His hood he cast back, showing the white orb of his ruined eye. He put his face close to that of the corpse and made three sharp intakes of breath, followed by one long, sucking inhalation. Then he stood straight, replaced his hands in his sleeves, took a step back and waited. Few saw the strain on his face, but it was there, a tremble to his limbs from the effort. Ghosting is not what it used to be. Harder, some say.

Have you ever seen a ghosting? The nature of the era dictates the need for it is lesser, although violence and great sorrow still require it be done according to the old rites. Those ghosts that refused to go present the likes of Guider Kressind with a stiff struggle. Green and silver light crept from the dead man's nose and mouth, questing tendrils at first, which twined and pulled themselves into a rising cloud of thready vapours. Aarin exhaled his held breath upon them, and they condensed into a loose image of the dead man. He glared at the crowd, then streaked skywards with the shriek of the departing.

"Not a bad job," said Trassan. "Quick, no fuss."

"Do you mind, goodfellows?" said a woman. "Show some respect to the Guider and the dead!" It was not the Karsan way to speak out so, a gentle tutting and a rolling of the eyes were the norm. But they were being rude, so fair play to the woman.

Garten smiled. He was a sensible man, overly thoughtful and sometimes prone to vacillation because of it, but in the company of his kin a different, somewhat rakish, side emerged. "That's not a Guider," he said. "That's our brother."

Trassan and Garten watched Aarin step down from the scaffold.

"You must agree," said Trassan to the woman, who was now tutting and rolling her eyes in the aforementioned manner of the Karsans, "that he did the ghosting well."

"A fine ghost," agreed Garten. "Shall we go and talk with him?"

Trassan shook his head. "He's busy. We'll likely all meet tomorrow anyway to see Rel away."

Garten handed his wine cup back to the vendor and puffed out a plume of steam. "Let's go and eat then. Then we might discuss this proposal about which you have been so close-mouthed." Garten said this with a smile, but his brother's reticence to say why he had wanted this meeting had started to annoy him several days ago.

"Naturally, a man must eat, but later," said Trassan. "If we are quick, we still have time to head to the museum. I wish to see the Old Maceriyans' god before dinner."

"How many times have you seen him? Dozens. Mother dragged us all round that place too many times to count."

"She did. But the truth is, I want to ask him a question."

Trassan had a marvellous new device with him, a tiny timepiece no bigger than his palm, but as accurate in marking the time as any market clock. He consulted this 'watch' as they walked toward the Royal Museum of Karsa. By his reckoning they had time for a quick drink and still make the exhibit he wished to see, so they stopped and had three. Per Allian's water pipes and sewers had made the water safe enough to drink, but Trassan held the old distrust of it and drank only beer. For health reasons, he insisted. A respectable attitude.

As brothers meeting after long apart, they drank immoderately of the stronger type of ale. They became rowdy, and this was not acceptable. They were forced to relieve themselves in an alley, and then to run for the museum to make the last admission. By the time they reached the bottom of the building's broad stairs, they were panting. They giggled and shoved at each other as they scraped their boots free of mud. A pair of young ladies were hurried along past them by their chaperone. Garten, more decorous than his brother, nudged Trassan in the ribs at this. They feigned sobriety as they ascended the stairs, approached the paybooth, handed over their money, and went inside.

Perhaps it was the hush of the place, or the weight of history pressing down from every brick of the building. Whatever the reason, once the brothers were in the main body of the hall they behaved in a manner more fitting to their station. They walked rapidly along the main hall's central exhibit, an aisle of bones lined by soft, velvet ropes, as if such a boundary could delimit this age of reason, keeping it uncontaminated by the savageries of the past. They walked by the remains of extinct creatures. A complete skeleton of a horse, that beast of burden of the ancients, then on by a pair of elephantine skulls of animals hunted out for use in forgotten wars thousands of years gone by. A modalman's four-armed skeleton reared up, ivory in the gaslights. There were plaster dummies of men from the Years of Woe arranged in vignettes of desperate combat. In the museum, their time of endless war is grouped alongside the horrors of the elder days. A fitting comment on that uncivilised age.

The brothers came to the Maceriyan gallery. A broad, high arch of patterned brick and stone led from the main hall to the museum's most prized exhibits. The guard looked annoyed as they walked under the arch. His hand dropped from the grille that would shut it for the night, which he had been about to pull closed. Other visitors were heading for the exit, the museum's cleaning staff were already beginning the laborious task of polishing its marble floors. The brothers were late. Only minutes remained before the closing bell would chime.

Garten glanced at the relics of Old Maceriya and Pre-Maceriya as they went by, things dragged from the earth by archaeologists these last one hundred years. Machines of unknown purpose stood upon plinths, their parts locked by corrosion. Statues missing a leg, or an arm, or a head, were carefully presented on iron rods. Monumental sculptures crowded alcoves fifty feet high. Glass cases showed off the personal effects of the nameless dead, each one carefully pinned, numbered, and annotated in the careful hand of antiquarians.

The lighting was low in the museum, and getting lower as various side galleries and individual rooms were shut up and their lamps doused. The galleried windows along the tops of the walls were dark. The air was musty and unmoving, as dry as that of a tomb. The ghosts of the Maceriyans were long departed, and the building had been properly warded in any case, but

Garten could not put aside the fear that if they lingered too long in the hall, he and his brother would be lost to the ancient dead, forced to join them in procession night after night. An earth tremor set the exhibits a-rattling, doing nothing to lessen this impression.

The odd noises that precede the closing of any large building prompted Trassan to stride faster. His shoes squeaked upon the floor. His pocket watch was in his hand, its protective clamshell open. He frowned at it every third step or so, as if the lateness of the hour was its fault, and not his for insisting upon another drink.

They went past a lofty side hall which housed a massive pediment taken from the temples of balmy Ferrok and reconstructed in Karsa's hall of antiquities. Decorated by an elaborate frieze, it was regarded widely as the museum's greatest artefact. The brothers spared it no thought, and headed for the resting place of the world's putative last god. Although we all know another resides in Perus, and a couple more besides.

Trassan came to an abrupt halt. The case—in truth a sizable room walled with glass—was empty. The glimmer lights inside were out. Bottles and clay amphorae were scattered on the floor, just visible in the dark.

On the ornate framing of the case, in large letters, was written: 'Eliturion, God of Wine and Drama'.

Trassan was disappointed. He cast about until he spotted a sorry looking man pushing a wide broom up the gallery. "Excuse me!" he said. "Where is the Maceriyan god?"

The man looked up from the floor slowly, as if he had not raised his head in months. "Yes, goodfellow?"

"The god?" said Trassan impatiently. "I wanted to see the god!"

"Oh, yes, goodfellow. The god, sir. He finishes early on Karsday, at fourth bell. He is no longer here today."

Trassan frowned. "We paid full admission! It is the only exhibit I wished to view."

"It states plainly, goodfellow, if I might be so bold, on the signs without. The god finishes at four."

"We shouldn't have had that third drink," said Garten. "We can always come back tomorrow," he added placatingly.

"No," muttered Trassan. "No."

"If it pleases you, goodfellows," said the servant, "the divinity likes to take his drink in the Off Parade, he'll be there all night, in one of the public houses. If you wish, I can give you the names of those he favours. He will not be too hard to find."

They waited for the information. The man looked at them expectantly and cleared his throat politely. Trassan grudgingly reached for his purse.

The Parade was Karsa's grandest road, a recent avenue driven right through the heart of the old city by royal decree, linking the palace and the rebuilt Halls of the Three Houses. Palatial apartment buildings and townhouses in the Maceriyan revivalist style lined the way. All was vibrantly new. Vulgar, they say, but time will change that. The trees that would one day make the parade a tunnel of leaves were but saplings in nurseries of iron. New stone sparkled, elegant women and men walked arm in arm down the street, shining dog-drawn carriages and glimmer cars clattered along the flawless, tarred and gravelled surface. None of the cobbles or sets one finds in the older grand areas, no, but Erecion Gandamyn's fine creation. No expense had been spared.

Off Parade was a different matter. The rebuilding of the city to Prince Alfra's grand design had not yet progressed more than three streets back from the Parade, and there the warrens of the unimproved Karsa reasserted themselves. Cramped and sometimes dangerous, there was a feverish atmosphere to the area, as if the inhabitants and buildings were aware that soon all would be razed to make way for Alfra's vision, and were spurred to greater revelries.

Trassan and Garten pushed their way into the widest of these narrow streets, leading directly off the Delian Way, itself emanating from the Parade. You know it? They did too. This was a familiar haunt; Off Parade is a place where rich and poor mingled with something approaching parity. The delights to be found there are manifold, attracting men of all classes and tastes. You're here, after all, and only some of you are scum.

Hooting charabancs tottered on spiderlegs, glimmer stacks glowing, steam belching, their drivers shouting at the throng to part lest they be crushed. By the side of the road, a ten-strong dray team barked and howled, eager to be away, as barrels were rolled out the tailgate of their wagon and into the cellar of a salt merchant. The shouts of hustlers, streetmerchants, barbers and more blared out, amplified by phonograph. Dogs barked, rakes whistled, whores shouted. Faces swam in and out of gaslight, indistinct, suddenly revealed in the harder light of glimmerlamps, only to be snatched away by the next shadow. Such is the face of our modern world.

They went to three public houses named by the museum drudge. The god was not in any of them, because he was in the Nelly Bold, of course. Indeed, from what Trassan had heard of the size of Eliturion, he doubted the god would have fit through the doors of any of them. They were dark, noisy places, not fitting for a divinity in his or Garten's opinion. The Nelly Bold was where the god was famous for being, he reasoned. But Trassan insisted on inspecting all.

"They are, after all, on the way," he said, ordering beer at every one.

It was on exiting the third such establishment that Trassan was robbed. A hand went for his pocket watch. He fell for the feint and instinctively reached for it, only to be relieved of his wallet by a second hand.

There was a flurry of movement at his feet, and a youth burst up from the ground, pushing hard into the crowd. Trassan had the presence of mind to trip him, and he stumbled. "Stop thief!" he bellowed.

The crowd, turning toward the commotion, inadvertently parted. With a desperate, terrified glance backward, the boy regained his feet and lunged heedlessly forward, flattening bystanders, Trassan in hot pursuit. His cry of "Stop thief!" had been taken up, and echoed off the tightly packed buildings. Trassan charged after the boy, upsetting a stack of linen as he blundered into a stall. Ignoring the holder's angry shouts, he forced his way on, following the wake of flapping arms and outrage the boy left as he pushed deeper into the Off Parade. Trassan caromed off a man, sending him sprawling, went round a corner into a threatening alleyway, and then was unexpectedly into a space in the crowd. In the centre of this clearing, fenced by faces, two men of the watch had the boy pinned to the ground. He wriggled and shouted, but was held fast. A third watchman kept back the gawpers. Trassan lunged for the boy. "My wallet! Give it back!"

"Stand back, master engineer! You obstruct us in our duties." The watchman shoved at him without restraint. A thick-faced man, his eyes lacking the vital spark of humanity. He was the kind of man to be wary of, but Trassan was angry.

"That boy," panted Trassan, "took my wallet."

"How do we prove that?" said the watchman kneeling on the boy's back.

"It's a difficulty, goodfellow," said the first watchman without regret.

Of course, thought Trassan. The thieftakers would divide his money among themselves, "owner unknown" they commonly said. He was having none of that.

"Ask him," said Trassan.

The watchmen's faces soured.

"Go ahead," said Trassan. "Do your duty, as you say you should. Ask the boy if it was me he robbed. He has no reason to lie now he has been caught."

The watchman nodded. "Right you are, goodfellow," he said sourly, but Trassan was of high birth and the crowd was paying close attention to their exchange. Trassan got a glimpse of a defiant, foreign face as the watchmen barked questions at him.

"He says it was you, goodfellow, but he is a thief, and what worth is the word of a thief?"

"And it was me. I am no thief; do you doubt the worth of my word, the word of a goodfellow and master engineer?"

For a moment the watchman stared into Trassan's eyes. Trassan tensed.

"I believe you have something of mine," he said levelly. "Hand it over."

The watchman looked down suddenly, some internal calculation returning unfavourable results. "Yes sir, here you are, sir."

He held out Trassan's wallet. Trassan snatched it. It was noticeably lighter than it had been.

"Thank you," Trassan said. "Now I will go about my business. You go about yours."

The watch hauled the boy upright roughly, landing blows on him as they hustled him back onto the main way. Trassan supposed he should feel glad for it. After all, the boy had robbed him. But the boy was pinched-looking, and Trassan was sickened by it, and wished he had not spoken.

Garten's hand caught his elbow.

"I lost you there, brother." He had his sword out in his other hand, its length was pointed downward, but the gleam of naked steel bought them some space in the crammed alley. "They caught him?"

"They did," said Trassan. By now the street was returning to normal.

"You should file a report."

Trassan grimaced. "I have no stomach for that. Let's go before the watch return and insist that I do."

Trassan and his brother pushed their way back out of the alleyway, braving a crossing of the open sewer at its centre to get out the quicker. They went back into the more genteel area of Off Parade, where there were signs of new construction and preliminary explorations for the building of Allian's sewers, towards the Nelly Bold.

Ah, the Nelly Bold! A name worthy of legend. She stood at the intersection of three streets which were undergoing modernisation. Much of the square had been repaved with the hard black rock of Karsa's cliffs, the streets lined by new kerbstones. A triangular seating area had been fenced off by gleaming rails. Three saplings, sickly from filthy air, were caged at each point. To the north side of the square an entire block had been flattened. Gaps in the roofline further back toward the Parade indicated that this area was next to suffer the attentions of the architects. The surveys for the sewers were being conducted in a most direct manner. More buildings would fall later to provide space for a new boulevard.

Not the Nelly Bold. Somehow, she had been saved when countless other buildings of note had not. Is it her indomitable skirts of stone, or her impressive height? Five storeys, higher by far than the slums about her. Is it the venerable history of the place, standing as she had there for three hundred years, when this was nothing but a wind-blasted heath, and the sea could still be spied from her topmost windows? Is it my presence here, for it is my favourite hole? Or was it, perhaps, good Ellany's strategic application of monies and other favours? Who knows? Perhaps it is unimportant. The Nelly Bold would remain, and that is that. She was wearing a fresh coat of paint in anticipation of new suitors. Modern glimmer light shone from the tall windows and from lamps upon her front. Her sign was bright and new. The brothers paused outside. Another tremor rocked the Earth. Neither the crowds or the pub paid it notice. Of more annoyance was the rain sweeping in from the sea, chill and thick.

"Now this is more like it," said Trassan, and reached from the door handle.

"I hope he's in there," said Garten, shivering.

I see from your faces that you anticipate what's coming, as you should, for the place I describe is this the very one where I sit now telling you this tale and the brothers are outside this very moment. Now, look to the door. It opens.

In they come.

CHAPTER SIX
The Nelly Bold

FUGGY AIR AS thick as bricks walled the threshold of the Nelly Bold. But although the Nelly Bold appeared a down at heel establishment, it was, for a large part, sham. Doormen appeared silently, taking the brothers' coats and hats in exchange for garderobe copper chits, and the two brothers found themselves not so uncomfortable after all.

To go from the dark and cold to a noisy house discloses to a man the true state of his mind. Outside, the brothers had felt sober as Guiders. Inside, their drunkenness was revealed to them entire.

"The god is here!" shouted Trassan. "I'm getting a drink, then I'm buttonholing the bastard."

"Cider, I'm sick of beer. Why that face?" he said to his brother's expression of distaste. "You come to The Nelly Bold to appreciate the rougher side of life. Cider! And, and food!" he yelled after his brother, who although only three paces away had been swallowed by the crowd. "I'm starving!"

Trassan emerged back through the press, and grabbed Garten.

"Eh?"

"Look who I've found," he said, dragging his brother after him. Scowls followed them as Trassan jostled arms and elbows.

"Look!" Trassan pointed to a man sitting in a booth, all alone. He was shorter than either of them, more slender, with long pale hair arrayed on a large lace collar. He wore a broad-brimmed hat, even indoors, and was nursing a glass of wine.

"Guis? Guis!" shouted Garten. "Where have you been?"

The two brothers were obliged to shout together to attract Guis's attention. The scowl he wore at the disturbance melted into a fragile smile when he saw who addressed him.

"Trassan? Garten!"

The two younger Kressinds forced their way to their brother's table.

"What a fine bit of luck!" said Garten.

"Can we join you?" said Trassan.

Guis shrugged amiably. "It's not like I have company."

The brothers exchanged hugs and took their seats. Trassan waved frantically at a harassed looking serving girl. He held up three fingers, she nodded wearily.

"Cider, ale and...?"

"Wine," said Guis. "A bottle."

"Wine!" shouted Trassan.

The girl waved at her ears, then pointed.

"She can't hear me," said Trassan.

"Are you surprised?" said Guis. "This is a rowdy night."

"Ah, she's coming back," said Trassan.

"The god is over there then," said Garten, craning his neck. Back off the main room was a large booth, almost a room in itself. At the very back a giant sat, a caricature of a rambunctious rural goodfellow, all good cheer, rosy cheeks and loud laughs.

"He is," said Guis.

"Terrifying," said Garten sincerely. He had never seen the god out of his case.

The god looked Garten right in the eye, winked and pressed one enormous finger against his nose. Faces about his table turned to look at the brothers. They raised their tankards and shouted salutations that were lost in the hubbub of the crowd.

"Why are they looking at us?" said Garten.

"He's been expecting you, he's been talking about you."

"What?"

"You've never been in an alehouse with the god?" said Guis. "Why Garten, you are duller than you look. It is his habit to tell stories." Guis patted at his shoulder where something stirred in his hair. "It is his habit to embarrass at least one of his listeners while doing so."

"God of wine and drama," said Trassan, pleased to have been anticipated.

Garten was dismayed. "It is no small thing to draw the eye of a god."

"Don't worry about it," said Guis. "He does it to everyone. To be frank, he can be a bit of a cock. He enjoys disturbing people."

"Where is that girl?" said Trassan. He fidgeted in his seat, craning his neck this way and that.

"Where have you been, brother?" asked Garten. "We've missed you."

"Away up north, in Stoncastrum. I've been there for seven weeks or so," said Guis.

"Have you moved?" said Garten incredulously. "Why didn't you tell us. You should have written, sent a message, anything."

"It's just a short stay. I've been busy. I have a play on. I would have sent notice but, you know." He smiled, but sadly.

"You should not keep your movements to yourself so. Does mother know you are back?"

Guis shrugged. The accompanying smile was a little sour.

"Well!" said Garten with forced cheer. He clapped his hands together and rubbed them. "We're all here now, that's the important thing. Three Kressind brothers in one place at one time, that's worthy of celebration."

"We'll all be together tomorrow," said Trassan ruefully. "Rel's getting kicked out of the country. I assume you're coming to see him off?"

"I did hear," said Guis. "Any idea why?"

"Ah," said Trassan dismissively. "He fucked the wrong man's wife, is what I heard. They've had him banged up for a fortnight in the regimental prison. Big fuss about nothing if you ask me."

"He'll be missing Katriona's wedding."

"I can't help but think that was intended," said Trassan. "Alanrys is a sod, no matter what father thinks of him. There's something going on there. Father pulled some strings," said Trassan. "Apparently it was before the wedding or fighting Ocerzerkiyan corsairs."

"He'll be halfway across the continent in a week," said Garten.

"Katriona will be livid," said Guis.

Trassan huffed in agreement. "She is." He picked up a pewter salt cellar and fiddled with it. There were few objects Trassan would not worry at. He was a devil with knickknacks.

"Leave it be!" Guis scowled; it settled into deep lines worn into his face by its many predecessors.

"Have you still got it then?" asked Garten. "Let's say hello."

"It's not a pet," said Guis sharply. "It's a fucking great pain in my arse."

"If you were nicer to it, then it might not be," said Garten.

"Are we getting drinks here or not?" said Guis, desperate to change the subject.

"No sign of that girl," said Trassan. He dropped the salt cellar. It rolled on its bulbous side in a slow arc, spilling white grains upon the wood. "Hang on." He stood up and shoved his way out of the booth.

"Tyn! Tyn!" said Garten softly. "Are you there? Come out. It's me, Garten. Come and take some salt."

"Name not Tyn," said a small, papery voice, somehow managing to make itself heard. A patron, sat at the head of a nearby table, glanced over uneasily.

"I've got to call you Tyn. If you don't like it, tell us your name."

"Name not tell," said the voice. "Name not mine to tell. Not yours to know. Name not tell. Geas."

Garten tugged off his glove and licked his fingertip, dabbing up salt from the table. He held it up near Guis's shoulder. "Come on, I've got salt. Come out."

The thing in Guis's hair blew a raspberry, but came forth nonetheless. First a spindle-fingered hand parted Guis's hair like a curtain. Then a face emerged on a neck as delicate as a grass stalk. He was as ugly as could be, a hairless bat crossed with some goggle-eyed ape. Its nose was all twitching folds and frills. A roar of laughter from a nearby table sent it darting back. It emerged again, ever so timidly. Then with a sudden rush it scampered off Guis's shoulder and ran down his arm, hopping from the table onto Garten's outstretched hand. It was tiny, the size of a small rat, yet possessed of humanoid anatomy in miniature. It wore no clothes but for a tattered mouse fur loincloth and a pair of pointed boots. A topknot tied in a bow of red thread was the only hair on his scalp. The arms were disproportionately long, the hands and feet big. A delicate chain ran from a twist of iron wire at its neck to a fastening on Guis's necklace.

Tyn stood in Garten's palm for a moment. He flinched at every sound. It looked up at Garten, asking for approval. Garten nodded encouragingly. In a flurry of movement Tyn pounced on his finger to lick greedily at the salt. Garten laughed at the sensation.

A gasp at Garten's shoulder. He turned to see the serving girl, her hand to her mouth, lips and eyes wide and white. Tyn spun around in fright and shot up Guis's arm.

"My brother's pet," explained Garten.

"It is not a pet," said Guis darkly.

The girl continued to stare.

"Can we order, do you think?" said Garten gently. The girl nodded.

"Where is Trassan?" said Guis.

"Who knows. Let's get him a drink and some food."

"And what if he's already on his way back here with some drinks?"

"Then we'll have two drinks apiece. That's a lot less than I intend to drink. I have children, a wife, and a patron who demands I be available at all hours. I don't get out much," said Garten.

"How is Charramay?"

"I don't get out much," repeated Garten flatly.

Guis laughed.

"Oh do fuck off," said Garten, which only made Guis laugh more.

TRASSAN FORGOT ALL about finding the girl. The god was watching him, ruddy cheeks split by a knowing smile. In the museum Eliturion seemed smaller. Out in public he was immense. His drinking cronies followed his gaze, and soon Trassan was being stared at by a table's worth of drunken men.

"Good evening, Trassan Kressind!" boomed the god, waving his arm in an arc over the heads of his friends. "You sought me at the museum today. Here I am. You wish to ask me something, so why do you not ask it?"

His fellows made loud noises of agreement. "Ask him, go on! Ask him! We've been hearing all about you!"

Trassan ignored them. If there was anything to be offended about, he could be sure Guis would have become offended by it on his behalf. Trassan put on his most confident smile, and stepped nearer.

"They tell me you know all that is to be known."

Eliturion inclined his head. "One might say such a power lies within ambit of the god of drama. For what is history but a story done, the present a story in the telling, and the future a story yet to be told?"

"'Drama is truth, not fact'," quoted Trassan.

"So said Damarteo of Hethika," said Eliturion.

Trassan smiled back and bowed slightly.

"Very pithy," said the god. "But balls. Damarteo of Hethika was an enormous tosser, and I knocked him on his backside for it two thousand years ago. There is no such thing as absolute fact, only truth. Truth is to be found only in story. I am therefore, the master of what is to be known."

"Tale-telling more like!" shouted one of the braver bravos.

"That is exactly what I said, dunderhead. Hush now." Eliturion clucked irritably at the man.

"That is nonsense," said Trassan. "Damarteo has it quite the other way around."

"And as I said, Damarteo of Hethika was a tosser. Go on then, Trassan Kressind. Are you going to ask me or not?"

"If you are the master of truth, by your own reckoning, then surely you know what I wish to ask you?"

Eliturion snorted. "Of course, of course." He let out a godly belch, thunderous and pungent. "But you have to ask. There are rules, even for me."

"Then I shall ask. Will I be successful in my venture?"

"And why do you ask that?"

"You know why I ask. You are being evasive."

The god essayed a sly smile. "Perhaps."

"Will I be successful?" pressed Trassan.

Eliturion stared at Trassan for an uncomfortably long moment. The god looked right through him and out the other side, like his head was hollow and his eyes glass windows.

"That very much depends on your definition of success, young man." The god sat back. "There you go, one question, one answer. You got what you wanted."

"I beg to differ," said Trassan hotly.

"Well then, you got what you asked, which is what you get if you don't phrase your questions to a god right. If you do not have what you wanted, choose your words more carefully next time," Eliturion smiled benevolently at his cronies as they roared with laughter. Trassan did not think it so funny.

"Such a thing, when a god requires toadies," he said.

Eliturion barked out a laugh. "When did a god not require toadies? What is a worshipper if not the worst toady of all? These men at least are honest in their sycophancy. They ask nothing of me but to drink with me and hear my stories! Gods take and give little in return, and what their caprice furnishes their worshippers with is often very far from what they desired. As you, my friend, have just discovered. You are fortunate, to badger me in the pub. No entrails or priest's fees or other humbug to be dealt with. Why do you think old Res Iapetus chased out my brothers and sisters? No man likes to bend his knee for no reward."

"You remained, and you still have your worshippers."

"Do not provoke me, Trassan Kressind."

"Is that a threat?"

"Only if you hear it so, I am not one for threatening. If you don't like my sooth speak to my cousin. He might prove more enlightening, if you survive the experience. All I want is a good time. Forever. I don't like to be annoyed. It prevents me from enjoying myself."

Trassan gave a wide and mostly sincere smile. He bowed deeply. "And I merely jest, for it is known far and wide that of all the creatures who walk upon the shivering earth, Eliturion, last of the gods, enjoys jesting most."

"You know your mythology. It's all bollocks. Still." Eliturion sniffed and raised his giant cup. "Your health sir."

"And yours," said Trassan.

Trassan rejoined his brothers. Their drinks had arrived and Garten was tipsy.

"Where you been then?"

"Talking to a god!" said Trassan grandiosely.

"We ordered you some food," said Garten.

"I hear you've some mysterious project on," said Guis.

"Not mysterious, but freely known!" said Trassan. "I have been engaged by Arkadian Vand in the construction of the world's first oceanic iron ship."

"Ah yes, I did hear. But brother, will it not sink?" said Guis archly. "Being made of iron?"

"Floatstone doesn't sink," said Garten. "And that's made of, you know, stone." He hiccupped. "Excuse me."

"Floatstone's full of holes," said Guis.

"Ah, then it should sink the quicker," said Garten.

Guis and Garten clanged their tankard and glass together.

Trassan shook his head. "Funny. An iron pan will not sink when placed in water, but displaces the water, allowing it to float. We are harnessing this phenomenon to create a ship of unsurpassed size and power. It is nothing new. There are several smaller vessels plying the Olb on the mainland made solely of metal. Only this is of unsurpassed scale."

"Unsurpassed excepting the three that sank."

"Details," said Trassan. "And mine is still bigger."

"How are you going to power it?" said Guis, genuinely intrigued. "Glimmer engines? How'd you get enough to make it move? How do you keep it fuelled?"

"Could just use normal steam," pointed out Garten. "Like Tallyvan Landsman, he's making quite the fortune on coal-fired steam, so I hear."

"Got to get the coal, got to carry it. How do you manage that? It'd require a whole new supply network," pointed out Trassan.

"True," said Garten. "You could make one."

"Logistics bore me." said Trassan. "There is a new procedure. A new type of engine, that will carry enough fuel and enough power to drive a ship the size of a town." He leaned in close. "I designed it."

"How's it work?" asked Garten.

Trassan's eyes flicked back and forth between his brothers, as if debating whether to reveal his secret. "Iron." He said finally. "Iron that holds a glimmer charge."

Guis slapped the table "Now I know you've gone crazy. They're inimical to one another."

"Not if the iron and the glimmer are treated and combined in precisely the right manner, not if the iron is married with silver iodide. Silver is the glimmer metal. Iron can be encouraged to hold a charge if alloyed with silver iodide under strictly controlled circumstances. Strike the alloy, upset the patterning, and it produces a steady stream of glimmer energy as the iodide decays." Trassan became animated, sketching the process in the air with his gloved hands. "The glimmer is released slowly. As it encounters the iron, it is annihilated, generating great heat. Hot enough to make the iron cells glow red hot. If you array them in battery, introduce water... Well, I need not describe the potential of superheated steam." He went on to do so anyway. "Imagine, the force generated by water heated not to evaporation, but to three or four times that. Even five. I believe we can reach as high as six, but it puts a terrible strain on the machinery."

"Seriously?" said Guis, placing his glass back on the table.

"I can say no more. There will be an announcement soon. Vand wanted construction underway before the methods are revealed. We can't hope to keep it secret forever, but we can keep it secret long enough to be the first to use it."

Guis looked at him for a long moment. "You haven't actually got it to work properly yet, have you?"

"Well..." said Trassan reluctantly.

"I know you," Guis said. "You're playing a longshot. Does Vand know?"

"Of course he knows!" said Trassan, his face sharp. "Look, the technique works. The hypothesis has been proven. I've had fifteen alchemists replicate the results, not charlatans mind, but proper magisters. There is a problem in scaling up the production, but such things only remain problems for a short while. You should see the power you get out of these devices, gentlemen! It's going to change the world."

"Once you crack the problem," said Guis speaking his gently mocking words into his wine glass. "Good luck."

"Does this have to do with what you want to talk to me about?" said Garten.

Trassan became uncomfortable. "Yes, but I cannot discuss it here, I'm sure you understand."

He said this to Garten, but truly it was addressed to Guis. Too late, for the elder had already taken offence. Trassan would tell one brother, but not the other. From such things spring discord among siblings.

Guis struggled to shrug it off. Trassan would have a perfectly good reason, he told himself. One that would come out once whatever deal he needed to do with Garten was done. But a nagging sense that his brother did not trust him to keep silent soured his mood, if only because he would not trust himself to keep a secret either. His good mood blackened. He retreated within himself, a snail withdrawing from insult within his shell. His grin froze, becoming something wolfish. His eyes would not meet theirs. From this alone it was hard to tell he was offended, but his manner changed, losing its diffidence, becoming caustic. This was not an impression gained from his words or his actions, but rather something felt, like a switch in the wind, and was all too obvious to his siblings. The conversation dragged on for a while, family matters, jokes that fell flat. The others probed Guis about his doings in the Stoncastrum, but this most verbose of men bit his words hard when upset and they were reluctant to leave his mouth.

Garten knew his brother best. He was more alive to the moods of men than machine-obsessed Trassan, and became concerned. He coaxed Guis, tried to obliquely reassure him without suggesting he had become offended, which would make matters worse. Despite his best efforts, Guis remained morose, and became angry.

"Oh come on Guis! It's probably something to do with the Admiralty. Am I right? I'm right." He turned to his other brother. "You're building a ship, right Trassan? You need something from them. You want me to help, right? You can say as much as that surely! Guis doesn't need to know the details."

"I can't say anything. I can't, I'm sorry," said Trassan.

"I think I better be going," said Guis, and stood, jarring the table. "I'll see you tomorrow."

"Guis..."

"Trassan, it's alright, I understand. Tell me all about it when you can. I'm just being a bit of an idiot. You know what I'm like, I get things stuck in my head it..." Guis smiled tiredly but honestly. "I'm tired. I better go."

They exchanged warm farewells, yet cooler than their greetings.

"Well," said Garten as Guis pushed his way out to the door. "That was tactless. You should know better, he hates it when he thinks he's being excluded."

"Nonsense! I tell him everything, and I will tell him everything about this too." He intended to as well. To him Guis was an advisor, one of his most trusted confidantes, but one to be presented with all the facts and quizzed extensively on his opinions of them. Not with half-baked plans, with which he had little patience, nor secrets, which he struggled to keep. Guis's mercurial nature hid a certain wisdom, but it must be utilised carefully. Trassan instinctively understood this, although would not have framed it quite that way himself. "It is not that I do not trust him, brother. It is that he does not trust himself." He slapped Garten on the shoulder and smiled. "Come on! I'll say sorry to the old drama queen tomorrow. He'll turn up to see off Rel. We'll sort it out then, it'll be fine. We can't go running around playing sop to his ego. It only makes him worse. Now, let's have another drink. I feel like staying out all night."

Garten's eyebrows rose.

"You don't?" said Trassan.

"Well, you see, job." Garten smiled at some private matter and swirled the dregs of his drink. "Wife. All that."

"Bah! When was the last time you had a holiday? You're staying out with me, by the gods. Besides, I've got something to show you, I can only show you now the tide is low, and it's best seen at first light."

CHAPTER SEVEN
The Darkling

GUIS DID NOT go straight home but went instead to the Carcaron's Gold, a quieter place, expensive—too expensive in truth for his depleted resources. The atmosphere was altogether more private. This was a place monied lovers came, or men with business they would rather hide.

Guis stared into his wine cup. He drained it, filled it, then drained it again. A knot sat between his shoulders, a boulder in his gut. A cruel anxiety that was not his own crushed his heart. He went over again what Trassan had said, the manner he had said it. Already his intellect had processed the exchange accurately, but his emotions were not his to command.

A malady of the nerves afflicted Guis. He took pains to see his self-loathing reflected in others' love for him. He took bitter satisfaction when his poor behaviour engendered the rejection he feared.

The worst of it was that he knew it was all nonsense. Helterskelter down the passages of his mind, there was a part of him that did not suffer, a Guis as might have been. It looked upon the greater Guis in horror, and despised what it saw as weak. He had been told once that those insane who know they are insane are close to sanity. He ruefully reflected such self-knowledge did not provide a cure.

He shook his head mechanically, four to the left, four to the right. *If I do this no harm will come to those I love. If I tap the table, if I tap the table but four times, all will be well. All of it.* He did it, four sets of four, digging his nails harder and harder into the wood until they parted the grain.

The ritual did no good. Nor did the alcohol. He could not regain his mask. Forebodings of imminent disaster gripped him.

"Careful, master," hissed Tyn in his ear. "You are slipping. We should leave."

"Nonsense," he said, ignoring the slur in his voice. "I need to find some women."

"To what? To look at them, frighten them, and not approach? To leer at them in drunkenness? To speak with them and challenge them to hate you? This I have seen so many times. You must go home. The Twin is large in the sky; this is a night of potency, you should not be out. Go home."

Tyn tugged at a knot in Guis's hair. Undoing it would calm his emotions, but such was Guis's state of mind he would rather suffer. He poked at Tyn, scaring the creature around the back of his neck.

Guis rubbed the insides of his wrists four times each with the opposite wrist. All these acts he performed when no one was looking. If caught, he pretended as if he was doing nothing untoward.

They calmed him a little for a space, ultimately the anxiety redoubled. He reached for his silver cup. A violet spark leapt from its lip, earthing itself in his forefinger with a crack.

"Fuck!" he said, shaking his hand from the pain. Some of the other patrons looked up at him. He doffed his hat at one sardonically, deepening the man's glower further. The man would have fled if he could see the image in Guis's mind; unbidden, the thought of him digging his thumbs into the other man's eye sockets and popping the organs therein. He shook the thought away, appalled. The images were the hardest to deal with. He feared them to be his deepest desires.

"You should have let me untie the knot! Now it is too late!" whispered Tyn into his ear. "Such behaviour is dangerous. He has seen you. We must go where I can protect you. It will be difficult here."

"No, no." Guis was still trying to push the thought away. What kind of a man was he, to think such things?

"Look at the shadows. Look!"

Guis lifted his wine-heavy head. The motion induced a spasm of nausea. He was drunker than he realised. A night like this could end in one of two ways; garrulous frivolity in one drinking pit or another—his black thoughts kept at bay for a while—or *it*. He squinted at the coign between floor and wall. It was often from there the Darkling came first, reaching spindly figures out and threatening to make the worst of his thoughts real.

"Do you see?" said Tyn. "The shadows thicken. We must go!"

He had half a bottle of wine left. Fuck them all, he thought, what did he care? "Let him come," Guis mumbled. The bottom of the bottle bumped on the table as he dragged it to his lips. He drained it in a series of desperate gulps. Wine helped him forget his problems. He needed wine.

Tyn yanked hard at Guis's hair. "We are going," it said. "Now."

Tyn abandoned secrecy and rode openly back to the apartment, leaning out far from Guis's neck vigilantly. Guis slipped and cursed in the mud. Rain hammered down, wilting the brim of his hat.

"They do not care for me," he moaned. "My family have abandoned me. I am loathsome."

"Hush," said Tyn, peering into every dark place. A footpad shrank back into the gloom when it caught sight of the creature squatting on Guis's shoulder. But it was not peril such as this that Tyn sought. "If that were true, why were they pleased to see you?"

"They were pleased, but it did not last. My brothers. I embarrass them. I cannot help myself. They do not care for me. My father hates me! I do not..." Guis steadied himself against a wall, leaning his head forward and forcing Tyn to scamper onto his back. He belched messily, saliva streaming from his slack mouth, but he did not vomit. He wiped his mouth. "I do not think anyone does."

"Hush, hush," said Tyn. "You are not to think bad things, you are not to dwell on them." Tyn's gaze darted about. There were no glimmer lamps in the alley, a stinking sidestreet deep in the Off Parade. Yellow candlelight showed around shutters or slanted through curtains. There was not nearly enough light to keep the shadows back.

"I am a disappointment. I have neither Garten's diligence nor Trassan's ingenuity, Aarin's focus or Rel's good nature."

"Hush. Hush now! Go home, go home now. You will bring it upon yourself!"

Immersed in his own self-pity, Guis would not listen. "And what of my sister! I have but a whit of that girl's brains. That is why my father hates me. He hates me."

"Get on, foolish manling," said Tyn. Its voice lost every trace of servility, deepening, becoming gruff and wild. "Get on or you will perish and I will dance upon your soulless corpse before I fly back to my freedom!"

This roused Guis. He staggered the remaining ten yards to his building; an ancient, decrepit tenement with two lower storeys of brick and three upper storeys of warped timbers. It took him three attempts to get the key in the lock. The door's opening took him by surprise, and he fell forward. The door slammed into the wall of the narrow shared hall with an unconscionable bang.

"Shhh!" Guis giggled. "Shhh! People are sleeping."

As quietly as he could, Guis mounted the creaking stairs and climbed up to his room.

Guis was poorer than he had been, but not yet in poverty. The room was very large, occupying all of the third floor, ten yards by eight. Outside a ragged hole split the clouds. Rain still fell, but the stars shone through. The Red Moon had gone from the sky. White moonlight streamed in through square-leaded windows, illuminating everything in cold shades of grey and midnight blue. A curtained bed took up a portion of the room. A brick fireplace occupied the centre of one of the shorter walls. A screen hid a commode. A small copper bath hung upon the wall. Four tables of varying sizes were dotted about, and several mismatched chairs. All of these were covered in piles of books and papers.

Guis's work, the varying legibility of the handwriting testifying to his mental state when he wrote each.

Guis sobbed, part in self-pity, part in fear. Something was stirring in the thick air of the room.

"Everyone hates me." He tripped on a stack of books, sending them skidding across the polished floor. He flopped face down. "I hate me," he said.

"You are not to think so! You are not to be so, you must find balance. Find your peace within, my master. They love you, they love you, do not think they do not."

"They do not!" said Guis. A lie, his intellect said. The terrible truth, his heart rejoined.

"Be calm. Light your candles. You must do so, or I will struggle to help you."

"I am! I am trying."

He would have torn the little being from his shoulder there and then, if his instincts warned him against it. Without Tyn, he was defenceless against his own thoughts. He dragged himself up and went stumbling about the place, knocking his possessions into disarray. He lit big-headed matches that exploded with sulphurous ferocity, and touched them to the wicks of his candles. No tallow for Guis. He remained a goodfellow, at least for now.

One, two, four, six candles. The moonlight was replaced by naked flame's soothing flicker.

"There!" hissed Tyn. In the corner, a patch of shadow that would not depart before the candle glow, a physical darkness.

"To the bed! To the bed! Get inside the circle!"

Around Guis's bed was a circle of silver filings mixed with salt. Unlike the rest of the room, this part of the floor was clear of detritus. He stepped over it and sat on his bed.

The shadow drew itself up, taking on the rough shape of a man. The candlelight dimmed, its colour drained away. Sounds from outside became brittle.

Guis screwed his eyes shut.

"Do not concentrate! Do not think on it!"

"How can I not?" said Guis. His terror dissolved into bitter, drunken laughter. "Too late."

The shadow thickened, its outline became more certain. A pair of glints in the shadowy round of its head suggested eyes.

"Think of something else, my master!"

"I cannot, I cannot!" He slammed the heels of his hands into his forehead. "I can't stop thinking about it!"

"Stop this, my master! You must stop it."

"I can't, Tyn. I'm tired. Tired of this. Tired of it all. Let it come. I deserve my fate, the loveless son."

"Then sleep, sleep." Tyn made a pass with his hands, as if drawing down Guis's eyelids with its finger tips.

Guis's eyes, already heavy with wine, slid shut and he fell sideways on the bed. Tyn leaned with his collapse, expertly riding the playwright as he fell. He scampered up over Guis's collarbone to stand upon his upper arm, not taking his eyes from the shadow.

The skin of reality rippled. Light returned, intruding now into the shadowed corner, separating the night-black skin of the thing from its refuge.

"Go Darkling, go, nothing for you here!" said Tyn softly. "Back to the shadow with you, get away from the light. Back to the cold, back to the night."

The Darkling remained manifest, its half-formed shape indistinct but too invested in the weft of the world to be dissipated easily.

Tyn growled at it. "Begone!"

The shadow creature's form thickened.

"Begone!" Tyn said. He held his hands wide. His eyes blazed. Smoke rose from his flesh beneath his iron collar. The scent of rich leaf mould filled the room. Tyn's eyes flashed green.

The Darkling melted back, becoming shadow once again.

Tyn shut his eyes. When he opened them, they were bereft of power, and he stood smaller. He rubbed at his burnt neck and grimaced. "Poor Tyn," it muttered. "Poor Tyn is trapped. Poor Tyn will never be free." He stared at his sleeping master. Hatred etched itself into his face.

The moment passed. Tyn's anger burned out. His expression changed to one of affection. He padded along Guis's arm, climbed down and stood on the bed. He reached a hand out to Guis's cheek and stroked it tenderly.

"Sleep, good master. Sleep."

Guis rolled onto his back and let out a somnolent, wine-stinking sigh. Tyn climbed onto him again and stalked up and down until satisfied the magic was done. The rain started again, as it fussed and primped at Guis's shoulder, tying new warding knots into his hair, crooning a song which brought to mind wild places. Raindrops tapped at the windows, driven by gusting wind, run-off spattered noisily into the street mud from a broken gutter. But the night was quiet. When its duties were done, Tyn took another look around the room, sniffing at the dark places suspiciously. It was a long time until he was satisfied. Warily, he coiled the braids into a nest in the hollow of Guis's neck. There it slept the remainder of the night through, face twitching as it dreamt of dark forests.

CHAPTER EIGHT
The Silver Ship

A WET NIGHT gave way to a fine morning that found Garten and Trassan on a bench on the south cliffs. From the safety of Malladua, they looked down upon the Totterdown, a cleft in the cliffs full of prettily painted buildings that wobbled higgledy-piggledy to the high water mark. Insular and sometimes dangerous, its inhabitants had been there for generations. They carried on regardless of the city that had swallowed them, eyes forever on the sea. All of them were fishers, anguilloniers, potmen or gleaners.

Malladua could not be more different. So new the stone gleamed, ordered, planned, named in Maceriyan, and fronted by the great walls of the cliffs. High above the water, it offered the cleaner air of the sea with none of the peril. A meticulously-tended green twenty yards wide ran all along the cliff walk in front of fine terraced townhouses, lawns studded with flowerbeds and ornate lamps. A round plaza paved with slabs of granite was central to this linear park. From its seaward edge, a statue of Demes, the father of Alfra, looked out over the marshes with blind bronze eyes.

The brothers had not slept. The hour was early, that time when the world is luminous with the coming sun. It was too late for ne'er-do-wells, too early for most good folk. In the predawn stillness sounds carried far, shouts from the waking markets, a bell tolling out thanks to departed gods, and the ceaseless cries of Karsa's gulls. Smoke wound up from the city in uncountable blue threads.

"What are we doing here?" Garten shivered. He had lost his hat, and it was cold. He keenly felt every last drink of the night before. Daylight reveals drunkenness's shabby nature all too readily. "It is going to start raining again soon. Look at those clouds."

Trassan had a spyglass. Garten vaguely remembered stopping by his house to fetch it. "Just wait, will you? The sun will be up in a moment, that weather is miles out to sea. Trust me, this is worth it. You can only see this after a Great Tide, blasts all the muck out to sea. It'll be swallowed up by the silt in a few days."

"What will?"

Trassan laughed. "Just wait! This is a surprise."

Acid burned Garten's gullet. He swallowed it back. There was a leaden pressure growing at the back of his skull that pulsed as if alive. Each beat squeezed bitter spit into his mouth. "I don't feel all that well. I need bacon. Very salty bacon. I'll be fine if I can have some bacon. Please. Bacon."

"We'll get you bacon after we've seen this and after we've seen Rel."

"I don't think Charramay is going to be very pleased with me."

"She'll not know! You can come and sleep it off at my house."

The sun crested the horizon, a sliver of brilliant light peeking between cloud and earth that joined the distant sea and mud of the marsh into a single sheet of molten metal.

"Ow," said Garten, shading his eyes.

Trassan stood and scanned the mud.

"There!" he shouted.

"Ow," said Garten again. He rubbed his head. "Why do I always listen when you say 'one more drink'?"

"Look! Look!" Trassan hauled his brother to his feet. "There it is! Can you see it, right there, a flash of silver brighter than the rest?"

"Yes. So what? If I look interested can I have some bacon?"

Trassan tugged him over to the rail around the viewing platform until they were right on the edge of the cliff, by the brazen feet of Alfra's father. Trassan pointed. Garten looked hard. Trassan handed the spyglass to Garten.

"See there? Can you see it?"

"What am I looking for?"

"An object of sculpted metal, unharmed by the sea."

"Is that it? A spine of metal emerging from the mud."

"That's it."

Garten saw something tall, seven yards or so, sharp as a shark's fin. A pool excavated by the rush of the tide glinted around it. As his brother said, the metal was free of corrosion or fouling and shone with reflected sunlight.

"That, brother, is a Morfaan ship."

"And? People have known about that for years, it's in plain view," said Garten. "It's on all our charts. You dragged me out here to see that?"

"Then did you know an engineer by the name of Gann tried to retrieve it? He failed. Whatever that piece of metal is, it's attached to something very large."

"That I did not know."

"He attempted it ten years back, before you joined the Admiralty," said Trassan.

"Right. Well, it's very nice, but why are you showing me?"

"Because, brother, you're looking at the past there, but also the future."

"Every magister with big ideas says the same thing. The wisdom of the ancients! A new world! Bollocks. I don't see what the fuss is about. The Morfaan were decadent, and they fell. Ours is the superior civilisation."

"That's father talking. You don't really believe that."

Garten shrugged. The motion forced out a sickly burp. "Maybe I do, maybe I don't."

"Imagine if we could make a ship like that."

"Come on Trass, no one knows how to replicate their metallurgy. Father told us that often enough. What has all this to do with me? I feel lousy and its freezing. Do we really have to be out here? What is it you need from the Admiralty? If it's permission to dig that out you'll need to speak to the Shoreman's Guild and the customs people. The foreshore's not our purview. Sorry."

Trassan smiled, not taking his eyes off the ancient vessel buried in the mud of the bay. "I'm not interested in salvaging the wreck. Well, I am. But I don't think I could. However, there is something better. I'm going to tell you something that no one else knows. I trust you can keep it a secret."

"I'm your brother, Trassan."

Trassan put his hand on Garten's shoulder. His eyes were alive with excitement. "Vand has discovered the location of an intact Morfaan city."

Garten raised his eyebrows. "What? How long have you known this?"

"Not long, I swear, or I wouldn't be here with you right now. He'll announce it soon. His excavations in Ostria have been most illuminating. He found a map. It dates from some time before the Maceriyan period, when the Morfaan were in decline. Most of the places marked there are familiar—the ruins at Ostria, naturally, Under-Perus, Mohacs, the Glass Fort, the rest. But there is one site, so remote, that he took a gamble that it might still be whole." Trassan gripped his brother. "He had a seeing performed, it's there alright. Still there, whole, untouched. Deep in the south, surrounded by ice, but it's there, in the Sotherwinter. It's fortunate that the *Prince Alfra* was under construction," said Trassan.

"Right," said Garten, who did not believe it was a coincidence for a second. "You're planning to go there."

"Yes, yes!" said Trassan. "In the iron ship! The greatest adventure of this modern age!"

"And to get there you'll have to pass beyond the Final Isle."

"I will," said Trassan encouragingly. "What I need from you, brother, is a free charter of trade for my ship, a Licence Undefined."

Garten lowered his spyglass. "Piss off. Nobody gets a Licence Undefined but the Ishmalani. We can't have captains going where they will. Crossing the Southern Ocean is out of the question without proper consideration. The treaty with the Drowned King forbids it."

"I'm serious. This ship will be able to do things no other vessel built by men has ever done. Not even the king will be able to stop it."

"I'd take that back if I were you. We're dangerously close to the water."

"A boast. I have no intention of crossing the dead. That's why I want the official documentation."

"Then it doesn't matter what this ship of yours can and can't do, brother. Be more careful of your bragging. The ocean is his domain." He frowned. "No. I can't do it for you. You'll have to go through official channels."

"No! You *can* do it for me, without all the delay." Trassan paused. "What if I were to tell you that I have a Ishmalan captain? Would that make it easier for you?"

"How much did he cost you?"

"Everything is in place," said Trassan soothingly. "It will all be perfectly legal. If I'm going to do this, I have to go next spring. I need your help."

"Apply openly," said Garten. "Don't drag me into it."

"Come on, anything with Vand's hand in it will be debated endlessly. He's as many enemies as friends. It'll be kicked up from the Admiralty and end up in the Three Houses. The last thing we want is the politicians to get involved. Get me my charter, let them argue over it afterwards."

"Yes. Right. I see." Garten looked at his brother seriously. "And you're not planning to go anywhere unusual. No. Just a simple request, that's all. Utter rot. No one will believe you. You'll have to go through the official channels, public inquiry. It'll be judged in the national interest, you'll get it, although I don't see the king allowing you an easy passage. You'll just have to wait."

"We don't have time. There are other parties interested. Rumour has it Vardeuche Persin already knows what Vand has uncovered and is preparing an expedition of his own. I'll be kicking my heels here for another year while he's looting the city. We don't want the Maceriyans to get there first, do we?"

Garten huffed. "Trass..."

Scenting triumph, Trassan pressed on. "There's a city, Garten. An entire Morfaan city! Can't you see what this means? Do you really want all that to end up in the hands of the Maceriyans? Look, you can trust me, we're family. I'll cut you in. There's a lot of money to made out of this. But it all has to be done discretely. If I go through the proper channels, then the Houses are sure to block us at every turn. Half of them are in the pockets of Judan, Horozik and the rest."

"And they're in the pockets of Persin." Garten weighed the spyglass in his hand as he mulled over Trassan's words, his growing hangover forgotten for a minute. "All right," he said cautiously. "I'll see what I can do. No promises!" he said in response to Trassan's grin. "Understand this, I'm doing it because you're my brother, not for the money."

He raised the telescope to his eye again and looked out to where floatstone ships laboured up and down the horizon.

"But I do still want the money," he said. "In case you think I'm going to do it for free."

Trassan chuckled. "Spoken like a true Kressind." He smacked his brother's arm. "Come on, if we're quick, we'll be able to catch Rel before they kick him out of the country. Then we'll get you that bacon."

Garten sucked air through his teeth. "It's not like that. He's not getting kicked out."

Trassan leaned forward onto the rail, and looked down directly to the marsh a thousand feet beneath him. "It is exactly like that," he said.

CHAPTER NINE
A Night in the Drum

THE WATCHMEN JOKED about a woman they had both had dalliances with as they dragged the hooded and handcuffed Tuvacs from the street. He was limping from his beating, but they pulled mercilessly, their fingers digging into the soft flesh beneath his biceps. A door opened, and he was shoved up into a watch wagon.

He saw little through the sack on his head; little glimpses of a world crosshatched with rough fibre, a windowless box with benches down each side. Three other men staring bleakly ahead while his handcuffs were fastened to a bar running under the bench. The door closed, leaving them in near total blackness. An uncomfortable ride, two more men thrown in. Another dash over rough streets brought him to the Drum, the old castle of Karsa City, and its most infamous prison. There he was chained to the others and jogged through a nail-studded door he had heard so many black stories about, down slippery stairs into the cacophonous gaol. Cries wailed from grilles in doors. Pleas for release, for water. Curses. The watchmen slammed their truncheons into the wood and shouted for quiet. The stench was revolting.

They stopped. Tuvacs snatched his breath as the watchman unlocked a door. His arm was grabbed roughly again. Hands tugged carelessly at his wrists. The handcuffs came off, followed by the hood. He was still blinking at the smoke and stink when he was tossed onto a filthy stone floor.

"You'll see the magistrate tomorrow, thief," the watchman said. "Keep yourself quiet until then."

The watch sauntered off, bashing bars and doors with their sticks and taunting the prisoners.

The bang of the door at the end of the corridor cut their talk abruptly off. The shouts from the other cells subsided. Somewhere, a man was weeping.

Tuvacs lifted up his head. Damp straw stuck to his face. His cell was small, but there were half a dozen men crammed in there. One of them stared at him with unfriendly eyes. Tuvacs got to his feet and backed up, finding a seat. The man next to him bared his teeth. Tuvacs was careful not to shift his gaze too quickly, nor to leave it on the man's eyes for too long.

The man he found himself sitting next to leaned over and spoke from the corner of his mouth. "Clever boy you are, not looking scared, not looking too long. Sign of weakness in here is a death sentence. Best leave it to the magistrate to dish those out." Beneath the grime and the crusted clothes the man had the light blue skin of an Amarand. "Don't expect to find the likes of me in here, do you? Not quite what you think of us, is it?"

The man elbowed Tuvacs in the side. Tuvacs leaned back. The man on the other side of him pushed hard back.

"Watch it," he growled.

"Be careful in here boy," said the Amarand. His breath was rotten with bad teeth, overlaid with the sweet smell of poppy. "Get yourself killed."

Tuvacs said nothing. He gave the Amarand a hard stare, then found a patch of wall to stare at, surreptitiously examining the men in the room from the corners of his eyes. There were seven of them. Most from the very lowest levels of society. One had the flat stare of a real killer, and wore better clothes than the rest. A mercenary, he thought, or gang muscle. No one bothered him. A small man in the corner looked out of place, a baker or something similar. Two other men menaced him with harsh whispers, slapping and poking at him.

"Look at them boy, itinerants, robbers, thieves, cutthroats. You've found yourself in a right fine place and no mistake." The Amarand's hand found its way onto his upper thigh. "You stay close by me, and I'll see you right."

Tuvacs looked at the hand, then at the man's face. The Amarand withdrew his hand, and held both up. "No hard feelings, eh? Can't blame a fellow for trying eh, pretty thing like you. Shouldn't be in here. If you were mine, I'd treat you right." He nodded as if this statement was a high truth.

"I am not anybody's mister," said Tuvacs.

"Oh ho ho? That right?" The Amarand sat back. "Immigrant. Street kid by the look of you. All street kids belong to someone at some point. It's a hard world boy, or ain't you heard?"

"Not me."

"We'll see."

"Leave him alone, you fucking outland queer," growled another. He looked directly ahead, not at the Amarand at all.

"Just being friendly."

The other man glared at him. "Your kind of friendly is fucking disgusting. Lay off him or I'll tear your cock out at the root."

The Amarand laughed.

"I ain't seeing nothing funny."

In the corner the baker was whimpering out pathetic words. "Please, I don't want no trouble, leave me be, I'll call the guard." The slaps and pinches became harder.

"Touch me and you'll get the joke," said the Amarand. "I got the eye." He pulled down his lower lid, exposing his conjunctiva. A startling pink against the blue. "Mageborn, ain't I?"

"Ain't got no magic, blueskin. If you were mageborn no way you'd be in here," the man harrumphed, but went back to staring at the wall.

Five minutes later, the baker was screaming. The men beating him grunted with the effort of their blows. The other prisoners studiously ignored the attack, moving as far away as they could. No one came. Eventually, the baker stopped crying out. His tormentors kicked a few times at his limp body then lost interest. They sat down, panting.

Tuvacs made himself stay awake.

Time was difficult to measure. The lights of the torches never changed. He could have been there five hours or five minutes when the door slit slammed back and a watchman looked through.

"You!" he said. "Oi! You Mohaci!" He meant Tuvacs.

"What?"

"Your lucky day."

The door opened. Three watchmen stood outside, clubs and shortswords of dull steel in their hands. "Come on then," said the speaker. "Get out now or take your chances with the magistrate."

Tuvacs got up.

"What happened to him?" said the guard, jutting his chin at the baker.

"He slipped," said one of the men who had beaten him. He and his partner laughed.

The watchman's face clouded and he turned to one of his colleagues. "Get him out of here and up to the physic." He pointed his shortsword at the baker's assailants. "I'll be reporting this to the magistrate. You have anything to do with it?" he said to Tuvacs.

"No," he said.

"Right answer. Out you come."

Tuvacs was marched up two flights of stairs, into a cleaner part of the building. A door was pushed open, and he was shoved into a room.

"Here he is," said the watchman. Thin windows showed glimmer-lit streets. The dead of night.

A man in a long blue coat stood at the other side of a table. His coat had no sleeves, and was trimmed with white fur on the front and around the arm holes. A rich man's coat. "A fine looking lad. Well fed. Good, good." He smiled and spoke directly to Tuvacs, somewhat slowly, as if Tuvacs were an idiot.

"Do you speak Karsarin?"

"Yes," said Tuvacs. "I'd be a fool if I couldn't. We are in Karsa City, are we not?"

The man laughed, three distinct noises like soft barks. A neatly trimmed beard framed unbelievably white teeth.

His face remained wide-eyed, somewhat fixed, a mask he hid his true self behind.

"And Mohaci? You are a native of that land?" he said. "You speak the tongue?"

"Yes," said Tuvacs. "Mohacin, good Low Maceriyan, a little High, a bit of Makar, some Khushashin, twenty words of Otzerk, and the secret tongue of the Gravo gleaning gangs."

"Excellent!" the man slapped gloved hands together. "How old are you?"

"As old as I need to be to get out of this place."

"A little insolent too. Very good. I'll need a bit of that. Now," he said, harder, "how old?"

"Sixteen," said Tuvacs. He paused. "I think."

"Why are you in here?"

"I was unlucky."

"That's not what I meant."

"I robbed an engineer in the Off Parade, and got caught."

"No murder, rape, larger thefts?"

"I do what I need to survive, that is all. I am not a criminal."

"Courts say otherwise, boy," said the watchman.

"Good, good. Very well, I'll take him. Marvellous." He looked Tuvacs up and down with a gleam in his eye. "I'd quite given up hope. A lot of the Mohaci in Karsa are a little reluctant to go back, got too much invested here, but you, well, I suppose you don't have much choice, eh?"

"I don't understand," said Tuvacs.

The guard took a purse from the man, counted out fifteen silver thalers.

"He's bought out your conviction, boy. You're his now."

"What?"

The guard ignored him. He produced a document, a wooden pen, a pounce shaker and ink from a drawer. "You swear to guarantee his good behaviour, provide food, lodging and apprenticeship for seven years?" he said to the man.

"That I do, that I do," said the man. He signed with a flourish.

"You're off out to the Black Sands then?"

"A lot of money to be made out there," said the man.

"Glimmer trader?" said the guard. He shook pounce over the ink after inspecting it, and blew it off.

"No, goodman. Glimmer prospecting provides only a chance of wealth. Servicing the prospectors, on the other hand, is a guaranteed source of income."

"You need him to trade for supplies then?" said the guard. The man seemed not at all bothered by the guard's curiosity.

"Buy it out there? Are you mad? Shoddy foreign rubbish. I'm taking Karsan-made with me. Karsan's got a fine reputation. There's quite the premium."

"But the cost of transportation..."

"My my," said the man, taking a keener look at the guard. It was not an entirely friendly scrutiny. "Quite the drawing room merchant, you are."

The guard shrugged. "I don't want to be minding the likes of this scum for the rest of my life," he said defensively. "Man's got to have ambition."

"Indeed he has, indeed he has. Well. There is no great cost. We shall hire two box cars, one for my merchandise and men, the other for more merchandise, my lead dog and her mates."

"Four week's travel. A long time on a train."

"If we're lucky. These things do stop, you know. We'll be fine."

"I always thought of going out there myself."

"Look at this, boy," said the man.

Tuvacs, who had remained silent throughout this exchange, looked back. "He was doubtless desperate to come all the way across the whole of Ruthnia to this city. You have to ask yourself, if the Black Sands are such an easy place to make money, why did he not go there? The eastern deserts are much closer to Mohacs-Gravo than to Karsa." He mangled the name of Tuvacs' home in that way all Karsans did. "I'd consider that carefully before you enact your career change." He flicked a copper bit at the man. "With gratitude for your help."

The guard caught the coin and secreted it as quick as a conjurer. With the coin came a hint, and it was taken as deftly. "Right then. Thank you, sir. You," he said to Tuvacs, "are free to go. Stay out of trouble. You break this contract, you break the law and then you'll hang for sure."

Tuvacs stared at him.

"Charming. I'll be pissing off now. Way out's that way." He pointed at a door on the far side of the room.

When the guard had gone, the would-be merchant drew in a happy breath and rose up a little on his toes. "Here we are, *here we are*!" He stuck out his hand. "I am Mather Boskovin."

Tuvacs hesitated. Just like that, he'd gone from free man to serf. His heart skipped a beat. What about his sister?

"What is happening here?" he said. "One man cannot buy another."

"Indeed no, because that is slavery, and bondage of that kind is quite illegal. I have bought your crime, you just happen to come with it." Boskovin's hand remained extended.

The Amarand's words returned to him.

"I'm fucked, aren't I?" said Tuvacs. Boskovin's smile tightened a little at the profanity.

"Now now, no need for such language. I suppose you are, from a certain viewpoint. But I can provide you with food, shelter, training, and adventure. What lad would turn that down?"

"I have a sister. I can't leave her behind."

A small 'v' developed between Boskovin's eyebrows. He could have been putting it on, but he looked concerned. "Regrettable. Nothing to be done for it. She is better off with you alive and distant than you swinging from a rope, and believe me boy, you would have been swinging come the noon. You have time to send her a letter. Is she safe for the moment?"

"More or less," Tuvacs said.

"I can get her employment."

"She's no whore. She's pure. She's too young. I won't let it happen."

"My boy, there is no such things as pure or too young. There are beasts that walk on two legs everywhere, and I refer not to the dracons. No, nothing like that. Millwork. A cousin has a small mill. Dice maker, would you credit it. Best I can do."

"No deal," said Tuvacs.

"Deal? Deal?" scoffed Boskovin. "There is no deal, I am doing you an immense favour! I am well within my rights to do nothing at all. Do you want me to do nothing at all? That way is a sure way to the brothel for your sister."

Tuvacs shook his head.

"Good lad. Now shake my hand."

"Tuvacs," said Tuvacs. "That is my name." He shook Boskovin's hand.

"Tuvacs," Boskovin said his name like he had tasted a delicious sweet. "Do you have a given name?"

"Alovo. No one calls me that."

"Tuvacs it is then, my lad. Look at it as an apprenticeship. The terms are the same, although I admit the penalties are harder. Your time with me will soon be done and you will be a better man for it."

"Seven years? And then I am free?"

"And then you are free, and accredited, and what's more paid, my boy."

Tuvacs' expression said he did not believe this.

"It is true, I promise. The money is not quite so good as if you were a... aha... crime free apprentice, half, in fact. But you will leave my service one hundred thalers richer."

A hundred thalers for seven years of his life. A pathetic sum.

"If you can read," went on Boskovin, "you are free to read the documents yourself. Perhaps on the train? It is a long way. Now come along, it has taken me an age to find an agreeable Mohacin speaker. We leave this morning, and I am quite late already."

CHAPTER TEN
The Hospitality of the Third Dragoons

DAWN WAS AN hour gone and so was the sun. Garten and Trassan arrived at the gates to the barracks of the Third Dragoons. The city streets were already busy. Light drizzle fell, pulling acrid pollutants from the sky.

The barracks were new. High walls of heavily rusticated stone blocks in the Maceriyan revival style enclosed the parade yard. The gates in the tall gatehouse were vulgar, cast-iron confections of twisting heraldic beasts. Prince Alfra's coat of arms was mounted in the middle of the gates, and repeated on the top of the building in stone: two dracons rampant, holding a shield emblazoned with a single scallop shell. The gates were chiefly ceremonial, a display of power rather than a defence. But they still needed opening, and Trassan and Garten were kept waiting for five minutes after knocking until they were.

A cheery guard in the burgundy jacket of the Third, heavy with gold frogging and buttons, checked their papers. He smiled, and opened a smaller gate to the side of the main. The brothers were led across a courtyard far bigger than the circuit of the walls might suggest. The outer edge was cobbled, the middle sanded for cavalry drill. Kennelled dogs bayed for their breakfast. The sharp, reptilian smell of dracons emanated from stables in the arched cloisters to the north and south sides of the square; their heavy doors were all shut. The dragon-kin slept late.

"Captain Kressind already has a visitor," said the dragoon, a cheery sort given to smiling.

"Aarin," said Garten.

"A death talker," said the guard.

"A brother of ours," explained Garten.

"They come in all types in your family, don't they, goodfellows?"

"That they do," said Trassan.

The guard walked them to an ironbound door where another dragoon stood at attention. He stared ahead, ignoring them.

The gate guard reached for the ring of the latch. "Captain Kressind's a popular man with most here, goodfellows, we'll be sorry to see him go. He and the colonel don't see eye to eye, that's for sure, but we men are fond of him." The guard swung the door wide. It opened onto a flight of stone steps leading under the building. "Careful now, they are steep. Captain Kressind is in the cell at the end.

Trassan and Garten went down. Trassan ducked the low arch of the staircase to save his hat. Garten still missed his.

The gaol was clean and cool, a relief to Garten's throbbing head. The odour was of straw and cold stone. It was brighter than they expected, with slanted lightwells leading up to barred windows either side of the staircase, and oil lanterns hissing every five feet on the walls. The cells were cages with gridded bars for walls and a door, but each had its own window high in the wall.

Rel stood with his hands resting on a crossbar. His wrists were manacled. He wore his riding boots, regimental grey trousers and a white shirt. He was dirty, but unharmed. Aarin was talking quietly with him. Rel caught sight of his other two brothers and his face lit up.

"Brothers." Aarin nodded in greeting.

"You came to see me off then?" Rel said.

"We're your brothers, aren't we?" said Garten. "And please, not so loud."

"Out with Trassan?" said Aarin.

Garten nodded with a wince. Rel smiled.

"Lucky. I'd kill for a decent beer. The stuff they give us down here is sour and turns your stomach."

"You have found yourself a fine palace," said Trassan.

"Believe me, this is a lot nicer than the other cells I've been in," said Rel.

Garten shook his head. "Never say that in front of mother."

"Where's Guis?"

"Sulking," said Trassan.

"Typical."

"Still, we're all here, aren't we?" said Garten.

"So, what is it this time?" said Trassan. "I heard you tumbled some old money aristo's wife."

"Well, yeah, yeah I did," said Rel. "But that's no reason for this!" He shook at the bars. They did not budge. "Bastard couldn't even let me wait fifteen days for Katriona. I can't believe this. I've done nothing to

Colonel Alanrys. He's always had it in for me. He's been waiting for me to screw up, and I did."

Aarin raised his eyebrows. "With your predilections, little brother, he was never going to have to wait forever."

"One rich man's wife!" protested Rel.

"The *wrong* rich man's wife," countered Aarin.

"I don't even get to cross the Neck when the Great Tide is in. Do I get to see the sun setting as I bid farewell to my homeland? Whitecaps crowning the turbulent channel, picking out the whirlpools Gorgoantha and Sryman either side? Do I bollocks. Just miles and miles of sucking mud. He waited on purpose for after a Great Tide. He'd be here crowing now if it were the done thing."

"I hear the Maceriyan Channel stinks when the tide is out," teased Trassan.

"That was terribly portentous and dramatic," said Garten. "You should be the playwright, Rel."

Rel looked down at his feet glumly. "And the least that sod could have done is turn up. I might never see any of you again."

"Don't be like that," said Garten. "You'll be home soon. You'll see. One big adventure and you can bore us all with it until we're all fat and old, and then start on our grandchildren."

"Looks like he's already getting fat," said Trassan.

"Says you! Garten, what did mother say? Katriona?"

"Oh! I almost forgot," said Garten. "Mother did write to the colonel to allow she and Katriona into the barracks."

"You mean Katriona asked?" said Rel.

"Well, yes."

"And of course Alanrys said no. Well. And too much to ask that father come," said Rel.

"He is still angry with you," said Aarin.

"Furious," corrected Trassan. "'A disgrace! Wastrel! A shame on the family! Does he know how much this is costing me? I should have let them flog him!'" He mimicked their father's voice, although he left out the man's speech impediment. They never mocked that.

Rel pulled a face. "He actually said that?"

"He actually did," said Trassan. "But he's not as angry with you as he is with Guis, so you're winning there."

"The station's too hectic for mother's nerves," went on Garten, "and she wouldn't allow Katriona to go unchaperoned so close to her wedding. Katriona gave me this letter to give to you." He pressed a square of paper sealed with dark blue wax into Rel's hand. Rel pulled it back through the bars. He cracked the seal and scanned it.

"She's prepared your bags. They'll be waiting on the train. You should have everything you need, and most of what you want," said Garten.

"She's too good to us," said Rel sadly.

"At least once you're on the train you can change out of those rags," said Trassan.

"They're not rags!" protested Rel. "This shirt was tailored by Karosian and Bwyn. Tyn stitching!" he said, tugging at it. "It is very fine." He grimaced at it. It was stained all over, wide sweat patches under his arms and round his neck, grubby from being slept in for a week. "*Was* very fine."

"I'd throw it away," said Garten.

"I'd burn it," said Trassan.

"It does smell a little, brother," said Aarin.

"Listen to Aarin, he spends his time surrounded by corpses," said Trassan. "If he says 'a little', it means 'a lot'."

The door rattled open. Two others of the Karsan third Dragoons came in, grinning meanly. One carried a ring of polished keys. A brass fob depicting the regimental arms hung among them. The other guard brought a sack. "Captain Rel, your next duty awaits."

Rel stood up and sighed. "This is it boys, off to the fucking end of the world. And look, Alanrys has sent his two biggest lickspittles. Nice to see you, Plovion. Juresk, looking as hideous as ever I see."

The uglier of the two—and Rel was not wrong, in his brothers' opinions—loured. The other answered. "Shut it, captain; while you're in there and I'm out here you've no right to be speaking to us that way. Your rank is suspended."

Plovion unlocked the door to the cell and undid Rel's manacles.

"If it were down to me, I'd leave you here to rot," grunted Juresk.

"Good job it isn't then." Rel smirked as he rubbed at his wrists. "You're only jealous you didn't get to tumble Lady Anellia yourself. Best you've ever had charged you double, you're so ugly. Isn't that right, Plovion?"

"How the hell should I know?" growled Plovion.

"Sorry, I thought you did your mother's accounting. My mistake."

The guards both tensed up. Trassan and Aarin stepped in front of their brother, smiling without warmth.

"If you're intent on a fight, boys, I'd happily make the time. Leaving two corpses behind me would be quite the exit, don't you think?" goaded Rel.

Aarin cleared his throat. He stared at Juresk and Plovion. The scars around his white eye were livid and menacing. His head shook the tiniest degree. That was enough. There were few men who would anger a Guider.

"Just get yourself ready," said Juresk nervously. He pushed a regimental jacket at Rel, then the sack. "Papers are in there. Be outside in two minutes or it'll be the worse for you."

"Now why would I duck such a prime posting?" Rel said.

"You are a disgrace, Kressind," said Plovion. "Get your uniform on, then get out of here."

"Ah ah ah!" said Trassan. "We're all Kressinds here. Insult one, insult us all."

"Begging your pardon, your reverence," said Juresk nervously to Aarin.

Plovion elbowed him, but said nothing to the brothers. He went away for a minute, and came back with Rel's sabre, sheathed in its steel scabbard. Rel took it with a nod and hung it from the belt about his waist. The guards went away. "Two minutes!" reiterated Plovion, cleaving to this last scrap of power.

Rel did up his buttons. Dirty though he was, he looked more of a gentleman in his jacket. "I can fight my own battles," he said pettishly.

"Evidently not," said Aarin. "Not all, anyway. I have this for you." He pulled his hand out from his sleeve, in it was a plain leather pouch, tied at the top with silver wire. Rel accepted it with suspicion.

"There are bones in this?"

"Yes!" snorted Aarin. "It is the magic of the dead, little brother."

Rel passed it from hand to hand and wiped his palms on his jacket. "What is it for?"

"Protection," said Aarin. "The Gates are regarded as a soft place for a soldier by some, but there are many perils out in the Black Sands. If you ever find yourself out that way, this is proof against some of them."

"How will I know when to use it?" said Rel. He fiddled with the wire.

"You'll know," said Aarin. "And don't ever open it!" he added quickly.

"No fear there," Rel said, and tied it to his belt.

They walked to the foot of the steps. "Well," said Rel. The barking of drays and clatter of wheels on cobbles sounded down the stairs. The light from the open door and windows at the top dimmed in sequence as a carriage drew up. "I think that's me. Brothers, it's been fun." They embraced him one at a time.

"You'll be back," said Garten.

"You better be," said Trassan.

"Be well," said Aarin. "And be careful."

Rel pulled back and smiled. "When have you ever known me not to be?"

"Captain Kressind!" shouted a voice down the stairs.

"I'm coming!" Rel bounded up the steps. He stopped at the top, silhouetted in the daylight, waved, and was gone.

"He's still like a big bloody puppy," said Garten.

"Aye, with a sword and a gun," said Aarin.

"Lost gods help us all," said Trassan.

Orders and proclamations and all that sort of military shouting that meant little to the others sounded outside. A bugle blew. The carriage drew off to the yipping of dogs.

Trassan smacked his lips and grimaced at the taste he found. "I do believe I am sobering up, and my head is beginning to hurt."

"About time," said Garten. "I hate to suffer alone. There was bacon promised."

"Indeed. Might I treat you goodfellows to breakfast?" said Trassan.

They agreed that that would be pleasant, and together went in search of food.

KARSA CITY STATION was a maelstrom of people. The noise was horrendous, with trains coming and going. The locomotives filled the high glass ceilings with clouds that stank of spent magic.

The carriage dropped Rel by the main entrance. Two of his fellow officers accompanied him to make sure he definitely got on the train. These were better disposed to him than either Juresk or Plovion, and aided him in retrieving his things and finding a handler for them before placing him on the train and bidding him farewell.

The whole exercise was conducted so quickly and under such stress that Rel did not remember to be sad until he had found his seat.

There was Katriona's wedding, Alanrys had made sure that he'd miss that. Rel had beaten the colonel in a fencing match, but it wasn't that that brought his wrath down on him. There was some grudge he bore his family. He wondered which of his uncles were responsible, or even if his father was. And he wished

Guis had come to see him go. Katriona couldn't, but Guis could, and he should have come. The six siblings would rarely gather again, whatever happened.

His thoughts turned to his friends and his lovers as the waysayer's whistle blew, answered by the long, mournful hoot of the locomotive. With a mighty huff the train jerked forward, jolting the couplings. Metal grumbled. Against its great protestation, the engine dragged the train forward. The crowd slid by, slower than a walk at first, quicker and quicker as the engine's wheels bit and gained traction on the rails.

He would never see Ellimia or Druva again, or any of the other girls. And although only Ellimia and Druva really meant anything to him individually, the collective loss of the rest hurt almost as bad.

They pulled out into open air. Streamers of glimmer-tainted smoke spiralled past the window. Rain marked the glass with spots and streaks. He felt unspeakably low. The crowd madly waved to loved ones he could not see as the train pulled away. There was one figure who did not wave. He stood apart from the rest of the crowd, even though he was surrounded by them. Rel's eyes went past him, but snapped back in recognition.

He sat up happily. "Guis!" he shouted, and banged on the window. The other passengers tutted at this un-Karsan show of emotion. "Guis!"

Rel's eldest brother put two fingers to his temple and saluted sardonically. Rel waved back. Guis's sinister companion blinked at him from behind a curtain of hair, eyes points of yellow light in the shade there.

"Guis!"

"Good luck," Rel's brother mouthed. Clouds of smoke and steam puffed past the window with increasing tempo. The groaning of the train lessened as the strain settled evenly. They picked up speed, and Guis was gone.

Rel elbowed a scholarly looking gentleman next to him. "That was my brother!" he said cheerfully. The man tried to look like he was somewhere else. "The bastard came after all."

CHAPTER ELEVEN
The Second Wedding of Katriona Kressinda

THE RAIN STOPPED the day before Katriona Kressinda was due to wed a second time, a brief interlude in the weather the more superstitious society watchers trumpeted as a good omen. But a wedding as extravagant as Demion Morthrock's to Katriona Kressinda was not to be missed, rain or not. The old aristocracy dismissively referred to it as an industry wedding and sneered at its common excess. They came nonetheless, along with everyone else.

Gelbion Kressind hired the Grand Hall of Karsa for the occasion. A tall confection of a building, stone white as sugar tracery and as intricately decorated. New buildings for new money, the old families said.

The Kressinds were not the wealthiest merchant clan in Karsa, but today they were paying to look like it. A stream of carriages drawn by matched dray teams arrived at the grand staircase to disgorge passengers as elegant as the building. The great and good of the city had barely time to step out before their transports were whisked off to allow the next to arrive. Servants dressed in a fantastical livery reminiscent of the Old Maceriyans greeted them at the door with drinks and flattery. A nine foot confection of spun caramel dominated the Great Hall's rotunda, depicting the angels and devils of long ago. Men and Tyn in fancy dress wordlessly formed tableau depicting great events in Karsan history including, tellingly, the founding of the Kressind Works. The tableaux broke apart and reformed elsewhere to great approval. Jugglers and acrobats and exotic, firebreathing Oczerks walked the party. A Torosan godling, sweating in his traditional furs, brought gleeful terror from the guests with his mock roars and posturing. In three ballrooms there were three different forms of dancing. The great and good of the Karsan industrial elite commented with equal approval on the glories of the building and the bride both. As the evening wore on and the wine flowed, the old aristocrats too gave grudging praise.

The ceremony was short, though sumptuous. Everyone was eager to get on to the Mingling, the feast that followed, and the revelry after that.

All the Kressinds were present, down to cousins of the least degree.

Guis avoided his brothers for the time being, his apology to them not yet correctly formulated, and so he wandered through the throngs of guests, exchanging pleasantries with those that approached, evading the rest. He grew engrossed in a display of petty magics by a pair of Amarand witches in tight silks. They conjured bright lights from the air and birds from their hands. They wove visions of the heavens and hells over their heads. They made figures in the sugar sculptures dance and set the cars of dogs and antelopes upon unsuspecting worthies. All the while they climbed up over one another, twisting themselves sensuously through each other's limbs. Their bodies and display enchanted Guis, until Tyn crawled up the collar of his coat.

"Be away, good master! This is true magic, not slippery hands of charlatans. Not good for you."

"Of course it is true magic," murmured Guis. "My father would pay for nothing less today." There was more to it than that. A quickening in his own veins. His heart ached in sympathy, his mind burgeoned with possibilities sexual and magical. When a flamescape of distant Aranthiya disintegrated with a demonic laugh, leaving the witches perturbed, he knew it was time to leave.

He tore his eyes from the display and moved away while the witches searched the crowd for the mageborn who had disrupted their art. Affecting boredom, he examined fruits arranged in yard high stacks on silver platters, and watched a troupe of acrobats build pyramids of their bodies. Their skills were entirely of the mundane kind, and he became bored in earnest.

Greater Tyn, dressed in clothes to match the human servants', moved among the crowd. Guis had never seen so many in one place, but of course the Morthrock clan were known for their Tyn. Half the height of a man, broad shouldered in the main, far larger than the creature that shared his life, but Tyn nevertheless. Their unlovely faces were made more grotesque by the finery and make-up they wore. Iron collars were at the throats of every one. They waddled around the party, offering drinks and dainties to the guests. Guis stopped one. It was impossible to tell if it were male or female, or indeed tell one individual from the next. They all looked alike. The Tyn looked at him oddly as he took a glass of wine. It could smell its own kind on him, he was sure. Guis's creature seemed timid of its larger cousins and remained hidden from them. The Tyn nodded hesitantly, and moved on.

A horn sang too close to him. He turned around in startlement and nearly spilled his wine down the front of his sister's wedding dress.

"Hello, brother. Doing your best to ruin my dress, I see."

Katriona embraced him, and he held his glass out awkwardly. He fought down vile, unwanted images of him lying with her, of gouging out her eyes. There was a tug in his hair as Tyn unknotted a braid. He relaxed, and carried on as if he had not seen such things in his mind. What else could he do?

"Not you, not you. They are not your thoughts," whispered Tyn in his ear. "Peace, good master, peace."

He took a deep breath, stood back, and smiled genuinely. Now he was grown, and Katriona had ceased to be an annoyance, Guis could see she was beautiful.

"Sister, you look amazing."

She smiled, proud and bashful. "Thank you, brother."

"I mean it, unfashionably slender but athletic and delectable in a manner that, in realms other than ours, is regarded as the very acme of attractiveness."

"Now now, you're spoiling it," she said, still smiling.

"No, really," he joked, "you should put some weight on. Excess weight speaks of wealthy indolence. You'll appear worryingly active to many men. They'll wonder what they might do with you, if you are dashing about all over the place and getting in the way."

"I try my best."

"You do look fantastic. I mean so genuinely. As beautiful as the handmaids of the gods themselves."

She grinned, displaying even teeth. Katriona had never suffered a blemish.

"A fine party," he waved his glass around.

"A time to strike deals and reaffirm alliances," she said. "You can thank father for all this. It is precious little to do with me. And anyway," she added sharply, "you would know a lot more about it if you had been present for some of the planning of it."

"That's why I wasn't present," he said. His sister raised her eyebrows. "Ah, ah, I'm teasing you, sis. I've been away in the north."

"Your play. It has been doing well?"

"Reasonably well. I'm not rich, but I no longer fear that I will be on the street by winter. And it is warmer there. You heard it was playing?"

"Some of my brothers still speak to me, even if you don't," she said. Her admonishment was undone by her pleasure at seeing him.

"I am sorry," he said, and meant it. "You do look beautiful."

She smoothed her dress down. "If you are going to turn your dubious charm on me, I should be flattered. You are forgiven then. But why are you all alone?"

"Drinking quietly and trying to stay out of trouble. Obviously it wouldn't do to get too close to father, but I bumped into Trassan and Garten before Rel left, and I am afraid I behaved like an arse."

"What happened?" said Katriona. "Oh Guis, I thought things were better with your nerves."

"They are, they are. Don't worry. Tyn here does his job well. Why, I am almost sane. No, this was entirely down to me, I'm afraid. Trassan and Garten are up to something, Trassan wouldn't tell me what, I got in a snit about it. The usual."

"Oh Guis."

"I know, I know, I was drunk. I am working my way up to apologising." He paused, and asked sheepishly, "I don't suppose you know what Trassan is up to?"

"I haven't a clue," she said. "Not that they'd tell me, I'm just a girl."

"You know it's not like that."

"Exactly, and so should you. You are too hard on yourself, and that makes you hard on the rest of us. Loving you is difficult, Guis, but it is worth it." She took his arm. "It truly is. Arvane always spoke highly of you. A lot of people do, if only you would see it."

"I am sorry he is not here with us any more, Katriona."

"If he were, I would not be marrying again would I? Arvane was a good man, but he was also a good soldier. And good soldiers often die. I am not the first young widow in the world, and I wish dearly I could be the last. But I am one among many." A touch of fragility entered her voice. Her kohl-lined eyes moistened. She blinked her tears back and smiled. "Look at me! Weeping on my wedding day. If you've five minutes to spare for me, will you walk with me?"

They relaxed into each other's company and talked of this and that, greeted relatives both loved and disliked, they watched Irricans play tunes upon silver trumpets that stirred the heart, they took drinks from Tyn, and clapped at several clever *tableaux vivants*.

After a time, Katriona had to go. "I have a bride's responsibilities, brother, and I am neglecting them," she said. She kissed Guis on each cheek.

"Who is that strange woman, the one in the mannish clothes with the pipe?" asked Guis.

"Her?" said Katriona, looking around. "I'm surprised at you. That, dear brother, is the Countess Lucinia Vertisa of Mogawn."

"She's the Hag of Mogawn?" said Guis, mildly surprised.

"Yes. Her father and Demion's were close. There are good relations between the Morthrocks and the Vertis. Relations, brother, I wish to keep in good order," she tapped him on the arm with her fan. "I would appreciate it if you were not your usual offensive self around her."

From anyone else but Katriona, Guis would have fallen into one of his traps of despair. Frankness defined their relationship, and he took no offence.

"I have no intention of saying anything unpleasant to her. I'll willingly mock a man for his foibles, but it is the worst thing in the world to mock someone for their physical characteristics. They cannot help them."

"Saying that to her would be precisely the level of bold tactlessness I wish to avoid," she said reproachfully.

"I won't even allude to it. She is not a beauty by any yardstick, and her clothes and manner are a little out of the ordinary, but I think 'hag' is unwarranted, sister. I have heard some colourful descriptions of her. I do not recognise the woman from them. She seems... lively."

They watched her awhile, as she laughed without restraint.

"People are cruel, and foolish. They call her that because she does as she pleases, and will take no man as a husband. She is thirty-five and not yet married. She was educated at the academy of Goodlady Halyonaise in Perus, apparently she was quite the favourite."

"A yellow sash?"

"A frightful one!" said Katriona mischievously. "Rumour has it they were lovers. Half the stories they tell about her are nonsense, but the other half are true. Generally the more shocking they are, the greater the truth, so says Demion."

"He told you that? I thought the man never spoke around you."

"He is rather awkward, but he did ask me to marry him."

"He must have worked up to that over months!"

"Guis!"

"Come on, he's been besotted with you for years."

Katriona frowned a little. "Leave him be, Guis. For today, if you can. He is a good man."

He is not Arvane, thought Guis. He felt compelled to say it, to speak the truth no matter how hurtful. He fought to keep it in.

"What do you think of her?" he said, returning his attention to the Hag.

"I find her fascinating. I intend to get to know her."

"Kindred spirits, and all that," said Guis. "But I'd advise against the pipe."

Katriona gave him a sisterly shove.

"Watch the wine!" he said.

"I'll spill it if I desire. It's my wedding."

"She's fascinating." The hag joked with a pair of young blades, all dressed in ribbons at the principal joints of the body, as was the fashion for the youthful this year. Guis was disdainful of them, he doubted they could use the swords at their belts. His disdain grew as they laughed with her, only to speak to one another behind their hands once she moved on. "Tell me sis, how are you going to preserve your independence?" He nodded at Morthrock. "I see him there politely listening to Great Aunt Cassonaepia, he's managed five minutes and his smile is yet to crack. There's steel in that man. Even you might not be able to master him."

She elbowed him sharply. "Don't you worry about me, brother," she said sweetly. "Nobody may rule the mind of this woman, no matter how much steel he has."

"A certain steeliness is a man's friend on his wedding night."

"Behave yourself," said Katriona. "Show a little decorum." She gave him a peck on the cheek. "Thank you for everything."

"For what?" he said, taken aback. "What have I done?" Guilt clouded his mood. He had done very little for his sister in recent years.

"For being my brother, you arse!" she said, sotto voce. "All of you, the whole brawling, arguing, stupid gaggle of men I had to grow up with. I love you all. You better find fitting wives or I shall be most unpleasant to them." Her face softened. "And you particularly. Were it not for you I do not think I would have survived Arvane's death. I thought my life over before it had begun. You showed me it was not."

"Well," said Guis. "He was my friend. I miss him too."

She touched his cheek softly.

Guis forced jollity into his voice. "And now perhaps you should attend to your other guests. I am going to introduce myself to the countess."

"Be good!" she called after him.

He turned back to face her and gave a self-deprecatory bow.

*   *   *

"GOOD DAY, COUNTESS," he said.

The young men courting Lucinia Vertisa's attention looked daggers at him, but she turned and welcomed him warmly. "And here comes the eldest son! Guis, is it not?"

Guis nodded. "It is. You know your Kressinds well."

"Your father is a man of great repute."

Closer to, the Hag was even less hag-like. She had an unfortunately masculine face, square shoulders and a thick waist. That she was dressed in barely feminised male clothing of garish colour with a matching fan in a man's style did not help her. She lacked many womanly charms, but she was not repulsive. He had seen far uglier women pursued ardently, ordinarily those attached to large fortunes, and no one called them hags. Despite her plainness there was a vibrancy about her that was attractive.

"I thank your family for inviting me," she said.

"On behalf of my family, I am glad you came. In truth, I lack the authority to make any representation on their part."

She smiled. "Naturally. I hear of your estrangement from your father."

"We are all gossiped about, countess."

"That we are!" she agreed. She took a fresh glass of wine from the tray of a passing Tyn and handed it to Guis. "I trust you do not mind me defying convention, but you appear to be running dry."

"And I trust you refer to my glass and not my conversation."

"My my! Are they all as dry as you?"

"Not quite. Katriona is drier."

"She has it all then, I see," the countess said. "She is quite the beauty. The breasts, the lips, the hair... All those attributes that so trouble the gaze of men."

"Quite. She is well aware of all that, but refreshingly reluctant to abuse her gifts. Do not judge her by her looks, she is a modest woman."

"We are all judged by our looks, goodfellow."

"That we are, countess."

She looked at him curiously.

"She is—I have often remarked—the perfect balance of our mother and father's humours and intellects. Beauty ensnared, I am sorry to say. I fear marriage will be hard on her. Morthrock dotes on her, but she never had any time for him before his proposal, although he has been besotted with her since we were children. She is very spirited. I cannot quite puzzle out why the change in heart."

"Perish the thought! What will they say?" The countess watched Katriona for a while. "She will be well. She lights this room. Look at her husband."

"Morthrock? What of him? Tell me what you see. I am intrigued."

"A sound fellow. Our fathers were friends, you know. But he has always been a mild sort. Observe how he is less noticeable than your sister."

"It is only right, it is her wedding day."

"Ah, but his charisma is of a meaner measure. She'll outshine him any day of the week. Let us look at him."

They drew together like spies. Guis was a head taller than the countess, and had to bend a little. She leaned scandalously close to him.

"See now," she whispered behind her fan. Demion was still stolidly absorbing Aunt Cassonaepia's viperish conversation. "He is not ugly, nor is he handsome. He has a passable enough physique and face. He is a little thick around the middle, perhaps, but no more so than others of his generation."

The countess was correct, he thought. "Morthrock has always struck me as flabby, not so much in body, but in mind and habit."

"Once, I had a cat," she said unexpectedly.

"Oh?"

"My father wished to have him castrated, for he feared the cat might grow wilful and scratch me. I was against it. The kennelmaster was to do it. He explained how his drive for sexual relations might turn him against me, and that if he were relieved of his stones then he would not. He would, in the goodman's words, remain 'an affable little chap'."

"What a sinister phrase."

"Just there," she said, "stands an affable little chap. Whereas there," she indicated Katriona, "is a cat whose stones are very much attached."

Guis laughed loudly. The Hag smiled at this response, becoming energised by it. "Why do you find him objectionable?" Guis said.

"I did not say that I found him objectionable, goodfellow. What I intended to convey is that your brother-in-law is entirely unremarkable. Do you see, he possesses no great passions, and can rarely be stirred from a position of distracted geniality. He is the sort of man who is easy to overlook. You can see it in his face, and in his bearing. Today he is outshone by his bride, you say. But anyone with half an eye can see it will always be so. He is a candle against the sun."

"As is polite to say of all brides on their wedding day."

"It will be said of her much longer."

"I suppose that is true. Still, he will be happy. Demion had been besotted with my sister for years."

"That is all the more reason she will dominate him, mark my words."

"I can only agree. Well read. You describe the boy I knew, and doubtless the man he is. You really are a magister."

"Simple observation, goodfellow. I work no magic, and would not be accepted as one even if I could."

"Being a person of the female persuasion?"

She performed a mocking curtsey. "I follow the latest treatises of course, but theory is all I might muster. I have no talent for the esoteric arts, and no desire to employ someone who has so that I might experiment with the greater magics. There are plenty of magisters falling over each other in their desire to build bigger and better machines to ape the Morfaan and Old Maceriyans."

"Like my brother," said Guis.

"I content myself with gazing at the stars. There are mysteries among them enough to satisfy the most inquiring of minds. And I do have an inquiring mind, sir."

"As I said, a magister."

"Not as the common usage of the word would have it," she insisted.

"There is little common about me, countess. Nor anyone here. I will speak properly."

"I am but a talented amateur," she said with mock humility.

"That is not what I have heard."

"People talk a lot about me."

"They do." There was no point pretending otherwise.

"It is you, I hear, that is the magister. You are mageborn, are you not? But you are neither mage nor magister." Her manner became sharply appraising.

"That I have put behind me. I was not fit." He changed the subject. "My sister says that half of what they say about you is nonsense, but that the more scandalous half is true."

"I very much hope that is correct. Very well, if you must call me something, I prefer the term of empiricist. I measure the world as it is, and do nothing if I can help it to change it. The creator struck an equilibrium in all things. I seek to understand it, not how it might be manipulated."

"Empiricist it is then, goodlady. You may have heard that I am a playwright."

"I have, I have even seen one of your plays."

"Truly?" said Guis.

"Your star is rising."

"Even as my bank balance falls."

"We are both seekers of truth, you and I," she continued. "For what do we do but look into things and attempt to uncover the heart of the matter?"

"You possess a telescope?"

"A very fine one, the lenses are from Marceny. Mogawn is ideally situated. The stars over the sea margin are unobscured by the filth of Karsa's factories. Tell me," she said. "Would you like to see it?"

Guis hesitated. "I cannot say I would not. To look at the stars with great clarity... What would anyone with but a little poet in them say to such opportunity? We live in times of great progress. I am fascinated by the new sciences."

"As your plays so eloquently attest. But?"

Guis shifted uncomfortably. "I am a teller of tales, goodlady. I cannot guarantee that what I witness of you and yours will not work themselves into my plays."

"So long as what you say is truthful, what matter? In fact, I insist you do write something. Ah!" she said, and tapped his chest with her folded fan as if claiming him for a dance. "I will make it my condition. You may come to visit with me, but you must write of it. Are you happy now? Please, it would be my honour to host you at Castle Mogawn."

"Countess, I would not wish to impose," said Guis. His objection was more than perfunctory ritual.

"And what gentleman would? I insist. I am mistress of my own house and offer my invitation unreservedly. If you are as interested in the new as you say, then I have something very special to show you."

Guis paused. He was a Kressind. His speaking with this woman would fuel the scandal broadsheets for a week on its own. If he were to go to her castle alone the embarrassment to his father would be immense... He smiled.

"Something amuses you?" the countess asked.

"No madam, I am merely pleased at your offer. I would be delighted to visit with you."

"Very good! Very good. I shall have my servant, Mansanio, contact you and arrange it all."

Guis nodded. "It is agreed. I will reply within..." He broke off. His eyes narrowed. "Excuse me, but I must ask something of my sister."

"Oh," said the hag, disappointed. "Until next time then."

Guis bowed his head. "Until next time." Then, with as much haste as was seemly, he went to his sister's aid.

CHAPTER TWELVE
The Revelry

ALANRYS WORE ALL the glory of Karsa upon his left breast in an array of glittering medals. His uniform was an elaborate version of that of the Third Dragoons. Over his brocaded jacket he wore a short overcoat held together at the neck by a gold chain, the sleeves cast over his back and pinned with the cuff facing upward. His right jacket arm was stiff with insignia woven of copper thread. He carried a tall shako under his left arm. A sabre swung from hangars on his belt. His belt, boots, and pistol baldric were of ribbed black dracon leather, polished to a gleaming shine. He was handsome, the very image of a dashing sauralier, his face the subject of a thousand fantasies. His moustache and whiskers were immaculate. Most praised were his eyes, gorgeous pools framed by the handsome crags of his features. It was these that Guis liked the least. They were the eyes of a predator, colder than a dracon's.

Katriona was pale under her make-up. Alanrys had her left hand in his right. He spoke to her quietly, a smile that to anyone else but Guis and Katriona probably looked sincere.

Guis stepped up to the colonel.

"What the hell are you doing here?" he said.

Alanrys lifted one perfectly plucked eyebrow. "Your father invited me. I am an old friend of the family."

"You are no friend of mine, or my sister's. Let her go."

"Or what, Guis?" Alanrys's smile turned upon Guis threateningly. "I'll not be ordered about by the family madman. Now, if you were Garten, or perhaps even that drunken sot you call your youngest brother, I might take note. But you are not quite the swordsman either of them are. Do not give me cause to call you out, the world would be such a dull place without your little plays. Besides," he said, "I'm rather busy of late. I doubt I'd have time free to dispatch you. Perhaps you could save me the bother and drink yourself to death? I hear you are making sterling progress already."

Guis boiled. Katriona winced as Alanrys squeezed her hand. "I am so sorry Captain Kressind could not be present. His journey would not wait." He locked his eyes on hers. "I did what I could to keep him here, but the Gates are such an important posting. You should be proud of him."

Guis pushed himself between Alanrys and his sister. She stepped back, her hand slipped from his. Alanrys made a show of throwing his own up in search of it, a play of regret on his face. He locked eyes with Guis for a long moment. Guis stood his ground.

"As you wish. Good day, Goodlady Morthrock. I wish you all the happiness for your future. Good day, Guis."

He bowed, sidestepped a chattering pair of lordlings, and disappeared into the crowd.

Guis shook his head. "You'll be safe from him now."

"You think Demion can save me from that?" she said. She stared hatred after him. "I fear he'll dog me for my entire life."

"No sister, I don't think Demion is up to that sort of thing," said Guis. "But I imagine you can use marriage as a shield to protect yourself. He can't carry on behaving this way toward you, not without damaging his reputation."

She slipped her arm through his. "Thank you, Guis."

He laid his hand over hers. "You've saved me more times than I've helped you. I still owe you a great deal."

"She should have married Alanrys."

"Do you think, father? She hates him," said Trassan,

Gelbion Kressind grunted. "What has like or dislike to do with it? It's marriage boy. He's a hero of Karsa!"

"He's a monster."

"There's too much of your mother in you children. What kind of a man do you think makes a hero? Not the likes of you. Only strong men can perform such deeds. It is up to their country to decide if they are heroes or not. Heroism is an ugly business, Trassan."

Gelbion Kressind was old before his time, twisted by apoplexy four years gone. His left leg moved stiffly, and the weight on that side he supported on a stick. This he held awkwardly across his body with his good right arm, his left arm also having been affected with weakness. His arms were thus awkwardly crossed. His posture was otherwise unaltered, and he stood as tall as his weakened limbs allowed. In his face the full ravages of his condition were apparent. His left eyelid drooped, the skin slack around it as if partially melted, while half his mouth was frozen upwards in a perpetual sneer. But the real damage was deeper inside. Gelbion Kressind had been a man of influence, of power. Forced to withdraw from the politicking of the Second House, he had become bitter. His ambition was thwarted, and become poison.

"If only she'd been born a boy," said Gelbion.

"She is talented, father."

The right side of his mouth twisted to match the left. He banged his stick on the floor. "She is a woman. She cannot inherit, and she's ruled by her emotions. See how she dismissed Alanrys like a peasant, calling that worthless brother of yours to help her. She is the most like her mother of all of you. Weak! One setback and she sinks into misery. Is she the first young widow in this world? No! So it goes if one tries to engage with women as equals. The cycle of their menses rules their minds. Women are flighty and inconstant, Trassan. You would be good to remember it."

"I think you underestimate our sister, father," said Trassan. His father scowled intently, a master craftsman inspecting inferior work.

"And what would you know about it, childless and wifeless as you are? Spend six months sharing your bed with the same woman, then you'll know. It's about time you left your dalliances behind boy. Settle down."

Trassan persisted. "Katriona is intelligent. She..."

"It matters not one jot! You can teach a woman many things, but you cannot make her a man," said Gelbion. He had trained away much of the speech impediment the apoplexy had left him with, but he slurred when angry, and dribble spilled from his lips. He dabbed at his mouth with a handkerchief held in his feeble left hand. "Even if she overcomes all that nature has put in her way, how by all the banished gods will she ever get anyone to take her seriously? Look at that over there, that creature your brother was cavorting with," he said with disgust, "conducting herself so shamelessly. There is a woman who would be as a man. Do you see how she is laughed at, how despised? Her cunt rules her mind, she is filth. A bitch sniffing around the dogs. She acts like a man and seeks to outdo them to prove her point. She is a countess! Where is her dignity? A disgrace. How Demion Morthrock has the temerity to invite her to this celebration..." Gelbion slammed his cane down again. "If you love your sister as I do, my boy, you will not encourage her. Shame and infamy is all that awaits her."

Trassan nodded. "Yes father."

"Good boy, good boy." He patted at his son, anger suddenly spent. "Now help me to a seat and sit with me. Standing so long suits me poorly." Trassan took his father's elbow and guided him across the polished floor. Guests moved aside. Trassan caught their reactions. The pitying glance, the patronising smile, the expressions of distaste. "Tell me about this latest venture of yours. I am glad to see you putting your mind to good use, unlike that pointless elder brother of yours."

Trassan stole a look over his shoulder at Guis. Their eyes met, and Guis raised his glass in salute. Trassan smiled back. At least Guis had stopped sulking, that was something.

"The witches are proving popular."

Gelbion's ruined hand twitched. "Their time is done. Not so long ago they'd have been at court. Look at them now, performing tricks for coppers. The magisters' science is infinitely preferable. This era will see magic tamed, and it will herald prosperity for all."

They reached a chair, and Trassan eased Gelbion into it. Gelbion stuck his bad leg out and sighed. "That is better. There are some things, Trassan, that will never change. Never mind Alanrys. Demion is a good enough match for Katriona. An alliance between the Morthrock and Kressind families will stand us in good stead. Especially you. You're an engineer. One of the best, trusted of Arkadian Vand himself. Bloody fool that he is, but it counts for something."

"He is sorry he could not attend."

Gelbion sniffed. "Well. Vand's a bloody fool and you're a bloody fool to follow him so closely. A genius when it comes to building, but a dog of a businessman, and I won't have you going the same way, do you hear? If you continue as you are, you'll be the one to take over after me. Don't look so damned surprised, or I'll change my mind. Don't say anything. You've a clumsy mouth and you would only make a mess of it. That, my boy, we will have to work on, but what other choice do I have? Garten's sworn into service of the crown, Katriona's a bloody female and I wouldn't trust Guis with my legacy if the rest of you fell off a cliff, Rel's an idiot and Aarin has his vocation. Well done Garten for providing me with grandchildren, confound him for producing girls. No, it has to be you."

THE DAY WORE into night. Katriona departed with her husband to a fanfare of trumpets. As custom dictated, with the departure of the bride and groom the Revelry began. Music became softer. The lights were dimmed.

The water flowing from silver fountains in the hall's alcoves ran pink then red as it was replaced by wine. Rooms were opened upstairs for trysting. Guests retired for a while, returning an hour later in their evening costumes—dressed as diaphanously clad Wild Tyn tree maidens, priapic devils, lustful outlanders and other, more outrageous garb. Hirelings in revealing attire insinuated themselves into the crowds to entertain the guests. A myriad of physical types drawn from across the Hundred. All beautiful. All paid for by Gelbion Kressind.

"Would you look at that," said Trassan, turning his head to track a glittered woman whose costume left nothing to the imagination.

"Patience brother," said Aarin, who had finally arrived. "There is the matter of etiquette. Guests first."

"I'd leave off altogether," said Garten. "You can be sure father will be interviewing every whore afterwards. Sanctity of the Revelry be damned."

"Still," said Trassan. "I'm tempted, aren't you?"

Guis grinned drunkenly. "I'm not tempted to have our father discover my sexual preferences, no. But by all means, you go ahead."

The brothers spoke in a quiet corner close by a wine fountain.

"You are a little distracted this evening, Trassan," said Aarin. "Is there anything wrong?"

"No, not at all. It's just well, all this flesh... That's what's distracting me."

Guis took a goblet of wine from a naked serving woman. "Trust you. Personally, all this is rather over the top."

"It is a wedding night," said Aarin. "Vows are suspended. Love celebrated."

"Spoken like a priest," said Guis. "But I find it disturbing," he added lightly. Trassan saw that something troubled him. Guis caught him looking and raised his wine glass in mock salute, but the darkness was in his eyes; there was movement on his shoulder.

"Let her have her fun," said Garten. He was quite drunk. "She's a pretty one," he said, nodding at a girl.

"You'd get to find out if Charramay wasn't here."

Garten sighed. "I never would. I just like to look."

"A voyeur then?" said Guis archly.

"Not like that! I'm window shopping, is all. I'm a good man. I'm in love."

Trassan made a face. "Please."

"Well this is a fine gathering," said Guis. "Trassan distracted by tits, Aarin glum with the dead."

Aarin raised his hands to protest. Guis pointed at him. "No! You do appear glummer than usual, Aarin."

"The order of the Guiders is not what it once was. We are underfunded, and undermanned."

"No one wants to spend all their time with ghosts and corpses any more?" said Trassan.

"I suppose not. Today I caught a deacon washing funeral shrouds. They're not supposed to reuse the cloth, but they do," Aarin said regretfully.

"Doesn't sound so bad," said Garten. He swayed on his feet.

"It is but the least of the things that I have encountered recently." He would say no more, no matter how they tried to draw him on it.

"I feel like dancing," said Guis. "Only it's not the same without Rel." He raised his glass. "To Rel, wherever he is."

"To Rel," the others said.

"And to Katriona, I hope she's happy," said Garten.

"I hope she knows what she's doing," said Guis.

They talked, they drank. The evening wore on. Their eyes strayed more and more often to the women. Garten determined to drink himself insensible before he betrayed his wife. "After all, the wine is as free as the sex," he said, before collapsing in a corner and falling asleep.

Their group was joined by others, conversational tides pulled them apart. Trassan found himself separated from his immediate kin. He was by this time quite drunk. The evening took on an hallucinogenic air. Couples no longer went upstairs, but copulated openly in the corners and along walls. Laughter and soft sighs out-competed conversation. Other guests—the older ones, the firmly attached, the already sated—talked in polite knots. A juxtaposition that struck Trassan as faintly ridiculous.

He moved to a wine fountain. A small hand caught his wrist. He turned to see a young woman he did not recognise, wearing a half-smile and little else. She had long blonde hair worn up in a plait wrapped around her head, large eyes lined with blue and green and flecks of gold. She wore a flimsy shift split all the way up both sides. The shoulders were pinned together with large brooches with serpents coiling upon them. At her waist, the front and back were held together with chains linked with golden locks.

Trassan furrowed his brow. It was an effort staying upright.

"Aren't you a little young for all that?"

"All what?" she said with feigned innocence.

"The gold locks. You're a sybarite. All that pleasure and pain business. I thought you had to be jaded to enjoy that."

"And are you jaded?"

Trassan took a slug of wine. He smiled and shrugged. "I suppose I could be."

"I could not help noticing that you are alone."

"I seem to have lost my brothers," he admitted.

"I am not talking about your brothers."

"A woman?"

"A lover."

"No, none of that. Not here anyway." He felt a twinge of guilt. Customarily, all vows were suspended for a Revelry, but as with Garten's Charramay, there was no chance Veridy would be pleased about this.

He decided to blame the wine if he were found out.

She stood up on her toes to whisper in his ear. "Come with me," she said. Her breath was cool and sweet, and he felt self-conscious for the stink of wine on his. She did not wait for an answer before she led him away. He decided not to think about it, and followed after her.

They made their way through the party. The light was low as a cave, and red as blood. She was surefooted, he less so. He passed Guis's friend, the army officer Qurion, who winked at him, trailing his own woman.

Trassan peered behind him.

"Was that the Hag of Mogawn?" he said.

The girl looked back at him. "Hush," she said.

She led him up the leftmost of the hall's twinned grand staircases. Upstairs no one was talking. They stepped over entwined bodies, through a door into a large stateroom. It had been prepared for this stage of the wedding. There were couches and heaps of cushions, thickly piled carpets everywhere. No lights burned. Glimmer shine from street lamps and light from both moons streamed in through the windows, highlighting half-hidden curves of flesh. The girl led him to a round couch by the window. Curtains stirred in a breeze. Cold. Trassan shivered. The girl was unaffected.

She unpinned the brooches at her shoulders, but held her dress on with her hands. The breeze pressed the cloth against her body highlighting her breasts and the mound of her genitals.

"Who are you?" he asked. He was captivated by her eyes.

"I am whoever you wish me to be, Goodfellow."

"Oh, right. You're one of..." He couldn't bring himself to say what he was about to say. "You're one of father's," he finished lamely. He felt inexplicably disappointed.

She released her dress. Her clothes slithered to the floor and pooled about her feet. She laughed. "If you like." Pink moonlight sparkled off the glitter on her breasts.

Trassan reached for her face. They kissed.

She drew him down onto the couch.

CHAPTER THIRTEEN
Eastwards

FROM KARSA CITY to Macer Lesser, through the highlands of Maceriya, from there to the permanently shadowed Umberlands where there was the city of Perus, then on through the remainder of Maceriya to the borders with Daiserich and Brodning, across the broad lands of the Grand Duke to the forested plains of the Queendom of Pris, from there through the quarrelsome minor fiefdoms of the Olberland, whose pocket handkerchief territories made up near half the number of all the Hundred Kingdoms, the train clacked on and on and on.

Autumn came earlier to the Karsan Peninsula and the Isles than the continent. On the far side of the Karsan Sea, summer's rearguard fought. Almost as soon as Rel was past the Neck a dry, drowsy heat descended, thickening the air of the carriages and inducing a state of extreme lethargy in all aboard. The heat worsened Rel's despondency. He drank too much, he ate too little. If he were honest with himself, and in this state of mind he was bitterly so, he was moping.

There were some richer moments. The passage over the Neck from Karsa to the mainland was stunning despite the absence of the crashing sea. If it made his melancholy greater, at least for the time it took the train to run across the Neck he felt as if he were the hero of his own story, cast out, but sure to return home in triumph. He imagined the look on his father's face as he returned after performing some notable deed or other, and relished it.

These notions of grandeur evaporated in the face of reality. On rare occasions a spectacular piece of scenery roused him but the effect diminished the more tedious farmland and trackless forest he traversed. The ringing of bells and cries of the train waysayer announced the name of each new land they crossed into, but to Rel the land either side of the borders looked very much the same. Five weeks in Hamadan gathering his papers did little for his mood. The city of aesthetes was definitely not to his liking. He swore he could hear Alanrys's laughter echoing from every hushed courtyard.

By the time he reached the grand chasm of the river Olb and its thousand tributaries, said to be the great natural wonder of the entire Ruthnian continent, he could not care less.

The train chuffed doggedly alongside the canyon, rattling over the many bridges linking the various scraps of Olberland to one another. He gazed woefully at the splendour of small castles atop pinnacles of rock, the six-winged silhouettes of dragonlings coasting over purple moorlands, intricate as models, and decided to hate it all.

He drank some more.

The canyon narrowed. They crossed at speed a bridge of stone whose many piers were topped by monumental statuary. Dead gods, dead heroes, the usual dead things commemorated in dead stone. A broad river that fed into the Olb glinted in the canyon far below, worming its way through banks of mud. They were many hundreds of miles from the sea, near the limit of the tide's long reach, yet still this far away the ocean exerted its suzerainty. It ordered the rivers of the world to kneel and rise at its command and rise and kneel they did, crawling upon their bellies to pay obeisance at sandy shores.

The waysayer rang his bell as they hit the halfway mark of the bridge.

"The Imperium of Mohacs! The Imperium of Mohacs!"

"I'd like to shove that bell of his somewhere it won't ring so well," said Rel. The only other person in the compartment with him rattled his three-day old newspaper.

Rel went back to sulking at the view. Presently, he fell asleep.

When he woke again it was high afternoon, the sun burning in the cloudless sky. His face was hot, and had stuck to the window. He sat hurriedly, wiping at his mouth. A parade of awesome buildings rose in the distance, shrouded in thin smoke.

"Mohacs," said Rel. "Or is it Gravo?" He turned around, but the man with the paper and the middle-kingdom scowl had gone, leaving him alone in stuffy opulence. The train swung wide around the city. He saw signs of the chasm that divided it from its sister city, a strange break in the skyline. The station was in Mohacs.

"Must be Gravo over there," he said to himself. He returned to his seat as the waysayer announced their imminent arrival at Mohacs station.

Train wheels squealed. The whistle hooted. The city engulfed them. Everything was colossal, overblown in the pompous eastern style, all towering stone needles and flat domes. Boulevards opened in slowing zoetrope, light dark, light dark. Rel caught a flash of a long street crowded with small palaces. The heyday of the Imperium was long past, but after being absorbed by the Hundred, Mohacs had reinvented itself as the de facto centre of the southeastern Hundred and had remained wealthy. There was money on display, and plenty of it.

A riotous geometry of colourful stone and bronze made up Mohacs station. Just before they passed under a soaring glass roof, the double track split into eight separate sidings, the platforms either side gloriously decorated. The shades were all suggestive of autumn to Rel. Either he was influenced by the season, or the Mohaca had a sense of irony regarding their current place in the world.

The people outside were dressed in clothes from all over the Hundred, their skins were all hues: blue, black, brown, white, pink. Every sort of human being, though no Tyn. Having grown up in Karsa, Rel found their absence odd. The people were mostly wives, excitable children and their servants. Behind them an army of porters marshalled their barrows, like some pre-Maceriyan army arraying its chariots for the charge. He decided to wait for the crowd to subside before alighting.

A man bounded across the platform. Such was his exuberance that he was impossible not to notice, and

Rel followed his progress until he lost him by the train. He didn't expect him to come bursting unannounced into the carriage. Rel's heart flipped, and his hand leapt for the sword lying on the seat.

"Mester Rel Kressind?" the man said in heavily accented Karsarin. "You are he. I have it here, marked. Your carriage, your number, your description."

"Who the fifteen hells are you?"

"You were not informed, not told?" the man was aggrieved by this news, in the manner of men the world over who believe their colleagues to be idiots. "I am Zhalak Zhinsky! Khusiak, and honoured servant of the Glass Fort." He clipped his heels together, and bowed sharply, snapping back up so quickly he was in danger of wrenching something.

Rel could see the man's origins plainly. He had the ruddy skin and folded eyes of Khusiak, drooping moustaches that terminated in paired sets of three ceramic beads. Physically, he was precisely as a Khusiak should look, at least according to his storybooks, but was dressed in a keenly tailored five-piece suit, this year's Perusian fashion. He wore it well, but the combination of man and gear was a double dose of outlandishness.

"Your journey was good?" asked Zhinsky.

"A few spectacles, a lot of boring scenery, one swift dalliance with a young woman that almost ended in a duel. It's been a really uneventful trip. Fifteen days. If I never see another railway again, I think it will be too soon."

This elicited a gale of laughter.

"Did I say something amusing?"

"Forgive me! Forgive me. You might change your tunes, as you say, after a few days in the saddle of a dracon. They are not quite so comfortable as all this. No room service!" he wagged a thick, calloused finger.

"I can ride."

Zhinsky raised his eyebrows. "Maybe you think you can."

"We are leaving as soon as possible, I suppose."

"Yes, yes we are. You are eager for your posting? That is good!"

"Not really," said Rel. "An unlucky guess as to our timing. My life has become that kind of parade."

"Ah, that is unfortunate. Well, we will see how you find the Glass Fort. There is some adventure there, if one is in the mind."

"Marvellous," said Rel insincerely.

"Come now!" admonished Zhinsky. "I get your bags collected. I have dinner booked, very good officers club. Very fine food, very fine women. We get to know one another, you and I. We have long journey ahead of us."

Rel stifled a yawn. "If it's all the same to you, I would like to go to my lodgings, please."

"This is Mohacs-Gravo my friend! Capital of the old Imperium. There is much to see here. A shame not to, a shame for you. You regret it in one month maybe, definitely after two. Much cold and boredom awaits you."

"Thank you for your efforts on my behalf, but I am very tired."

Zhinsky's face darkened. "You, it is as I thought. You are spoiled, and soft! As soon as I get the summons to embassy here I decide this." He made dismissive gestures at Rel's clothes. "New man, new money. No nobility in your sort. You go to the Gates of the World my friend, is there any fire in you merchants' sons? I see your sort many times heading to the Glass Fort. You are the... the..." he struggled for the Karsarin word.

Rel was so taken aback by the Khusiak's sudden change in manner, and the accompanying insolence, he did not become angry. He stared, boggle-eyed at him, as he continued.

Zhinsky face's was becoming an uncommon shade of purple. "Cast-offs of the world!"

"Have I transgressed some custom regarding hospitality? I have, haven't I? Father always said I was clueless."

Zhinsky ceased his tirade. His mouth shut. He stood back. "You have. I offer you great service, you turn it down, this grave affront to me. This not Karsan way?"

"Not really. My brother Garten is the diplomat. I'm not much good for that kind of thing I'm afraid," said Rel. "You have my apologies."

Zhinsky grunted, and looked Rel up and down like he was seeing some unusual specimen for the first time. "I wish to ease your journey, is all. You should enjoy this place, where we are going there is much to be bored. No women, no good drink, no theatres, shadowplay, or restaurants. If I in your boots, friend, then I enjoy civilisation like I never see again."

"The way you say that suggests it might be a possibility."

The Khusiak roared with laughter. "I like you! I do! Always with the joking. This is a good attitude!" His smile vanished as quick as it had come. "You will need it."

"Very well, I suppose you are right, let us go and see the sights a little. Did you say something about women?"

"I did! I did!" said Zhinsky. He smiled expansively. His teeth were off white, slightly crooked. Two of the lower set had been replaced by gold.

"Well, lead on. But tell me, if you're on the way to the Gates, doesn't that make you a discard as well?"

"No my friend, it does not. We of Khushash take the Gates very seriously. We live by the Black Sands and see what live there. All Khusiaks you will meet there are warriors, not spoiled merchant boys, be sure of it! Now come, let us see how little merchant boy drinks!" He pulled a serious face. "You can drink, can't you?"

THE TRAIN WHISTLED and slid to a jerking halt. Tuvacs was shaken awake. Thin bars of sunlight let in by gaps in the planks striped the interior of the boxcar. The others were up and muttering, gathering their belongings. Boskovin was nudging the last sleepers awake with his toe. Marko was already awake, but Lem and Julion, younger men, were fast asleep.

"Up! Up, you laggards! Get up! We're here! Mohacs-Gravo! Mohacs-Gravo! Last stop on the line, now the real journey begins.

Whistles sounded from outside and the door slid open. A field of arms waved for attention, dozens of pauper porters. A group of them, fully laden, passed behind the clamour at the car door. Starvelings, they nevertheless bore huge loads on straps tight about their foreheads. They walked, eyes at the floor, hands clutching at ropes securing the bundles and boxes, following in single file after a fat outland merchant.

Tuvacs' own language was being spoken. Everything was overwhelmingly familiar after so long away.

"Boy! Boy! Tell them to get away from the car. Shake yourself out of your daze and do your job!" Boskovin waved at the desperate porters.

"Go away!" shouted Tuvacs in Mohacin. "There is not work here for you, my master has his own men. Go away!"

"Please please please little brother!" they shouted. "We need work, we shall work cheaply. Tell your master, let his men rest! We have families that wish to eat."

"I am sorry big brother," said Tuvacs. "He will not spend his money. Begone! He is ready to use his stick," he said, not knowing if it were true.

The porters broke up, some visibly distressed. Tuvacs' heart was heavy. These men of Gravo were his own kind.

"Well done boy," said Boskovin. "Men!" he shouted. "Unload!" He turned back to Tuvacs. "Are there holding areas for cargoes here?"

"Yes, I think so. I am sorry master, I have been here only once, on our journey away."

Boskovin clasped Tuvacs' shoulder. "Very well. I am sure there must be. You and I will find out where, and then we shall visit a kennelmaster. Do you know of one?"

"I know where they can be found."

"Excellent." Boskovin winked at Tuvacs. "An excellent purchase you were. Marko! Marko! Get Rusanina out. She'll be wanting a walk."

Boskovin jumped out of the car, then stood a moment in the bustle of the platform rubbing his legs. Tuvacs joined him. "Fair long trip, addles the head, then to be straight out into this! Still, boy, time cannot be bought, only freely traded. Marko! MAR-*KO*! Get me my bloody dog!" He yelled. He slapped Julion's back. "Not there! Stack it there! I want the four of you around it all the time, this place will be thick with foreign thieves. The boy and I are going to find secure warehousing. Get it ready to move out."

Tuvacs found a harassed looking official. The man looked down his nose at Tuvacs.

"Get on your way, urchin," he said.

"Goodman, goodman, it is not for me I approach you. My master, from Karsa, he has business here."

Boskovin was dealing with an altercation at the edge of the small space his men had carved out on the platform, porters trying to grab work, possibly thieves among them. His men shoved them back and Boskovin, seeing Tuvacs waving, pushed his way through the crowd.

"My master, Goodfellow Boskovin of Karsa," said Tuvacs.

There followed a lengthy debate about the customs worth of Boskovin's possessions. "Tools, kitchenware for the Gate and the railway there."

"Trade goods are taxed at one in five of expected worth," said the official. Tuvacs translated.

"No, no! Tell this blasted idiot that they're not for sale. We're the damned victuallers! They're artisanal equipment, not trade goods."

Tuvacs translated the lie.

It went back and forth like this for a while. Eventually they reached agreement, and Boskovin handed over a heavy purse of coins.

"Daylight robbery," he muttered through an insincere smile. "I'll bet half of it'll end up in his pocket, bloody foreigners."

"Please goodman," asked Tuvacs of the official. "We need storage for our equipment. Where is there space?"

The official pointed over the heads of the crowds, out past the rail terminus. "There, down toward the east end."

"Thank you." Tuvacs relayed the information to Boskovin. He felt lightheaded, the noise and smell of the station dizzied him after so long in the car. And to be home...

"Come on boy! Keep it together. You're the only thing between me and a damned fleecing at the hands of your filthy countrymen." Boskovin spat on the marble tiling, drawing looks of ire from the Mohaca. He dragged Tuvacs back toward the train. The engine whooshed loudly, letting out clouds of steam that glittered with residual glimmer. Clouds boiled in the high glass ceilings. The wind shifted, blasted a wall of warm, sharp-smelling fog across the platform.

Tuvacs coughed, instinctively batting at the sparks of exhausted magic settling on his clothes.

The steam cleared. The men were rearranging the equipment on baggage carts, haggling heatedly in broken Low Maceriyan with the cart handlers.

Boskovin was talking to his dog. Rusanina was a magnificent dray bitch, very tall, her withers level with Boskovin's shoulders. Her head was three times the size of Tuvacs', her mouth full of ivory spear tips.

"Bad place, much noise," she said. "Too much scent. Can't think." The dog growled out its clumsy words with patient effort, swallowing hard between every sentence. She looked over the tumult with canine disdain. Her consorts were afraid. The two smaller males stood behind her, heads bowed and tails between their legs. One let out a grating whimper.

"Sorry old girl," said Boskovin, ruffled the beast's thick fur. Rusanina leaned into the caress and half-closed her eyes with pleasure. "Can't sleep yet. I need you to come with me to see the other dogs."

"I come now?" she asked.

"Yes. We're moving the gear first, then the boy here will take us where we need to go."

She glanced over the heaps of material. "I not pull. Not enough dogs to pull."

Boskovin rubbed under her chin. "No need to pull yet, my love. The men'll pull the gear."

Rusanina growled. Tuvacs stepped back.

"She's laughing, boy; she finds it funny that she doesn't have to work, don't you my lovely?" He scratched harder under her jaw. "Don't you be afraid of old Rusanina. She's a gentle one."

"I deadly when needed," she said.

Boskovin laughed. Tuvacs did not find it funny at all. The dog looked like it could tackle a dracon and come off better.

"Come on," said Boskovin. He laid his hand lightly on Rusanina's shoulder. Tuvacs fell in behind him, sheltered from the chaos by the dog to the side and the merchant to the front. The crowd, dense as it was, parted magically in front of her. No one wanted to get in the way of a dray her size.

Trains hooted, there were scents of spiced Mohaca food that had Tuvacs' mouth watering. He had been too long eating bland, rotten Karsan fare. They passed the engine at the head of their train. Steam hissed from its pistons, water dripping from spill pipes. The engineers were checking it over, noting down readings from gauges. There was a loud crack and a blaze of blue light as one of them opened the door to the glimmer chamber. Uncanny heat blasted Tuvacs in the side of the face. Rusanina barked nervously and sidestepped, her mates slunk away from the machine, walking parallel with Rusanina so that Tuvacs was walled in by high, furry flanks.

The dogs walked stiffly. They radiated animal tension.

"I want to run," grumbled Rusanina, as if she had read Tuvacs' mind. "Too long on train."

"Soon my love, soon," soothed Boskovin.

They turned right, walking now perpendicular to the trains. Tall trees grew from pots the height of a man, their leaves blackened with soot and discoloured with glimmer burn.

There were five locomotives arrayed at the terminus of the tracks. The heat of them made Tuvacs sweat. Hot metal stank up the air. The power of the glimmer throbbed from their boilers in pulses. Caught in the interference patterns created between them, a pressure built in Tuvacs' head.

An engine blasted magically-heated steam from its pistons, sending up roaring billows either side of itself. With an ear-splitting shriek it started backwards, clanking and huffing like a dragon hauling itself from its lair. Rusanina's mates howled and yipped. She barked at them, barely stopping them from bolting. The engine's huffing increased in volume. It strained backwards against its load. Sounding a long, mournful note, it disappeared into a hot mist of its own making.

"This way, goodfellow," said Tuvacs. He led them off the platform area into a less crowded part of the station. The went through a gateway whose metal scissor grille was folded back.

The cargo area was cool. After the hurly-burly of the platforms the silence was welcome. Men came and went, dropping off and picking up goods, some were merchants, others agents. Tuvacs asked one of the servants where they should go. Once there, he negotiated with a man for lockable storage. Tuvacs bargained well. The man pulled a pained face when given his payment, muttering loudly that it wasn't enough, that he had been robbed, but he took them off down a side way. Cast-iron pillars supported many arches on either side, each gated by a folding, lockable grille. He brought them to an empty bay where he had Boskovin sign papers—Tuvacs was no help to him here, for he could not read—and handed over a key. The Mohaci narrowed his eyes resentfully at the Karsan party and strode off. The men unloaded the carts, and the cart handlers went away. Tuvacs translated, and he managed to get a deal that satisfied everyone.

"Tuvacs and I are going on a little adventure," proclaimed Boskovin. "The rest of you'll wait here near the station until we get back. Julion, you're staying with the gear for the first two hours."

Julion groaned.

"You'll not be here long. You'll be relieved, you miserable whoreson! Improve your attitude, or you can sit the whole day out here."

"Alright, Mather, alright!" he said.

"Marko, Gordan, find a tavern. Stay in it. Lem, go with them and bring Julion a drink and some food. Rusanina, have your husbands stay here with Julion. If they have to piss or take a shit, they're not to do it on anything important."

"There is an area for it, master," said Tuvacs.

"Lem, find where it is, take the dogs, bring them back here." Now it was Lem's turn for disappointment. "You'll be in the tavern soon! None of you are to get drunk or wander off, do you hear? No fighting, no whoring. I plan for us to leave as soon as we can. I'll not be chasing you out of cathouses. If you're not here when we leave, you'll stay here. There's a train setting out from Gravo tomorrow, and I want us to be on it. The boy here's going to take me to find a draymen, Rusanina will choose us a good team. We'll be back soon."

Boskovin, Tuvacs and the dog set off. Rusanina barked harshly at her consorts when they tried to follow; they sank lower into themselves, and went to stand by Lem.

"This is all going swimmingly," said Boskovin happily as they left the station.

"HERE SIR! HERE, the finest dogs!"

Tuvacs shook his head. "Not this one. I do not trust his face."

"How so?" asked Boskovin.

"It is his manner, he is too desperate. He looks like he has nothing to lose."

Boskovin nodded. "I'm getting gladder by the minute I bought your crime out, boy. What about here?"

They stopped by a kennels with an ostentatious archway made of punched metal. There was no barker outside to drag people in.

Tuvacs nodded. "This is a good place. The way here in Mohacs-Gravo is that those who do not need to advertise, do not advertise."

They stepped through into a walled compound. Dogs were tethered all around the periphery. When Rusanina came in, they began baying loudly and leaping about at the end of their lines. A man hurried out of a small door let into one wall. When he saw the men, his face lifted. When he saw Rusanina, his face fell.

"Welcome sirs!" he said in passable Maceriyan. "You are here looking for dogs?"

"We are," said Boskovin. "I need one team of eight. I have my own lead." He rested his hand on Rusanina's back.

"A Sorskian dog?" said the man.

"Yes," Rusanina answered.

The kennelmaster's manner veered between wonder and wretchedness. "I have not had the pleasure of seeing such an animal," he said. "She will pick the dogs?"

"Of course," said Boskovin. "So no rubbish."

The kennelmaster sighed resignedly. "Sale or rental?"

"We are going to the Gates of the World."

"Sale then," said the kennelmaster. His mood picked up.

The kennelmaster went about his patter, pointing out various of his teams, then individuals within each team.

Rusanina sniffed, craning her neck forward, passing her nose over the air. She approached one team. The dogs greeted her warily, allowing her to smell their necks, facial and anal glands. She was brief, and did not provoke them.

"No good, no good," she said. "This one smell sick. This one crazy. This one angry with two-leg master and four-leg leader. This one old." So it went. The draymaster allowed them to inspect two more teams, but Rusanina was dismissive of them all. They passed a group of lead dogs who bared their teeth at her, but she held her head high and ignored them.

They left the man wheedling at his gate.

As they went from kennelmaster to kennelmaster Tuvacs found himself looking over his shoulder. The Street of Dogs ended at the canyon that separated the twin cities. Here the upper reaches of the Olb flowed. Not ten miles further upstream, the distant sea finally relinquished its dominion of the waters and the tides held no sway. Like all dirty businesses, the kennels were located in Gravo. But even here was wealthy compared to where Tuvacs had grown up, on a shelf carved into the cliffs, raised by a gang of gleaners. He wondered if he'd see anyone he knew; it could be dangerous if he did, for he had broken his bond when he and Lavina had run away. He doubted it, and doubted too if anyone would recognise him. It was three years ago, and he had filled out greatly.

Mohacs' side was higher than Gravo's, and the richer city was in full view. He kept his eyes firmly on that. If he ever returned to the twin heart of the Imperium, it would be to live on the other side.

They found a suitable place. The prices the kennelmaster charged were double some they'd been quoted, but Rusanina was satisfied, and that was what was most important to Boskovin. Contracts were exchanged, a deposit paid and the remainder of the monies displayed. The chosen dogs were marked with blue dye. Boskovin sealed the deal with sweet plum brandy. The kennelmaster promised delivery of the teams to the station within three hours.

The evening deepened. The warmth of the day was bleeding off.

The traffic worsened, and it took them a long while to recross the canyon back into Mohacs, and twenty minutes to find the tavern where Marko and Julion were, once there. The men were half-drunk, reluctant to leave.

"It's going to be a cold night," said Julion when they stepped outside. The men shivered and stamped their feet.

"Then work harder," said Boskovin. "We don't have long. Get the gear packed up. The dogs will be here in two hours from Gravo. Get the carts put together."

The men grumbled as they made their way back to the station. Under glimmer lamps, they unpacked their dog cart from its cases and bolted it together. It was a skeletal, light thing made of steel and wood, designed for rugged terrain and easy repair, with wheels that could be removed to allow it to run on its runners. Presently, the kennelmaster arrived with the dogs. Rusanina inspected them all, ensuring they were the animals they had paid for. The rest of the money changed hands. For an additional small fee, one of the kennelmaster's men stayed on to guide Boskovin's men through the cities to the station on the far side of Gravo.

Almost as soon as he had arrived back home, Tuvacs was to leave.

CHAPTER FOURTEEN
The National Interest

GARTEN HAD HIS office deep inside the Admiralty Building. Trassan sat therein, upon an uncomfortable chair; too small, the ribs too fine, the padding hard. Being so enabled it to achieve the high curved effect on the cushion so beloved of Molliger Holm's workshops, but it was damned unpleasant to sit on. Trassan moved his backside across it, trying to find a position that did not feel like he was permanently damaging his coccyx. He failed, so he stood and began to impatiently pace.

A huge clock upon a marble table installed solely to house it clicked loudly. Ceilings in the Admiralty were high, the pronounced echo they produced encouraging the bureaucrats responsible for Karsa's sea power to whisper. This one was twenty feet above the polished oak floor. Give or take. Trassan calculated the overall dimensions of the room—six hundred feet squared, far too big for its tiny fire to heat. Then he figured out the loading stress required for the beams holding up the roof. The ceiling was broad, vaulted, heavy with complicated plaster cornicing and roses from which hung three large brass chandeliers. The candle holders in them had been modified to take glimmer lamps, and not long since; the solder lines were still brighter than the surrounding brass. The smooth spaces of the ceiling were dominated by a massive fresco of Tiritys, exiled god of the sea, and his twenty-one daughters. One, Ionatys, had been hideous where the others were beautiful. In the painting, she cowered in a deep cave, rejected by her sisters. She had had the last laugh, Trassan recalled, being the only one of Tiritys's children to escape Res Iapetus's wrath. Allegedly she still dwelt in the deepest parts of the ocean, creeping out of the sea to devour the children of coastal villages. It was a Farisles legend, one from the immense cluster of little lands that huddled around the far southern edges of Karsa. Trassan had no idea if it were true or not. He suspected so, there were worse things under the water than Ionatys.

One of them was why he was there.

The clocked let out a miniature carillon. He glanced at it, a monstrous ormolu thing under a heavy glass dome. Independent wheels set into the face gave the phases of the White Moon, Red Moon and Twin relative to one another, a huge dial occupied the bottom third of its face, a tidal table crammed with writing so miniscule a jointed arm bearing a magnifying glass had been fitted to the clock case to allow one to read it. Four cavorting dolphins held it aloft, an emperor anguillon coiled around its base, mouth ready to strike at one of them. Altogether the clock must have weighed as much as a man. The gold plating must have cost the sanity of at least one gilder. He calculated how much quicksilver they must have got through. Anything to stop him looking at the hands creeping around their digits and reminding him how late his bloody brother was.

The door banged open. Garten strode in, flicking through a dossier as he came. His heels clicked loudly on the parquet.

"Trassan!" he said with a smile. "I am sorry to keep you waiting. The High Legate's illness has the place in uproar. I've had the palace bombarding me with messages for the last three days."

"That's not your purview, surely?"

"Not Admiralty business, no, but Duke Abing has been given the nod as the emissary to Maceriya in the ah, unfortunate event of the Legate's death for the election. I've been given my own nod that I will accompany him."

"Well done," said Trassan. "You're going up in the world."

Garten threw the dossier down onto his enormous desk. "It's not a certainty. It would just be my luck to do all the work only for some sycophant to get the job. That would upset Charramay, she's dead set on my going."

"How is Charramay?"

"She and the children are fine," Garten replied distractedly. He pulled out his chair and sat. "Take a seat."

"No thank you. That chair is bloody uncomfortable."

"Heh, yes they are. But they are very fashionable."

"Right."

"And they help us prevent people outstaying their welcome." He smiled again, less broadly this time. "Look, Trassan, I'll get to the point." Garten's expression became serious.

"What is it?"

Garten pushed at a paperweight on his desk, glass with the emblem of the Admiralty imprisoned inside. "I'm afraid I have some bad news."

"You can't issue the licence. Why in the fifteen hells not?" Trassan's cheeks flushed.

"Look, I did warn you. I looked into it, and the answer was no. Emphatically so. I've been warned off quite forcefully. There are protocols to follow, Trassan. The treaty with the Drowned King; your expedition is going to go right across his territory."

"So?"

"It has to go through the proper channels, Trassan."

Trassan paced back and forward. "For fuck's sake, Gart! This is in the national interest. Who the hell is going to object? Do we want the Maceriyans to get there first? You have heard, haven't you? The moment Vand put the notice of his discovery out, Persin announced construction of his own fleet."

"Yes. Yes I did hear," said Garten quietly. "'Race to the Pole!' was plastered all over the papers, brother. And still is."

"Floatstone! Did you hear that? Four refitted ships. He's going to be ready long before the *Prince Alfra* is completed."

"Your ship is faster. You told me only an iron ship had a hope of getting through the ice to the shore."

Trassan rubbed his head. "Yes. Yes, but there is another way, to leave the vessels and travel over the ice. Very dangerous, but there is always a chance he might make it. Do you want to risk that?"

"What I do not wish to risk is the safety of this nation's trade routes."

"Really?" shouted Trassan. His voice boomed from the high ceiling. "What you do not wish to risk is your career, more like. You would deny me the chance of advancing the cause of our country to move your peg a few rows up the game board? What do you think the broadsheet editors might feel about that?"

A cough interrupted Trassan's tirade. Garten's secretary was poking his head around the door at the far end of the office. He looked comically small so far away.

"Is there anything wrong, master?" said the man.

"No, no," Garten said. "My brother and I are engaged in a robust discussion."

The man looked from brother to brother.

"That is all, Meesham," said Garten.

"Very good, sir."

The door clicked shut.

"Do us both a favour, Trassan, and keep your voice down," hissed Garten. "This is an office of dignity, not the province of dockers and shipwrights. Any licence that infringes on the rights of the Drowned King must be signed by Duke Abing. As it is, with you wishing to drive a spike of iron right across the king's territory, it'll have to go to a full inquiry. And don't think to threaten me, you stupid bastard. I'm on your side!"

"It doesn't feel like it. Why can't you issue the licence now? The inquiry will almost certainly grant it in the national interest."

"I fully expect it to. And that will be my recommendation."

Trassan looked out of the window. Wind had cleared the sky of fog, and it was cold, full of rain. "A recommendation, is that all you can do? If it's so certain, why not just issue it?"

"Because I can't! Look, a recommendation is a lot better than nothing."

"Not by much, brother. Not by much. You are going to look like a fool for this. Imagine that Persin gets there first, and plunders the whole site. That will be on you."

"Of course I've taken that into consideration! But the wheels of bureaucracy turn to the urging of their own engine, not to that of public opinion."

"Fuck the proper channels."

Garten shuffled papers, tapping them on the desk until he judged them properly aligned, then laid them down. "If it were anybody else, Trassan, I might not offer my recommendation. It is my judgment that there is a high chance you will fail. Then you will provoke the Drowned King for no reason. The last thing Prince Alfra needs at this time is an army of the dead creeping around the high tide mark. Can you not understand that? Perhaps, do you not think, it's better that Persin upsets the undersea kingdom and the king looks to Maceriya for a time? Do you see?"

"Perfectly!" Trassan threw up his hands. "I understand that you have no confidence in your brother, and you would risk our national interest for the sake of your own advancement."

"And you would imperil the safety of all ships that fly our nation's flag for the sake of yours. We have a special relationship with the Drowned King. He watches over our ships, he favours our passage over others. It is a keystone of our naval policy. We are especially vulnerable to him if we anger him."

"I am sure you are making our father very proud."

Garten paused. "I do not take this lightly, Trassan. As a matter of fact, I spoke with father. He was not particularly enthusiastic about having our family name associated with a crippling blockade. I also got the impression he was not much in favour of your adventure."

There were other reasons Trassan could not explain. The favouring of him over his brothers as inheritor of their father's industries would split their fraternity apart.

"You could have spun that yarn differently."

"Lied you mean?"

"No! The truth."

"Truth is a matter of opinion. Brother, I am sorry. I truly am. But neither I nor Karsa can risk to indulge you. Vand has influence, as do I. The enquiry will be over quickly. There are many who are keen to invest in this venture. And it is in the national interest. But we must show the king his rule is taken seriously."

"It will take months."

"It might have taken a year. I will do what I can to hurry it along."

"So useful having a brother highly placed in the Admiralty."

"Not highly placed. Not yet. And if I do what you ask, I never will be. I shall do everything I can to help—"

"Except giving me the licence."

"Lost gods hunt you down and tear you up!" said Garten, suddenly losing his temper. He leaned forward across his desk and jabbed a finger at his brother. "You can be a selfish little cock sometimes. Listen to yourself! This is my fucking job! This is what I do! I am not going to go against all my own experience and the procedures of this entire institution, dedicated as it is to protect one of the most valuable aspects of our entire economy in order to gratify your impatience."

The door opened. The functionary nervously poked his head around the door again.

"Are you sure there is nothing wrong, sir?"

"Go away!" both brothers shouted simultaneously.

Garten took a deep breath, and regained some of his characteristic composure. He groaned softly. "You are one of the few people on this Earth, brother, who can rile me up so. Go back to your yard. Continue with the construction of your ship. With a careful play of your hand, and a modicum of luck, you will be away in the spring as you intended and then you will beat the Maceriyans to the Morfaan city. I wish you all the luck in doing so. You'll have as much help as I can give."

Trassan looked at the floor. "It won't be enough."

"Trassan, it will be fine."

"Garten, we need the licence to continue work."

"What?"

Trassan chewed his lip. "We are close to running out of money."

"Preposterous! Arkadian Vand is one of the richest men in the western Hundred."

Trassan became nervy. "I shouldn't tell you this, and by our mother's life you must swear not to tell another soul."

"Go on."

"Vand has put everything into this that he has. Between this and the excavations in Ostria, he's got nothing left. Persin's appropriation of his designs has virtually bankrupted him. His factories are not as lucrative as they should be because of that, and the disaster at Thrusea six years ago cleared out his coffers. We were going to use the licence to raise investment."

"Vand close to bankruptcy? Hard to believe."

"Blame Persin. He does, you would not credit the enmity between those two."

"Well I am sorry, but you are going to have to come up with another way to raise your finances." He got up from his chair. "I am going to have to ask you to leave now. I have a great many things to do. The High Legate's illness has the entire government running around like dracons in a chicken yard. We are living in delicate times."

He held out his hand. Trassan reluctantly shook it.

"I am sorry, Trass, I really am."

"Save it," said Trassan angrily. "I won't forget this, Garten."

"I was afraid you would say that."

"What did you expect?"

Garten moved to embrace his brother, but Trassan moved away. "I'll be seeing you."

"Trassan, don't be like that, wait!"

But Trassan strode across his brother's vast office without looking back, his cheeks burning with fury.

CHAPTER FIFTEEN
Morthrocksey Mill

BREAKFAST AT DEMION Morthrock's house on the Parade was a frosty affair. Katriona came down from her room, he from his. They ate stiffly in silence, sitting in their morning clothes, before retiring for the second dressing to change into their daywear. Morthrock glumly thought it was a pattern that looked to become set. Married life stretched out its miserable, rocky road in front of him.

He hurried his breakfast, and got up to go. "By your leave, my goodlady," he said.

"You do not require my leave to go from your own breakfast room, husband," she said. She did not lift her eyes from the newspaper. The front pages carried a large headline on the High Legate's worsening sickness and the political manoeuvrings it had engendered. Trassan's ship also merited many column inches. It had done ever since Vand had announced the discovery of his frozen city.

To these she paid cursory attention, however. She was a curious one, poring over the business notices for an hour or more every day. He attempted to break the ice, one last time.

"Would you prefer some lighter reading matter, wife?"

"No, goodfellow, I am content," she said. A forkful of kedgeree hovered by her mouth as she scrutinised stock movements. Some fell onto her paper. She did not notice.

"Goodlady... I... Let me." He said. He came to her side and scooped up the mess with a napkin, careful not to stand too close to her. He moved awkwardly around her to prevent their touching. She glanced up at him.

"Thank you," she said.

He blushed. Closeness to her brought up a potent mix of emotion. The memory of their first night together embarrassed him. He had never expected her to fall willingly into his arms, but it had been so cold he had not attempted to share her bed since.

He made to go. She stopped him with a hand on his arm.

"You are timid around me. Why?" Her tone was unrevealing. Was she angry, challenging him? He could not tell.

"I am not a monster, Katriona," he said. "I have never been much use at anything other than cards. And then not all the time. This marriage was of our mutual choice, but I am aware that your heart will always belong to Arvane. I... Perhaps I was a fool to hope otherwise. I will try to be a good husband to you. Gods know I've not been much good at anything else. I refuse to force myself on you." Although, that was what he had done; it certainly felt that way. This was not how he hoped things would turn out.

She looked into his eyes searchingly. He could not tell if she found what she was looking for. He blinked stupidly.

"I shall make a proposal to you, Demion Morthrock. Let us try to get on. Let us try to make this marriage work." She brushed a grain of rice that Demion had missed from her paper. "Gods also know that I have seen enough misery in marriage. I refuse to be a miserable wife. I acquiesced to your request for my hand because you have a gentle reputation. I have shared your bed." Not very enthusiastically, he thought dejectedly. "Do you not think we should be friends?"

"Well, I, well, yes. Yes, I suppose we could be friends. We should be friends!" His heart quickened.

"And friends, especially husband and wife, should share in all things. Is that not what the vows we took said?"

"I suppose so..."

She smiled brightly at him. "Excellent. Then tomorrow you may show me the mill."

The request threw him. "I... I'm sorry?" he stuttered. The napkin, stained with news ink and kedgeree, dangled from his hand.

"We are married, whether we want to be or not. We might as well enjoy it. Let us be friends. Let us share everything. You are supposed to be a man of business, a short trip for a happy wife. Show me our family industry."

"Well," he said. "Well." It was all he could think to say. "Well." He was such a fool!

"You do agree, do you not?"

There was nothing he could think of that made a reasonable argument as to why he should not show her the mill. She was his wife now, she shared his name. Why then did he feel as if he stood upon a precipice?

"It is a dreadfully noisy place," he said doubtfully.

"I'll survive. Surely you cannot hope to have missed that I find such things interesting? Why not tomorrow at half of the sixth bell, the workers will be already at their tasks. I would not wish to get in their way."

"Yes. Yes, half of sixth. Very good." He nodded, even as he questioned what the hell he was doing.

She returned to her paper. He had to remind himself he did not have to wait to be dismissed before he bumbled his way out of the room.

THE MORTHROCK MILL was in Karaddua. The name evoked a rural idyll, but the village it had once belonged to had been buried by row upon row of miserable grey houses. The city continued for a mile beyond Karaddua before the tattered fringe of the countryside began to break up the factories and slums.

The Morthrocks' carriage clattered down a wide road of setts made uneven by subsidence. Six black dogs pulled it, fine drays. They wheezed in the unhealthy, chemical reek clinging to the district. Towering chimneys punctuated the rule-straight sentences of housing. Long banners of black, glimmer-tainted smoke streamed from the top of each. The sky around the horizon was clear, but Karaddua was lidded with a brown roil that crept lower to the ground with every passing moment, shutting out the blue.

A tram rattled past, bell ringing and dogs barking. Morthrocks' team yipped in greeting. Katriona looked out on women labouring at their stoops and windows with scrubbing brushes. Their cleaning never ceased. One threw a bucket of grey water not quite in their path, and fixed the carriage with a hard eye. A small girl in a filthy dress and bare feet stood on a street corner. She held a hoop in her hand, but did not play with it. Their carriage, gleaming when it came out from the coachhouse, had accrued a layer of grime. Katriona looked through a haze of dirt.

"It is abominably filthy here," she said.

Morthrock nodded. "Our family's business is a dirty one."

"And all these people live among the muck."

"They come from far and wide for employment, my dear. It is necessary that they dwell close by their place of work. There is a living for them here that there is not in the countryside."

"It seems inhumane."

Demion banged on the carriage roof with his cane. He was surprised at his irritation with Katriona's reaction. Rationally thinking, it was better this way. If she were shocked she would leave well alone and get on with being the good wife, and he was rather hoping for that outcome. But he found himself affronted. He realised that he wished her to be proud of his family's enterprise, even though it had never interested him, and had left its running to others since he had inherited it.

"My father provided doctors, and schools for every child until the age of seven, employment for life thereafter, all benefits they still enjoy. These people are fortunate. They have the opportunity for advancement. They could be beholden to some old money lord and dwelling in a shack. Instead they have freedom here."

Katriona looked again at the ranks of houses. Filth trickled along gutters.

"This is a poor form of freedom."

"This district will soon be linked to the sewers. The

embankments on the Lemio and the Var are in place. There is no flooding in the lower reaches any more." He pointed to a lamp. "There is glimmer lighting, put in only this last year. I admit the people could have better lives, but every year brings new advances, new benefits. It will not always be this way. Industry enriches us all. Here is the opportunity to make something of oneself, if one but has the mettle."

"My father says the same thing," said Katriona. "I never believed it."

"My father did a lot for them." He awkwardly patted Katriona's hand. He felt even more awkward when she did not withdraw it, but instead grasped his hand tightly.

"And what have you done for them, my dear Demion?" she said.

He wanted to retort, perhaps sharply. He wanted to ask what her father had done for anyone, growing rich as he had from factories and mills such as his. But he could not. He had always found it hard to speak whenever Katriona locked eyes with him. He had assumed this inability would leave him once she was his. If anything, it was worse.

"Ah, well. Yes." The carriage slowed, saving him. "Aha! Here we are!"

A tall wall topped with a fence of spiked, cast iron wheels bounded the mill. Four sets of double gates pierced it, each decorated with moulded brick reliefs depicting scenes from pre-Iapetan mythology. All were open. Large wagons went in and out of two. A tramway came out of the third. The driver called out his commands to his team. The dogs barked and turned sharp left into the fourth gate.

They passed under the archway, and into the Morthrocksey Mill.

THE MILL ENCOMPASSED several blocks, a town in its own right clustered around the Morthrocksey stream. A wide main street divided it into two. On either side of the gate end were tall, modern buildings with large windows. In these were situated the mill offices and most delicate, recent machinery. At the far end, some five hundred yards away, were the foundries. From one of the three came a ceaseless stream of smoke, shot through with orange sparks, the others were cold. Down the left hand of the street ran the Morthrocksey. The river had been imprisoned in a straight channel of smoothly coursed masonry. For much of its length down to the Var it had been culverted. The plans were that it would be incorporated into the sewer system, but for the moment this brief stretch emerged still into daylight. What water that had not been sucked up by the factories was bright orange, a stinking trickle that ran through miniature rapids of rubbish. Where the refuse grew thick it dammed the oily flow, rainbow patterns on the surface there, crowned with extravagant mounds of dirty yellow foam rimed with brown scum. The smell of it was intolerably potent.

Katriona held her handkerchief up to her nose as Demion opened the door and stepped out.

"I told you this was no place for a lady," said Demion with a mixture of admonishment and sympathy. He held out his hand to help her alight from the carriage nonetheless. "We'll start with the production floor first. This way."

Three Tyn came out to handle the dogs, their iron collars hidden under scarfs whose bright colours were undimmed by the dirt that caked them everywhere else. Child-sized and vulnerable by the drays, they crooned into the dogs' ears. The dogs shut their eyes and lightly licked at the Tyn. The Tyn moved around the whole team, checking their feet and harnesses.

Demion waved at them. "Fine dogs, aren't they?" he said cheerfully.

The Tyn watched him with diamond eyes. One spoke. "Very fine they are, master, yes, very good. Very good. But..."

Another Tyn shushed him. They shared hard looks.

Demion sighed. "They are always doing that. They have their ways. Katriona, no! Leave them..."

Katriona shook off his hand and approached the Tyn. They came no higher than her chest. They appeared sexless, near identical, with long noses and shocks of grey, coarse hair. One, from its skirt and headscarf, appeared to be female.

"No, please. What would you tell us?"

The female Tyn curtseyed. The one holding the dog's head looked to the floor, evidently nervous. "Begging your pardon, goodlady," she said; her voice was surprisingly deep. "We don't mean to tell you your business."

"Why?"

"Tall kado don't like it much when we're telling them their business," said the one holding the lead dog. At close quarters, his relative youth to the others was apparent. His face was less wrinkled, there remained black in his hair. His utterance earned him a kick from the other male. All wore hobnailed clogs, so it must have hurt, but the younger male made no sound.

"We don't mean to be forward," said the older one hurriedly.

"I do not care if you are. What would you tell me?"

The Tyn looked at each other. The young one spoke hesitantly. "Begging your pardon, goodlady, but the left wheel dog has a problem with his leg."

"Lokon, did you know this?"

The lead dog shook his head. He had a little Sorskian blood in him, but though he understood human words well enough he could not talk.

"Well then," said Katriona. "What is your name?"

"Tyn Jumael," said the younger Tyn.

"You are the groom?"

"Stableboy, goodlady."

"Perhaps you could see to it for me then?" She fished in her clutch bag for a purse, and pulled out a copper bit. "For your trouble."

The Tyn looked at it, and then at her.

"Take it, please."

"Thanking you, goodlady," said the Tyn. He practically snatched it from her. She smiled. "I will see to it for you." The female Tyn scowled distrustfully, and went to oversee the uncoupling of the dog team from the carriage.

"What was all that about?" asked Demion as she rejoined him.

"There is a problem with one of the dogs."

He nodded. "Ah. They have a way with animals, as with many other things."

"There are many Tyn at the Morthrocksey mill?" Katriona watched them in fascination.

"A hundred or so. You like our little workers?" said Demion approvingly. "They labour hard and are honest, leaving aside their abilities, which are formidable."

Katriona and Demion stopped to allow a two-storey goods wagon to rumble past. Fourteen huge dogs strained in their harnesses. They were unmatched, mongrels, picked for size and strength.

"Why do they work here?" she asked. "In the stories they are frolicking in the woods."

"The wrong kind of Tyn," said Demion. "These are not of that sort."

"That does not answer my question, husband."

"Oh, you know, they have nowhere else to go, I suppose."

"Have you ever asked them?"

Demion looked uncomfortable. "They are a secretive people. They are bound to the place. They've lived here for, well, forever, I suppose."

He led her over a bridge, and to a side door of the building. There a man in a formal suit waited, much thinner and a little younger than Demion, but the family resemblance was noticeable. He was accompanied by a female Tyn, her sex apparent only by her garb, although in her case her clothes were vibrant in the extreme, She wore layered skirts, three scarves, and a large, lopsided hat atop a headscarf that hid her wild hair, a style currently favoured by lower-class women. Her arms were hung from wrist to elbow with copper bracelets, many with numerous charms depending from them. Three mismatched necklaces sat on top of her scarves. The clothes were all heavily patterned, and to human eyes the colours and designs clashed unpleasantly.

They were antitheses of each other this pair, she short and broad, he tall and thin. Drab to colourful. Male to female. Human to Tyn. She was solid, he wan, his hair lank under his foundry-master's hat. Both dipped their heads in deference to Demion as he approached them, but the man did so with a hangdog expression, a weary expectance of hard work that would not end. The Tyn projected pride and curiosity.

"This is my cousin, Holdean Morthrock," said Demion. "He er, well, he runs things here on a day-to-day basis."

"Goodlady," said Holdean in a voice barely over a murmur. He took Katriona's hand in fingers as limps as sprats and made a mime of a kiss over them.

"And this," said Demion, looking down and smiling, "is Tyn Lydar, queen of the Morthrocksey Tyn."

Tyn Lydar performed an uncomfortable looking curtsey with such solemnity that Katriona smiled.

"Please to meet you, Goodlady Tyn."

"I am just Tyn, goodlady, to the likes of you," said the Tyn.

"No no," insisted Katriona. "You are a queen, and I am not. It is you that should be goodlady, and I goodwife." Katriona performed her own curtsey.

Tyn Lydar smiled uncertainly. "If you say so, madam."

"Well then!" said Demion. "My wife would see the mill, let us show it to her."

"Very good, Master Morthrock," said Holdean. "If you would like to come this way?"

The door, a nondescript twelve-panelled affair, one found on buildings throughout Karsa, swung wide at Holdean's touch.

Noise landed a blow upon the ears, followed shortly by a second hit to the nose from the smell. Not as unpleasant as that outside, but just as strong, thick and greasy. Katriona stepped into a world she had so far only read about. Her father had refused to allow her into his own works.

A vast room awaited her, lit by light slanting in from tall windows. The ceiling was high. A furiously spinning axle ran along the ceiling below thick wooden beams, disappearing through a hole in the far wall. Every ten feet a leather band ran out from the axle to a flywheel. These were attached to further wheels by another axle. More, smaller bands ran from these drive wheels over individual workdesks. Levers by the desks allowed the workers to engage or disengage their power band, so activating the machines they worked at. There were a great many machines, of three common designs. Tyn and humans stood at them, working metal.

"The lathe room, madam." Holdean spoke straight into her ear, and his breath tickled it in a manner that she found disagreeable.

"We make all kinds of things in here," boomed Demion. "But they're all parts for the engines."

"These are assembled in another building?" said Katriona.

"Yes," said Holdean. "We have everything to produce glimmer engines. Metal comes from the smelters at the end of the site. Ore is refined into ingots, that are then cast into whatever shape we require at the foundry, my chief area of responsibility." He said this as if it were a death sentence, and not the path to respectability.

"Do you not find the enterprise at the mercy of ore prices?"

Holdean looked at her curiously. "No. Indeed, that was precisely what Uncle Demiaron wished to avoid. Ore is available from many sources, refined metal from fewer."

"Each tier of processing narrows the pool of suppliers," shouted Katriona over the racket. "By taking the process back to the providers of raw materials you should have a wider choice of supply, and therefore more command of the price."

Holdean and Demion shared a glance. Demion shrugged.

"That is the theory," Katriona went on, "but does it in effect work? I have read, as a matter of fact, that it is a fallacy."

She walked on ahead, not truly desiring an reply.

Katriona headed down a row of workers, looking over their shoulders. Exposed machinery clattered and whirred everywhere. Showers of metal sparks fountained from cutting machines. Young boys stood to hand behind these workers, pails of water in their hands. There were more children crawling about in the guts of the machines. They crabbed their ways around pistons and shafts that could rip the flesh from their limbs as if they were hunting frogs in the woods, pulling out sharp curls of swarf and putting them into buckets. All of them had cuts on their legs and arms.

"You have a lot of children here," said Katriona.

"Many," said Tyn Lydar. Nothing could be read from her voice.

"They are given schooling four days of the week until they are seven. They only work two days, and have one day free every threeweek."

"Surely everyone has the Freeday free, weekly?"

Holdean pursed his lips regretfully. "Oh no, goodlady, that is not so, but we are progressive here."

"He means," said Tyn Lydar, leaning in close to her, "that they are as progressive as they need to be."

Demion laughed uneasily. "You see! It is as I said, the workers may indicate with their feet as to their preference of employer. It is not like the old days."

"Do you have any difficulty with labour associations?" asked Katriona.

"It is precisely why we provide so much care to our workforce!" spluttered Demion. "To avoid that sort of thing."

"But the associations have been agitating a great deal in the last three months, have they not?" Katriona was looking around the factory carefully.

"What kind of a woman have you married, cousin? Is she a yellow band?"

"She is a Kressind," said Morthrock. Katriona glanced round at the pride in his voice.

"There are some," conceded Holden. "But not as much as some of our competitors have suffered. Indeed, our enlightened policies to both Tyn and human worker are being blamed in some quarters for the recent disturbances."

"You have suffered none here. I have not read of any in the papers."

Holdean drew himself up. "We keep an eye out for agitators, we'll have none of that here."

"You are very interested in it all," said Demion. "You are putting me to shame." He tried to sound jocular, but it came across as forced.

"My father taught me to keep careful account of my investments," Katriona said.

"My factory is your investment?"

"Marriage to you in my investment. It is to our mutual benefit that you succeed." She watched over the humans and Tyn working at the benches. "What kind of shift pattern do you employ?"

"I am sorry?" said Holden.

"The shift patterns," she repeated. "What kind? I did read in last month's *Engineering Digest* that a greater efficiency can be achieved through staggered shift patterns." The two men stared at her. "I read it, that is all. I am quite sure I understood it," she said. "I am the daughter of Gelbion Kressind, he has a long interest in modern manufactory. My brother is Trassan Kressind, who they already suggest may succeed Arkadian Vand as the world's foremost engineer. Why should I be any different? This," she said, looking again around the workshop, "is in my blood."

"I am surprised that a woman would be so interested in all this clatter," said Holdean. The look on his face was annoying her. He was looking at her as if she were a pet who had performed some unexpected and wholly delightful trick.

She gave him a stare that made him step back. "It is a great surprise to me, cousin, that a man would not," she said. "Your Tyn here are ruled by a woman, why do you find it so surprising that I, a woman also, would take an interest in the male's world? And why, for that matter, is manufacturing and industry regarded as the sole province of men?"

Tyn Lydar chortled.

"Now, surely you have seen enough? Perhaps you agree that a mill is no place for a goodlady of your refinement?" ventured Demion.

"Five generations ago, my family was sailing cargoes of pickled fish on a single floatstone barge across to Lesser Macer and back. Any refinement I may have has been beaten into my soul by industry."

"I see," said Demion. He blinked in that way he had when wrongfooted. It annoyed both himself and Katriona.

"How many individual workshops are there in operation here, Master Holdean?" she asked.

"Over forty, cousin."

"Not more? What of the others? There is redundant capacity at Morthrocksey?"

"There have been some difficulties. Competition," he said. "We have had to let some become idle."

"How many buildings are currently out of commission?"

Holdean looked uncomfortable. Demion coughed and flexed his spine. He looked at the roof.

"Mills three through seven, madam."

Katriona drew in a slow breath. "What is your total number of workshops, assuming a workbench density such as I see here?"

"One hundred."

"Very well then. Still forty then, including glimmer blend and foundry, smelters and furnaces?"

"About that, yes."

"You see, my dear, too much to see," said Demion, somewhat desperately.

"On the contrary, husband. I wish to see it all. Come along then," she said when none moved. "We better be quick about it if we want to be back in time for dinner."

Tyn Lydar gave a long, gravelly purr that turned into a chuckle. "Of course, goodlady, of course." She fixed Katriona with a knowing eye. Katriona coloured, sure that the creature could read all her plans as if they were plainly written upon her face.

The Tyn smiled and slipped a hand into hers. It engulfed her own fingers and palm entirely. Warm, more leathery than a human hand and covered in calluses. Tyn Lydar patted her fingers with the other hand. Perhaps she could read her mind. Perhaps she did see what Katriona intended, for the abilities of the

Tyn were varied. Then Tyn Lydar looked at her in a way that clearly conveyed a sentiment that made her heart skip.

Ally.

CHAPTER SIXTEEN
At the Gates of the World

GRAVO WAS DIRTIER, poorer, and set lower in the local topography than Mohacs, as if the landscape were commenting on their relative status. The south-eastern lip of the canyon was, owing to some quirk of geology, some hundred feet lower than the north-western.

The station had grown since Tuvacs and Lavina had fled the city. There were many more platforms, and a great number of engines. There were hundreds of people there, dozens of trains by platforms of wood and heaped earth. Pleasantly carved though the woodwork on the platform's seats and facings were, the structures were open to the elements. There were no grand buildings. Gravo's station evinced a marked contrast to that of its sister.

Dawn was not far broken, the light still had the brassy cleanliness of very early morning, and yet already the smokestacks of the glimmer refineries circling Gravo's north belched out black smoke speckled with glowing motes of blue. Tuvacs drew satisfaction to see the factory's exhaust drifting out over the richer half of the twin city.

"These are new," he said to Boskovin. He dared conversation with his leader. Most other men who had power over Tuvacs in the past, Travnic excepted, would have struck him down for the impertinence, but Boskovin was not of that ilk. Karsans were classbound, but there was a species of easy humour that greased interactions between rich and poor. Perhaps that was why Boskovin did not rebuke him. Tuvacs was forming the impression that Boskovin was simply a decent man.

"When was it again you left this place?"

"Three years, master."

"Yes, yes, mostly new. Boom time here in Gravo. The Mohaca try to muscle in on the refinery of the glimmer here in the east. The Maceriyans aren't happy about it, but what can they do? 'One Hundred as one, equal in all,'" he quoted from the Treaty of the One Hundred. "Gods know most get around all that, but the Mohaca are still powerful, and they're putting a lot into this line. Before this, there was only the west-east mainline from Perus to the Gates, via Kasub in Khushasia, but this poses serious competition. I've heard it said that Gravo could outstrip Maceriya's production of refined glimmer within five years or so."

"We could have gone through Maceriya?" said Tuvacs.

Boskovin nodded. "That's right. You did not come that way yourself?"

Tuvacs looked down. "I do not know, master. I was young, the journey was long."

"It is much quicker, not such a detour to the south."

"Why not then?"

"Tolls, boy. The Maceriyans slap a big fat tax on anyone heading out to the Black Sands. Damn fools are too short-sighted to see that that's playing right into the Princes of Mohaca's hands, they're driving the trade south-east. In fact, if Maceriya wasn't so central it'd be happening quicker. Still, there's a lot of trade down this way, and if the Khushasians can get the Croshashians to agree, then they'll continue the track up as far as Ocerzerkiya. If they can get it across the Red Expanse, we're talking real foreign trade then." He spat. "Actually, I'm sure the Maceriyans can see what a balls up they're making of it, but the Rail Guild's overly powerful in Maceriya. They won't give up such a large part of their income easily, no matter who puts pressure on them. But they are fools. They can't see the bank for the penny in front of them. It is very complicated."

"I understand, master."

Boskovin smiled broadly at him again and ruffled his hair. Tuvacs repressed his flinch. He was too old for that. He was nearly a man. Men did not ruffle other men's hair.

"You are a bright boy. Still, best not think too much on it. That sort of thing can drive you mad. Best keep our eyes and minds on our own business."

"There was a time when one of the gleaner gangs would not join with us to work, even though we would have made money."

"This is similar." Boskovin was pleased with the comparison. "Self-interest and suspicion, you see, often trump the greater good. That's why I'm off to the Gates. Make some money, but that's just the start. I'll show them how it's done. Now, let's see if you can figure this out, bright boy. Why tools? Why don't I just go and get a stake in a mine train, start importing glimmer sands myself?"

Tuvacs thought a moment. "Because you will be one among many, will have great distance and many strong men to contend with. Offer equipment, you can remain in one place. Those who work need tools to work with."

"Exactly so! My, you are a rare find!" He threw a companionable arm around Tuvacs' shoulder and hugged him close for a second. "Now, enough education for one day, let's get our dogs on this damn train."

Tuvacs translated as Boskovin dickered with marshalling yard men and train guards over fees. They chartered three box cars for the dogs, goods and their gear. Boskovin put one of his men on each; the luckless and ever complaining Julion moaned about having to watch the dogs again; Gordan doubled up with Marko to watch the goods. Boskovin smiled wickedly at Tuvacs as Julion grumbled his way into the dog car.

"He complains so much, I enjoy aggravating him," said Boskovin. Tuvacs found himself grinning back.

They made for the passenger cars. People were already boarding, two hours ahead of departure. Those with fourth class tickets clambered onto the roof and staked out the best spots.

"Don't worry lad," said Boskovin when he saw Tuvacs looking. "We get to go inside."

Tuvacs climbed up the boarding steps with a last nervous look over the platforms back at Gravo and shining Mohacs on the cliffs beyond. He had come back without incident. When he had arrived the day before, he had half expected Markovitzski or Kostarno to be there on the platform of Mohacs station waiting for him. Of course they were not. What did he matter to them? He had left Mohacs-Gravo behind before, and was leaving it again. He touched his hand to the folded promissory letter in his pocket. Boskovin was a good man. His sister was safe. He felt nothing for Gravo. Coming back proved to him that he had left Gravo behind.

REL'S HEAD HAD more or less stopped throbbing by the time the train departed Gravo. The carriage he was in was supposedly first class, but was as mean as any he'd ever ridden; no compartments, every inch packed with people. Those here had at least the semblance of respectability, as Guis would doubtless have put it. Guis was a fucking snob, but Rel found himself in agreement with his absent brother; this was no place for goodfolk. Narrow, uncomfortable seats upholstered with threadbare velvet faced each other and were jammed too close together. There were blinds on the windows which could be closed; for that his head would be forever grateful. And it was at least clean. He groaned and leaned his head on the cool glass. Getting through the horrendous press at Gravo was almost more than his hangover could take.

After an interminable wait, the train departed. He settled into the rhythm, trying to ignore the bodies jammed around him and find an equilibrium between being soothed and nauseated by the carriage's movements. He had little recollection of the night before. Zhinsky had a seemingly endless supply of fiery liquor that he supplemented their drinks with. They had been to a show, something with a lot of singing that had gone on too long, and bare-breasted women. Something erotic involving a snake. Then at least four different drinking establishments. There had been a... a restaurant? He remembered food so spicy it made his mouth burn. Zhinsky had laughed at him because of that, but then he had quickly realised fucking Zhinsky laughed at him for fucking everything. There had been women too, paid for in a brothel whose dirtiness made him shudder in retrospect. Early morning, predawn, and they were howling like wolves into the great chasm of the Olb dividing the cities and pissing daringly from the edge. An overall picture of the evening then, if lacking the details.

Did he have a good time? Probably. He hoped so, because he was paying the full price.

Rel groaned. He let the train rock, let it rock. The wheels clack-clacked over the rail joins. *Clack-clack*. The pain in his head receded. He was left with a tight feeling in his eyes and a rolling gut, bitter saliva in his mouth. He cleared his mind, let it fill with the profundities that foreshadow sleep but flee from wakefulness unremembered.

At least Zhinsky wasn't there.

He did not dream.

"Little merchant's boy!" boomed a voice. Rel jerked awake. His mouth was sticky and disgusting. He couldn't remember where he was for a moment; the rocking of the train he took for an internal dysfunction brought on by drink. But that was responsible only for his head, now feeling as vast and inhospitable as a desert.

"Let me sleep," he groaned.

"You sleep all day! We two hundred miles from Mohacs-Gravo already. You sleep it all away, farting and mumbling in your sleep! You should apologise to these good people." Zhinsky grinned around the carriage. "I sorry for the little merchant! He had a big night."

"Leave me be, will you?"

"Oh! Oh! The little merchant's boy shows his teeth."

"I'll show you a damn sight more than teeth if you don't lay off."

"You think you can use this?" He kicked Rel's sabre, then sat down next to Rel. He leaned in close. His breath smelled of the spicy food they ate last night. "Never make threats to a Khushashian sauralier, my friend, if you do not intend to carry them through." The sauralier moved his hand under his coat. Hard metal dug into Rel's side.

"Is that a knife, Zhinsky?" said Rel.

Zhinsky laughed. "Oh, a good jest. A good jest! I warn you, not terrify! You in foreign lands now, little merchant. I your guide, you learn culture or you be in big trouble." He shook his head, still laughing, his beaded moustache rattling. "I give you this!" He held out his little flask, made of tin chased with geometric hunting figures. Rel recognised it from the night before. "Cure for poison is more poison."

"That's nonsense," grunted Rel.

"Yes, nonsense," said Zhinsky with an encouraging nod. "Drink, it make you feel better anyway."

Rel took the flask. "Very well."

He unscrewed the cap and slugged back a measure. He gasped, it was even rougher than he remembered.

"You feel better no?"

"Not really. Excuse me." Rel lurched to his feet, slaloming toward the door at the end of the carriage as it swayed. He yanked it open, sending a blast of steam down the carriage. There was a narrow balcony at the end of the carriage. He rushed to the railing along its edge and was noisily sick over the side.

"Gah," groaned Rel. He wiped his mouth with the back of his shaking hand.

Rel stood up straight. Wherever they were, it was colder than in Mohacs-Gravo, and drier and sharper than the air in the islands of Karsa. The train was moving slowly, pulling itself up a steep incline. Rel leaned out and looked forward. The hill seemed to go on and on, so long that his mind tricked him into seeing it flat.

The door banged. "We go up! Up!" said Zhinsky.

"Right. Thanks for that."

"Do not complain little merchant boy. You feel better, no?"

"Well, well. Actually..." Rel took a deep and shaky breath. "I do."

"Good! Good! Have another drink. You feel better still."

Rel gestured to his mouth. "I, you know, the..." He made a little vomiting gesture.

"Ach! It do not matter. Drink!" He thrust his flask at Rel. "Properly now!" admonished Zhinsky as Rel raised it delicately.

Rel took a big pull. He flapped his hand, gulping when it threatened to return, but the liquor stayed down.

"You feel even better now, yes?"

"Yes. Thank you, goodman Zhinsky." Rel held up his hands to ward off the flask, proffered a third time.

"Suit yourself." Zhinsky glugged back four times as much as Rel had and let out a pleased sigh.

"We travel north now for more than two thousand miles," explained Zhinsky. "These great plains of Mohaca, many battles here once between Khushash and old Imperium of Mohacs. But they never conquer us!" he said proudly. "When we cross River Mohak, then we are in my country." He gave a satisfied nod that encouraged agreement. "There is no better place in all the world!"

Rel smiled weakly. They all said that, foreigners. Conceited bastards. He smiled weakly.

"It looks like rich land," said Rel. "Where are the farms? Is it because of the wars?"

"It look rich, all this grass, but there many droughts, hard winters here. Few rivers for bringing water. River Mohak and River Olb both dig deep into ground. Their little feeders, their..." He waved his hand around.

"Tributaries?"

"Ah! Tributaries? Tributaries!" Zhinsky spoke the word with delight. "You teach me better Karsarin, I take special care of you. That my deal. Good?"

Rel supposed it was, he made a noncommittal gesture.

"Difficult life here, bad for farming," Zhinsky went on. "Many herders we have, and some who hunt the last wild raukor, but they few now, and most Kuzaki you will see drive their cattle and not hunt no more. They are kin to my people, proud and great warriors, easy to upset, but good hearts, big hearts."

The slope levelled off into a vast prairie, and the train picked up speed. The horizon was foreshortened by a dark green, uneven line, clouds stacked high over it.

"The Appin mountains," Rel said, quite keen now not to be seen as a total fool.

"That is so. We go toward them, they come toward us. Northeast. We spend much of the journey riding in the mountains' shadow. Tonight we cross the high reach of the Mohak. Tomorrow we pass the Sentinel, the mountains' watchman, then it a few hours on train to the range."

Rel spent the night in a fuzzy stupor more than real sleep. He woke in the early hours ravenously hungry. Zhinsky had packed food in his day sack, and he went outside to eat, picking his way over the sprawling legs of sleeping passengers. He sat with his legs dangling through the railings in the freezing, grey predawn. The air had a sharp edge that promised winter.

He picked at the hard brown bread, so different to the bread at home, but bread still. He stared at the Appin range as he ate. They had grown to an uneven wall, capped by white where the snow never melted. The roof of the world. There were no mountains in Karsa like that.

The Sentinel caught him by surprise, appearing from his left from nowhere. Some fold in the landscape smoothed out, revealing the mountain. Little more than a mound at first, as they approached he began to get a true impression of its scale. Rising as straight as a pillar from the plateau for four and a half thousand feet, no foothills to soften the contrast. Wizened trees clung to cracks in its wrinkled cliffs. Two thousand feet up slumped shoulders allowed thicker forest, so isolate as to never have been trodden by man. He wondered if Wild Tyn dwelled there. It was the sort of place they should. Over the russets of the autumn trees and deep greens of conifers, striated grey cliffs resumed, stretching up endlessly to the sky where the early sun bathed its eastern flank with orange light. The western side was black as night, cloaked in mystery. That something so massive could be there amid all this flatness was astounding. The train went into the mountain's shadow. The temperature dropped. The grass was white with frost. Rel looked up with something akin to awe. His every sense was alive. He took a bite of his bread and chewed slowly, relished this breakfast at the edge of the world.

He was beginning to enjoy his adventure after all.

SEVEN DAYS LATER. Zhinsky roused Rel at noon. He rubbed at his neck, stiff from sleeping on the hard wooden seats. He started when his eyes focussed.

Zhinsky had changed. His incongruous suit was gone, replaced with a pair of baggy wool pantaloons ballooning over a pair of tight riding boots. They were clean but much patched and weatherstained. His shirt, by contrast, was new and its linen dazzling white. Like his trousers, his shirt sleeves swelled out, flaring around his biceps, complicated pleats drawing them in just below his elbows. The lower portion was heavily embroidered in red, green and yellow, especially about his wrists. Three large silver buttons closed the cuffs. Over this he wore a goat fleece jerkin, the hair turned inside. He wore a pointed hat of the same material, the back of it fashioned into a bifurcated tail that covered his unbound hair. Zhinsky had upon him many silver charms and bracelets, and had beaded his hair like his moustache.

"Now you look like a Khushiak sauralier," yawned Rel.

"I did not before?"

"You looked like I don't know what before. It was the suit."

"We are whatever we are no matter what we wear, my friend. I wear this, I sauralier. I put on lady's nightdress, I still sauralier. I take you out of that fussy red coat, and put you in clothes like mine, and you still be spoiled merchant boy. Clothes do not make the man. The man makes the man."

"They say the opposite in my country."

"Your country sounds much blessed with idiots, goodfellow." Zhinsky clapped Rel on the shoulder; Rel sincerely wished he'd stop doing that. The sauralier had hands like rock. Rel scowled and rubbed his arm. Zhinsky grinned the wider.

"Come my friend. We approach. Soon you will see the land of opportunity!" his gold teeth flashed in his smile. "Follow me." He switched languages. "We are speaking Low Maceriyan now." He stopped, and asked with a serious expression, "You do speak Low Maceriyan, yes?"

Rel gritted his teeth. "Low and High and Ancient Hethikan. I am an educated man."

Zhinsky frowned. "So that is what is one looks like. A big waste of money, eh?" He grinned and thumped Rel's shoulder again.

Rel winced. He followed Zhinsky up the carriage with exaggerated, plodding strides, being used to the sway of the train after so long travelling. He was in a foul mood, as he often was on awakening, but a part of him felt the anticipation of relief. He was extremely weary of trains.

They went out onto the little platform at the end of the carriage.

A round-bellied mountain jutting from the others gave a false end to the range. The train pulled around its feet, and the view ahead to the Gates of the World opened up.

The Gates were a cleft in the mountains, so precise it looked made. Not a pass, not a high, hard road winding along snow-choked rock where the mountain would allow it, but an actual gap that came down, down, down, almost level with the plateau. A lake, deep blue and cold, fronted it. The water came some way to the south, full of captured clouds. The larger part of its stretched away to the north for miles.

Commanding the pass was a slender tower on the northernmost side.

"The Glass Fort?" asked Rel. "It does not look like the pictures I have seen."

Zhinsky smiled and hit him on the back.

"No! No my friend, it does not look like the pictures, because that is not it! That is the Rearward Watch. The fortress itself in Farside."

"It is so big. I thought that was the castle."

"If this is impressive to you, the Glass Fort will steal your breath, my friend. Here, drink this so you are prepared for the shock." He passed Rel his flask. Rel absently shook his head.

Constructed in ages past by inhuman beings, in this era the Gates of the World was affronted by the meaner efforts of men that surrounded its opening. The mountainsides had been stripped bare of trees for miles in either direction. Log flumes ran from ruined forests of pale stumps. Raw landslips wounded the slopes. A tented shanty of considerable size infested the lake shore. Small boats disturbed the crystal waters. There was a rich scent on the air, the unmistakable reek of unplanned human habitation. Doubtless it would be unbearable in the streets. Northwards there was a stock yard. Hoppers bridged the rails, tall warehouses next to them. Over everything was a haze of wood smoke, coal smoke and glimmer discharge. After several days travelling along the untouched splendour of the mountains, the despoliations of industry were marked and ugly.

The train passed onto the lake's littoral on tracks crammed between the silent cliffs and the dark water. In places the water went right up to the rock, here wooden piles bridged the gap, carrying the tracks. The water lost its reflected blue and white and became black and sinister. As they approached Gate Town, Rel saw an increasing amount of trash in the water—offal, broken barrels, shattered planks. On one beach of grey sand, two men fished a bloated body from the lake with boat hooks.

"I am sure you know how to use your sword, little merchant boy," said Zhinsky. "Keep it close to you. Gate Town is a squalid place."

"My father is not a merchant," said Rel, but Zhinsky made no acknowledgement he had heard.

Human noise joined human activity. The clinking of hammers on rock in the quarry, shouts, the whistles of glimmer engines, the sounds of a dozen small industries, music, the howls of dogs, the buzzing whine of sawmills. An explosion rumbled out, a slow billow of rock dust from a mountainside revealed its origin.

The lake shore widened. Wooden buildings appeared in increasing density. They passed a slaughterhouse, the screams of animals outmatched in awfulness by the stench. A swirling cloud of flies, scavenging true birds and dracon-birds lifted from open barrels of viscera as the train rattled by. A slick of thick blood ran under the tracks to turn the lake red.

Gate Town's passenger terminal was rough and ready, a single platform of unfinished planks bleaching in the weak mountain sun. A station building was under construction, but as yet was nothing but three courses of brick and a framework of scaffolding. The platform's lower boards disappeared into the churned mud of Gate Town's main street. The settlement had the air of impermanence. Half the buildings were tents or part tent; wooden bases with canvas sides and roof. The timber of the more solid structures was pale and new. Only the glimmer warehouses in the goods yard were of stone. Gate Town had been built quickly. It looked like it could disappear just as fast. The people were dirty. Half swaggered, half skulked despairingly. A lot were drunk. Some wore fine clothes, but they were crusted with the filth of squalid living. Rel saw the national dresses of fifty lands, and the tattered finery of last year's city fashions.

"This a desperate place, it attracts desperate people," said Zhinsky. "There is fortune here, and death. Only desperate people would want to mine the sands. We get off here. The train goes on to the yard, there your luggage will be. I will send for it. We will go directly to the fortress. It is not wise to stay here." Zhinsky's usual bluff manner was absent, his accent less pronounced. He looked around him attentively.

Zhinsky shouted his way through the alighting passengers in a rough mix of languages. From the platform edge he whistled loudly, attracting the attention of a dirty man waiting with a two-dog cart. He nodded in recognition and urged his dogs forward. His dogs—mongrel, piebald creatures—were paired in all things; paired in size, paired in looks, paired in filth. They reached the platform.

"Jovankic!" Zhinsky shouted at the man. He tipped his hat. Zhinsky and Jovankic proceeded to exchange words in a language Rel did not recognise. There came one of those awkward moments all who are struck dumb by unfamiliarity with a foreign tongue must endure; Zhinsky clapped Rel on the back and gestured at him, spouting a rapid stream of nonsense that could have been complimentary, insulting, or neither. Rel smiled and bowed his head. There was little else he could do.

Jovankic indicated they should board. Zhinsky stepped lightly right off the platform into the cart. Rel followed, the little carriage rocked with their weight.

"Hyah!" shouted Jovankic. This at least Rel understood. The dogs strained forward, struggling to drag the little cart free of the grasp of the mud. Jovankic yelled angrily at a sixteen-dog wagon that sped past, spattering them all with dirt. A glimmer walker clanked past, spider legs fastidiously pecking at the road.

"Twenty years ago," said Zhinsky, "there nothing here at all. Only garrison and customs officials. Then the new processing, glimmer from the black sands, boom time! This place very good if you want get rich quick, very easy to die quick too. No law here, only us in the fortress. But I am soldier, not policeman. What to do? This frontier my friend. Money or death? The gods decide."

Jovankic piloted them skilfully through the chaotic streets. The town was ostensibly laid out on a grid pattern, but the system had been flagrantly abused. Tents were pitched in what should have been thoroughfares. Buildings with greedy footprints reduced roads to alleys.

"It's very muddy!" shouted Rel.

"Rains come here at autumn and they are early this year. It stay like this till spring," said Zhinsky, then brightened. "In four, five weeks' time it freeze solid, so merchant boy not get so dirty, eh?" Another comradely punch. Rel gritted his teeth.

They passed a rowdy tavern. Lights blazed inside even though it was slightly past noon. Past this last wooden building, Gate Town gave out as quickly as it began. A few rows of small tents, then bare rock.

So near to noon the shadow of the mountains was off most of the town, but it waited, biding its time by the mountains' roots. They crossed the boundary between light and dark. Out of the sun, autumn bit. The noises of Gate Town lessened in volume, scared away by the eternal silences of stone.

Jovankic's dogs found the old road and turned sharp right onto it, running dead straight at the Gates of the World. The paving was pitted and worn yet where whole, remarkable. Morfaan workmanship, old as time. A rail line joined the road, covering a third of the surface with ballast, but there was still space for two carts to pass abreast. Looking back, Rel saw that it went down a slight slope and ploughed on right through Gate Town towards the goods yard, the railway arcing off in a graceful, brown iron curve to link with the track there. The old road was left to bottom out in the lagoon of slurry that was the town's main crossroads. He thought he could see the original outline continue on through the confusion of tents and shacks until it plunged directly into the lake.

"Road was on causeway, they say, and lake smaller once," said Zhinsky. "The arche—archao—the digging man! Jakkar, he is called. You meet him sometime. He say much about this place but pah! What does it matter? Morfaan long dead."

The sky appeared starkly through the gap, a dazzling blue slot framed by perfect Morfaan stonecraft.

"The other side," said Zhinsky, pointing. "Three miles away. The walls are unmatched, completely straight. Nothing so perfect in this world anymore."

The dogs picked up speed as they passed into the gap.

"The railway goes right to the black sands?"

"Yes," said Zhinsky. They spoke quietly. The gap was as quiet as a sepulchre after the roar of Gate Town. "Across Farside. It only five miles wide here, the Black Sands close. Another town there, Railhead. Farside much wider further north and south, one hundred miles wide in places, but here the desert creeps close to mountains."

They passed deep trenches cut into the floor and walls of the canyon, those in the floor bridged over with timber that boomed as they sped over it. "These are the famous Gates of the World, the actual gates." Zhinsky said. "The gates are gone, and the slots are too deep to fill in."

The road passed out of the gap, emerging onto a narrow, fenceless plain of closely cropped grass of green, studded with golden tussocks. The mountains north and south extended arms far out toward the east, revealing the position of the Gates as occupying a natural indentation in the range. To the north the monolithic wall of the Appins fragmented into hundreds of individual, densely packed conical mountains. Away to the east the steppe gave way to a black desert. There was no mingling of the two landscapes. The grass ended, the sand began, neighbours for millennia but strangers to one another still. Evenly spaced obelisks marked their boundary, one every three quarters of a mile.

"The Sentinels, also Morfaan. They keep out the badness in the sands," said Zhinsky. "Is your job, little merchant boy, to patrol them."

A haze clogged the desert horizon, robbing Rel of a sense of perspective. There was no telling how far he could see, nor how tall the mountains were. The railway and the road continued side by side over the grass. The road stopped by a small town, Railhead, he guessed, equally new and impermanent as Gate Town. The road vanished, but the rails plunged onto the sand, the glinting of their metal the only feature for miles. In the distance where the desert met the sky he thought he could see a structure of some sort, but it was at the limits of his vision and disrupted by the haze in the air.

Zhinsky took a deep breath with evident pleasure. The air was clear and pure.

"Is this where you are from?"

"Farside? No. I come from Great Khushashia, not this province," said Zhinsky, his eyes still closed. "But I spend much time here. It is my home now."

"Zhinsky, tell me. Where is the fort?"

Zhinsky's eyes snapped open. He looked at him in astonishment. He said something to Jovankic, and the dogs broke into a trot, then a gallop, barking for the pleasure of the run. They went out from the mountain for half a mile or so, where the driver brought his animals around in a wide loop, sending the cart into a lean. They carried on, riding back towards the mountains.

The rock containing the gap extended out from the mountainsides in a wholly unnatural way, square as a block of ashlar, so that the slot resembled a gate in a castle wall. Zhinsky pointed upward.

"There," Zhinsky said. "There are the forts of the Gates of the World, the last great fortress of the Morfaan people, and mightiest castle of this or any age." He spoke with respect, his accent, once again, suspiciously less thick.

Either side of the gap atop the squared-off mountain were twin fortresses. The base of their walls blended indistinguishably into the cliff face as if grown from it. Of the southerly one, ruins were all that remained. The walls were reduced to half their original height and riven through, the towers tumbled into heaps of bubbled slag. Where the finish to the seamless stone remained, it was pitted and dull. The tangled wreckage of the Morfaan's imperishable metal fouled the cliff top about it, as shiny as if newly placed, although it was not. Far from it. The magister-archaeologists could not agree when it fell, only that it was many thousand years ago. The fort on the other side was yet whole. A grand edifice of dark towers and soaring ramparts. The walls quickly shed the dullness of the rock as they climbed, taking on the glassy sheen that gave the fort its name. There were seven bastions on the wall towards the desert, each faced with a giant statue; slender, alien beings that looked out onto narrow steppe of Farside and over it to the Black Sands. They were the Morfaan, the builders of the Gates, once rulers of the Earth. Identical roads climbed the cliff face to dark entrances in the rock, three switchback turns to each. A lone, two-dog cart climbing toward the intact fort gave scale. It appeared tiny, a model from a flea circus.

"Ah," said Rel.

"Ah indeed, my friend," said Zhinsky. "You give me much amusement." He shook his head. He spoke to Jovankic rapidly, telling him of Rel's question if the laughing was anything to go by.

"Do not worry! Do not feel shame!" Zhinsky grabbed his shoulder, for what must have been the fifteenth time that day. "It is easily done."

Zhinsky shouted some more in his unintelligible tongue. Jovankic cracked his reins and the dogs sped toward the road that led to the Gates of the World.

CHAPTER SEVENTEEN
A Desert of Some Opportunity

ONCE THE MONEYED passengers had disembarked, the train pulled away from the platform toward the goods yard. "Get ready!" shouted Boskovin. "Boy, you're coming with me." Boskovin's men were hauling out cases and duffel bags from the luggage racks over the benches. The few people still in the carriage and not working for Boskovin stayed out of the way. Tuvacs dodged between them as best he could, going to stand by the carriage door with his master.

The train went slowly, stopping again three quarters of a mile down the track in a goods yard lined with stark buildings of grey stone. Here there was no platform at all, only the black spoil from the glimmer mills. Iron pegs were set every three feet in a diamond pattern, strung together with rust-red wire. The doors opened, and people jumped out straight onto the track side. A crowd sprang up from nowhere as the passengers on the roof clambered down, and townsfolk arrived to tout for work. At first it was chaotic, but Tuvacs noted that they all headed for the defined paths back to town. No one, he saw, stepped over the wires.

"Bloody beggars!" shouted Boskovin. "Tell them we don't have any money for them, Tuvacs."

Tuvacs tried, but the gaggle of cripples dogging his master spoke no Mohacin. He tried the little Khushashian he knew, then Low Maceriyan. If they understood, they did not relent.

"Away! Away!" shouted Boskovin. Lem and Marko came up, batons swinging, bashing the poor from their path.

Boskovin surprised Tuvacs, digging into a pocket and hurling a handful of coins at the beggars.

"Hit them, curse them, push them away," said Boskovin to Tuvacs. "But never forget that one day that could be you."

A myriad languages came at them. Khushashian in the main, and there were a fair number of Mohaca here too. But there were people from all over the Hundred, and all words were swept up into one, incomprehensible babble.

There were others there, hucksters calling out the names of lodgings, whores smiling yellow-toothed smiles framed by poppy red lips, agents promising work on the railway or in the mines on fair conditions. Boskovin pushed his way through them all, his men following. They came to the box cars where their goods and animals were transported. The door to the first rattled open as they approached, and Julion popped his head out.

"How do they fare?" shouted Boskovin. He was an energetic presence, his own excitement and urgency galvanising his men.

"One's sick, boss. I'm going to have to kill it, I reckon."

The faintest frown flickered over Boskovin's forehead. "And Rusanina?"

"She's fine. Won't stop complaining, it's doing my head in."

Relief then, bright in Boskovin's smile. "Let it, Julion, she's worth four of you. Get them out!"

He strode on to the other two cars, Marko and Lem came after, shoving people away. Gordan jumped down from the one carrying their trade goods. A group of customs officials in poorly dyed blue uniforms were moving up the train, consulting with gang chiefs and bossmen at each boxcar. All manner of goods were being unloaded from the train's long freight tail. Boskovin's men worked quickly, stacking their own materials for inspection.

The customs men reached them. One was obviously Mohaci, and Tuvacs addressed him.

"Goodman, please give my master advice as to the process here. It is his first venture into Gate Town."

The Mohaci man stopped and watched Boskovin bellowing orders. "He seems to know what he's doing." His attention fixed on Tuvacs. "You're new to this. Never tell someone like me you do not know what is going on. I could have charged you four times the rate and you'd never know."

"I..." Tuvacs' prepared speech stumbled to a halt.

"Take the lesson to heart, but not the shame. Learn fast here, or die quicker. What has your master got?"

Tuvacs pulled out a manifest.

"This is in Low Maceriyan. What does it say?"

Tuvacs pulled it back, this was not going to plan. "I cannot read."

"Good job I can speak Low Maceriyan, isn't it?" One of the customs man's fellows came to his side. "I'll deal with this, you move on up the train, or we'll be here all fucking day," he said. The second man went on. The customs official shook his head as he read the manifest. "I tell you, I've been doing this for seven years. You get all sorts, on and off the train. Excuse me!" he called, switching to Low Maceriyan. He spoke it with only a slight accent. "Yeah, you, big merchant man. You, goodfellow!"

Boskovin came over.

"Good day," he said.

"Explain this. What's your business? Bit odd bringing all this material here if you ask me. A lot of it we produce here." He went down the list. "Shovels, lanterns. And the dogs. You could have three teams by lunchtime if you wanted." His eyes went to Rusanina. "Although you'd be hard pressed to find the likes of her. Why buy them in Mohacs-Gravo?"

"Bringing the dogs all the way from Karsa was too expensive. Buying the dogs here would have cost a fortune, and they work them hard here. Poor quality. Everything costs a lot here. So, easiest and cheapest to bring the dogs out from Mohash-Gravu." Boskovin mispronounced the name. The official and Tuvacs glanced at each other in amusement. "All my goods are Karsan made. Karsan make, Karsan premium."

"No doubt you'll be selling the same shit as everyone else once you've got yourself a name."

Boskovin inclined his head in way that could have meant anything.

"Fine. It's all in order." The official took up a wooden paddle that dangled by a loop from his belt. He put the papers onto it and rolled a stamp across them. "You got trading papers? A licence?"

"Aye, right here," said Boskovin. He reached inside his coat.

"I don't need to see it. Get it verified at the station in Railhead. They manage trade licences there. Show them your stamped manifest."

"Even if I plan to set up here?"

"Even if you plan to set up here. They have the appropriate machinery to verify the document, and a telesender to check with Kasub and the Mohacs-Gravo rail office if it doesn't check out. Do you have an issue with that sir?"

"Of course not."

The guard flashed crooked teeth in a not altogether friendly smile. "Well that's alright then, isn't it?"

He pushed the manifest back at Boskovin. Boskovin went back to his men, speeding up as he walked as if freed from some peculiar kind of bureaucratic spell. The customs man finished filling out his own records. He handed Tuvacs a wooden chit with a number on it. "Tell your master to keep this. It'll tally with our records. Congratulations, you are now entitled to apply to conduct business in and around the property of the Mohacs-Gravo Kasub Railway. You want to do business further out west, you need to clear it with the Maceriyans, got that?"

Tuvacs looked at the chit. Boskovin would need this to do business. He had been passed a small measure of power.

"What is all this?" asked Tuvacs. He kicked at one of the wires. It thrummed like a harp string.

"Don't do that boy," said the customs man. "Bad idea for us all. Iron lines. Stops random magic. Lot of glimmer in those warehouses, in this sand. We're careful here, but the stuff gets everywhere. Once it accumulates, there's a danger of discharge. Doesn't happen often, not like in the desert. You'll see far bigger webs out there. Got to pin the world down out in the desert."

"What do you mean?"

The stationmaster squinted at him. "When you get out there, don't stray from the webs, not for any reason, not even for a few yards, do you hear? They'll bang on about it when you get to Railhead, but you have to know, they are not spinning you any yarns. You get more than a few steps from the web, you might never find your camp again. Do not venture too far out into the sands. Do you understand me?"

"Yes, goodman."

The customs man looked over at Boskovin. He was directing his men as they assembled the dog wagons, two this time. "And don't trust these outlanders. Just you watch yourself, alright boy?"

"Yes, goodman."

The man winked at him. "Good. I hope you make your fortune. Good luck. Try not to get yourself killed. You seem quite pleasant." He sauntered off.

"Thank you!" called Tuvacs. The official raised his hand over his head without looking back.

Their dog carts assembled and loaded, Boskovin's expedition put five dogs to each and set out from Gate Town. The din of the place dropped away with suddenness, and they were into the great square-sided chasm that was the Gates of the World.

Timeless silence there, whose damp and muffling reign could not be interrupted by the talk of men or huffing of running dogs. A small locomotive filled the gates with a drawn out whistle, end to end and back again.

Iron wheels clattered on iron rails. Men seated on open carts at the rear of it shouted down at Boskovin's crew. Even their noise perturbed the stillness of the place only as much as a smooth pebble tossed into a mountain lake; an insignificant break in the skin, swallowed by the vastness beneath.

The train outpaced them, obscuring the path with glimmer-shot steam. Then it was away, hooting again. The voice of the machine muted by the scale of the cut.

The exhaust cleared. The way through the mountain revealed itself. The dogs burst through into sunlight. Warmth hit Tuvacs and he blinked against the sudden brightness.

Grassland of rich variety stretched away from them north and south. Ahead, lay an endless expanse of the black sands, dark grey and twinkling in the sun.

"Look, my boy, look!" said Boskovin, placing one hand at the small of Tuvacs' back and pointing with the other. "The Black Sands. Here the greater part of the world's supply of glimmer is extracted. It draws the hopeful and the hopeless, the rich and the poor. All with money to spend." He smiled happily. "We arrive at a desert of some opportunity."

Tuvacs had little time to reflect on the fact that this was his new home. They hit Railhead, and the rest of the day was a rushed set of meetings, haggling, arguing and frontier bureaucracy. Tuvacs could not credit that the withered crone propped up in the corner of the railway office at Railhead could manage so much as a card trick, let alone a long distance sending. In the end it did not matter, they had their licence.

Boskovin made right for a vendor of similar implements to those stacked upon their dog carts.

The trader, a grizzled man of Birestinia, was unimpressed with their wares.

"A couple of generations back, you could pole glimmer rocks right out of the desert from the edge of the grass. All that's gone now, we're forced to go deeper and deeper into the desert. The tracks, trains, supply depots. And the damned ironweb. It all costs money. Do you have any idea how much the ironweb alone costs to maintain? Should be spun of gold, wouldn't be any dearer. No my friends, you make your money while you can. The days of the independent prospector are coming to an end."

"This one looks like a vagrant but speaks like a stockbroker," mumbled Julion to Tuvacs.

"That's disrespectful," said Tuvacs.

"I'll start being respectful when I find someone worthy of my respect."

"The world will always need glimmer," said Boskovin.

"Aye, it will. But only those with serious capital behind them can afford to get at it. Getting the glimmer has become a major operation. Sure, you might stumble on a small vein in the desert still, sometimes even in the mountains, and it's a lot safer there. Nobody is disputing that. But there are two issues with that. The amount of glimmer being traded is so big that the price has come down. You make a small claim, it's not the paydirt it once was. And the real reserves are out here in the desert, the big mines. And only business has the resources to get to that. These new men here? They're coming for a pay cheque. There are no more lucky strikes to be had. And I don't know if you seen them, goodman, but there are five forges putting out tools almost as good as these."

"From what you are saying, I am out of luck," said Boskovin. He put on a performance of despondency a child could have seen through, although the merchant seemed blind to it. He moved in, feigning sympathy equally badly.

"Well, I don't know. But then," he tutted, "things are getting worse, not better for the likes of us."

"The same old story!" said Boskovin theatrically.

"Rumour has it the Cullozzi brothers are setting up a foundry; the price will crash. If I were you I'd get rid of them quick."

"There will be some market for my tools?" Boskovin brightened.

"Sure there is. Sell them to me, I'll see what I can do."

Boskovin smiled and wagged his finger. "You nearly had me! You very nearly had me there."

"I don't get your meaning."

"If there is no market left, you would not offer to buy my tools. I am no newcomer to business."

"Just hang on a minute..." said the trader.

"What would you offer me for them?"

"Deal's off."

"Just tell me."

The old man rubbed the back of his neck. "Four copper a piece."

"Well then, if I were fleecing a naive incomer, I would want to at least double my profits. So you are probably selling yours for ten copper?" Boskovin snatched up a shovel.

"Yeah, around that," said the merchant grudgingly. "A little less, a little more. Depends on the day and the trade."

"Well thank you, but no deal. I appreciate the information."

"If you say so."

They left. Outside the shop—little more than a wooden platform with three canvas sides and a shingle roof—Rusanina waited. She got to her feet and trotted at her master's side, her consorts walking meekly by her.

"He's right," said Boskovin quietly to his followers. "He's selling at five less than I was hoping to make. Looks like we've arrived one or two summers too late."

"It's been a waste of time then," said Julion. Tuvacs had already learned a hearty dislike for his long-suffering air.

"What will we do?" said Tuvacs.

"Shame on you there, Julion! Making the boy fear for his employment, when there is nothing to worry about! In business, my boy, one must take notice of the changing ground, see where the flood will strike or new land rise from the water. This is one of these moments." Boskovin put an arm around Tuvacs. "These businesses still need tools. If we are smart, we can strike a better deal. Mass supply, lower item price, that is unfortunate, but much large volume of sale. And it just so happens I have contacts with mills back home. Now what do you think of that?" Boskovin grasped the back of Tuvacs' neck and shook it.

"It sounds very clever, master," said Tuvacs.

"It is! This will not be the first fortune I have won, my boy."

Behind him, Julion muttered. "It won't be the first he lost either."

"Patience now, Julion! There are other ways to turn an honest coin. So, the miners do not require tools with such urgency as they did any longer. A shame, but they always require something else. What is it?"

"Food?" said Tuvacs.

"Indeed! But more than that, my boy, they need entertainment. Specifically, they need *liquor*."

Gate Town had appeared shabby and impermanent. In comparison to Railhead, it was a metropolis to rival Perus. 'Building' was too grand a word for Railhead's collection of shacks, framed tents and lean-tos. The smell of the desert was sharp on the air, a dryness that prickled the inside of the nose. The wind coming of the sands was cold, winter's herald.

"It's fucking freezing here," said Julion.

"I like," said Rusanina. Tuvacs started when she spoke. He was never going to get used to that.

"Yeah? You spend most of your time lying in front of the nearest fire!"

Rusanina growled. Her consort's ears pricked and they stared with yellow eyes at Julion.

"Steady!" Julion said, holding up his hands. Rusanina grumbled deep in her chest, a sound Tuvacs had learned was her version of a laugh.

"What do you expect?" said Boskovin. "This is not the Hethikan riviera!"

"I don't see why we couldn't keep our base in Gate Town," said Julion.

"Because the money is here, Julion. Six years this one has been with me, Tuvacs, and what has he learned! I suspect nothing. You my lad, seem a far brighter spark."

Julion's lips curled.

"Marko! What news?"

Boskovin's headman fell into step with them, Gordan with him. "I think we've got what we need."

"The dogs?"

"They're being fed."

"We mightn't be needing them. See if anyone's buying," said Boskovin.

Marko lips pulled thin. "A change of plan?"

"Since when are plans something to be kept to?"

Marko shrugged. "This way, Mather."

They ducked tent guy ropes and squeezed past tuns overflowing with rubbish.

"When this place is a little more established, I might offer to establish a refuse collection service. A lot of useful material is going to waste here," said Boskovin. "There is always money to be made. Even in shit, there is gold."

They came to the rail line. It split as it entered Railhead, then split and split again into a small goods yard. A single line fought its way free of the sidings to cross from grass to sand. They were only twenty or so yards from the edge of the desert. The iron web, began some ten yards out either side of the track, red oxide against black sand.

They crossed the track. The plume of a train rose skyward far out in the desert.

"How far do you reckon that is?" said Julion.

"I don't know," said Tuvacs.

"I thought all you foreign types were good at such things."

"I grew up in a canyon, that could be the other side of the world for all I know."

"Huh," said Julion. "Maybe it is."

Boskovin, his dogs and Marko had gone a little further ahead, into a fan of sidings.

"There you are," said Marko. He nodded at a boxcar.

"That's it?" said Julion. "That's the best you could do?"

"Julion, I am truly growing tired of your constant moaning," said Boskovin. "A lick of paint, some elbow grease, we'll get this looking grand. Can you not see it? A rolling saloon! You and Gordan can take the dog teams out to the outlying mines, sell off our tools, while I'll have Tuvacs staff it..."

"Why him?" said Julion.

"How many languages do you speak, Julion?"

"Two."

"Yes, and your Low Maceriyan is awful. Whereas Tuvacs here is quite the linguist. Having him on hand will make the clients happy. You don't need to know the local lingo to carry an armful of shovels."

"Bloody foreigners," said Julion.

The others went to inspect the boxcar. Tuvacs wandered away. The black sands enticed him, and he found himself drawn over to them. The line between the steppe and the sand was remarkable. If one looked closely between the blades of grass grains of black and quartz winked back, blown in by the wind. But there really was a line delineating the landscapes, sharp as if cut by shears.

He passed by one of the pylons lining the edge, an ancient edifice of iron pitted with corrosion. A newcomer to town had pitched his tent against it, and a trio of troopers from the fort in gaudy uniforms were shouting at him to take it down. Tuvacs crossed the tracks again to distance himself from their quarrel.

He came to the very edge of the grass. He stood with his toes hanging off the turf. There was a drop of six inches of so, yellow grass and green grass atop a bluff of brown soil giving way to the sand. A single sod grew three feet out, and crumbs of soil patterned the black close to the edge. Past that there was nothing but sand. Within the confines of the ironweb were various pieces of half-buried rubbish. Beyond it the sand was pristine, not a footstep on it.

An urge came over him. He stared at his toes. One step, and he would cross into a world alien to his own.

"Do not step onto the sand." A voice, female, speaking accented Low Maceriyan. Startled, Tuvacs turned. A girl of around his age leaned against the sun-bleached side of a boxcar. An old woman squatted at her feet. Both wore layered robes in varying shades of cream and brown that covered every part of them but their faces. Coins on short lengths of chain fringed her face. The old woman had a similar headdress made of twists of bright thread.

"You are watching me?"

"We are resting," said the girl. "My grandmother tells fortunes to the outsiders in this village."

"You translate?"

She nodded.

"That is also my job," he said.

Tuvacs took a step back from the desert edge, its spell broken. Unaccountable relief swept through him.

"The desert had you. Do not look long at it, and never step on it. Even here it is not safe."

"Are you from here?" he asked. "I don't see anywhere other than this place."

"We are Zashub," she said. "From mountains to the south."

"I can't keep track of all the tribes there are here."

"It is the same for all foreigners, they are stupid. Ignorant."

"I am not as foreign as some."

"You are," she said.

"I am Mohaci, from Gravo. That is not far."

"That is a long way from here."

"My friends are from much further, from the far west, from the islands."

"The lands of the little ones?"

It took Tuvacs a moment to understand. "The Tyn? I suppose."

"We have stories about them, that they do not hide in secret places, but live like men in houses. Is this true?"

"Yes. It is true. We told the same stories in my city. But it is not as the stories say. There are not many, and I never saw one. Not close, anyway."

She looked disappointed. "Did you see the sea?"

"Yes I did."

"You have really seen it?"

"I have," he said. Here was a novelty, there were a few places untouched by the ocean in Ruthnia, even Mohacs-Gravo witnessed its power. But they were no longer in Ruthnia, he thought.

"What is it like?"

He nodded at the desert. "Like that. Only wet. And... angrier."

She smiled. "That is very fine."

The old woman snapped something at the girl, then gestured at Tuvacs.

"Grandmother wants to know, why do you worship the rails?"

Tuvacs was taken aback. "Worship them?"

"Yes. You spend much time laying them and riding about on them. That is worship."

She was so sure of what she said, he wanted to laugh. He swallowed it, fearful of causing offence.

"I don't, really. It's for transport. That's all."

"That is all?" she said. "There is something arrogant about it. It ignores a boundary that everything else on the plain respects. The foreigners do not respect much." She looked at the man arguing with the fort troopers. One repeated himself over and over as the man bawled in his face. The other two soldiers were kicking down his tent, freeing the iron obelisk of canvas and rope.

"Have you been here long?"

She shook her head. The old woman was muttering to herself. Her granddaughter ignored her.

"Why are *you* here?"

"Why are you here?" she asked.

"To make money. Because I have to be."

"That is why we are here also." Something attracted her attention. Tuvacs started as a wet nose was pressed into the back of his neck.

"You," said a gruff canine voice. "Master wants. Too much dawdle."

Rusanina's eyes were level with his own. She stared at him hard. He reached out a hand and gave her an experimental pat. She whiffled, then took his affection and returned it, almost knocking him from his feet as she nuzzled him.

The girl giggled. "That is very fine."

"We go now," said Rusanina. "You work." She circled him and poked at him with her muzzle, forcing him back towards the boxcar.

"Goodbye, Mohaci boy," said the girl.

"My name is Tuvacs!" he called. "What is your name."

"I am Suala the Zashub."

"Perhaps we will see each other again?"

"Perhaps," she replied.

At her feet, her grandmother grumbled and shook her head.

CHAPTER EIGHTEEN
The Iron Ship

THE SITE OF Arkadian Vand's venture occupied one third of the New Docks. Upon taking possession of the site, the first thing he had done was construct a spur line from the railway that ran from the industrial districts. That had taken a lot of money, and a lot of politicking, and a small adjustment to Per Allian's plans. An enormous shed of corrugated iron had followed. In itself, the Vand Shipyard was a wonder, larger than the largest cathedrals to the banished gods. Such things were common in the foundries and mills of the city, of course, but to see its like rising above the centre caused quite a stir. Prince Alfra himself, who had intended the docks to bring commerce to the heart of the capital, but who had also wished to prettify the third ward with water and the graceful rigging of ships, was said to be thrown into something of a personal turmoil.

What was inside, though smaller, was a far greater marvel: the *Prince Alfra*, the world's first ocean-worthy iron ship. Trassan hoped that calling his ship as he might calm his royal highness down.

"They said we were mad to build a ship up here. 'How will they get the stone in?' they said." Arkadian Vand, the self-proclaimed greatest engineer in the world, thrust his hands into his pockets. "The bastards aren't laughing now, are they?" He chuckled, his expression inviting Trassan to join in.

Hammers rang across the dockyard. Box cranes clunked along overhead rails, miniature glimmer engines puffing hard. Chains rattled. The *Prince Alfra* sat waist-deep in an empty stone dock barely big enough to hold it. The shed caught the noise of industry, concentrating it. The racket within was deafening, all-pervasive, and not easily defeated. Trassan and Vand had to shout. Doing so made Trassan's nervousness worse, and he was nervous at his master's visit, despite Vand's evident glee at his progress.

"As you see, master, we have finished the main superstructure and are in the process of applying the hull plating." Trassan pointed at a steam tractor that whistled as it approached the side of the ship. It held a slab of iron in its delicate claws. Men and Tyn shouted, waving the driver on. The iron made a dull boom as it met the ship's ribs. Wooden beams were braced against the top, men set iron poles along the bottom edge to lever it in. With a tremendous hooting, the tractor reversed. The men shouted, and worked their poles free. The plate slipped into its final position.

Seven teams of three riveters ran forward, one of the three in each team carrying an iron bucket full of glowing rivets in gloved hands. Half of their number ran around the side and into the vessel. They set to work immediately, one placing a glowing rivet into the pre-drilled holes around the plate's edges, the other two, one inside the ship and one outside, placed to hammer them flat. They sang as they worked to synchronise their blows. In five minutes, all eighty rivets were in place. Tyn iron whisperers came forward, to ask of the metal if it were sound.

"Do we not have more whisperers?" asked Vand.

"We have nine, but so much iron affects them. I have them working in shifts, otherwise they fall sick."

Vand nodded. "You are still making remarkable progress, Trassan. I am impressed."

Vand looked upward to the high roof. The ship's side rose sixty-five feet over them. "Very fine work, very fine work indeed."

Veridy, Vand's daughter, smiled at Trassan behind her father's back. "Stop it," he mouthed. Her smile widened. Trassan could not help but grin back.

Vand turned around. "Is something amusing?"

"No, master."

"It is a very fine ship, Pappa. I was merely trying to attract Goodfellow Kressind's attention in order to inform him of my sentiment." She coughed and put a hand to the hollow of her neck. "This clamour is quite destroying my voice, and there is a fearful amount of smoke here."

"Yes my dear, of course," shouted Vand. "No place for a woman this, but she insisted on coming. I'm not surprised." He looked back over his shoulder. "My ship is as beautiful as I envisaged."

Trassan's smile became fixed. The ship was primarily of his design. Not that that would stop Vand from taking the lion's share of the credit.

"Perhaps we should retire to my office? It is a little quieter in there, and we can see the whole of the vessel from there," Trassan said, gesturing to the ugly pressed iron box atop a gantry from where he could observe the entire site.

"Lead on, Goodfellow Kressind."

VAND UNROLLED A chart and held it up to the light. He scrutinised it carefully. "Damn eyes aren't getting any better," he said. He peered down his nose.

"Pappa spends far too much time reading in his study," said Veridy.

Vand shot his daughter an admonishing glance. "Please, Veridy. Have you solved the problems of attaching the inner skin?"

"I have," said Trassan. "I have men going inside the hull space; cramped, but they do a good job."

"Good," said Vand, he rolled up the sheet and went to the windows which ran around three sides of the office, allowing the occupant to look to the bow and stern of the ship. "The world's first oceangoing iron ship." He sighed contentedly. "In truth, it's the fourth," he said looking back at Trassan. "But this will be first successful one."

"I am sure it will," said Veridy. "Trassan is very skilful, Pappa."

"Oh, oh, yes, he is, he is! Why else would I choose him as my student. And," he said looking between the two of them, "potential son-in-law. No! Silence, the pair of you. I'm not blind. I might be getting old, but nobody takes Arkadian Vand for a fool." He looked back at the ship. "*Amity* broke its back rolling down the slipway," said Vand, "Sunbright of thirty-nine. The *Penalopy* foundered, her seams split, and she sank."

"Gannever of forty-two."

"Forty-three," corrected Vand. "And lastly the *Grand Ruthenian*. Boiler explosion. No one has dared tried since. But I dare. Arkadian Vand dares."

That they were Trassan's plans he was daring with, and that the *Grand Ruthenian* had been Vand's own vessel went unremarked upon. Triumph glowed from Vand's every pore. One did not interrupt a man such as Arkadian Vand in a mood such as that. Especially, thought Trassan, when one owes him everything one has, and is bedding his daughter besides.

"Right then." Vand rapped his knuckles on the window. "I'm very impressed by all this Trassan. You have my permission to court my daughter." He looked back at him. "Not that you will have time. You will prepare the site for a visit from the worthies of Karsa."

"I see," said Trassan.

"I'm glad you are taking it on the chin. Money for all this doesn't just fall from the air, young man. We're going to need more cash. I'll need to do a once over with your foreman, Hannever, to make sure the bloody thing isn't going to go the way of the other ships, but it's time to announce to the world that the *Prince Alfra* is almost ready. There will be a lot of interested parties, of that I am sure. Military, too. Think of what a navy could achieve with a ship such as this. It need fear nothing on the waves." He looked meaningfully at Trassan. "Or under them."

"We're not really ready."

Vand slapped his palms together. "I'll be the judge of that. You are a capable engineer, Trassan, but you have inherited little of your father's talent for business. Leave that side of things to me." Trassan shrank inside a little. Vand had this effect on him, and many others. "We don't have much choice, do you see my boy? If you could have secured us an early licence, then raising the capital for completion would be so much easier. With Persin openly declaring for the South, we'll have to win them over with the technological wonders here, to prove we can beat him to the prize."

"There is nothing I can say against that."

"Quite so."

"Can we at least make sure that the paddlewheel assemblies are in place?"

"Why?"

"I think it will look the more complete."

"Your estimated time of completion to that phase, Goodfellow Kressind?"

Trassan did a quick mental calculation. "The 33rd of Frozmer, master? I could make it ready in time to be a part of the half-winter celebrations. Surely there is merit in that?"

"Possibly," said Vand. He considered a moment. "Very well. That gives you nigh on twelve weeks, the best part of two months. Seventy-four days. A generous portion of time. We shall see what we can do, but be warned, I will be starting the funding drive for the completion soon, like it or not. You will perform the presentation of the ship; I have little appetite for speaking to crowds. Still, it may do no harm to stoke interest now, but keep our hand concealed. Play coy, that's what I'm always saying to Veridy. Not that she ever listens."

Veridy slipped her arm into the crook of her father's elbow. "Papa!"

"Veridy, go outside a moment and wait. There's a good girl. Don't worry, I shall give you a few minutes to exchange breathless words with Trassan once I have had my time with him." He stood tall. "Less breathlessly than you are accustomed to, naturally, now that you know I know."

Veridy nodded to Trassan and went out. Trassan tried very hard not to watch her go. She had a habit of swaying her hips in her skirt just so that...

"Trassan!" Vand snapped fingers in front of Trassan's face. "What are you doing, man? Pay attention."

"Master, sorry." He cleared his throat. "My apologies."

"Tell me why your attempt to secure the Licence Undefined failed."

"I had hoped my brother would provide me with one without question."

"And he did not."

"No, master. He proved to be annoyingly diligent in his duties. He seemed to be quite open to the idea initially, but he is being groomed for advancement by Duke Abing, and will not issue a licence without a full run through the Three Houses. He says it is a formality, but formality is the devil where the unbreathing lord is concerned." Trassan would not speak the name of the Drowned King near the ship, to do so was to invite misfortune.

"Well, well, that's something," said Vand. "But it's the time that will take; not insurmountable, but with Persin on us like a dog after a chop it makes it all the more ticklish. Have you tried your father?"

"I have. That rather put Garten's back up. He's my brother, but I think I might have misjudged him."

"Don't be glum, boy. It's not the worst that could happen. Chances are that we'll see it through without a hitch, and that once the licence is granted—and it will be, for this of all my ventures is surely in the national interest—"

"That's what Garten said."

"—then we'll see a surge in share sales. It will be fine!" said Vand briskly. "Always need a bit of a race, keeps life interesting. Always judge a man by the quality of his rivals, that's what the Hethikans used to say. Who knows, Trassan, you keep this up, and you can have your own Persin to worry about. Motherless cur that he is, I'd be insulted to have a lesser enemy."

Trassan nodded. He had, of course, corresponded with Vand about the licence issue, but he had been dreading telling him about Garten's lack of enthusiasm.

"Now, we'll meet again in a week when I'm back from the dig at Ostria. I'll send my daughter in. No funny business, do you understand."

"I have been meaning to ask you, master..."

"By the gods man, not now! Let's get this ship out of the way first, and have you back from the voyage. I'll not be wanting to make Veridy a wife and a widow within weeks of each other. One thing at a time."

"Yes, master."

"Very good." He opened the door. "Five minutes, my sweet."

"Yes, Pappa."

Vand leaned out onto the landing and took something covered in a bright cloth from a servant. He put it on Trassan's desk.

"What's that?"

"A gift, I could say," said Vand, "but I would really mean chaperone. Five minutes, do you hear?"

"Yes, sir," said Trassan.

"Yes, Pappa," said Veridy.

Trassan shut the door. Veridy let out the most outrageously girlish giggle and pranced into his arms.

"He is just outside, you know."

"Ah, as he said, he's known for ages."

"I thought we were discrete."

"You were," she smiled widely. "Don't be taken in by his claims, he's trying to unnerve you."

"He's succeeding."

"Nonsense. He's as perceptive as a block of pig-iron when it comes to me."

"What?"

"I told him."

"Why?"

"Because, stupid, he would have worked it out sooner or later." She gave him a little kiss that turned into a bigger one.

They pulled apart.

"I can do that only because you have impressed him, otherwise he'd have you hanged. It is a beautiful ship."

"He surveys it as an old man leers at the friends of his daughters," said Trassan.

"I rather thought it was how an agricultural gentleman might gaze happily at his favoured dray."

"Dray or wife, it doesn't matter, it's mine, not his."

"It is his money, Trassan."

"It was *my* idea."

"And *his* teaching."

"Oh do not let's argue about this again. I've not seen you for weeks."

They went to kiss each other again. A tutting interrupted them. Both of them turned this way and that, before settling on the object on the desk. Trassan disengaged himself from Veridy and lifted the cloth. He let it drop and groaned.

"I might have known."

"There is no need to be rude, goodfellow," said a voice from under the cover.

"What is it?" asked Veridy.

"A Tyn," said Trassan.

"In there?"

"A Lesser Tyn, the little kind." Trassan drew back the cloth. Inside a beautiful cage sat a tiny Tyn no bigger than Trassan's thumb. She was otherwise as perfect as a doll, like a high-born woman shrunk down to fit in a matchbox. For all he knew, she might have been. She wore a red velvet gown and an iron collar as delicate as a twist of grass.

"I prefer just Tyn, if you please," said the tiny woman.

"Fair enough," said Trassan. "Can you tell me your name or is there a geas on you?"

She raised a pair of perfect eyebrows. "You know something about this sort of thing?"

"Don't ask," said Trassan.

"Then I will not. My name is Tyn Iseldrin. I like Issy."

"She is beautiful! Where on earth did he get her?" whispered Veridy, wide-eyed. She bent down to look.

"I could ask the same of you." Issy cleared her throat. "Don't loom so child, it is impolite." Veridy backed off. "Better. I require genteel conversation, four thimblefuls of honey a day, and one of milk. Bring no mirrors into my presence, that one is a geas," she explained. "And I advise you not to talk too much about your employer, because I am bound to report to him all that I hear and see. I'd keep your hands off each other also. You are not married yet. This is my purpose, to see that you remain unentangled until such time as you might be. Married. Not entangled." She grinned. There was a feral air to her smile.

They drew apart a good couple of paces.

"And although it is not necessary, I like to read."

"Well, well!" Trassan ran his hand through his curly hair. He began to laugh, and stopped. "Fine! And what does so fine a lady Tyn as yourself enjoy as reading matter?"

She gave another sinister grin, showing teeth as sharp as a kitten's. "Agricultural papers," she said. "The very latest. The ones that deal with mechanical aids."

Trassan risked taking both Veridy's hands in his own. The Lesser Tyn tutted, and shook her head. He let them go.

"Not long now, darling," he said. "I'll make a good job of this. It's my final test, I feel."

"You stopped being his apprentice a long time ago."

Trassan looked down at the endless labours going on, in and around the ship. "If I pull this off, I'll be his equal."

Vand rapped on the door.

"You better not fail then, had you, Trassan Kressind?" Veridy planted a kiss full on Trassan's lips and stuck her tongue out at Issy. "Tell him, for all I care," she said.

"Tsk!" said Issy. "I will."

Vand poked his head around the door.

"That is enough time for you two now. Trassan, I wish you to take me all over the vessel. I will inspect every inch of it. Every inch," he repeated ominously.

"Yes sir. I'll find Hannever, and Tyn Gelven. He has the most up to date information one could wish for. And...?" Trassan looked at Issy.

"Oh, don't worry about me," she said. "I'm not going anywhere." She sat down on the gilded couch built into the side of her cage and folded her arms. "You and I are going to be the most excellent of friends," she said, with the most perfectly menacing expression Trassan had ever seen.

CHAPTER NINETEEN
The Glass Fort

JOVANKIC'S CART DROPPED them inside the gate, where they were made to wait. Zhinsky winked broadly at the guards in a shocking disregard for military etiquette. The gates were withdrawn into the seamless glass of the walls and must have been immense; the gateway was forty feet wide and eighty high. Stern-faced Morfaan looked down upon Rel from either side. There were marks about their necks and at the top of their outlandish swords, as if someone had tried and failed to hack them away. The bailey extended a long way back up the mountain, the rear of the fort being significantly higher than the front. Far above, up near the peak, was a tall tower made small by distance. It was round and fat-bellied as a gun bastion, but its Morfaan proportions managed to make it appear as graceful as a palace.

The fort was huge, far bigger than it appeared on the outside. The rearmost portion of it was built directly into the mountainside. The stone there had been simply scooped away, giving the same glass finish to the rock as the walls had.

"Melted," said Zhinsky, tapping Rel on the shoulder and pointing. "They melted the rock. How do you suppose they did it? Look at that, and remember this: you are away from comfortable certainties now, little merchant boy. This is the edge of the world. The rules of your kingdom do not apply."

"Wait a minute, Zhinsky, what exactly is your role here, besides my greeter?"

"A little of this, a little of that."

"Well, as much as I've enjoyed your company, perhaps you better call me captain now. We are bound by military rules here."

"Are you sure, little merchant boy?"

"I'm afraid I must insist.

Zhinsky chuckled. "As you wish, little captain."

The overall impression of the fort was one of great age. For all that the bailey played host to lumber and stone buildings, built by Rel's own kind, and rang to the practice of arms and the shouts of men, the place had the sense of a monument to the dead, rudely sequestered to this other purpose.

A Khusiak serving boy was sent away by Zhinsky. He left laughing his head off. Shortly after, a young man in a Maceriyan uniform came to the gate.

"You are Captain Rel Kressind, Third Karsan Dragoon Sauralier?" he said. As much as Rel was a judge of Maceriyans, he appeared cultured. He wore full uniform, bright and heavily decorated in the Maceriyan manner.

"I am," said Rel. He walked forward and shook the man's hand.

"Lieutenant Veremond, 15th Perusian Lancer Corps. Pleased to meet you. I will be your guide for the first couple of days here." He gave a weak smile. "Not that there's much to show. Don't let the size of the place fool you, it's repetitive. You will settle down in no time. Not much to do or see here. Then it's endlessly arbitrating customs disputes and riding until your backside goes numb."

"I better make the most of my first day then, while it is all fresh."

Zhinsky ambled up. "I be seeing you. Veremond here is a good man. Very thorough. Not bad rider for a non-Khusiak either."

Zhinsky clapped Veremond and Rel on the shoulders and went away across the square, whistling.

Rel was surprised when Veremond saluted him. Zhinsky winked and waved.

"Why did you salute him?"

"Why did I salute him?" said Veremond. "Oh..." A look of understanding dawned on his face. "No reason. We just do. Local joke, that sort of thing. Good old Zhinsky." He looked after the Khusiak. "Right. The colonel is expecting you."

"But I've yet to wash. It's been a long day. It's been a long few weeks. I've come two and a half thousand miles."

"He won't care about that. We all stink of the road out here, and lizard. There isn't much water, but you'll get used to that as well. If we all stink, nobody stinks."

Rel nodded. "All right."

"But I would put your uniform on, sir. And button it up. Estabanado's a stickler for that."

Veremond took Rel to his quarters and departed on some errand. Rel's room was small. The bed was a long, thin platform seemingly grown out of the crystal walls.

Besides that there was a wooden table, chair, pewter wash jug, bowl, chamber pot, candlestick and a chest. Nothing else. A small window opened up right through one wall. He would probably be able to see out of it if he stood on the chair and stretched, but the thickness of the walls would preclude much of a view. It let in a little light and a lot of cold.

Rel did, after all, have time to soap away the worst of the stink from his armpits, arse and groin, and rinse the dust from his face as he waited for his luggage to follow him up. The water was so cold it made him gasp.

He had his jacket on anyway. He did up all the buttons, pulling faces at the dirt ingrained into the designs on them. He polished at them with his sleeve until his cases arrived. They had seemed few on the train but filled his room so completely he thought himself excessive.

To his jacket he added his high-waisted trousers, riding boots and sash. He opened his armschest, but dithered over his cuirass and weapons. He put them on anyway. There were no servants to help him and he struggled with his armour fastenings. The weight of his ironlock carbine felt odd after such a long absence, and he opted to leave it behind. He locked it in its case, it was worth a small fortune. He burnished his sabre's sheath, and rehooked it upon his belt. When he got his helmet out of its wooden case he found the crest of dracon feathers a little bedraggled, but that could not be helped.

Veremond came for him shortly after. He nodded in approval. "You're wise to make the effort," he said. "This way."

He led Rel down long corridors in the walls; all of the same jointless material. He had never paid much attention to his father's lectures on construction or anything else for that matter. It bored him, but he couldn't help but think that Trassan would have been fascinated by the place.

"I will admit it is impressive at first viewing," said Veremond. "I recapture a little of that first impression when I show people about. One of the reasons I volunteered to meet you sir."

"It is quite amazing. How old is it?"

"No one knows. Ten thousand years some say, two thousand say others. I've heard both and every number between. I have shown more than my fair share of academics and magisters about, they often like to talk. They all get the same look on their face you have now sir, and they all believe they are right. They don't have to live here though. It is unbelievably cold in winter. After the first one of them, you begin to yearn for good honest brick and timber."

"It's cold now," said Rel.

Veremond gave him a regretful look. "I'm afraid that it is not."

They went downstairs into a long, tall hallway where there was a deal of traffic. "This is the main way, it runs right the way around the wall, through all the towers to emerge either side of the main gate. You'll soon find your way about, but in general here on the south side are the headquarters, northside is the kitchen and stores and so forth. We're here," he stopped by a door. It too was of the heavy, stone-like glass that made the walls, decorated with a crisp, alien design. He opened it onto a windowless antechamber lit by a single lamp. "Colonel Estabanado's office is through there. I'll wait here." He pointed at a trio of chairs; stiff-backed and miserable, as if they had committed some misdeed and waited to be punished themselves.

Veremond rapped on the inner door. "Enter!" came the reply. Rel went within.

Colonel Estabanado was writing at his desk in an office that was as dark and cold as Rel's quarters. There were rich rugs and furnishings, but so little light that their colours all ran into one sorry greyness. Many books filled locked cases lining the three inner walls. The outer wall, to which Estabanado had his back, had one small arrow loop rather than a window. A wooden firing platform gave access to it, reached by four steps. The room smelled of old paper and damp.

Rel came to stand at attention before his desk.

"Captain Rel Kressind, Karsan Third Dragoon Sauraliers reporting for duty, sir!" he said, clicking his boots together.

Estabanado's pen scratched over paper for a full minute. He tipped pounce onto the paper and lifted it to pursed lips. He took his time, fastidiously blowing from one side of the paper to the other. A blower, thought Rel. Not a tapper. Fine puffs of powder curled off the paper and drifted onto his desk. The colonel folded his message, then wiped his desk down. Only after this performance was completed, most definitely for Rel's benefit, did Estabanado look up. The first thing he said to Rel was hardly encouraging.

"I would not like you to think that your family's station affords you any special privileges here at the Glass Fort, Captain Kressind."

"No sir," said Rel.

"Your father bought your rank."

"Yes sir."

Estabanado snorted derisively. "You thought you could do what you liked. You were wrong. Your transfer papers." He held out his hand.

Rel handed over the leather tube that contained the papers. Estabanado took it. He left his gaze on Rel's face. He had a hangdog expression, mouth turned down under this neat beard, eyes pouched and tired. His skin was light brown, typical of Correados, but around his face and hands it was tanned a darker shade. The sign of a field officer. Estabanado might be severe in manner, but he was no pen pusher.

He popped the top of the dispatch tube and took out the papers. He went over them quickly.

"Adultery," he said, flicking from one page to the next.

"Yes sir."

"In my country, this is a capital offence. Karsa is a land of lax morality. You should not be here." He tossed the papers onto the desk. "You should be dead." He folded his hands over one another. "This fort is no place for criminals, Kressind. Few of the men who are here want to be, many have been sent here for punishment. Some, I know, think their posting here is unjust. But they are not common felons. Are you a felon, Captain Kressind? That is the question."

"Not by the laws of my country, colonel."

"A lawyer's answer. I will not stand the antics of rich boys with purchased commissions. All soldier here with equal effort. All who don't are equally flogged. Am I clear?"

"Yes sir."

"I will not brook any display of disobedience. You are men of many lands, but all of you are under my command, and I will be obeyed in all things. Is that clear also?"

"Yes sir."

"I see from your record that you have some talent. Therefore, at my discretion, your rank remains intact. For now. However, you will not be assigned a full squadron of men." Estabanado poured himself a drink of brandy from the decanter on his desk. He did not offer Rel one. "There are simply not enough. This fortress can house three thousand men, if need be. But I am not given such resources. No clear and present threat, I am told."

Rel said nothing. Estabanado sipped his brandy.

"You are a dragoon. We have no medium cavalry as such. I will instead place you in command of a troop of twenty light under Major Mazurek."

Rel did not hide his surprise very well.

"Something amiss, captain?"

"No sir."

"There is. Speak."

Rel risked looking at Estabanado.

"I did not say at ease, Kressind."

Rel's eyes snapped back to regard the wall again. "I am sorry sir. This is my first command. I have not yet finished my training."

"You have training, that is more than some of the other ranking sauraliers I have. Dregs, some of them. Few enough in the Hundred take the garrisoning of this fort seriously. I do."

"Yes sir."

"Whether your rank is bought or not, I will not say anything against Karsan training. You strike me as lazy, Kressind, but if any of your training has gone in, then it makes you a better asset than some of my less... dissolute officers. I am giving you a chance, do you understand? One mistake and I will take your rank away."

"Sir."

"Very good. Be on your way. If you have any questions or problems, take them up with Mazurek. Do not trouble me. He is in overall command of our sauraliers. He reports to me. If I hear anything at all that displeases me, then you will suffer. I am not a lenient man."

"Sir," said Rel.

"And Kressind?"

"Sir?"

"Twenty men and dracons represents one third of all the cavalry available to us here. Do not do anything foolish with them."

"No sir."

"Dismissed."

Rel did an about turn and stiffly walked out. He felt he had got away lightly, and that did not bode well at all.

Veremond had gone from the anteroom outside the colonel's office. In his stead, Zhalak Zhinsky was sitting in a chair. He sprang to his feet when Rel emerged.

"Hello little merchant boy! How did you like our glorious leader?"

"He seemed well enough. Stern, but straightforward. I can follow a man like that."

"Very astute," said Zhinsky. "Now I suppose we go to see Major Mazurek?"

"He told me to report to him, yes. Where's Veremond? He said he would wait?"

"Oh, he is a very busy man. I take you. Come on! Come on!" Zhinsky frantically beckoned. "The major's office this way." He led Rel out into the main thoroughfare and set off at a terrific pace.

"Hey Zhinsky."

"Yes, oh wise scion of the Kressinds?"

"I appreciate it's just your way, and I like a good banter as much as the next man, but Estabanado seems quite the stickler for the rules. Perhaps while we are in the fort you should call me 'sir'?"

"First he wants captain, and now he wants 'sir'?" Zhinsky roared with laughter. "Sir?"

"Something funny, Zhinsky?" The military air of the fort had reawoken the soldier in Rel.

"Oh little merchant boy, I thought you and I were friends! After all Zhinsky has done for you." He put on a sad face. "Ah! Here! This is Major Mazurek's office." He held up a finger to his lips and winked. "Shhh! Mazurek is very lazy. He is probably sleeping. Let's give him a surprise!" he said, and reached for the door handle with his other hand.

"Shouldn't you knock?"

But Zhinsky had barged into the office. He took off his hat and threw it onto a pile of papers occupying a sideboard. Miraculously, it did not fall over. The whole office was in a similar state, a clutter of paperwork and objects covered with a fine layer of dust.

"Pah!" said Zhinsky, coughing and flapping his hand in front of his face. "This place so dirty. That Major Mazurek, eh? You must be thinking he is a dirty fellow."

Zhinsky went through a pile of papers, a frown on his face. It lit up when he found a bottle under them. "Aha! I know where the good stuff is." He plonked himself down behind the major's desk. As nonchalantly as could be, he kicked a stack of papers onto the floor and set his dirty boots onto the wood. He stretched back, uncorked the bottle with his teeth, spat the cork out and took three big gulps of the major's liquor.

Rel looked about himself in consternation. "What are you doing, man? He could be here any minute!"

Zhinsky took the bottle away from his lips and smacked them appreciatively. "Why the bother? I thought little merchant boy like the party? That is what his papers say."

"You read my papers?"

"Of course! Why shouldn't I?" He drank again, and shuddered with delight. "Now that is good. Do you want some?"

"He'll have us up on charges!"

Zhinsky peered around the room as if there might be someone lurking under the furniture. "Who?"

"The major! His paperwork, his whisky."

"This not whisky? Whisky? We not in Karsa, merchant's boy. This is little water."

"Does it matter what it is? It's his! You drank it!"

Zhinsky sighed, took his feet off the desk and put the bottle down with a clunk.

"I never have liked paperwork," he said.

"But..." said Rel. Then, "Oh. I see."

A grin split Zhinsky's weather-beaten features, wider than the canyon of the Olb. He laughed and laughed and laughed, so hard he had to hold his belly with both hands. Then, suddenly, he stopped, and his mien became deadly serious. "I am Major Zhalak Zhinsky Doroetsev Mazurek. First two my names, next to last my mother's, Mazurka is where I am from." He shrugged. "Simple. I learn you Khusiachki. It be good for you."

Rel gaped. Zhinsky smirked.

"Good joke, yes? Come! Do not be looking like the grounded fish! I enjoy joking. Is good for morale."

"Why didn't you tell me?"

"How do I get to know you if I do and you are bowing and scraping and sir this and sir that? This way is much better. I was in Mohacs-Gravo, you there. Good idea of mine." He ran his eyes over a pile of paper that he had not kicked off his desk. He sighed at it. "Now Captain Kressind. You were saying something about me calling you all the time 'captain' and 'sir'?"

"Sorry," said Rel, snapping to attention. "Sir."

"As you are seeing, I have much work to be doing. Go find Veremond. He finish showing you about. I see you later, say four of the clock?"

"Yes sir," said Rel.

"That is all arranged then! You are, as we say when we do this properly, dismissed captain."

Rel backed out of the room, feeling shaky. As the latch clicked down he could hear Zhinsky sniggering to himself inside.

CHAPTER TWENTY
Captain Heffi

CAPTAIN HEFFIRA-NEREAZ-Hellishul vovo Balisatervo
Chai Tse-ban stepped out of a hansom cab and onto the
Bottomquay. He was a large man, and the cab rocked
on its wheels as he relieved it of his weight. Some of his
kind hid their religion, but not the captain. His ample
girth was accentuated by a wide and extravagantly
ruffled golden cummerbund. He wore his hair shaved
but for one, long lock that cascaded from the right hand
side of his head, arranged by ritual prescription upon
the shoulder of his embroidered jacket. From the tips of
his square-toed shoes to the oiled ends of his side-knot,
he was obviously and proudly Ishmalan. The cabbie
caught the coin he tossed and examined it with a surly
eye. The cabbie eyed the three gold rings in the captain's
nose, the hoops in his ears and the jewels on his fingers.

"Thank you," said the captain. He said it pleasantly,
but with finality that made it clear there was no more
money forthcoming.

The cabbie tugged the peak of his cap, although his
expression belied this respect. He flicked his whip at

his dogs. They had taken the opportunity to lie down as dogs will, and stood with wide, red gapes, rumbling their displeasure.

The cab drove away, the noise of the iron rims of its wheels silenced by the thick layer of muck on the cobbles. The captain breathed deeply of the air. The sharp tang of salt, the reek of the Lemio and Var as they ran down their spillways either side of the locks. There was rubbish on the wind, and shit, and spices from far lands. And fish. Always there was fish.

"It is good to be back at the Locksides," he said loudly and sincerely.

The wharfs of Bottomquay were accessible only during the least of the Lesser Tides, and therefore attracted the lowest tolls. There was a minor rise on, and smaller floatstone vessels crowded the grubby docks, crews frantically unloading before the water turned. Fine, silty mud was thick underfoot; from this a good part of Lockside's unique aroma issued. A hundred feet above were the higher docks, positioned at the mean of the tides. A little above that, beyond the reach of all but the highest of tides, the first buildings began; the Lowhouses. Bottomquay was inundated far too often to build on, and the steep cobbled roads leading up to the Lowhouses were thick with men and women, taking wares up to the stores and funiculars clinging to the cliffs above.

The locks themselves dominated everything, one of the great engineering feats of the age. The Slot, they were called. That name had once belonged to the cleft into which the locks were built, but most now did not remember the Lemio-Var waterfalls, or the Tyn that had dwelled underneath. Already one hundred years old, the locks were still unmatched in their size and boldness, and caused the most jaded seadog to stop and stare. There were twelve of them, one for every hour of the day, they liked to say. The upper seven were cut directly into the rock, deeper the higher one went, stepping up directly into the city along the original path of the conjoined Lemio and Var, now forever divided. The angle of the cliff was less severe there than elsewhere in Karsa, but still precipitous, and so the lower locks were built far out into the marsh on footings of giant boulders, carved and fitted without mortar. Giant coffers of pitch-blackened timbers rose from these, the trees that made them brought all the way from the forests of Shefir overseas. Gates of the same six-foot thick wood fronted each locks. The bottommost lock was a black line ahead of Heffi. The tarred timbers of the higher locks went up and up. Big floatstones sat in two of them, their masts poking over the top of the walls, high over the buildings. Waiting for the gates to open and draw them one level closer to the heart of the city, they were the toys of a giant left upon the stairway of titans.

How Captain Heffi loved the sight of them. The locks meant home, and he never failed to be cheered by them. He patted his belly happily, and headed off into the crowds of stevedores, sailors, dockworkers and those who earned their trade serving them. He'd not got halfway to the Anguillon and Anchor before he was stopped by an agent seeking a Ishmalan captain. Three more times it happened before he made the door. All but one were Ishmalan like him, and all knew him personally. They called his name with enthusiasm.

"I'm not interested," he told them one after the other, after the customary handshakes, backpatting and small talk. "I have employment. I am contracted for the foreseeable future. A grand venture, no less."

He would tell them no more, and when they asked for further detail, he smiled and walked on.

Presently, he reached the rusty grille that let into the private steps of the Anguillon and Anchor. Often covered by the tide, they were a quick way to the inn two hundred feet above when it was out. A long, dank climb up, and he emerged directly into the pub's yard.

IT WAS TO see an agent such as those that had hailed him that the captain had come. Their meeting had been arranged a week in advance, because both were busy men. Orerzensonam rose from the booth he was waiting in, and the two greeted each other like the old friends they were.

"Heffi! Heffi, Heffi, Heffi. Old heart!" The agent slapped the captain affectionately on the shoulders as the larger man engulfed him in a hug.

"Orry. Good to see you," he said. "I'm glad you could make the time for me."

"I can always make the time for you, Heffi. Always. The best captain on the seas!"

"Now you are flattering me, my friend."

"Nonsense, nonsense! You know me, eh? I speak only the truth."

"Ha! The biggest lie of all."

"How is the world treating you? Has the One sent anything fine your way?"

Orry was of the same sect of the Ishmalan as his friend, less ostentatious perhaps, but they did not hide what they were. They ritually touched their foreheads at the mention of their god.

"He has, he has," said Heffi. "I came the long way round, had to go down the Lockside, up the water steps. I needed to remind myself what I came from, because life is very good."

"So I see."

Heffi slapped his gut and the two laughed.

"It is good to see you."

"It has been too long. Is the food here the same?"

"Dreadful as always. The fish stew will kill you."

"Fine. Then let's drink."

They ordered a jug of dark sailor's porter each, and some food anyway. "Just bread!" insisted Heffi darkly. For a time they talked of this and that, exchanging news of their intertwined families, whose members were scattered across the known world.

After the first pint, they turned to business, slipping into the secret tongue of their kind. A rich creole of Low Maceriyan and Croshash, spiced with words used in no other living language.

"Is it true? The *Prince Alfra*, the iron ship! Is he as magnificent as they say?"

"It's common knowledge," said Heffi. "So it is true."

"Common knowledge! That the ship exists, *that* is common knowledge. What the ship is like? That is not." Orry looked at him expectantly.

"I can't tell you."

"Draught, beam, displacement?" ventured Orry. "To go to the Sotherwinter it must be–"

"Nothing."

"Masts?"

"No. Nothing at all. I can tell you nothing, Orry."

"Come on, there are thousands of workers at work, old heart."

"And you know nothing, because they're all under the threat of Tyn glamour, made large and worrying by the efforts of one Magister Tullian Ardovani. They come in, they work, they go home, and for the life of them they cannot speak of what they have done. Arkadian Vand is not a fool."

Orry raised his eyebrows at the name. "Ardovani? The sea witch! I see. But you're..." He waved his finger around.

"Talking? Privilege of being captain."

Orry laughed. "You'll tell me spies are struck blind."

"I could tell you that."

"I see." Orry let his inquiry drop and grew businesslike. "Alright then. How many are you after?" He retrieved reading glasses from a pouch in his pocket and pinched them onto his nose, then dragged a ledger from a knapsack on the bench, licked his finger, and opened it up. He looked at Heffi expectantly.

"It's not just the normal complement I need," said Heffi.

"Oh? Do you mean quality or quantity by that, old heart?"

"Orry! I mean both!" said Heffi. "Quantity *and* quality. We're after any you can find who are familiar with the operation of glimmer engines. I need rod shifters, mechanics, tenders... The lot."

"Fine, fine."

"And sailors. A lot of sailors. Especially those with experience of the deep south. There will be ice."

"Right, right, old heart. How many?"

Heffi took several gulps of his beer. He set it down hard on the table and wiped the suds from his beard.

"Two hundred ordinary seamen," he said. "Give or take."

Orry looked at him incredulously. "You're serious? You are serious!"

They laughed, Orry rather more cautiously than Heffi.

"Can you do it?" asked Heffi.

"What kind of ship is this?"

"Like none you've ever seen before. Can you do it?"

Orry looked down at the rows of columns in his ledger. He shrugged.

"No. Well. Yes, yes. Yes I can do it. It'll be difficult but... How many of the People do you need?"

"As many as possible. It's a difficult voyage. Now," he said. "Can you get me Tolpoleznaen? He's the best steersman by sea or river."

"Afraid not. He's on a lucrative contract up past the Little Islands way. He's due out in three days, won't be back for a year and a half."

"Double his fee," said Heffi.

"He'll not break contract for that."

Heffi shrugged. "Triple it then. I will have him."

Orry set his pen down. "Heffi..."

"I want him on board. Whatever it takes."

Orry sighed. "I'll put out the word, see if I can get him before he leaves port. Anyone else you want?"

Heffi thought. "Volozeranetz. Suqab. And is Drentz still sailing?"

"He says he is quitting."

"He says that every year," they said together. They smiled. The little tension between them melted.

Orry shook his head. "I can just hear the racket! Two hundred you say? There'll be no ship able to sail for weeks."

"Our kind will get rich from it."

"I'm sure you'll be getting richer still," said Orry.

"I am being paid an obscene amount of money," Heffi said agreeably, lacing his fingers over his gut. "But there's a lot of opportunity available for others, especially our kind. I am generous. I am sharing."

"The People of the One will profit first?"

Again, they touched their foreheads at the mention of their god.

"Of course! I am of the true faith."

"Haven't you heard? Religion is highly unfashionable," said Orry.

"Not to me. Not to us. The blind no longer believe. They chased their gods out, but it ever was a false faith."

"So it was." Orry took out his pen, and began making notes on scraps of parchment. He paused. "Remember the words of the first fathers, Heffi."

"Which ones?" said Heffi.

Orry looked up over his glasses. "'The love of money is the falsest of all loves,'" he quoted.

"Amen to that!" said Heffi, and raised his porter. He smiled broadly, but there was a hollowness to it. It stretched his face uncomfortably.

Heffi did love money, and a little too much at that.

CHAPTER TWENTY-ONE
Qurion

AUTUMN DEEPENED. THE rain gave way to early frosts, the first coming not long after Katriona's wedding. Come mid-Leffall the leaves were falling quickly, and the nights were unseasonably cold. Guis stayed in a lot, preparing his latest play. His self-imposed exile, or sulk, depending on how generous he was feeling towards himself, lasted until Qurion came to see him.

A letter from Rel had distracted him from his work, and he was sat close by the fire rereading it when the knock came at the door. Tyn started on his shoulder and dug under his collar, his tiny hands causing Guis to shrug irritably.

"Don't do that!" he snapped. "It tickles."

"Master grumpy," said Tyn in his reed-thin voice. "Master drunk too much last night."

The door shook on its frame. "Oi! Guis! You're in there! I can hear you!"

Guis looked at the door. "Qurion," he muttered. "It's open!" he called. "Let yourself in."

The door flew open, and Qurion strode into the room. He was tall, black haired, his yellow uniform immaculate, his moustache fastidiously waxed. He had a confidence in his bearing so great it threatened always to topple into the comic, but somehow managed to remain magnetic.

"I'm in town, as you can see, and you're coming out for a drink." Qurion pointed a white-gloved finger at Guis and smiled.

Guis turned back to his letter. "I can't. I've got a letter to write and then I've got to get the stage directions finished on this for tomorrow." He waved his pen at an untidily piled manuscript. "I'm going back to Stoncastrum in two days. I'm on the dull bit. Done the words, got to do the actually having people saying them part. I hate it. Now's not a good time."

"Don't give me all your writerly bollocks about the pain, the art!" said Qurion, slapping the back of his hand on his forehead and casting his head back. "You'll be saying you've got a touch of the vapours next."

"Actually, it's going very well," said Guis. "I have no problem writing, so long as I am left alone to concentrate on it."

"Soft belly, you. Should have been a soldier, that would have sorted you out." He sniffed. "It's warm in here." He whirled his coat from his shoulders and cast it onto the bed. He dislodged a pile of papers and plopped himself into a chair.

"You should have been here last winter, no money for coal then."

"This year, your fire is high. It's going well," said Qurion.

"Yes!" snapped Guis, his irritation turning to laughter. "Yes, yes it's going really well. Would you believe, people came to watch my play?"

"Who'd have thought it? I'm glad for you. Going well, and you're off for gods know how long in two days. And I'm not often back, correct?" Qurion counted the points off on his fingers.

"That's correct."

"That's three very good reasons for coming out, set against one very dull reason for staying in. You're not winning this argument, you know that, right?"

"Qurion, Qurion!" Guis set Rel's letter down carefully, so as not to lose it in the mess of papers in his room. "I'm not coming out for a drink."

"Oh yes you are." Qurion leapt to his feet, grabbed him under the armpit and half dragged him from his seat. "You need to get laid, my friend. Stop you being such a miserable arse."

Guis protested. As much as he loved his friend, he hated it when he used his greater strength. Qurion did not desist.

"I'm not coming out," said Guis.

Qurion set Guis on his feet and dusted his coat off, frowning at a stain. He plucked a piece of lint from the lapel and gave him a quick, white-toothed smile. That smile usually had some otherwise respectable woman's skirts up around her waist before it had left Qurion's face.

"Yes you are."

"Tyn?" said Guis.

"Master?"

"You're going to have to go into your box."

"Master is cruel!" the Tyn poked its head out from under Guis' hair. "Tyn does so much for you, and now you say, into the box!"

"Where he's taking us, it's not safe for you."

"How do you know where we're going?" said Qurion.

"The kind of places you ordinarily bring me to, my friend, are not safe for Tyn."

"Shame! Shame! You are ashamed!" wailed Tyn.

"I am not, but I also do not wish to cause a riot. You have to go in your box."

"Pfft!" went Tyn, but clambered onto Guis's upheld hand just the same. Guis delicately undid the chain that linked them, and carried Tyn over to a small, ornately carved box. The creature clambered in, and Guis locked the door. Qurion watched, fascinated.

"You could just leave it behind. Bloody great burden if you ask me, I don't know why you just don't get rid of it."

Guis smiled sadly. "I can't."

"Why on earth not?"

"It's complicated. You know."

They stared at each other. Qurion forced a smile. "All right then, bring your monkey. Let's get out of here."

FORTY MINUTES LATER Guis was in a noisy salon drinking shit ale and worse Svavincan snapsa. His face glowed uncomfortably with the booze and the heat. The noise in there was so great he had to bellow to his companions. Companions, he ruefully noted, that did not currently include Qurion.

"What I don't understand about that man, is that he makes such a massive fucking fuss about dragging me out here for a drink, then promptly dumps me for some floozy. It happens every bloody time. Every time!"

"Charming, we not good enough for you?" said Hermanius. He arched an exquisitely plucked eyebrow and stared into his wine as if he expected it to give him an apology.

"You know what he's like, Guis!" said Bannord. Bearded and belligerent, a lump of a man, mostly muscle and heart. As made for good cheer as for war. "Led around by his cock that one. It's not his fault he's good looking is it?" He leaned in close. "Or that he discovered the secret."

"Oh?" said Hermanius. "Do tell?"

Bannord lowered his voice, "He found out that girls like fucking just as much as we do!" He bellowed with laughter. "He's so bloody persistent they just give in to him, because we're all so pissing busy writing poems and glowering." He looked knowingly at Guis over his beer. "Some of us are, anyway."

"I find many paramours, but they are all of high quality," said Guis drily. "I'm more careful in my selection than you are. I'll have you know I fence well above my grade."

"According to Qurion," said Hermanius.

"Patronising bastard," said Bannord. "So, we going to get ourselves some action or sit around here?"

"I came out for a drink," said Guis.

"Don't go all fucking mopey on us, you bastard."

"No, he's right," said Hermanius. He tossed his watch into the air, letting the chain snap taut, and catching it. Like Trassan, he was one of the first to own the new devices. Unlike Trassan, he had no practical need for it. "I'm in no mood for chasing skirt."

"Now, are you ever my friend?" said Bannord. "I wonder about you sometimes."

Hermanius raised an eyebrow. "Do you now? Whether I am or I am not in the mood for chasing skirt, I have no choice in the matter. I am helpless. And tonight, I am not in the mood."

"Oh for fuck's sake," groaned Bannord. "Not the free will shit again! I've had it with all that. I just want to get pissed. You want to get a proper job, soldiering'd be good for you."

"Qurion said the same to me tonight," said Guis. "Soldiers are so eager to get us all killed along with them."

Hermanius smiled, as tight and humourless a smile as that of a tax collector.

"Bannord doesn't think such things are important, Guis, I do."

"So do I," said Guis. He took a nip of the snapsa and pulled a face. "Either everything is random, so our decisions mean nothing to the progression of events," he said. "So we have no free will, or..."

Hermanius finished off the sentence. "... everything is predetermined by natural law, and we have no free will."

"He's a fucking philosopher!" said Bannord sarcastically.

"Just a philosopher tonight," said Hermanius. "Are you sure you don't want to be bothering barmaids? Let the adults talk, lieutenant."

"No, I want to say goodbye to my friend. I've been fucking constantly since I got back, and to be honest my cock is a bit sore." He slammed his beer down hard, making their drinks jump. "Woman! Woman!" he hollered in the general direction of the bar. "More beer! Besides," he said to his friends, "I've four more days of freedom left, so I can afford to take some time out. Unlike Qurion, I intend to spend some time with my friends."

"It is very nice to be so well regarded," said Guis.

Bannord snatched up Guis's beer in salute, then drained the tankard. "I'm glad you think so."

"So you've been listening to Lord Delieffarn," said Hermanius to Guis.

"I've read some of his work. If one is going to write plays, one has to have something to write about. You're going to get me another one of those, right Bannord?" said Guis, tapping his tankard.

"Get it yourself. I'm going for a piss." Bannord winked, and barged his way out through the press.

"But what about random events, navigated by those possessing free will?" continued Guis. "Surely that gives us some amount of self-deterministic capability. Magic, for example is the imposition of will on the material reality."

"You're quoting Unthien. You should have gone to the college," said Hermanius.

"I *am* quoting Unthien, and no I shouldn't."

"The issue with that proposition is that any purported random events are collapsed into a predictable pattern by free will, especially gross acts of magic. One man's exertion of will ripples out, affecting many others, becoming deterministic in itself. So you see, dear Guis, either way, we're merely riding the carriage, and have no way of directing the dogs drawing it where we would. We only think we do."

"That's a cheery thought," said Guis. He had, of course, ruminated much on this topic himself. Were his own nightmarish visions and feelings his doing, or was he free of responsibility for them? In effect, he supposed it did not matter. What mattered was that he felt the feelings, and thought the thoughts. Dealing practically with them was all that mattered, and on the practical level, alcohol freed his mind from the tyranny of himself. He came close then, very close, to revealing his troubles to Hermanius, a confession he'd mulled over many times but had never dared to utter.

Bannord drunkenly grabbed the pair of them.

"I say fuck fate, the same way that old Res Iapetus told the gods to go and fuck themselves, entirely fucking freely, I say we drink!" He scooped a number of large jugs and tankards from the tray of a servingman trailing him and plonked them on the table.

The moment passed, the glimpse of freedom Guis had from his condition receded. He gripped the handle of Tyn's case hard under the table. Inside, the creature shifted.

Conversation dwindled, leaving him caught in the dark vortex of his own anxiety. The pause was a sucking void he could not abide.

"I've been invited to stay with Countess Lucinia of Mogawn," he blurted.

"What? What? You've been invited to stay with the hag?" said Bannord. "Now there's a woman who likes fucking. You go to her, not only will you get fucked, you'll *be* fucked. You know what they say about her?"

"Do you really believe all the shit they say in your barracks, Bannord?" said Hermanius, rolling his eyes. "You're quite the most credulous person I've ever known."

"I've heard some shit that's not true, and some shit that is true. Remind me sometime, and when I don't mind scaring the crap out of myself, I'll tell you what one of the veterans told me about Farside skinturners. That sounded like shit, but that's true, and I heard that in the barracks,"

Bannord said pointedly. "Makes the ghouls we have skulking on the shore look pretty tame, let me tell you."

"She's not like they say at all," said Guis, feeling unaccountably defensive towards the countess. "She's got a sharp mind."

"She looks like a man, dresses like a man, has no manners, ideas that are derided and a notoriously hungry twat. She's a one woman scandal machine. You lay with her and you'll never hear the end of it." said Bannord warningly. Some of his humour returned. "But if you do, please take notes. I'm fascinated."

"Bannord..."

"Ooh, looks like someone's got the hots for the Hag!"

Guis's rage, never wholly leashed, erupted. "You know what? This was a bad idea. Fuck you Bannord. Goodnight, Hermanius."

Hermanius lifted his glass.

"What did I say now?" said Bannord.

"You know what you said."

From across the room, Qurion caught sight of Guis's exit. His eyes widened at Hermanius in question. Hermanius shrugged.

Hermanius watched him make frantic apologies to the floozy he was talking to. Well, he supposed. She wasn't actually a floozy. She looked on the face of it, quite well mannered. Probably someone's wife. Not that that would stop Qurion. "And now, there goes our hero." Hermanius affected a world weary expression, and gave Bannord an admonishing look.

"Screw the lot of you," Hermanius said. "Screw the lot of you, but most of all, screw the son of a bitch who made this godsawful wine!"

He drank it anyway.

* * *

GUIS REGAINED HIS head when he went outside. The cold, foggy air was a slap in the face he needed.

"Perhaps master should have stayed at home like Tyn suggested?" said Tyn from his box. Guis gave it a vindictive shake.

A gaggle of drunks spilled from the tavern out on a wash of warm air, noisy and eager for more entertainment. They staggered past Guis, hallooing and guffawing. Qurion came after them.

"And why are you being such an arse then?" he said.

Guis shrugged.

"It's getting like I can't take you anywhere."

"That's the second time I've flounced out of a pub in one week."

"That's really not like you," said Qurion with amicable sarcasm.

"You know what? It really isn't. I'm not... Look, I'm not as angry as you think I am my friend."

"Yes you are," said Qurion. There was an edge of enmity to his amity.

"No I'm not! Shit, I am, I suppose..." Guis took a deep breath. "You, it's you. You make me angry."

Qurion's smile vanished. The beginnings of a glower took his place. Threat and charm, that was all he had by the way of public faces. There was more to him, but he rarely put what was inside on display. Qurion's gifts limited him. He didn't try harder, because he did not need to. Such a shame.

"Let me explain," Guis said. "I owe you an apology."

"Too damn right."

"For years, I've been massively jealous of you. I think you know that."

Qurion glanced at him. "Not this again."

"Look, every time we go anywhere, you fuck off and have your hand up some woman's skirt before we're two pints in. I get left there nursing my wine while you're off. One wink and they drop their pants for you. I don't get that. You've always been bigger and better looking than me. You don't realise it."

Qurion sighed. "No, you don't realise it, my friend. I've seen you scare off women time after time with your intense artist dogshit. You're a clever man Guis, charming. You are not much to look at, but you have them eating out of your hand half the time, then you push them into the dirt."

Guis snorted. "You are a patronising bastard."

"I'm right though. They're just after a good time. Just like us. They want a quick tumble. not your bleeding heart on a platter. All you have to do is offer them that. You give them too much baggage." Qurion stared off into the fog. A four dog carriage clattered past. Glimmer lamps were mysterious balls of light on the other side of the road, distant as the moons. Water droplets shifted and danced to a tune only they could hear. "You could have it too." Qurion grabbed his shoulder.

Guis shrugged off his hand. "Don't you get it? I could not have it. Not like you. I have to work hard. And this is the part you don't get. I am jealous of you, but I do not want to be like you. I've sat there on my own in the pub watching you play lone wolf with other people's girlfriends. I've watched you chat up my women, flirt with my sister, your cock practically in your fucking hand. And not a thought in your head for your own wife.

She adores you, and you treat her appallingly. Wedding vows are *vows*, Qurion." He looked disdainfully at Qurion's uniform. "If you can't keep those, what can you keep?"

Qurion was furious, but Guis wasn't done.

"I remember when your father was fucking every doxy in the Off Parade. How much it hurt your mother, and how angry it made you. Well, look at you. The fruit never falls far from the tree, does it?"

"You call this an apology, you little shitbag?" spat Qurion. His hand was hovering near his sword hilt.

"Don't do that, Qurion," said Guis mildly. "I'm not as a good a swordsman as my brothers, but I'm still pretty good. There's one kind of swordsmanship I am better at than you, and it kills."

"And now you're threatening me."

"I'm getting to the apology part. You can't help yourself. I've been a bad friend to you. You've wanted a squadron mate, all this time. Someone to ride beside you on the chase. That's not me. I can't be your partner in that. I don't want what you want. So if you want to go chasing skirt, take someone else. I'm sorry I can't be the person you think I am. Trying to be has made me conflicted, and that has made me behave poorly."

"You're behaving well tonight, flouncing out like a theatre diva? I suppose you forgive as well."

"Something like that," said Guis.

"Who's the patronising fucker now?" Qurion bent over, thrusting his rage-reddened face into Guis's. He prodded him in the chest. "You are a sanctimonious hypocrite. You've played the same game yourself enough. It's not my fault you don't play as well as me."

"I choose not to."

"Fine. Fine." Qurion calmed, as if he were trying to rein back his anger. But then something snapped inside him. "I'll be me, you be you. You miserable fuck. Just remember, when you're wining and dining it up with the Hag, I got there first."

Guis eyebrows went up.

"That's right. At your sister's wedding during the Revelry. I assume that makes that particular instance alright by you, being by custom and all? Yes? Oh good. Now, I was having fun. I won't be seeing you around." Qurion turned around and pushed his way back through the door.

"Wait!" called Guis but Qurion had already gone.

"Surely, master is the king of contrition," said the box in Guis's hands.

"Shut the fuck up Tyn."

Guis stopped by a gin shop for a half pint of rough liquor on the way back. He wasn't sure who he was most angry with. He came to the conclusion that whether it was himself or Qurion, both of them were arses. He found this hilarious for a while. Then fell into a depression where he fulminated on his own inadequacy, and on Qurion's arrogance so much that the dangers posed by his broken mind were quite forgotten for one night. When he barged out of the gin shop and walked home, he did so without treading on the cobble cracks or scratching at the walls with his fingernails.

He lit a spirit lamp when he returned. He cast off his hat and was none too gentle with Tyn's box when he set it down.

There were two more letters on the table by Rel's. One was from the Hag. He drunkenly reread it, then screwed it up and tossed it onto the last embers of the fire. It flared up, and went to ash. He was angry with her for being what she was, angry with himself for not seeing past it. The persona he affected was not supposed to care about these things, but he did.

The last letter was from his mother. It had arrived yesterday, and he had avoided opening it. Now, slumped into the chair by the desk, he stared at it. The seal was in pale cream wax, elegant in design. Fine Tyn work.

He picked the letter up. He tapped it against his lips four times. The paper smelled of his mother's perfume. He ran the paper under his fingernails sixteen times. He growled in irritation at this semi-conscious ritual, and threw it back onto the desk. Fear bloomed in him, urging him to run the paper round and round his hands again.

"Mother," he said. It hit him then how drunk he was. He decided to read it. The seal cracked easily.

Dear Guis, it read. *It is several months since you last paid a visit to me. I hear from your brothers that you are shortly to depart for Stoncastrum again. I would dearly like to see you. Please come at seven of the clock, Martday evening. I shall be in my garden. I will not tell your father, if that makes it any easier for you.*

It was signed *your loving mother* in a series of loops. They spoke of a confidence she did not have.

He groaned and kneaded at his frown with the heel of one hand. Martday was tomorrow.

"Mother, mother, mother," he said.

He sat there woozily for some time. He kept the fear of the Darkling at the back of his mind, behind the bars of this conundrum: To go or not to go?

He reached no decision. Ephemeral fears and vile fancies dogged his thoughts, but the Darkling did not come.

He roused himself and fell into bed as the first rays of the sun sparked hard, frosty highlights from the city rooftops.

CHAPTER TWENTY-TWO

Moorwena Kressinda

GUIS REPLIED TO the invitation first thing in the morning before his trepidation turned to procrastination, and thence to implicit refusal. Come the afternoon, he sent for a public dog coach of the better sort to meet him at the Parade near the Grand Illia hotel. The driver raised his eyebrows at Guis's shabby dress. They cranked up a fraction higher when Guis told him he was bound for the Spires.

Feelings of inadequacy threatened to overwhelm him as the dog coach rattled up from the Var-side city centre into the Spires. The richest part of town was built on three ridges of soft sandstone that separated Karsa's double shallow valleys. The whole area was riddled with caves. The cliffs of Karsa were of hard black rock, but their tops were covered in thick layers of soft clay broken through by the stone of the Spires. The lesser crags that had characterised the area in the time of King Brannon had gone elsewhere in the city, quarried and built over as the metropolis swelled. But nowhere was the soft rock more accessible than at the Spires, and nowhere did it go so deep. The very first Karsans had made their homes there, barbarian people who had dug out their dwellings before the coming of the first king.

Over time the caves had been lost in the cellars of the vast mansions raised on the Spires. But from time to time a cave might be uncovered to reveal the mundane evidence of past ages. The province of a minor branch of archaeology, these finds rarely drew attention. Bones spoons that crumbled to dust at a touch, or fragments of rough fabrics and patches of rust where iron tools might once have been laid down to rest for the final time seemed so paltry compared to the inexplicable machines of the greater eras.

There was a split among the older families as to how these finds were celebrated. Some took each artefact carefully from its resting place and displayed it as proof of long family histories. Others preferred not to dwell on these relics of the rude past. Those who rubbed shoulders with princes and other potentates took unkindly to reminders of their humble beginnings. Living in caves was the habit of animals and Wild Tyn, not cultured men.

However, as the older families had been displaced by the newer, the former opinion was growing in popularity. To an impoverished lord whose social position was under threat, the bone spoon of an unremembered ancestor took on far more importance than any number of gold ones.

Guis's family was the newer sort of aristocracy, Gelbion Kressind buying the manse from a bankrupt baronet some thirty years back. If he had found such a cave on their property, no doubt he would have exhibited whatever was within gleefully, to show how humble the old families of Karsa City were in the beginning. His argument, often and vehemently aired, was that there was nothing special about the old money families. They had come from nothing, so why should they sneer at those newer to high rank who had come from nothing in their turn? Bone spoons, he was fond of saying, cut both ways.

The roads into the Spires split and wound round each rock like ferns uncurling in spring. The area wore its modern wealth openly. The soft stone lent itself equally to fantastical carving as it did to the construction of simple caves, and so the manses of the rich were a collection of glorious sculptures. The older were worn by the rain, but those of more recent vintage were lacquered with chemically activated resins. These gleamed as if perpetually wet. Another divider between the old and the new. Industrials, Wetrocks—Guis's kind had many derogatory names among the older aristocracy of Karsa.

The dog coach turned off the main road, rattling under glimmer lamps wrought from silvered steel, multiple lights hanging as fruits from branches clashing in the wind. Hard granite hewn from the sea cliffs surfaced the roads, dark capillaries in the pale flesh of the spires. The coach took another turn, then another, whirling past a false castle upon whose peak crouched a roaring gorgon of stone. Guis had never liked it. Not so much for the design, which was vulgar by any standard of taste, but mostly for its function as a landmark that told him he was nearly home.

They went around a tight bend. The road climbed. All of the Var-side was below him, covered in a soupy smog. The moons shone from the tops of the cloud. The

Spires were fanciful floatstone ships on a vapour sea. The image brought on a mild fit of vertigo. Guis turned to watch the rock wall blur past on the other side of the coach.

The wall gave out. Kressind Manse reared up suddenly in the dark. No fanciful carvings there. A tall house, stout as a tower, lacking even the modest decoration of the Maceriyan revivalist style. Small windows alive with yellow candleflame and blue glimmerlight, it appeared watchful rather than welcoming. Guis's stomach lurched at the sight of it. Many of the mansions here had appurtenances that hearkened to the fortresses of the Long Dark Woe, but Kressind Manse actually looked like one. A defensive structure in the heart of the wealthiest city district. It spoke volumes as to Gelbion Kressind's state of mind that he had chosen it as his home.

The coach entered a cut below the manse, a worn stone arch curved over the road, blocking out the house.

Guis banged upon the roof of the cabin.

"Stop here!" he shouted.

"Goodfellow?" said the driver. The dogs barked as he reined them in. The coach stopped with a lurch.

"I'll walk the rest of the way."

"As the goodfellow requests."

Guis paid the man. "Leave swiftly."

The driver cracked his reins. "Hup! Hup! Hup!" he hollered. The dogs bayed, went up the road, and came about. Guis drew himself into the side of the road. He waited until the coach had gone. Silence fell. A delivery wagon rolled by on the main street, the giant dogs harnessed to it with their heads down. Guis let it go. There were few people about. A typical weekday night in autumn.

Close by the arch, a natural crevice had been squared off to make a shallow alleyway. The stone had been carved to look as if it were made of blocks, but hints at its natural form persisted in unexpected undulations, some deep enough to preserve the stone's original texture.

Dead leaves and street trash clogged the gutters. Guis looked over his shoulder. He held out his hand to a shadow in the wall, gritted his teeth and concentrated. The leaves blew around his feet, although the night was still.

"Master! Master! Do not be foolish!" hissed Tyn in his ear.

Guis did not listen. He was damned if he was going in the front door. He stared at the stone wall, and made himself see it as a door. This was the hardest for him, fighting off the slippery images that attempted to replace what he wanted to see, trying to make themselves real rather what he wanted made real.

But this simple act of magic he could manage without killing anyone.

His fingers crackled with painful energy. A long spark leapt from his hand. The tip of it crawled up and down the rock in a sinister semblance of life. It found what it sought, and straightened. Light played through the stone, glowing from within. The spark winked out.

Guis breathed raggedly, supporting himself on the wall. A tightness at the back of his head told him the Darkling was awake, and aware of him. Tyn muttered his cantrips in his ear.

Before them was a door, no bigger than waist high, large enough for a Greater Tyn. He pushed at the ancient grey wood. It swung open noiselessly. He crawled through and shut it behind him.

The door faded away into stone again.

Beyond the door was a low dark corridor that forced him to hunch. As he moved forward his shoulders brushed a shower of sharp-scented sand from the friable stone into his hair.

"No more magic! No more magic to light the way," pleaded Tyn. "Please, please master!"

Guis fumbled in his pocket for a box of matches and a candle stub.

"Shut up!" said Guis. "I'm not a complete idiot." He lit the candle, revealing rough stone walls that danced with shadow. Tyn whimpered at the dark. Guis paid him no heed. He was in no mood for the Darkling today, and that gave him strength to deal with it.

He went upwards, through tunnels that smelled faintly of broken drains. His feet found treacherous steps that led past bricked up doors of odd and various size. An iron grille barred the way at the top of the steps. He pulled out a key, hoping his father had not discovered his secret way. The key stuck in the gritty mechanism and he swore. He twisted hard, the metal digging into his fingers. Suddenly it turned, and he opened the gate with a ghostly squeal. Guis blew out his candle and waited with his breath held. No one came.

He lit his candle again, and passed into the cellars of Kressind Manse. He stole up stairs that led to a small door in the corner of the gardens. There was no way to check who was on the other side of this, and so he stepped out without pause. Better that than stop, dither, and flee.

Chill night air, frost on the lawns, silence. He had arrived without notice.

Guis padded through cold grass toward a walled section of the gardens. A faint glow shone through a new conservatory built onto a base of ancient brick.

One final door, and he was in his mother's Moonflower garden.

The light of the flowers themselves lit the space, a square ten yards by ten yards. Paths paved with brick ran around the sides and crossed at the centre of the room. In the four smaller squares formed by the paths were large lead tubs, full of imported soil. These held the Moonflower plants, lambent as the White Moon, swaying hypnotically in their beds.

Footsteps. Guis watched from the shadows as his mother went about her garden. As she passed the plants the Moonflowers came alive, lifting up from their branches to fly across the narrow path, petal wings twirling. They sought out fresh branches, docking daintily. They crept on thread roots to positions agreeable to them, then pierced the thin bark of their hosts with the hollow thorns at the base of their stalks. Moorwena Kressinda trailed her fingers across the plants. She hummed a song she had sung Guis and his siblings as children before she had retreated from them. Luminous scales powdered her hands. The Moonflower plants shuddered. Moorwena encouraged them to fly with shooing motions, and soon the entire garden danced. She looked at peace, but she was not. Another lie, another secret. She wore long sleeves to cover the marks on her arms.

He felt sympathy and love for her. It was ruined as always by the thoughts that plagued him; these of forbidden sexual congress and matricide. These were the worst. He lived in terror that his body would respond. If it did, what would that make him?

Beneath his hair, Tyn stirred.

His mother frowned at a poor match between plants. She retrieved secateurs from her bench and returned.

A flower shrieked as she cut its stem. Thick amber sap spurted from its stalk. The wings shivered, locking position. His mother held the bloom up to her face and sniffed it.

"I know you are there, Guis," she said. "The flowers know."

Guis stepped out onto the path. The garden was awash with the chalky light of the blooms. It made Moorwena look like a ghost.

"That's better." She set the flower on a bench and went to Guis. She reached for his face with her hands dusted with flower scales and pollen. Guis flinched. She let one drop, let the other continue its course to rest upon his cheek.

"Thank you for coming Guis," she said.

"Mother," he said. "What do you want?"

"To see you of course!" she said. There was a tiredness inherent to everything she did or said. She had been beautiful once. She still was at first glance, before her insubstantiality became apparent. She was used up, wrung out by his father's fury and his illness. If Guis hadn't hated him before, he would have hated him for that alone. "That is why you came, to see me?"

Guis nodded. He dare not speak. He could not trust his thoughts.

"Then we are both happy. Come and sit with me for a while."

"Father?"

"He is in his study. He has no idea you are here." She took his hand and drew him after her to a bench. They sat.

She breathed out in contentment, and examined him. "How are things with my eldest son?"

"They go well."

She looked at his clothes, the patching and holes. "Are you sure?"

"I am fine! My plays are performing well." A half-truth. They were well received, they were not paying as well as he hoped. "This latest run in Stoncastrum should seal my fortunes for the next year or so."

She sighed and looked at her hands in her lap.

"I wish you would not occupy yourself with something as tawdry as the theatre."

"It is my choice, mother."

"Matters would be helped considerably if you were to obey your father's wishes."

Guis suppressed a shudder. The backs of his legs tightened. "Whose matters? I will not subject myself to the attentions of the magisters. They can do nothing for me. We were told by the metaphysic and physic that the best I could hope for was a dulling of my wit. At worst, I would be rendered an imbecile. As much of an embarrassment to father as I am, I am sure he would not wish an idiot for an heir."

"Don't talk like that, Guis. He only wants what is best for you."

"He wants what is best for himself," said Guis. "He wants a magister who will carry his name forward. A magister, who would bend his talents to increasing the family fortune."

"Many magisters do serve their families so."

"And many do not, mother! Father never did have much imagination. Who would want to involve themselves with the mundanities of business when he could tame dracons or raise the very fires of the Earth?"

"You are talking of the old mages, not of reality."

"The old mages are real, mother."

"There is the matter of your safety."

"Is there?" said Guis. "When I hurt Aarin, I told father first. I told him of the things that torture me, but he did not hear. I will not lie and say that there was no concern or fear on his face, but I will also not say that excitement and calculation did not outweigh his concern. I cannot be a magister or a mage, mother. My mind is broken. This gift I have is a curse." Bitterness crept into his voice. She never noticed anything, not truly.

"You are too much like me," she said softly.

"Perhaps. If I attempted to master my talent, I would become a monster," he said, rising from the seat. "I was hoping we would not have this conversation. I should go."

She looked up at him, her eyes as big as the moon her flowers were named for. "You should consider it, please. For me."

"I have considered it. Over and over again." Guis stepped in and kissed his mother's forehead. "I will not do it. I am managing fine as I am."

"For how long?" she said. "I do not wish to lose you. I cannot lose another."

There, thought Guis. There it is. Six children ignored for one dead. She could not even bring herself to attend his sister's wedding, but lingered here in her garden. She was broken by the loss of her child and the sickness of her husband. Broken, like him. But his sympathy for her was swallowed by his anger. No matter what afflicted her, he had needed her and she was not there for him. He fought his demons alone, and he was losing.

"You will not. I promise."

"I am sure I taught you that you should not make promises you cannot keep," she said sadly. Her eyes strayed to the flowers. She scratched her arm absentmindedly. She was a fine one to lecture him on promises.

"Father taught me one only should if the promise gained you what you wanted. Otherwise, they are not to be honoured."

"Your father has his own opinions on promises." She looked back to him, focused again. "What is it you want? Do you really have any idea? How long do you think you can continue on your current path?"

"As long as it takes, mother."

"As long as what?"

"Until I am satisfied. I am going away. I have a residency at a theatre in Stoncastrum, not large, but not small either. Do not worry about me, I will not starve."

"You need new clothes."

"And I will buy them myself!" he said in exasperation.

"You are too proud."

"I will not see you for a few months."

"You will come to see me again?"

"I will. I promise. And that is one I can keep."

She nodded, but he was losing her again. Her eyes returned to the flowers, and when he embraced her she was looking at them, he knew.

He took his leave. He looked back before departing. Already his mother had her sleeves rolled back, holding out her arms for the flowers.

CHAPTER TWENTY-THREE
The Second Queen of Morthrocksey Mill

BREAKFAST AT THE Morthrocks became less uncomfortable. There was little intimacy to it, but conversation was easier. Katriona made efforts with her appearance. Demion was a man, of course, and no more likely to comment on her appearance than notice it. But such things had a powerful effect on men that they were only dimly aware of, simple creatures that they were. Today she wore a high-necked gown, and anguillon rib stays that pulled her figure in, and sleeves that came to laced points looped over her index fingers. Her hair she had arranged every week by one of the best hairdressers in the upper Var-side Karsa. The effect upon Demion was subtle but pleasing. At first Katriona had pursued this course quite cynically, but lately she was not so sure, finding herself flattered by the compliments he paid her.

Demion spoke about this and that. Rarely about the business, but when he did Katriona made the odd comment, then the odd suggestion, then the odd insistence, until a habit of proper dialogue had become established regarding the mill. Initially reticent, she engaged more enthusiastically with him as he showed interest. Things were going better than anticipated.

That particular morning they discussed plans that Holdean had for expanding the manufacture of pots and pans—a very modest ambition, Katriona thought, but would not say. She must handle this carefully, she thought. Instead she made sensible, if equally modest, proposals.

"You are sharp!" said Demion.

Katriona stared at the food on her plate. She and Demion had been married nearly three months. She was delaying, she knew, in case he said no, and her life turned out to be exactly what her father had wanted it to be.

She could not abide that.

She came to a decision. If she did nothing, then she would never know.

"My father insisted that all his children had a solid grounding in all the necessary fields of learning so that any of us might run his business," she ventured.

"A sensible man, a prudent one."

"Then you will know that I have extensive instruction in bookkeeping?"

"Why, I suppose you must."

Katriona felt belittled. His face held no trace of condescension, but her annoyance bloomed, she forced herself to speak calmly.

"I was wondering if I might take a look at the accounts? Holdean is awfully busy. I am sure I could be a great help to him." She held her breath without intending to.

"Why do you want to see them?" he said. "They're another thing I'm not very good at, I'm afraid. It's my father's misfortune I proved so useless."

She hated this self pity. "You lived," Katriona said.

"I did," he said. He smiled, somewhat remorsefully.

"There is no need to be sorry," she said. She had not meant to raise the ghost of Arvane between them, but her eyes prickled. "You cannot be sorry for being someone you are not."

He breathed deeply and looked out of the window. The sky was flat and oppressively bright.

"The accounts. Very well."

Katriona plunged on. "I really do think that if you would let me have a look at them, then I could offer something to the joint—"

Demion held up his hands. "Katriona, I am saying yes."

"Yes?"

"Yes! If you wish to look at them, I have nothing to hide. I'm afraid my debts are entirely visible."

Disarmed by this easy victory, she found herself at a loss for words.

Demion wiped his mouth and stood, but he did not ring for their maids. He paced about, and went to the doors, placing his hands on the knobs. They were fine pieces. Demion's mother had had a taste for pretty, elegant things. He opened the doors.

"I will have my copies of the latest ledgers brought."

"I have already taken the liberty of examining them."

Demion halted, his hands still on the doorknobs.

"I do hope you are not angry with me, husband. I must be occupied!" For all his reasonableness, she could not keep her frustration from her voice. "What am I to do all day while you are engaged with your friends? I cannot simply stay at home and mind the household. I am capable! I wish to see the company accounts. All of them."

"I see," Demion said. He looked as if for all the world he addressed his words to his mother's doorknobs.

He closed the doors softly again.

"You know, you can drop this pretence. This deferring to me. I think I have an inkling of what you are about. I said I am no monster. I have no pride to cosset. I love drink and song and cards. If I could make the mill work for me, I would. If you have any ideas how that might happen, share them with me, please. Don't be so coy."

She was taken aback. She had not expected this.

"I am sorry?"

"I surprise you! I am glad." A smile transformed his face and he returned to the table. "You see? You had your reasons for marrying me. Do you not think I had mine for marrying you?" He gave her a long, sad smile that moved her heart, just a touch, but it moved. "You're born engineers, every one of you. Your father is a fool not to see it in you. We are married now. Do you know what to do, here, with this, to make my family's—*our*—family's industry shine the way it once did?"

She nodded, flustered. Surely it could not be this easy.

Demion knelt beside her. "Katriona, I have loved you ever since we were children. I know you do not feel the same way about me. I suspected that you agreed only to marry me so that you might find yourself a meaningful role, a chance to run the industries your father trained you for but kept you from."

"I was a guarantee. If all my brothers had died..."

"But they did not. And here I am, a little inept, a little lazy, and I confess a lot in love with you. What an opportunity! For me, and for you."

He dared take her hand. She let him. She looked down at him, shocked. His face was soft with good living, lined with too many late nights. His hair was thinning, and he was round in the belly, but there was a kindness and regard in his eyes that she had never noticed before. She felt ashamed with herself.

"You are not angry?"

"No."

"You are not hurt?"

He shrugged. "I might become hurt. You are a sharp woman. Sharp knives are the best, but can cut those who wield them carelessly, as they say. I am resigned to that, should it come about. I am cleverer than I look, Katriona. I am a gambler, and not a bad one. It is, indeed, one of the few things I am good at. This is another gamble. I have taken a risk, that if I give you what you want, then perhaps you might find your way to loving me as I love you. I am not Arvane, and I never can be, but I do have qualities of my own. Give me a little time, and you will come to see them."

"You are serious about this?"

"Absolutely. You are your father's daughter."

Her face fell.

"I do not mean in that way! He is callous, you are kind. What I mean is that you are a Kressind, Katriona. Your father's name is the byword for shrewdness. You are his daughter. I have three sisters. What men think about women is the utmost rot. I can never make this mill work properly. Unlike you, I have only my father's vices, none of his qualities." He held her hand tightly. "Tell me what to do, and let's do it together."

"Well," said Katriona. She breathed out explosively, a sob and a laugh tumbled together. Her hand flew to her mouth, her face glowed with delight. "I have so many ideas!"

"I am sure you do."

"But they are for later. First, we have to go over the accounts."

"Can you tell me why this is so important? Holdean presents them to me twice yearly. "

"I have read them. They appear to be in order."

"There we are. We have an outside accountant go over them. I see nothing amiss."

"They appear to be in order," she repeated.

Demion became quizzical. "What do you think you have found?"

She shook her head. "I... I'd rather not say until..." She cast about for the right thing to say. "Do you trust me?"

"I have chosen to. Is my trust misplaced?"

"No. It is not," she said. "Then wait. It might be nothing, but..."

"It might be something."

"Yes. Now, we will not know if there is something or nothing to this if I do not see the company's original accounts."

"Very well. Insistent. I like that. You always were forthright of character." He laughed.

"What is so funny?" she said, laughing herself. A large part of it stemmed from relief, but not all. She laughed because he did, and took pleasure in the sharing.

"I am learning something from you already."

"Then learn some more. We have to see them today. And do not tell anyone."

"If that is what you recommend, my dear, then that is what we shall do."

* * *

KATRIONA STRODE INTO the accounting office of the Mothrocksey Mill unannounced, Tyn Lydar at her heels. Tall windows let in weak autumn sunlight, but it was sucked away by the heavy wooden furniture and dark panelling that covered the walls. It smelled of polish, ink, dust, and old sweat. The three men who staffed it looked up from their ledgers in shock. Two of the three were seated on long-legged stools at high desks. The third was exalted over the others by his desk's greater weight and the large carved canopy curled over it. This third wore a tall hat to denote his seniority as Chief Accountant.

"May we help you, goodlady?" one asked. He was pale, dark-suited in the garb of accountants. The Mothrocksey company arms and examination proof badge pins were heavy on his sash.

"Good day," she said. "I am Katriona Kressinda-Morthrocka," she began.

"We know who you are, goodlady." The most senior of the Mothrocksey accountants came down steps from behind his desk. He spoke quietly and with an urgency that suggested he wished Katriona to lower her voice.

"I am here to see the accounts," she said.

"You are in the right place," said the man with a nervous smile. Delicate hands fluttered in front of his chest. "But I am afraid all requests to see the company accounts have to come from Goodman Holdean Morthrock."

"You are Goodman Temosten?"

"I am. Chief Accountant to your husband, and master of these offices."

"Will permission from my husband do?" She had anticipated such obstruction, and insisted her husband sign a letter of intent before she had left home. She produced this now.

Temosten took it, unfolded it, read it. "Certainly," he said. "It certainly will." He licked his lips. They were thin and bloodless. The other two accountants gaped.

"Get back to work, Gotreid, Medullan," Temosten said gently. There was tension to his voice. He went to a cupboard and unlocked it with a key hung around his neck. Leather-bound ledgers lined shelves from floor to ceiling. "Here are the accounts, dating back some thirty years. If you wish to see earlier ledgers then we will have to take you into the archive."

"Is the archive where you keep the company receipts, bills, invoices and the like?" she asked.

"Of course," said Temosten. "Where else, goodlady?" He smiled at her unctuously.

She smiled back, genial but stern. "Then where else would I go? I wish to see all the raw materials, not the ledgers. Do not be concerned, I have already been over Goodfellow Morthrock's copy of the accounts at Morthrock Hall. But, on second thoughts, bring me the ledgers too. It will be useful to have them to hand when I begin so that I might compare them."

"A-all of them?" stammered Temosten.

"When did Goodfellow Horras Morthrock's spirit go on?"

"Five years ago," said Temosten. "Although I do not see why that is relevant."

"I think you do," said Katriona. "Bring those ledgers, and those for the year preceding Goodfellow Horras's passing."

Temosten stared at her. "Of course," he said. He could say little else. "Might I ask what you intend?"

"You may," said Katriona, who was enjoying herself. "I am to conduct an audit."

"But why?"

"This is my husband's company. I do not have to divulge my reasons. But I will indulge you. I am taking an interest."

"An interest," he repeated.

"That is correct."

"You realise, goodlady, that we cannot help you. My department is understaffed, we are behind as it is..." he trailed away apologetically.

She smiled harder. "That is completely understandable, goodman. I am, however, adequately qualified to perform an audit."

Temosten's eyes widened.

"My father," she said by way of explanation.

Temosten had not quite capitulated. "Very well, goodlady. If you could wait until tomorrow, I will ensure that..."

"Now," she said. "I will see them now. When I leave this office, you will be leading me to them. Is that not so?"

Temosten bowed with stiff dignity, defeated. "As you wish, goodlady."

KATRIONA AND TYN Lydar were led down a long corridor covered in a threadbare carpet. The building was cold, although winter was weeks distant. One of the junior accountants pushed a trolley full of the ledgers in front of them. Temosten led the way.

"Why are these offices empty?" asked Katriona. "Should there not be more than three accountants for a firm of this size?"

"There were," Temosten said. "But Goodman Holdean had them discharged from employment. Times are not what they were."

"It appears not," said Katriona. She said nothing more until they reached the company archive. The other accountant would be on his way to warn Holdean that very moment.

Temosten opened the door to the archives. A shadowy room full of overburdened shelves awaited her. He bowed again, showing her through the door.

"Thank you, Goodman Temosten. You may go."

He was surprised at that too. Katriona smiled inwardly. This was probably far from the day the accountant was expecting. "And leave the key," she said. He pressed it into her hand reluctantly.

They went inside. The afternoon was wearing on. Night was not far away, and the towering bookcases and heaps of paper crowded in, making the place gloomy. Katriona lit a lantern. They brought in the trolley, and locked the door behind them.

The archive was in a terrible mess, and she experienced the prevarication of someone who, intent on a task, is brought to a sudden halt by the unexpected scale of it.

"I am intrigued, goodlady," said Tyn Lydar mildly, "to learn what this is all about."

"I will tell you, Goodlady Tyn Lydar, because it is you."

"You do me a great honour, goodlady."

"This is a man's world, no matter the breed. We women must work in concert, or we will remain shut up in our drawing rooms. What concerns me, Tyn Lydar, is that Demion's company was among the most profitable ventures in the entire city of Karsa before Horras Morthrock passed on. And now it is not."

She surprised herself, how easily Demion's name came to her lips.

"You suspect some mismanagement?"

"What do you think?"

"I cannot say," said Tyn Lydar. A strange note crept into her voice. Katriona looked back at her. Lydar stared up, all innocence.

"You cannot say?" said Katriona, her eyes straying to the Tyn's iron collar.

"That is exactly what I said."

"Really now. Consider this, Tyn Lydar. I arrive here to find many workshops closed up, and yet according to my husband's copies of the ledgers, the mill is consuming the same amount of raw materials as it was when all the workshops were open."

Katriona held up her lantern. Weak candle light blended with insipid grey daylight. "The shelves get worse as we go in! Are they all this disordered?"

Tyn Lydar pulled at her sleeve, guiding her lamp away from a loose leaf of paper.

"Best be careful in here, Goodlady Kat."

"This lamp has a glass cover."

"Some things, goodlady, they are eager to burn." Her eyes begged comprehension from Katriona.

"You are driving at something. What?" She held her lamp up. "No glimmerlamps, though we can afford them, such disorder!" She looked at sheafs of paper tumbling from files, at stacks of receipts punched through by dull desk spikes. "Nothing in its right place. Why are there no glimmerlamps? Has it always been like this?"

Tyn Lydar bit her lip.

"Did someone remove them?"

"You might say that, goodlady."

"Someone wants this place to be vulnerable. Is that what you are saying. Is there an enchantment on this place?"

Tyn Lydar looked at her feet. "Might be."

"Who commanded it? That is the pertinent issue."

Lydar's face writhed in conflict. "I cannot say. Geas." She panted. It pained her to reveal that.

"I see. You are under geas as an employee of the Mothrocksey Mill?"

"I am under geas as its property," she said. For the first time, Katriona saw resentment in the creature's face.

"Someone has ordered your silence."

Tyn Lydar did not move.

"Was it Holdean?"

Again, Tyn Lydar did not move.

"I cannot order you to tell me, can I?" She crouched down before the Tyn.

"Your gown goodlady! The dust. It is so dirty here, you will ruin it..."

"Lost gods eat my gown!" she said. "I know a little of geas. Tell me if I am wrong. I cannot order you to confirm to me what I think we both know, because only the one who has placed a geas may remove it."

Tyn Lydar nodded. A small grunt escaped her lips.

"The penalty you are under is pain. I am sorry," said Katriona. She stood. "We will get to the bottom of this, you and I." She laughed sardonically. "What a ridiculous pair."

"There is, in the Watermarket, if I might be so bold as to say, a certain merchant of the Gallivar Tyn. Shifty they are. Their clan is scattered, their home is lost, and so they are not to be trusted. No surprise that they are dealers in the Waters of Truth." She fiddled with the tassels on the hem of her robe.

"Are you trying to get around a geas, Tyn Lydar?"

"Now why would you be saying that, goodlady? I am but a humble Tyn. I can do no more than I am allowed, and no less than that either." She tapped at her iron collar with a yellow fingernail. A nail one would find on a digging animal, thought Kat. "You won't get me trying to cheat. Rules is the rules. Geas is geas."

"Fine. Very well. You can tell me no more. I thank you for all that you have... intimated."

Lydar gave a sly grin, exposed her peg-like teeth. "I am very old, goodlady. Wise by the measure of some. It takes a lot to stop me from saying what needs to be said. But the rest is up to you. I may say no more."

Katriona sighed. "Fine. Fine, fine!" She picked up a file crammed untidily with papers. Dust flew thickly from it. She sneezed. She stared at it for a good long minute. "This task will not complete itself. Do we have glimmer lamps?"

"Yes."

Katriona nodded in understanding. "Then as the wife of the proprietor I am ordering you to find me some. There," she added. "Orders to bound Tyn are more successful the more precise they are. I am correct?"

"You are."

"I am going to get to the bottom of this."

Tyn Lydar nodded approvingly. "That you are, goodlady, that you are."

CHAPTER TWENTY-FOUR
The Water Market

GUIS TURNED UP his collar. Banksrow was situated perpendicularly to the coast, offering no barrier to the wind. Strong gusts blew right up between the palaces of finance situated either side, creating stinging eddies of dancing leaves and grit.

"There are inconsistencies within the books," Katriona confided in him. "Money is missing. It has been hidden, but not exceptionally well. I can see that it is gone."

Guis nodded. "Your love of numbers is doing you a service finally."

"If you paid as much attention to yours as I did, then you might have the same facility."

"Yes, well."

They walked arm in arm along pavements where everyone else hurried away from the wind, faces down, hats clamped to their heads.

"It is everywhere, I fear. The prices for certain of the raw materials we consume in our simpler manufacturing processes are inflated."

"How so?" said Guis. Department stores replaced the banks, and they stepped into warm pools of light streaming from high windows, behind which goods from across the Hundred were arranged.

"I will give you an example. We have our own smelter, yes? We buy in iron ore. This is marked down as three pennies more expensive per ton than the current base commodity price."

"You really did pay attention to father," said Guis.

"Shush! This is important. I checked guide pricing with the Bourse. The information cost a lot, but I had them send me adjusted figures for the trades of all the bulk items the mill uses for the period since Frozmer of 456."

"And?"

"Everything we have bought is overstated in price. Three pennies may not sound like a lot, and indeed it is not. But when aggregated over hundreds of tons of consumable materials, then it adds up to hundreds, perhaps thousands of thalers."

"Perhaps this cousin of Demion's is simply incompetent."

"I did think so, but I managed, shall we say, to secure copies of company accounts from other firms serviced by the same suppliers. The amounts we were charged are consistently higher."

"You do not know how much money has been taken?"

Katriona shrugged. "Not at present, no. It all rather depends on how long it has been going on."

"Who is behind it? Could it be Demion? Is he in trouble, Katriona?"

"I can't believe it for a second. Besides, he let me look at the accounts precisely, or so he says, because he believes that I am more astute with numbers than he."

"Does he want to be caught, perhaps?"

"Guis!" said Katriona. It was a tone of voice that was always accompanied by the rolling of eyes. "If he is trying to expiate his guilt, he is going about it in an extraordinarily roundabout manner."

"Be careful, sis, he may be trying to implicate you to save his own skin. His father acted like a kindly old duffer, but he was a cunning old devil."

"You have known my husband since he was seven. Do you really think Demion is capable of that?"

"Well, bluntly, no. Who are the other suspects? I like this, it is like a play."

Katriona bit her lip. "We have many Tyn working for us, but they have no use for money."

"They may be securing it for someone else."

"I am afraid the culprit is closer to home than that." Katriona sighed. She stopped and pointed over the busy street to the Watermarket. For five millennia, its squat shape and shallow dome had been the grandest edifice in all southern Karsa, presiding over the Old Maceriyan city, its ruins, the fields that followed them and the town that followed that. Now Prince Alfra's redevelopments cast their shadows over it, attempting to outdo it in every conceivable way. But their architectural exuberance could not compete with its venerable presence, coming off callow in comparison. It was a respectable matron surrounded by dandies.

"Let's go into the Watermarket. It's too noisy out here. I need to think."

"A weak excuse to go and buy a love philtre. Married only a couple of months, and already you are out to snare a younger lover!"

"You are insufferable," she said.

"So they say."

"I'm not laughing, Guis, not today. If I get this wrong..."

"I understand," he said. "You won't get it wrong. You're too bloody clever."

"Language!" she hissed. "We are not in one of your seedy little artists' dives now, brother."

"You are such a prude. That's not bad language."

"Guis..."

"Sorry, goodlady."

They waited for the traffic master on duty to halt the traffic, then streamed across the road with dozens of other people. Collectors of the pure took advantage of the break in the carts and charabancs, dodging between well-heeled feet to scoop up the large amount of dogshit all over the setts. Katriona raised a tuzzy-muzzy to her nose against its bitter scent.

They reached the other side. The traffic controller blew his whistle. Recognising it for the signal to depart, the dogs in their traces bayed and leapt forward without prompting from their drivers. A steam whistle blew in answer. There were more and more steam coaches on the road every month. They puffed white clouds alive with dancing blue sparks as they clattered along the road on legs and wheels and Shefirian fired-rubber tracks.

The Watermarket loomed over them. Huge arches, heavy and somewhat ugly by comparison to modern styles, strained under the mass of stone they supported. There was always a sense of great weight to the Watermarket, more than that of masonry. The antiquity of the place pressed down hard.

They passed inside and the noise of the street diminished immediately. The temperature was constant throughout the year. Inside it was cool and pleasantly damp—as much of a relief from the chill winds of autumn as it was from the freezing days of winter or the heat of high summer.

There were many pools within, some stacked in complex fans that rose most of the way to the domed roof. Water trickled over warn lips into the bowls below. Worn carvings of sea life and drowned men decorated their rims and sides. The Watermarket's original purpose was long behind it. The pools had once contained the only pure water in the city. Now they had fish in them. The real draw of the place were the shops, three arcades of them arranged around the building's circumference. They ranged from boutiques frequented by the highest born, to strange little dens known only to a select few, full of dusty jars and dried things of dubious origin and run by foreigners, Tyn and Ishmalani.

"This place always raises a smile," said Guis.

"Why?"

He craned his neck to look up at the dome. Large slabs of quartz were embedded into the concrete to let the light in. "Because it was built by the Old Maceriyans at the dawn of their power. And in this age when their works are so highly regarded and so often mimicked, it is derided for being insufficiently Maceriyan! It is all so very functional, it lacks the refinement of their later works, it is ugly... On and on, so they go. One should have a continuity, don't you think? This building is five thousand years old."

"I did know that."

"And do you know Fenk Kespser wanted to blow it up when he built Bankers' Row?"

"I did not. You shame my ignorance, brother."

"We each have our talents and interests. You stick with your numbers, I with my history. I am particularly amused and exercised by the true seeming of things. And Trassan told me. He and I share a mutual fascination with architecture."

She slipped her hand from the crook of his elbow.

"What are you looking for?"

She flashed a quick, distracted smile. "What do you mean, dear Guis?"

"I understand. I see now. You have come here for something. Was I right about the love philtre?"

"Now what made you think that?" She tugged his forearm. "This way!"

She pointed to a small store, its glass front obscured by stacked baskets of obscure goods.

Guis was dragged uncomplainingly within. There was a strange smell, musty, on the borderline between enticing and unpleasant. A shop for magisters. Ingredients for rituals, most of them surely bogus, were stacked from floor to ceiling or hung from the beams in tight bunches. A glass-topped counter somehow contrived to find space within, full of more brown, leathery arcane bric-a-brac. Tiny wooden drawers filled the wall behind the counter, a wooden ladder that appeared slippery with a century's accretion of polish and grease ran on rails to allow access to them all.

Between drawers and counter sat a hunched Tyn of a kind neither of them were familiar with. He had immense ears. From these issued tufts of white hair, dense as rushes. Three pairs of glasses sat on his long nose. He was bent over a book so far it appeared that he meant to literally digest it. He read aloud at such volume he did not hear them enter. Only when Guis passed a half dozen cages containing lesser Tyn did he look up, for they chattered and squealed at Guis's companion. Tyn eyed them warily from under Guis's hair.

"You are a carrier, goodfellow," said the Tyn shopkeeper. He had a nasal voice that vibrated in the ears in a way that makes a man twitch.

"Me?" said Guis. "I am."

"Looking for a new one? That one worn out? Geas too onerous?" The creature slid off his chair.

"No, goodtyn. I am here with my sister." Guis gestured at Katriona. She had been staring fixedly at the Tyn since they had entered. Only now did he deign to notice her.

"Goodlady," it said with a bow. "What's a lovely like you want with an old Tyn like me?" It licked its lips. Katriona took a step backwards.

"I require a draft of the Waters of Truth."

"Of course, dearie! You have come to the right place." It came out from behind its counter. It had a peculiar gait, a hobbling skip that accentuated the hump upon its back. The Tyn went to a large onion bottle in the window, full of bright blue liquid. He removed a glass stopper and reached for a measuring beaker of pewter hanging by a chain. "Whatever you need to uncover, a good drink of this will reveal the secrets you crave."

Katriona caught the Tyn's wrist. She bent down to whisper in the creature's large, hairy ear. "Tyn Lydar, Queen of the Morthrocksey Tyn is my confidante."

"That is nice, my lovely. What does it mean to me?" The Tyn affected breeziness. It could not hide its grimace.

"Do not play ignorance with me. I want the genuine article, not the coloured water you sell to lovesick youths or tourists."

"I have no idea what you..."

"Shlee mafana," she whispered.

The Tyn's eyes narrowed. It wagged its head from side to side and yanked its hand from Katriona's grip. "Bah! Very well." It replaced the stopper. "It will cost you, Katriona Kressinda-Morthrocka."

Katriona was not surprised it knew her name. "I will pay four times the price of whatever you were about to sell me, in gold."

The Tyn was back behind his counter. It bent low, fishing about underneath.

"That is not the payment I require and you know it."

"Be careful, Kat," said Guis. "Don't start bartering for magic with the Tyn. As soon as they are in a position to, they will laden you with conditions you can't hope to fulfil."

"I know that! And I know what kind of thing you will ask me for," she sad to the Tyn. "I will not grant you a day of my life, or a kitten's breath, or my ability to enjoy the act of sexual congress!"

"Sis!" said Guis, scandalised.

"That's a good one. Did one ask you for that?"

"No. It is an example."

"Uh-uh-uh," said the Tyn, waggling its head. He grinned lasciviously. "You're that kind of girl, eh? I'll remember that one."

"No double-dealing Tyn magic or impossible geas."

The Tyn looked shifty. "Alright, alright!"

Katriona smoothed down her dress. "Now, the price."

"Well," it said, placing a small, unremarkable vial of water on the glass counter with a chink. "It's a warning."

"You want me to warn you?" she said, confused.

"No! You will take a warning from me. Warnings are not a cost, they are a price. Is that a deal?"

"There seems to be no catch in that."

The Tyn became sympathetic. "Goodlady, you have to take the Waters of Truth no matter what the warning is. The point is that you will know what is fated, and it will cause you anguish until it happens. That is the cost of this magic. Tailored for you, as it must be."

"Very well."

"And I'll also take that gold you were talking about."

"The very nerve!"

The Tyn held out his broad, spatulate hands. "The money is for me. This is a shop. The magic needs what the magic needs, but I still need to eat." He looked at Guis. "Ask your brother. He knows."

Guis stared grimly back at the Tyn. It pouted and blinked back.

"Fine! Do it."

The Tyn held out the small vial of water. Clear water, a few flecks of dirt in it, not the shocking blue of the bottled stuff on display. He coughed. His eyes rolled back in his head, showing only the whites.

"There will come a time when you must either be kind to the Morthrocksey Tyn, or not. Either way, it will end in trouble for you."

"That's it?"

The Tyn's eyes rolled back. He shook his head violently, making his ears flap. He dribbled, coughed hard, groaned and wiped his hand across his lips.

"You bet. But you have to take this, and you have to use it as you intended. Mark my words, only the use you had in mind! Not some other clever notion that might pop into that pretty goodlady head of yours." He leered.

"And if I don't? If your warning sends me shrieking for the hills and I dispose of this in the river?"

"You laugh about it now, goodlady, you won't once what I have said sinks in." It pulled a face. "You tall kado are so sure of yourselves. You might think of pouring that away. But don't you dare! You do and it'll be a hundred times worse. Magic's price, my lovely. Magic's price."

The Tyn gave Guis another long look.

"Come on," he said, taking his sister's elbow. "Let's get out of here."

She handed over a gold thaler, and Guis guided her out. They passed back into the quiet of the arcade.

"Who told you about this place?"

"One of my employees," said Katriona. "Why?"

Guis looked back. He half expected the shop to be gone. "That Tyn, he was not wearing a collar."

"So? If he has no collar, he can in all probability never leave that shop."

"You have to be careful round the free ones, they're almost as dangerous as the Wild Tyn."

"There are no Wild Tyn in all the isles of Karsa."

"Even so..."

"I understand," she said. "Better than you. You shouldn't make any distinction. They're all dangerous, brother dear. Every last one."

* * *

337

THEY LEFT THE Watermarket quickly, Katriona's purchase hidden at the bottom of her clutch bag.

"I say, I say! Goodlady Katriona? Is that you? Is that Goodfellow Guis?"

Guis pushed his sister on. "Keep going," he said.

Katriona did not heed her brother, but stopped before they got to the kerb of the road.

"Countess Mogawn!" she exclaimed.

"It is you! How delightful." The Hag was wearing a candy-striped suit favoured by the glamour boys of Perus this year. A monocle filled her left eye socket, a matching fascinator decorated with the emblems of the lost goddess Alcmeny sat on her head.

Katriona curtsied. "An intriguing outfit," she said.

"Isn't it? I asked my tailor to make me the most outrageous outfit he could. He came up with this. Terrible, isn't it? But absolutely perfect. I have a reputation to damage, after all."

Both women laughed. Guis thought she was trying too hard to shock.

A pair of servants puffed in the countess's wake under the burden of many bags and boxes.

"You're lucky to catch me. I must be back to Mogawn before midnight, when the causeway will cover over for the next week or so. My coach will be here in a moment. I've been shopping. I don't come to town often during the day. I'm more of a night owl myself." She ladled implication onto her statement. Katriona blushed. "Much fun to be had in Karsa of an evening. Although, my work of late has kept me from the city. That's the advantage of marriage, I suppose. If there is one." She smiled. "Forgive me. It is a blessed state, but not one for me. How is old Demion? Such a gentle soul, if a

"Well," it said, placing a small, unremarkable vial of water on the glass counter with a chink. "It's a warning."

"You want me to warn you?" she said, confused.

"No! You will take a warning from me. Warnings are not a cost, they are a price. Is that a deal?"

"There seems to be no catch in that."

The Tyn became sympathetic. "Goodlady, you have to take the Waters of Truth no matter what the warning is. The point is that you will know what is fated, and it will cause you anguish until it happens. That is the cost of this magic. Tailored for you, as it must be."

"Very well."

"And I'll also take that gold you were talking about."

"The very nerve!"

The Tyn held out his broad, spatulate hands. "The money is for me. This is a shop. The magic needs what the magic needs, but I still need to eat." He looked at Guis. "Ask your brother. He knows."

Guis stared grimly back at the Tyn. It pouted and blinked back.

"Fine! Do it."

The Tyn held out the small vial of water. Clear water, a few flecks of dirt in it, not the shocking blue of the bottled stuff on display. He coughed. His eyes rolled back in his head, showing only the whites.

"There will come a time when you must either be kind to the Morthrocksey Tyn, or not. Either way, it will end in trouble for you."

"That's it?"

The Tyn's eyes rolled back. He shook his head violently, making his ears flap. He dribbled, coughed hard, groaned and wiped his hand across his lips.

"You bet. But you have to take this, and you use it as you intended. Mark my words, only you had in mind! Not some other clever notion might pop into that pretty goodlady head of yours." He leered.

"And if I don't? If your warning sends me shrieking for the hills and I dispose of this in the river?"

"You laugh about it now, goodlady, you won't once what I have said sinks in." It pulled a face. "You tall kado are so sure of yourselves. You might think of pouring that away. But don't you dare! You do and it'll be a hundred times worse. Magic's price, my lovely. Magic's price."

The Tyn gave Guis another long look.

"Come on," he said, taking his sister's elbow. "Let's get out of here."

She handed over a gold thaler, and Guis guided her out. They passed back into the quiet of the arcade.

"Who told you about this place?"

"One of my employees," said Katriona. "Why?"

Guis looked back. He half expected the shop to be gone. "That Tyn, he was not wearing a collar."

"So? If he has no collar, he can in all probability never leave that shop."

"You have to be careful round the free ones, they're almost as dangerous as the Wild Tyn."

"There are no Wild Tyn in all the isles of Karsa."

"Even so..."

"I understand," she said. "Better than you. You shouldn't make any distinction. They're all dangerous, brother dear. Every last one."

* * *

little dull. I have always secretly held that he could be instructed to please a woman if given enough tuition."

"Countess!" gasped Katriona. She was pretending outrage. She had a smile of a kind Guis had only seen once or twice before on her face.

"Oh come now, don't tell me you are one of those old frumps? We were made to take pleasure in love, more so than men. That is why they try to deny it us. If I am regarded as shocking it is almost solely because of my embracing of this one, fundamental truth. And you, Guis. You seemed eager to come to Mogawn when we spoke at your sister's wedding some three months ago. Have you decided not to visit? You never replied to my invitation."

"A terrible lapse on my part, countess. I have been meaning to reply."

"Of course," she said, fully aware of the lie. "The life of a writer must be full of incident and drama. Where else would you find your inspiration?" Her eyes were provocative. "My invitation stands. I would dearly like to host you. I realise that there is a certain stigma attached to my company in refined circles, but I have much that you would like to see. My work is genuinely fascinating. I had heard you were something of a polymath."

"I read a little."

"You must not read, dear goodfellow! You must *experience*. Come to me, and I will show you the stars."

"Of course."

"Besides, I find you fascinating. Shall we say in three weeks? The final week of Frozmer is a fine time to be on Mogawn. Cold, but spectacular. If the ocean is generous enough to give us a calm night, there is no better time to practise astronomy. And other arts."

She gave him a long, lingering grin.

"I will be in Stoncastrum until the twenty-third of Coldbite," he said.

"Then come then. It is uncommonly cold then, but if anything the skies are clearer. There!" she clapped her hands. "It is settled. I will send for you. A coach. Bring warm clothes. As I said, Mogawn is cold that time of year."

Guis could not refuse without severe embarrassment. The necessity to agree neatly outdid his annoyance that she had bedded Qurion. And he realised that he wanted to go.

"Very well," he said. "I shall attend Mogawn on the twenty-seventh, if I may. I have matters to deal with here first."

"Better and better, for the Twin nears the end of his approach then. Until the twenty-seventh. Goodlady, goodfellow," she inclined her head. Guis bowed.

The countess's coach arrived, pulled by six dogs, heads crowned with plumes in her family colours. She got in. Her servants piled her boxes and bags onto the roof, and secured them under a tarpaulin. The dogs were well-trained, and pulled the coach away silently.

"My my," said Katriona.

"What?" said Guis.

"She really was not letting you back out of that now, was she?"

"What of it?" said Guis.

She gave him an impudent look. "She has her hooks into you, brother dear."

"I have no idea what you are talking about."

"Oh, absolutely not." She elbowed him in the ribs.

CHAPTER TWENTY-FIVE
Feast at the Fort

REL'S LIFE SETTLED into a dull routine. His training continued, and that he enjoyed, in spite of, or perhaps because of, Major Mazurek's unorthodox methodology. But much of his time was taken up with tedious sentry duties, the endless servicing of equipment and the writing of reports that said essentially that there was nothing to report.

The views from the walls were splendid, less enjoyable in the biting wind of late autumn. And such an autumn. To Rel it felt colder than the depths of winter. Snow crept lower and lower down the mountains. By the time Coldbite sank its teeth into the steppe, Rel thought he might die. He was provided a firebowl for his room, but the glass of the walls sucked away any heat that it provided. Most days it was cold enough to freeze his ink in its pot. The unglazed window let in the full ferocity of the weather. Inquiries after a shutter were met with laughter. He stoppered the gap with rags, but it did little to stop the cold. He came to regard it as a bitter irony that in a fort made of glass, there was none for the windows. He regretted not bringing more clothing, and spent what little funds he had on a heavy fur coat that he took to living in.

The one warm time of day was during the evening meal. Breakfast was a freezing affair with miserable food. But by evening the refectory had ample time to warm, fired by the heat of the kitchens underneath. Rel was very glad of this, as it was the custom of the garrison to turn out in full dress uniform to dinner and he had to leave his fur in his room. Dinners were a parade of bright colours and ostentatious buttons, presided over by Colonel Estabanado and his senior officers, all also in their pomp. Even Major Mazurek made an effort. An entire table had to be set aside to hold their hats while they ate.

It was at one of these meals that Rel was finally introduced to Kalesh Jakkar. Rel had struck up a friendship with the garrison's warlock, a blue-skinned Amarand by the name of Deamaathani. Amarands had a reputation for licentiousness and dishonesty. On at least one of those counts, Rel figured he probably could claim no moral superiority, and Deamaathani was personable, lively, and infinitely curious.

Veremond too provided a ready source of companionship. Inevitably their relative rank precluded true friendship. There was no such issue with Deamaathani.

Rel was sitting with Veremond at table, but it was Deamaathani who was responsible for introducing him to Jakkar. He performed his social function with a twinkle in his eye. Veremond groaned and ran his hand down his face when he saw who the warlock had brought to join them.

"Rel, may I introduce to you Kalesh Jakkar, the fort engineer, and unofficial archaeologist."

By his side Deamaathani had a small, round man whose face was mostly occupied by beard. Long and full to the middle of his chest, it crept most of the way up his cheeks, and all of the way down his neck. Those parts of his face that were not covered in this black thicket were overshadowed by eyebrows hairier than caterpillars. Grey eyes peered out, fiercely accusing whatever they lit on, though of what none knew. The hair on his head was similarly black, but there was less hair on his scalp than his face, the top being shiny bald, the hair, though long, confined to a wild sweep around the perimeter. What skin there was on display was ruddy, and growing more florid by the moment in the heat of the refectory.

The man held out a thick-fingered hand knurled with calluses, dark and dirty as a Tyn's.

"They sent me a Kressind, marvellous. There's much work to be done. I am responsible for the obelisks, along with all my other duties. It is good to have another engineer. You will help me."

"Charmed, I'm sure," said Rel. "And I am Rel Kressind, pleased to meet you."

"I know that," said Jakkar sharply. "Don't tell me you stand on all that ceremony." Jakkar turned to Deamaathani, his brows bristling even more. "You told me he was a good sort, not another popinjay more concerned with seating plans than battle plans! You deceived me. Ah, such is the Amarand character. Deceitful!"

"There is no deceit, he is a good sort. Saying hello pleasantly is not an unnecessary social adornment!" said Deamaathani sternly, although he was grinning.

"Bah," said Jakkar. He pushed himself onto the bench next to Rel. Rel moved up and Deamaathani took the seat to his left.

"He and I often eat together," explained Deamaathani. "He's been out for the last three months."

"Yes, yes," said Jakkar. "Inspections. Repairing, and where I can, cataloguing." He said this last like a challenge. "The obelisks."

"Well. I'm sorry to disappoint you," said Rel. "I suppose you're referring to my father's reputation."

"Yes, yes, what else? A Kressind aren't you? You have the type! Renowned engineers, every one." His stare challenged any of them to disagree.

"Not me, I'm afraid," said Rel. "I never really got the knack. I'm afraid you want my brothers and sister for that kind of thing."

"Oh, well. Useless. Never mind." Jakkar helped himself to a large portion of food from the pot in the middle of the table, one of six dotted at regular intervals the length of the board. Rel took rather less. The pomp of mealtimes at the fort was overblown as a coronation, but the food was simple soldier's fare.

"More beans," Rel said. "Marvellous."

"Do not dismiss the humble bean!" said Jakkar. He was fat enough that Rel reckoned Jakkar never dismissed foodstuffs of any kind. "It is full of much nutriment."

"They do little to kindle the appetite," said Veremond sadly.

"Jakkar has a great many interests," explained Deamaathani. "The proper maintenance of the human body among them. He is the best read man in this fort."

"I am the best read man for five hundred miles!" he protested. "Where's the bread? Bread! Bring me some bread." He shook his head disappointedly.

Rel leaned in close to Deamaathani. "He's an odd fellow."

"A lot of them are here," said Deamaathani. "Are you any different?"

Rel shrugged. "I cannot judge myself. That's for others."

"What?" said Jakkar. "What are you good for?"

"I haven't really decided," said Rel. "It was always intended that I go into the army, as befitted the fifth son of a true noble."

"But your father is a title buyer," said Jakkar.

"He is a real social climber."

"A title?" said Veremond, perking up. "I didn't know of this! That makes you a lord."

"Not me. My brother though. He will be Lord Kressind when father passes."

"I'll have to call you goodfellow and sir," said Veremond wryly. "You are nobility."

"You have to call me that anyway, Veremond, I *do* outrank you."

"Fair point. *Sir.*"

"Another soldier!" said Jakkar, as if only then noticing Rel's uniform. "We don't need more soldiers. We need more scholars!"

"The colonel does not agree," said Veremond. Jakkar gave him a black look.

"The colonel is short-sighted." The clattering of knives and spoons on pewter plates, the hubbub of voices and the fragile, edged quality that the glass walls lent to the sound made it hard to catch what the man opposite you was saying, but Jakkar spoke with such loudness that Rel glanced worriedly at Estabanado, sure he must have heard. "Look at this place!" Jakkar raised his hands and cast his eyes upwards. The others could not help but follow. For a moment Rel took in the soaring vaulting over their heads, made like everything else in the fort from seamless black glassy stone. "A world of wonders around us, and it is treated as a common barracks!"

"Come now, Jakkar," said Deamaathani. "This is not a common barracks. The place is full of disgraced lordlings. It is a fascinating place. There is no better collection of military uniforms in all of Ruthnia. It is a fine display. And then there is the interplay of character and etiquette. It is truly fascinating to watch. I could do it all day, I could. Look!" Deamaathani sucked his spoon clean and pointed it across at another table. "The military attaché from Macer Lesser will not sit with the attaché from Maceriya. Both of them vie for the friendship of the military attaché from Marceny. But, and here's the thing, the Maceriyan is a captain, the Marcenian is a lieutenant, and therefore believes that the lieutenant should be courting his attention."

"Why? Is the Marcenian some beauty?" joked Rel.

"The only beauties here are from the Queendom, and they keep to themselves," said Deamaathani. "The Maceriyan successors' kingdoms' shy wooing of one another is not about mutual affection. There's trade rights at the root of all that."

"Aren't these people here to be soldiers?" said Rel.

"Half of them are, the rest are sent with a whole library of orders to pursue. If you want an education in the application of national interest within the Hundred, then this is the place to be," said Deamaathani. "Deals are struck here. It is one of the few places that so many different nations mingle without the restrictions experienced at the Assembly of Nations. A delightful paradox—these men are all here for some minor misdemeanour or other, and yet they are given sensitive tasks that would stretch a diplomat. They try very hard, of course. All of them would much rather be somewhere warmer."

"Some of them are diplomats, I am sure," said Rel.

"There are a few," said Deamaathani. "You can tell; those are the ones the real soldiers will not speak with."

"I find it all immensely complicated, and therefore tedious," said Rel.

"You think the Maceriyan triad complicated? "said Deamaathani gleefully. "The various rankings and intrigues of the Oberlanders outmatch that by far. Listen, I am a master of the seventh magisterial art. I am equally well versed in true magecraft. I can imbue steel with will, bind fiends from the fifth hell to my command, and softly fry you where you sit with a gesture like that." He snapped his fingers decisively. "And I find their squabbles incomprehensible."

"I became a soldier to avoid complicated issues such as this."

"Really? You call seducing the wife of your commanding officer's close friend uncomplicated? You are more stupid than you appear," said Deamaathani. Veremond chuckled.

"I probably am," admitted Rel. "I trade a lot on my looks."

Deamaathani grinned. "Fine they are too."

"Really," said Rel, snapping his fingers. "Like that?"

"It takes a little more effort than just that," Deamaathani snapped his fingers again. "But I can do as I say, so tread carefully my friend."

"I always thought magisters were dry, dusty academics," said Rel. Deamaathani was anything but; young, vital and muscular as the soldiers.

"I am a warlock, a battle wizard," said Deamaathani. They all grinned at the ridiculous title. "Estabanado has me sending his messages because there is no one else with the talent to do so, unless you count that dried up old witch in Railhead, but it is not the pinnacle of my ability."

"There's not much money in all that fairy-tale stuff, is there?" said Rel. "That's what I heard."

"There are more remunerative branches of my calling, but nothing can match the feeling of raw power that manipulating wild magic in battle can bring."

"But you are a magister." said Rel. "Not a follower of the Iapetan School."

"It is possible to follow the new tradition and respect the old. Few of my colleagues accept this, but there is wisdom inherent in both paths. That is why I am here. It is an unpopular philosophical standpoint at the university."

"I wish you had arrived earlier sir," said Veremond. "He's never been so candid."

"I find him fascinating," said Jakkar. "And I am bored. I bore easily. Easily! You people are no stranger to magic, surely captain. Karsa is overrun by Tyn."

"I suppose so," said Rel. "I never really thought about it. They are just *there*."

"There are more Tyn there than you can believe," said Veremond. "Have you ever been to Karsa?"

"No," said Deamaathani.

"You see them everywhere, as workers, servants. Shopkeepers! I was rather scared when I was there the first time."

"So you should be," said Deamaathani. "There is one forest in Amaranth where Wild Tyn are reputed still to dwell. Nobody ever goes in there, because if they do, it is reputed that they do not come out again. It is not true, sadly. I went within its borders and found no Tyn."

"They don't like to be found unless they wish to be found," said Veremond darkly.

"I've never had any trouble," said Rel. "My tailor is a Tyn. He's always in his shop."

"In your land the Tyn live among you. Elsewhere, they are the subject of fear. Have you never thought why?" said Deamaathani.

"There was a king or somesuch. It's just a legend. I mean, they're just there. People, like you and I."

"They are not," said Veremond.

"You listen to your grandmother overly much," said Rel.

"Tyn. Interesting," said Jakkar. "But the Morfaan are the most interesting. The Tyn are woodland creatures, little better than beasts. They have never built, never triumphed, they simply are, tied to rock or stream or tree. And so they fall before those who are not, who do build and who do triumph and who can leave such ridiculous impedimenta behind. The true culture of this world was Morfaan. It has not been bettered. Nor will it be. I will prove it."

Veremond leaned back to get up. "Excuse me, sir. I need to make water." Veremond took his chance to whisper to Rel as he got up from the table. "Watch out for Deamaathani, sir, he's getting very friendly. You know what they say about the blues." He clapped Rel on the shoulder and departed, for the moment.

Deamaathani gave him a long look over his spoon. Rel coloured and, in desperation, plunged back into Jakkar's conversation.

"You may have something there." Rel said to Jakkar. "I thought the Morfaan ruins of Perus were impressive, but this..."

"The remains there are ruins, as you say. This is a living building, even if it is used as a barracks. Once mighty, there remains but a pair of Morfaan alive in this world. We have much to learn from their culture's remains. This place should be one of study. Not this ludicrous social display."

"We guard the way," said Rel.

"Your oath? Nonsense. There has been no credible threat from the Black Sands for three hundred years. The modalmen are depleted, the Uncertain Provinces of the sands pinned in place by the webs of iron. It is time we stopped being fearful of the past and investigate it for our betterment," Jakkar said.

"Jakkar is impatient, he feels he will die before the great age of discovery begins," said Deamaathani.

"Why don't you speak with the Morfaan themselves? They are on the Council of Nations."

"It is a sop to the past. The Morfaan have no power," said Jakkar. "The two that remain know nothing."

"You have met them?"

Jakkar nodded. "Twice. In secret, and it was hard to arrange. They are ignorant of the arts of their ancestors. Ceremonial. Adornment. They have the understanding of children."

"In what way?" asked Rel, genuinely interested in the face of Jakkar's brusque manner.

"Ask a human child how a glimmer engine works, would he know?"

"I suppose not."

"Do you?"

Rel waved his hand and pulled a face. "The generalities, yes."

"The specifics? Could you, goodman"—Deamaathani smiled at Jakkar's incorrect form of address. Rel suspected it was deliberate. Jakkar went on, waggling his spoon at Rel and spilling the gravy from his stew on the table—"build one?"

"No."

"And you are the son of the great Gelbion Kressind, brother to Arkadian Vand's pupil, and an adult to boot. So it is with the Morfaan. Children. I need practicality, pure knowledge!"

"My father says it is our turn now," said Rel. "Perhaps we should go our own way.

"Ah! That is why we should study the past. Your father would do well to remember what happened to the Morfaan."

"Nobody knows, surely?"

"They could do things we could not. Their artefacts defy the passage of time. They possessed a civilisation that if we could piece it together, all would see that it dwarfs our own. And yet they are no longer masters of this place. That should tell us all we need to know. This desert before us? Rich in remains. It is my hypothesis that the Black Sands were once, long ago, not a desert at all, but a rich land. We look to Old Maceriya for the centre of the Morfaan civilisation, but that is a remnant, nothing more. The last stronghold, a guttering torch passed on to the Old Maceriyan Empire by a dying people, before their light went out. I theorise that their homeland might have been here, in the sands."

"The desert is no place to live," said Veremond, returning to the table.

"Destroyed. In war," said Jakkar shortly. "Made unfit for life by weaponry and arts we could not comprehend. One must not underestimate the age of this place, nor the power of those who built it. This material, the glass of the Glass Fort. Impossible to cut, break or shape. But you have seen the ruins on the opposite cliff?"

"Yes," said Rel. He shifted uneasily. "I admit the question has bothered me: what did it?"

"Just so!" said Jakkar, jabbing his spoon again at Rel. "We are children playing in the burned palaces of our fathers. The Morfaan are a warning to us. We should heed it."

"Against what?" asked Rel. "They are no more."

"It is not them we should fear," said Jakkar.

"Then what is your warning against?"

Deamaathani smiled a humourless smile. "Hubris."

CHAPTER TWENTY-SIX
A Thief Uncovered

"AND HERE. THERE are changes to be made here." Katriona ran her fingers over a fine pen and ink diagram of the interior of the mill.

"This is a large change to the interior layout of a workshop," said Demion doubtfully.

"It is. I have been following the work of Thortha Bannda of Iruz. He came to the city last week and I attended his lecture." Katriona said.

"I had no idea he was here."

"He has gone now. Most fascinating." She pointed to a slim book. "His work."

"You propose to apply it to the mill?"

"I do."

"All the mill? His is a much smaller enterprise."

"It is, but he has proven it works, I see no reason why not take his procedures and amplify them in scale."

Demion cleared his throat in embarrassment. "You will have to apprise me more fully. I am unfamiliar with his thinking."

Katriona patted his arm. "Of course. Bannda proposes the institution of a line of assembly to quicken the industrial process. As we have it, this assembly of one thing by one worker from beginning to end is not a clever a use of their time."

"How so?"

"A Tyn or man has to know every step in the process. This requires time to learn. Moving from one set of tools to another takes time. Collecting multiple parts and materials in one place takes time. And if the worker leaves or dies, then training a replacement takes—"

"Time, yes, yes, I see. But what is the alternative?" Demion bent over the diagram.

"As depicted here. A long table, one that runs the length of the workshop. Each worker is responsible for one step and one step alone of the assembly process. That part done, the article is passed to the worker to their right, who completes the next step, and then onto another, who completes a third. Parts and pieces are delivered by others in bulk, all the same type. Each worker therefore requires only one set of tools, they do not need to reconfigure their bench for each task, and do not need to leave their place."

"All the parts and pieces are delivered separately?"

"Yes."

"What if they do not fit together?"

"They must be made to fit together. I have here," she dug under the papers and pulled out a sheaf of paper bound in cheap cardboard, "the most up-to-date rulings of Karsan weights and measures. If we adopt these fully, so that one tenth of an inch is the same whosoever might make a part or piece, we might standardise our components fully."

"Nobody fully applies those, it takes too much time."

"The reason they were proposed, my husband, is that they are efficient. Once the initial time is spent, much time will be saved."

Demion scrutinised the plans again. "The work will be repetitive. I don't know, Katriona. The assembly workers are among our best. Bored workers can become fractious."

"That is the beauty of this process. It can be performed by those of limited intellectual capacity. They can be gainfully employed, to our and their mutual benefit. Those of greater ability can train the others, and I also intend to move them periodically from one part of the process to the next, so forestalling boredom. The other processes in the factory will still require great skill; the smelter, the tooling shops, some of the finishing, all that. The lathes, grinders, bores and all else require setting precisely. All these are skilled tasks. The most able could be trained in multiple roles. When this succeeds, we will need to expand our operations, after all. But it is here, at the final stage where the parts are gathered and assembled, laboriously, that we experience a bottleneck. This plan will remove that, allowing us, I estimate, to increase production three or four times over. Even our most complicated articles, the glimmer engines, can be assembled in this way."

Demion pulled at his bottom lip.

"There are other benefits. Should an engine we sell to a client fail, a new part, exactly matching the old, can be sent to them. It is an incentive, husband, to buy our manufactures. With greater precision too comes the possibility of finer, more efficient engines. Don't you see how this will ensure our future prosperity?"

Demion thought a long moment. "Do it," he said. "Let's try it. Anything to improve our finances. I think you might be on to something here."

Katriona's secretary knocked and popped his head around the door. "Begging your pardon, goodfellow, goodlady, Goodman Holdean's here."

"Ah!" said Katriona. "Send him in, Hollivar."

"Right you are. Shall I have the tea brought in?"

"Please."

"Are you ambushing me? I feel ambushed. This is going to be very awkward for me." Demion cracked his knuckles.

"I do not shy away from my duties, nor should you. But I am not attempting to outmanoeuvre you, husband. There is something I must ask Goodman Holdean. We were speaking of finances. Better practice is not the sole answer to those," she said to Demion. "I believe he can shed some light on that matter."

Holdean came in, holding his hat respectfully in front of him. His hair had been greased and lay flat in last year's fashion. He was surprised to see Demion with Katriona.

"Good day, Goodman Holdean," said Katriona.

"Goodlady, goodfellow."

"Goodfellow Morthrock and I were discussing my new plans for the factory."

"Your plans, goodlady?" He looked at them. "I do not recognise the draughtsmanship."

"It is mine," she said.

"You drew these?"

"Yes, they are my plans."

In came Katriona's secretary bearing a tray with the accoutrements of tea drinking upon it. Demion cleared a space on Katriona's desk. Hollivar set the tray down and withdrew.

"Tea, Goodman Holdean?"

"Yes, yes I will." Holdean looked to Demion. "Goodfellow Morthrock, forgive me, but I am not completely certain of your intention. The factory is my responsibility. You yourself appointed me."

"I did, cousin, but Katriona has some very fine ideas," said Demion. "We should be open to new ideas."

"I thought she was looking into the accounts?"

"She was. It has rather gone beyond that now."

Holdean paled. His hands shook as he drank his tea.

"Goodfellow Morthrock... Demion. My position...?"

"Nothing to worry about man! You and Katriona will have to work together, that is all. You still have my trust."

Katriona smiled encouragingly. Holdean relaxed visibly. "Well then. Well! That is a relief."

"You thought your position in peril?"

"I don't like to say, Goodfellow Morthrock," he said. He gave a nervous chuckle. "My, oh my!" He took a drink of tea. Katriona did the same.

"I am glad that you are comfortable with Katriona's appointment. There will be some changes around here, for the better, I am sure of it!"

Holdean obviously wasn't happy, but he was smart enough not to say.

"You aren't happy about it, are you, Holdean?" said Katriona.

"Oh no, not at all! It is not right, if you ask me. Women are all well and good, but the female brain is simply not suited for business. Do you know, they are actually smaller than men's? The seat of intellect being smaller, then surely the intellect must be smaller also."

"I say there, steady on, Holdean!" spluttered Demion. "That's my wife you're talking to."

Katriona held up her hand.

"Are you taking money from the company, Holdean?"

"Yes I am," he answered wholeheartedly, although his face displayed utter horror. "I have been since Mester Morthrock appointed me."

"And how exactly have you been doing this?" Katriona said pleasantly. She held her tea up to her lips, but did not drink.

"It was very easy," he said enthusiastically even as his eyes bulged and rolled in panic. "Demion is not at all interested in the business, and I have been able to take his money as easily as if he dropped it in the street! I have been making deals with our suppliers, purchasing goods at normal market rates, but securing receipts for inflated prices and pocketing the difference. And entering into the books that I have been buying far more than I actually have." He looked helplessly at Demion. He tried to stand.

"Sit down," said Katriona icily.

Demion's knuckles whitened on the chair arms and he half rose, but he could not stand. The cords on his neck stood out with the effort, his face reddened.

"There you have it," said Katriona. "Really, Demion, did you not question where the money was going? Why this profitable industry had become suddenly unprofitable?"

"Is this true?" asked Demion.

"Oh absolutely, Goodfellow Morthrock." Holdean gritted his teeth to keep the words in. They escaped, somewhat strangled, but sincere and warm. "You are so blind it was almost too easy."

"By the blazes!" Demion looked from his cousin to his wife. "Why did you confess?"

"That is good tea, isn't it?" asked Katriona.

"It is delicious, goodlady."

"It is made with the finest Ocerzerkiyan herbs. And the Waters of Truth." She flung hers into the pot of the large plant behind her desk.

Demion looked in shock at his tea. "That's illegal!"

"So is defrauding your employers. All the worse that it is family who are robbed. If one betrays one's kin, who can one turn to? A sad aphorism, I always felt, and one unfortunately that Goodman Demion here will soon learn the truth of. Now, one final question. Who aided you in this venture?"

Holdean blurted a list of names. Unable to prevent himself from speaking, he said them quickly, but Katriona was ready and noted them all down. Four of Demion's own employees, including all three accountants, and six more in other firms.

"Thank you very much, Goodman Holdean. That will be all. You are released."

Holdean let out a cry and fair sprang to his feet. Red-faced, he waved his hat and shouted.

"What are you going to do? Discharge me and I'll let everyone know that you have Demion on a leash. He'll be the laughing stock of Karsa."

"Do so," said Katriona, "And I will inform everyone of your perfidy. You will be outcast and destitute."

"We'll see!" he said. "We'll see!"

"I think you should be going now, Holdean old boy," said Demion quietly.

Katriona called through the door. "Hollivar! Have Goodman Holdean escorted from the premises. He is not to stop or speak with anyone."

"Right you are, goodlady," called the secretary. Katriona had had three of the factory watchmen standing by. They were in the office in an instant. They grabbed Holdean's elbows. He tried to shake them off, but they held fast. His hat dropped from his hands and rolled upon the rug. They did not allow him to retrieve it.

"You'll not get away with this," said Holdean.

"I think you will agree that I have got away with this, and rather that it is you that did not. Good day, Goodman Holdean. Take him away," said Katriona.

Holdean did not go quietly. His shouted imprecations echoed down the corridor.

"So sad that men must resort to such crudity when they are confounded," said Katriona.

"Well, well," said Demion. "You, you are shaking all over! My dear, sit down!" Demion pulled out a chair for his wife. She sank gratefully into it.

"Such an interview is very bad for the nerves, husband."

"I thought you unaffected."

"Not so."

He took her hand. "Did you drink the tea?"

"Yes."

"Then I will ask you a question."

"Oh?" she raised her eyebrow, but made no attempt to stop him.

"Do you think you could ever love me?"

She did not answer immediately, but stared deep into his expectant eyes. Hope brimmed in them. "Perhaps," she said eventually. "Perhaps."

CHAPTER TWENTY-SEVEN
The Revelation

459 PROVED TO be a very cold year in Karsa.

The clouds of the Islands retreated, leaving the sky open to gimlet stars. In the cities, and in Karsa City in particular, their lights were dimmed by the smoke of factories. But these smogs were short lived and the clouds remained away. By late Frozmer, the year's uncommon rains were a distant memory. The mornings were frosty, the nights cold. The fifth week of the month saw the first snow of the year. It blew in from the southeast in wet flurries that disappeared as soon as they touched the ground. Not unusual in the isles, perhaps, but it caused the old folk to mutter charms against Father Winter, and spit and complain to whoever would listen that it was never this bad in the old days.

No one listened, for they said the same thing every year.

The more provocative broadsheets carried warnings of dire weather to come, foreseen by those magisters who dabbled in meteorology. Snow glimpsed in dreams, ice in nightmares. The patterns of clouds in the guts of dead dracon-birds.

For once, they were right.

Thrice magically warded by Magister Ardovani, Vand's shipyard was immune to the weather. Rain rattled off the corrugated roof. Weak sunshine failed to warm it. Storms tugged the sheets upon their nails without loosening them. Under this cover the activity on the ship never ceased. Hammers rang from sun-up until well after sundown into nights lit by glimmer lamps and paraffin. Arkadian Vand was forced to disburse the last of his liquid capital in silencing the complaints of the wealthier folk nearby. When he was not raging against their lack of foresight, he said to Trassan that nothing should detract from the great unveiling.

Every day Trassan came huffing in from the cold, trailing the sharp smell of bitter weather after him. A wall of industrial heat met him. By the time he had reached his office atop its stairs he had discarded his over clothes for his servants to collect.

The 33rd of Frozmer, three days before Coldbite and the official beginning of winter, was no different. Trassan dropped his overcoat over a cast-iron newelpost, deposited his gloves on a desk on the third landing, dropped his hat on his production manager's station. But the clothes he wore beneath were not his normal attire.

He burst into his office.

"How do I look?"

Issy looked up from the catalogue of seed drills and sundry other agricultural equipment she was reading.

"Not so noisy now!" she scolded. The catalogue was enormous to her, so large she must walk its pages to read it.

"I said, how do I look?"

Issy walked the length of her home to get a better view. The sight of so perfect a creature in a cage had tugged at Trassan's heart, and she now occupied a large model mansion. The interior he had furnished from a doll's shop with miniature reproductions of fine furniture. Unlike the bird cage, large parts of her house were private, screened from human view. The edifice was the most fashionable (and most expensive) one he could find. The cage remained as garden, and Trassan had added small plants and three platforms linked by ladders to its interior for her to wander. Altogether Iseldrin's home was an odd combination of toy house and aviary. Issy said she loved it, although she admonished him too, describing its construction as a heroic exercise in work avoidance.

It was to one of the platforms in the garden cage she went. From there she was close to the level of Trassan's eyes.

"You look sweaty," she said.

"The Goodlady Tyn overly flatters me," he said irritably. "I had to run here."

She shrugged. "Set off earlier then."

"I am not sleeping much."

She cocked her head, took in his pale skin, purple bruises under his eyes. "And you look like it. You are putting on weight too."

"You are infuriating!"

"*You* are infuriating. I cannot lie. That's a geas."

"You have more geas than seems feasible."

Her water had to be stirred anti-clockwise with a spoon of rowan, her food could not be eaten two days running from the same plate. Her name might be spoken freely except on the day of Omnus and all of the month of Little during leap years. There were more besides. Trassan had taken to writing them in a little book.

"Sit down," she said. "Call for some tea. Take a breath!"

"Yes, yes. Alright."

"It will be fine."

"Of course."

"You really are getting fatter."

Trassan stared at her. She grinned back with her sharp, sharp teeth. "You're welcome."

She stepped down the stairs gracefully, her coiled hair bobbing prettily. She still wore the same dress. Trassan had never seen her bathe, nor wear any other clothes, but she was never dirty. Her house was crammed with objects and papers, all were ordered neatly; it was as immaculate as his office was messy.

Trassan sat a moment, fidgeting incessantly. He stood and went to the door. The clamour of the shipyard came in as he opened it.

"Send me Tyn Gelven!" he called out. "And get me some tea."

He shut the door, and went back to his desk. He flicked through a disorderly pile of papers. They were all demands for payment. He scowled and pushed them aside. He drummed his fingers. He smacked his lips. He fiddled with a model of a new steam manifold he was designing. He tapped his feet. He...

"Stop fidgeting!" moaned Issy.

Trassan froze.

"Really! A grown man! You are like a child." Issy tore a strip from her catalogue and began to eat the paper, her custom with the journals she particularly liked. "You should calm down. Work is going well. I have nothing bad to say to your future father-in-law, except that you cannot keep your hands from the body of his daughter." She smiled around her paper and munched.

"That is great news," he said sullenly. He began spinning a pen around on his desk, until he caught Issy's furious look.

"Then what is wrong? After today, the money will come in. Your bills will go away as if magicked. Poof!" she waved her hand. A trail of glitter fell from it.

"I don't suppose you could do that for me right now so I don't have to go through with this?"

"I'm afraid not," she said. She hid a delicate belch behind her hand. "Excuse me."

The door opened and Tyn Gelven came within, chased by a blast of noise. He carried a tea tray with a teapot, two cups of normal dimensions and a tiny one the size of an acorn for Issy. "Good day master, Miss Issy." He said.

"You don't have to carry that yourself," said Trassan. "We've people to do that, you know."

Tyn Gelven smiled shyly. He was taller than the Tyn of the Mothrocksey, two-thirds human height. His skin was paler, but just as wrinkled. He had a long bulbous nose, pointed ears and a shock of brown hair that was coarse and dry as every other Greater Tyn Trassan had seen. "I'm begging your pardon, Master Trassan, but there's no need for them to be carrying it. I was coming up here, let them be getting on with something else."

One of the so-called free Tyn, unaffiliated to any of their many tribes, Gelven wore an iron collar nevertheless. A bright red neckerchief covered it. He wore a waistcoat of worsted wool over a shirt of dark blue.

"You're too good a man, Tyn Gelven," said Trassan. He took the tray from his foreman and set it on a pile of plans on the long table in the centre of his room.

"I'm begging your pardon master, but I be a Tyn."

"I know what I'm saying," said Trassan.

Gelven poured. He dribbled a tiny amount into the little cup and passed it through the bars of the house. "Miss Issy."

The lesser Tyn took it from her larger cousin with a bob of her head, and noisily slurped at it.

"Is everything ready?" asked Trassan. He paced the room in agitation.

"You look out of that window, master, and you'll be seeing that it is so. The central part of the deck is completed for the presentation, the paddlewheel housings have been finished. The stairs are up and being decorated. All is in order."

Trassan glanced through his grimy windows. The *Prince Alfra* was indeed nearing completion. The hull was whole. Only to the fore, in a section that ended a little short of the prow, was the deck planking missing. The rooms beneath that part were open to the air, metal and wooden boxes where glimlight joining torches sparked. The superstructure amidships had been sketched out in girders and plate. Mast housings waited open-mouth for their masts. The funnels, three in all, were in place.

He could not quite believe it. It was nearly done. The *Prince Alfra* still looked rough around the edges, and somewhat naked without the network of ropes, blocks, spars and masts that would take his shrouds and sheets, but he was nearly *finished*.

"The high-ups and brass knobs of your folk will get a very good idea of what you're building here, you'll see," said Tyn Gelven.

"And the testing?"

"You were there!" said Gelven. "You are excessively worrying, master."

"I know I was there," said Trassan. He had been until well into the morning. "What does the iron say?"

Gelven spread the fingers of his large hands wide. "Flawless, Master. Absolutely flawless."

Trassan drummed his fingers impatiently. "The temperature is still not all that I was hoping. The boilers were built correctly."

"They were. I went to the liberty of having Goodman Banruthen himself come over from his factory to inspect them in situ. He is well satisfied with their performance."

"He would be, his reputation rests on it."

"He is a good and honourable man, master. He was thorough."

"I am sure he was. But I am not satisfied with the pressure fluctuation. I think Banruthen has muffed up a seal there." Trassan ran his hand through his hair. "Vand should have given me an extra couple of days. I am sure Banruthen's men could have had all this ironed out."

"It is possibly the formulation of the rods, Mester Kressind."

"I calculated it perfectly, I'm sure," said Trassan.

"Then the fault lies in their manufacture, or in their fuelling. A binding of iron and magic, this is not men's work. Each to his own place. Each to his own power. The Mothrocksey Tyn are the masters of iron-in-water, it is to them you should go."

"My brother-in-law's people?"

"They would call themselves their own people, but yes. They."

"Maybe he can help then."

"Perhaps he could, sir. We can leave that for another day. Everything is working well."

"Yes. Yes, perhaps we better had."

Ollens, another of Trassan's foremen, knocked on the door.

"Hey, Trassan," he said. He had little time for social convention. Trassan liked him for it.

"Morning Ollens, how go the preparations?"

"Pretty well. Goodman Hannever says you are asking the impossible but that he will get it done."

"I'd whip him," said Issy. "He says that too much."

"Hyperbole is not a whipping offence," said Trassan.

"A pity," said Issy.

Ollens made an apologetic moue. "Goodfellow Trassan, there is but one thing..."

"Yes?"

"Well, Engineer Vand is here already."

"Ah."

"Yep, yep. He's waiting down by the temporary steps."

"What kind of mood is he in?"

"Well, you know, *that* kind of mood."

"Marvellous." Trassan picked up his hat and squared it on his head. "Gelven, Ollens, I will see you both at the demonstration. Best leave Engineer Vand to me."

He departed.

"Do you like my new house, Tyn Gelven?" asked Issy.

The greater Tyn looked to the lesser. "It is a wondrous dwelling, Miss Issy." He touched the covering of his own iron collar. "But a cage is a cage no matter how pretty it be."

* * *

ARKADIAN VAND PACED back and forth before the base of the wooden steps Trassan had had built up the side of the *Prince Alfra*. They switched back and forth three times alongside the paddlewheel housing, affording his visitors a view of the most impressive part of the vessel initially and then, when they emerged at the top, a vista of the entire ship.

Tables either side of the steps were being laid out with wine flutes. Hammering and shouting came from inside their hoardings where men tacked up swags of bright cloth in Karsa's national colours—red, yellow, and blue. The ship's belly stretched deep into the dry dock, resting on massive wooden chocks. The line of the quay came to around where the waterline would ultimately be. Close to completion, the *Prince Alfra* seemed even bigger, invested with the precursor to mechanical life, a readiness to emerge roaring steam at an amazed world. The wheelhousing was a vast semicircle, the paddlewheel inside so large each sighting of it amazed Trassan. He had never got over the wonder of seeing something conceived of in his mind and laid down on paper in miniature brought to life. One might suppose a grandiosity to come over a man upon creating such a monumental structure. Perhaps some did experience it that way. Trassan felt a certain humility, for he was dwarfed by his creation. What a difference a pair of months made! Now, nearly finished, nearly finished. Such a wonder.

It was a feeling he hoped he would never lose.

He wondered if Vand still felt it. He thought not. The elder engineer was agitated, so much so his irritation calmed Trassan's own jitters. He did not have Veridy with him. Trassan's mood sank further. It was to be one of those meetings.

"You better not fuck this up, Trassan," said Vand. "There's a lot riding on today. I don't want those fuckers going away with the wrong impression of my ship. We need their money."

"If it is so important, why don't you do it?" said Trassan, annoyed at Vand's appropriation of the ship.

"Don't come fresh with me, young man," said Vand, stamping his cane onto the cobbles. The ferrule spat sparks.

"What's all this?" he waved his cane at the wheel housing, the designs for which had been sketched out in chalk on the deep green basecoat. Gold lines would frame the teardrop perforations of the semicircular plate that covered the top half of the wheel arch. "It looks scruffy."

"Painters will work through the presentation. I want to give an impression of industry, without troubling the delicate sensibilities of our guests with the clash of hammers, heat, engine noise and so forth. Although there will be a little discreet riveting. There is a deal of theatre involved here."

"That is one of the reasons you are doing this." Vand calmed a little. "I do not relish this sort of work, but you have a gift for it. This tedious business is a necessary evil, for with no money there is no steel."

"Of course master," he said.

"Goodfellow Landsman is coming."

"Tallyvan Landsman, the coal man?"

"Aye, the coal man, the Black Lord. He is bound to be trouble. Watch him. Answer his questions carefully.

If he comes out of this looking better than we do it will only throw fuel onto his ridiculous fires. Coal! To generate steam. He'll set us back a century. But he is a wealthy man. He is confident, and dangerous."

"Don't worry."

"There are bound to be some of Persin's men here."

"I vetted the guest list with great care, master," said Trassan.

"It doesn't matter. Every man has his price. Persin has the backing of the Maceriyan government and their treasury to spend from. He can therefore set his prices quite high. There are not many with the spine to resist such inducements, and the likes of Landsman would dearly like to see me fail. So much the better for them if my failure comes with a little extra payment. Trust no one! If only our own rulers were quite so forward sighted, eh Trassan?"

"Yes master."

"One day perhaps you'll have a Persin of your own. Then you will know you count for something." Vand bared his teeth. Perhaps he meant to grin, but the effect was altogether more savage. "The tests?"

"Performed satisfactorily. I have some concern with overpressurisation."

"You will be able to effect a proper demonstration of the technology? It is vital, Trassan! Without the Licence Undefined, we are at the mercy of our own ingenuity. Persin will welcome Karsan gold as eagerly as we would. To all but the most patriotic, only the surety of a high return is of any consequence."

"It is an issue with uneven power output from the rods. For this demonstration I will keep the engines only to seventy parts in the hundred pressurised, well within parameters of safety. I have designed the engines with multiple failsafes. All will be well."

Vand nodded. "Good, good. We are to keep my involvement in this to a minimum. I am your backer and your advisor, the architect of the ship but happy to see his protégé step out on his own. If anyone infers any dryness in the financial wells, so to speak, then well..."

"Yes, master."

Vand slammed his cane down again. "You have done a good job of my ship, Trassan. Keep it up."

Vand stalked away. From the set of his shoulders it was obvious he did not want Trassan to follow him.

My ship, thought Trassan. *Mine. And one day, when your daughter is safely mine also, I will make sure everybody knows it.*

CHAPTER TWENTY-EIGHT
Accident at the Iron Ship

THE GREAT AND good of Karsa began to arrive an hour later. Trassan greeted them all personally. Servants wearing the livery of House Kressind served refreshments. Trassan had invited his father. He dreaded his arrival and wished for it in equal measure, although it was unlikely that he would come. As it turned out, he did not. Since his affliction he had rarely left Kressind Manse.

There were fifty or so of Karsa's wealthiest citizens, old and new money alike, and interested family members. Prince Alfra sent Baronet Gosarmand and Goodman Joefee of the Royal Works as a tacit show of support. Trassan took them all from stem to stern, pointing out those parts that had been completed, and those that had not. He understood firsthand now why Vand did not wish to speak to all these people, but as he described the finished ship his enthusiasm steadied his nerves, and he managed to be charming.

He took the group belowdecks after forty minutes. They visited one of the larger cabins, specifically outfitted to look as they all would when finished for the expedition. Trassan had Ollens keep a sharp eye out that no one used the garderobe. The plumbing was not yet connected.

He span it out as long as he dared before they descended ringing iron steps to the engine room. "The hull is double-skinned," he explained. "Better to survive impacts. Iron offers virtual impregnability against the predations of anguillons and sea-draco, while the lack of floatstone's characteristic chambered structure ensures it will be nigh on impossible for the unghosted dead to make their way aboard. That, and the inimical nature of iron to their being, provides us with a certain guarantee against them."

"You will have Tyn aboard? What about them?"

"The Tyn can tolerate iron for prolonged periods, indefinitely if the amount is small. They wear their collars from cradle to grave, after all. But of course you are correct. A section of the hold has been outfitted with wooden apartments for those who join us, in order to isolate them from the metal for at least a part of the time. I have recruited exclusively from the coastal clans, those unbound to place. My own Tyn assures me the riverine clans would quickly sicken."

Nods and muttered exchanges conveyed to Trassan that he was convincing them.

They passed into a passage lined with pipes. "These provide a heating system for the vessel, carrying hot water from the engines all over the ship for the benefit of men and Tyn. Without them, we might quickly freeze." He laughed gaily, as if the conditions of the Sotherwinter were a minor consideration.

"And can you wash, goodfellow?" asked a lady. A niece, he thought, of the Earl of Rocastorn.

"Indeed!" said Trassan. He smiled widely for her, as she was quite arresting. "Imagine being cooped up aboard a vessel like this with none of the finer things! Hot water we cannot draw directly from these pipes, because of glimmer contamination. But these pipes run through tanks, warming them for our convenience."

"How ingenious!" said the woman.

"Mere common sense, goodlady," Trassan said modestly.

They came to the end of the corridor. It grew hotter. Trassan stopped them before a door, and spoke in hushed tones. "Here we are goodfolk, the engine room. The heart of the might of the *Prince Alfra*."

Two engineers in spotless overalls spun a wheel-lock on the door, Trassan stepped within, and beckoned the visitors after him. "Mind your heads, the lintel is low. And I urge you, goodfolk, do not touch anything."

They stepped onto a mezzanine overlooking the engine room. Grilled iron made up the floor. A catwalk led on from the centre of the half-floor to a door on the far side. Offset from the catwalk was a spiral stair that led down to the main floor. Beneath were two of the three engines. They stood on four sturdy legs directly over driveshafts mounted laterally to the keel. A third engine was beneath the catwalk mounted athwart the keel. Each had an individual boiler set beside it. The glimmerrod assemblies that powered them had been hoisted out of the boilers, but were hidden from the view of the visitors under heavy black tarpaulins. In the gangways between the engines stood two lines of sailors, proud as soldiers on parade: a few were Tyn, but in the main they were men, and mostly Ishmalani men at that. Their curled beards and four-cornered hats made them eminently recognisable as such. Trassan had deliberately selected the more open followers of the One. The Ishmalani were the best seamen in the world, and he wanted it known he had many in his crew. His chief engineer Hannever led them.

"The engines for the paddle wheels," he said, pointing to the two either side of the keel, "and the third for the screw. The *Prince Alfra* trials new techniques for water screws. Indeed, it is my intention that, ultimately, ships will be powered entirely by propeller. As it is, the *Prince Alfra* can be propelled solely by water screw, however I adjudged that paddle wheels would afford us an extra agility. The *Prince Alfra* can turn on a three thaler piece! The engines for all three are of a revolutionary new design of my own devising."

Vand, quiet until this point, cleared his throat pointedly and stared at Trassan. Trassan ignored him. "Steam is fed from the boilers via these pipe assemblies directly into the piston head here. These are gimbal-mounted to allow for the driving of the shaft directly beneath. This rocking motion acts as a simple governor for the injection of steam. See these smaller pipes here?" He pointed to thin pipes of soft copper bent around the piston blocks. "Another innovation. These squirt small amounts of cool water into the chamber once the flow of steam is cut off. This causing a rapid condensation of the vapour. The ensuing vacuum draws the piston in, giving us an engine where the pistons are not merely pushed, but pulled. A two-way action that greatly increases power output. This is an entirely novel design."

He pointed out other features of the engines. He did not mention Vand once. Let him glare, thought Trassan.

This is my ship. My engines. He wants the appearance of a protégé stepping out, let him have the actuality.

"With the great weight of these engines in the centre of the vessel and low below the waterline, we have a ship of unprecedented stability and seaworthiness."

"Excepting, I imagine, when confronted with the tidal swell of a Major or Great Tide." The man who interrupted was Georg Landsman.

"There are few ships that are proof against the Great Tides," said Trassan.

"Floatstone is," said Landsman.

"Floatstone can be, with an experienced crew," corrected Trassan. "But floatstone is slow."

"Then why is Persin utilising it? I shall answer for you, goodfellow: because it is tried and tested!"

"Tried and tested has failed to convey anyone to the shores of the Sotherwinter before," said Trassan. "Floatstone is vulnerable to worse perils than the water. This ship is fast, it is armoured, it is powerful, it will not be slowed by ice, trapped by lack of wind, run out of fuel, or be overthrown by the leviathans and ghouls of the deep, goodfolk." He nodded. His men tugged at chains. The tarpaulins fell to the floor. A dull blue glow suffused the space as the rod assemblies were revealed.

The glimmer rod assemblies drew a host of appreciative gasps. Each were made up of a heavy block of iron and silver two yards by two yards. Multiple rods of refined glimmer were mounted, downward facing, into the iron, isolated from it by sleeves of pure silver. Trassan's men bundled away the cloths as he explained the cores' function.

"Each engine has its own glimmer core," he said. "Sixteen rods to a core. These are held in place with silver."

"Not iron?" asked a young man.

"No," said Trassan with a smile. "Direct contact with iron would cause both glimmer and iron to react violently."

"Herri Maun, from *All the Hundred*," a journalist identified himself. "Is it true that your engines work off this very principle?"

"It is. Another feature of my devising," he said proudly. "This reaction of iron and glimmer has long been regarded as dangerous. I see it as the power source of the future! Rather than a rod of refined glimmer, activated by magisterial rune stamp, heating the water, each rod is an alloy. They are imbued with a carefully calculated amount of iron plated in silver iodide. Once engaged the stacks are immersed in water. Ordinarily, words must be spoken by a practised magister to release the power inherent to the glimmer. It is this process that powers most locomotives, river boats, charabancs, indeed, the many lesser devices that you, goodladies and goodfellows, have about your homes. However, in my iron-glimmer engine, the decay of the silver allows gradual, controlled exposure of the glimmer to the iron, therefore generating a great excess of heat, far greater than that generated by purely magical means. This is an alchemical reaction, goodfolk, mediated by the new sciences. No human interaction is required. One could sail this vessel all the way to the grand port of Stamkar in Ocerzerkiya and back on one load of these rods. They need not be changed on long voyages, eliminating one of the principal hazards associated with current marine engines. Nor does one require a magister. The production of energy is a natural consequence of the material combination; it requires no will to set it in motion. As the energy output far exceeds existing engines, one can also build larger vessels, such as the *Prince Alfra* upon which you stand. Large vessels will sail more safely in the sea, carry greater cargoes and at greater speeds. This ship will revolutionise oceanic transport, goodfolk. You witness the future at first hand!"

More appreciative noises rewarded him.

"What you are in effect saying, Goodfellow Kressind, is that you are utilising the same principles, to a lesser or greater degree, as those employed in the operation of glimmer munitions," said Landsman.

"Why yes, yes I am," said Trassan, playing as if the idea had just struck him. "I was in fact inspired by the operation of the cannons at Growling Point."

"So you will admit that what powers your boat, goodfellow, is little more than a large bomb!"

Mutters of worry came from the crowd, gasps of a far less welcome kind.

Calm, thought Trassan, *go with his words. Do not deny*. "It is, you are correct. But an explosion, my goodfellow, is merely a plenitude of energy, spent wastefully. Here we harness it to our own ends."

Trassan lifted his hand.

The engineers donned smoked glass goggles and set to working the glimmer rod assemblies. Chains lowered the glimmer stacks into all three engines simultaneously; more theatrics that had taken a great deal of time to rehearse. Men swarmed over the top of the rod plates, bolting them down all around with spanners the length of their arms.

"For the purposes of this demonstration, we will activate only one engine," said Trassan. "As of the moment the screw is not mounted upon the shaft, so it is that we shall witness in action. Proceed Goodman Hannever," he called.

"Aye aye sir!"

Wheels were spun. Water gurgled in pipes as reservoirs fore and aft of the engine room decanted hundreds of gallons of water into the boilers. An engineer watched through the observation window. "Boilers full!"

"There, all engines are primed. But we will open the slats only on engine two. If you would, Goodman Ollens!"

"Aye sir!" Another wheel was spun. Blue glimmer light showed through the small porthole. There was a tremendous hissing from the engine.

"Reaction commencing!" shouted the observer.

"As you see, pressure builds rapidly once contact with the water initiates the reaction," said Trassan. "A useable pressure is reached far more swiftly than in a comparable coal engine, if such a thing as a comparable engine to this can be said to exist."

Landsman narrowed his eyes.

"Pressure at seventy percent!"

"Narrow the slats, if you would. Restrict the flow of water to the rods. Open steam valves," ordered Trassan.

Three Tyn in protective gear opened taps on the pipes leading to the engine. There was a deep, resonant *chuff*. Then another, and another. The pistons began to work, their heads rocking back and forth in their housings in smooth mechanical motion.

"This engine is somewhat quieter than earlier models, another result of the improvements I have enacted."

Arkadian Vand stepped forward. He held up his hands.

"As we can see my erstwhile pupil has done a fine job," he said. "I think perhaps we should see the engine brought up to full pressure, do you not think Goodfellow Trassan?"

"I have already promised the goodfolk that they will not be subjected to the full power of the *Prince Alfra* for their own safety."

"And they will not! One engine is all that runs. Bring it up to full pressure so that they might have the benefit of a proper demonstration. Or do you have no faith in your own designs?" His eyes glinted with anger. "You have done this before."

"Naturally," said Trassan uncertainly. "Fully tested." He gave Vand a questioning look. "But for all our safety we will take them only to three-quarters pressure."

"Take them to full pressure, Goodfellow Kressind," said Vand levelly. He was leaning forward, his full weight on his cane, his hand gripping the monstrous head tightly. His eyes were intent on the engines. "As your principal backer I demand a full demonstration of *your* technology. Show us the potential of your design."

The eyes of the crowd were on them both.

"If you insist. Goodman Ollens, take us to full pressure."

Ollens hesitated.

"Do it now, Goodman Ollens."

"Aye sir."

He threw the lever. The blue glow intensified. The noise rose. The pistons pounded faster and faster. The driveshaft became an oily blur.

Trassan held his breath. Nothing happened. He smiled. It was working.

A whistle proved him wrong. He grabbed the railing at the warning.

"That will be sufficient, Goodman Ollens, bring her down."

The engineers turned valves, shutting off the steam to the engine. The pistons slowed.

"Pressure's still rising!" Hannever shouted. He glanced worriedly at a large brass gauge.

"Close the slats."

"Slats are closed," said Hannever.

Trassan turned to face the crowd.

"Goodfolk, there appears to be a small problem with our boiler. If I might ask you to return to the deck where you will be furnished with further refreshments."

"Trassan! It's still going up!" shouted Ollens.

Trassan ushered out the guests. Landsman appeared very pleased. Vand curled his lip. "Best attend to your engine, Goodfellow Trassan," he said.

The goodfolk of Karsa effected a hasty exit, Trassan dashed down to the boiler side. The pressure was climbing. The whistle wailed deafeningly.

"The core is heating the water through the slats! That's impossible!" Hannever bellowed. A fierce heat radiated from the boiler.

"Not if the iron balance is off in one or more of the rods," said Trassan.

"What's going to happen?" shouted Ollens.

"If it's one rod, it'll burn itself out quickly," said Hannever. He checked the engine nervously.

"If it's more?"

"Dump the water," said Trassan. "Open the taps to the reservoirs, leave it open. Flood the chamber with cold water. It might help."

"How? We're not at sea now! We'll scald every bastard out in the yard!" shouted Ollens. He grabbed a lever, cried out and leapt back.

"We've no choice!" said Hannever. "Open the valves to the reservoirs then, keep the pressure down!"

There was a clunk. A bolt flew from a pipe join where the valve to the engine was situated.

"Get off there!" Trassan shouted to the Tyn around it. They needed little prompting, falling to the floor and running out of the engine room as quick as they could.

"It's not use, the pressure is still building!" yelled Hannever. Iron groaned. Something made a loud bang as it gave.

"Get out! Get out!" yelled Trassan. "Everyone out now! It is going to rupture!"

The whistle rose higher and higher, until the building pressure forced it off its mounting. It clashed into the roof, came crashing down spinning on the floor. All around men were abandoning their stations.

"Damn fool's pride is going to get us all killed," said Ollens. "Fucking Vand!"

"Get out!" yelled Trassan.

He and his men were scrambling for the doors when, with a terrible boom, the boiler skin split. Superheated steam rushed into the chamber. Men and Tyn screamed. Rivets spanged off metalwork like bullets. At least one man fell, shot through.

Trassan made it through the door as the boiler exploded.

A scalding shockwave sent him down, arms flailing. He banged his head, opening his scalp. Blood pulsed from the wound, hot and thick. He lay on the floor for a few moments, stunned, ears ringing. Groggily he got up and stood on feet that felt like another man's. The hissing subsided. The side of his face was red raw. He was one of the lucky ones. Moans of pain emanated from the engine room.

"Get help!" he shouted. "Get the physics!" The deck clanged as men rushed away. Others crept to the doorway to peer at the devastation within.

Trassan stepped through into a steaming hell. Wreaths of vapour curled around everything. From this searing fog came the groans of the wounded. His feet plashed in an inch of scalding liquid, a slurry of blood, water and blanched flesh gurgled down the bilge drains.

The housing of the boiler had cracked, a great three-foot long rupture ran over the curve of the tank. Pipes had been flung loose. Some had shot out with the force of cannon shot, one denting the inner plating of the hull to the depth of two feet, tearing out the rivets around its perimeter. The whole thing was wrecked, and there was damage to one other engine. Carnage was all around. There were four slumped shapes in the fog, collections of rag and boiled meat that had once been men.

The slatted box surrounding the core was buckled. Through the gaps he saw that two of the sixteen rods were blackened sticks, wizened as charcoal. A trickle of water ran from the reservoir, hissing where it touched the core. He reached for the wheel to close it, then snatched his hand back. He plucked a pair of steaming, soaking gloves hanging from the engine and donned them. They sizzled on the metal as he turned the valve shut.

Something grabbed his shoulder.

"Help me." A hoarse whisper. Trassan turned, and looked into Hannever's face.

The man was dying. His flesh had been flash-cooked by the eruption. His skin hung off in flaccid rags, revealing muscle that was the white pink of perfectly done meat. His eyes had been poached white. Where his fingers touched Trassan, it left smears of fat. The skin broke at the contact, cooked flesh parting to showed gleaming white bone.

Hannever stumbled. Trassan caught him. Inside his clothes, a chunk of meat slithered off in Trassan's hand.

Trassan lowered Hannever to the floor. "Stay with me, Hannever. Stay with me, help is coming!"

But Hannever was dead. The rich scent of boiled meat coated the back of his throat. He held up his gloved hands glistening with the juices of the dead man. His stomach spasmed. He vomited into the water lingering on the deck. His head spun with shock.

"What have I done?" he said. Ollens' words came back to him. Vand's pride. But it wasn't Vand's pride that had caused the disaster. Not entirely.

It had been his.

CHAPTER TWENTY-NINE
Rel and the Godling

"I FAIL TO see," shouted Rel, his voice muffled by the wire basket of his sparring mask, "how me fighting four opponents at once is fair!" He kicked out with one foot, pivoted on the other and twisted his hips. His boot landed squarely in the chest of Hankel Froond, a Suverend from Zhinsky's command. The man folded over, the wind knocked from him.

Zhinsky stood at the edge of the training floor munching on an apple. Every so often he would shake his boots to dislodge the sand sprayed onto them by the sparring soldiers.

"You know why, little merchant boy! It is because there are three hundred and fifty-seven men of the Kingdoms here in the fort, and it could take five times that many. When you can beat five men easily, then I am knowing that the Glass Fort is well defended. This makes I, Zhalak Zhinsky, happy, and it make Colonel Estabanado happy. Sad for all, not so many men as good a fighter as my little merchant boy, so you need to be fighting..." He cocked his head to one side and calculated. "At least nine men, and beating them. Keep fighting!"

Rel stepped back, his practice sabre blurring in an arc to catch those of Veremond and another Maceriyan named Poussel simultaneously. His fourth opponent, Vormeen of Macer Lesser, took his chance as Rel strained against their blades and came at him from the side. Rel shoved Veremond and Poussel backwards, and backhanded the man across the face with the basket of his sword's hilt so hard it caved the mesh of his mask in. The man shrieked and fell on his behind, blood pouring from his nose.

"Sorry!" shouted Rel. Froond was getting to his feet. Rel mimed a killing chop at the neck. Froon slapped the sand in frustration and hung his head.

"That's one!" Rel shouted gleefully.

"Good good! I would watch your back, little merchant boy!"

"Let me handle this my own way!" said Rel. He parried two strikes from Poussel and Veremond, aimed a flick at Veremond's head that had him duck back. He caught a riposte from Poussel, turned the blade and ran an upward slash along the inside of the man's arm. Rel's blunt training blade thumped into Poussel's padded jerkin.

"Two!" he called, ducking Veremond's return slash. A sweeping kick pushed the Perusian's ankles together. He did not fall, but skipped back. Vormeen, shook blood from his hand and came on groggily. Rel spread his arms wide as if to say *Really?*, batted aside Vormeen's half-hearted thrust. His own sabre bent in half as he lunged and thrust it with bruising force into Vormeen's sternum, knocking him back onto his behind. "Three!"

"Ha!" Zhinsky clapped. "He will have big love mark there, little merchant's boy."

"I keep saying," said Rel through gritted teeth, "my father is not a merchant."

Rel fought flawlessly. He and Veremond traded blows, a parry for every strike.

"You are toying with him! Finish him, finish him now!" shouted Zhinsky.

"It's not as if I'm not trying!" complained Rel. He feinted, stepped aside, and delivered a high, overhand downward thrust as Veremond stumbled toward where he had been.

Veremond rubbed at the scratch on his neck. "Four!"

"Maybe you not quite so useless after all," Zhinsky said. "The rest of you, yes, all of you. You are needing to be getting better. Shame on you."

Rel tore off his mask and dropped it. He saluted with his sword and exchanged it for a towel. Sweat ran off his face in a sheet. He screwed up his eyes and sponged them down.

"Damn stuff stings."

"Such a complainer. Not befitting a master swordsman."

"Master?"

"Well, you are not bad." Zhinsky threw his apple core over his shoulder. "Gudrun here says many good things about you." He waved at the master-at-arms, a bald-headed, thickset man who looked like he could not possibly have been anything else but a warrior. He leaned against one of the training posts set back from the training floor.

"Father made us all practise sword, grappling, various armed combats, all the arts of defence. He told us that a true nobleman should know how to fight, even though most of them don't. My brother Garten is the fifth best fencer in Karsa."

"Oh very good. And you?"

"Twelfth, as it happens."

"Not so good then."

"On the contrary. I am getting better. Garten's past his prime. I am better than Garten was when he was my age."

Zhinsky pursed his lips. "Very good merchant boy. I am impressed."

"Good. Can I sit down now?"

"No! Not yet," said Zhinsky, wagging a finger. "Little merchant boy wants to sit? Now?" he said, mumming wide-eyed surprise so effectively a laugh went up from the men in the salle. "I am interested to see, how with fancy fencing will you beat this?" He pointed a finger past Rel, grinning wickedly.

Rel turned around. The floor was empty of opponents. A boy resanded it from bucket while a second hurriedly raked it flat.

Zhinsky was pointing at the gate beyond the floor.

"What?" said Rel.

"You see."

The gate slid upward, unnervingly noiseless in the Morfaan way. The corridor was dark behind it.

The most enormous man Rel had ever seen stepped through, his grin matching Zhinsky's. The corridor had not been dark, the man was so large he had blocked out all the light.

"Merchant boy, meet Halvok. He is a Torosan. You ever see a Torosan before?"

Rel shook his head, dumbstruck. "Yes. Once or twice. There are three here."

"Four," said Halvok.

"But you have never seen one like him, eh? Halvok is nine and a half feet tall. Prodigiously tall! Have you ever fought one?"

"With all due respect, major, are you fucking joking? No! I have not fought one, as evidenced by the fact that I am stood here before you and not dead in a hole in the ground."

"That's fine. I am sure Halvok is not offended, is that not so?"

"No problem to me boss," Halvok said. His Low Maceriyan was surprisingly pure, though his voice was deeper than thunder. "Not many of my sort around. Too big, you see. We need a lot of space. I had an uncle go Karsa way once. Came back. Didn't like it. No offence meant, Captain Kressind, sir."

"None taken," said Rel quietly.

Halvok grinned. He stepped into the duelling square. He undid his uniform jacket and slipped it off, revealing a meaty geography of muscular slabs on a chest the size of Ruthnia itself. Ridged muscles covered his arms in the same manner mountains cover continents. "How you at wrestling, sir?" said the Torosan.

"You really want me to fight him?" said Rel, an unwelcome squeak entering his voice. He coughed.

"Oh, I want everyone to fight Corporal Halvok. Is that not so, Halvok?"

"Aye major. You and Colonel Estabanado."

"I think we should explain to Captain Little Merchant why." Zhinsky conjured a second apple from a pocket and took a bite.

Halvok smiled affably at Rel. "See sir, there's a lot worse than me out there in the desert, so they says anyways. Big things, mean too. Modalmen and that. Fighting me is good practice, and I ain't so big as a modal."

"Don't you mind being the punching bag for the garrison?"

Halvok laughed. "Nah sir. I like the work out. And we take it in turns, me and Moris, Fleki and Borid."

"The other Torosans," said Zhinsky. He crammed another bite of apple into his mouth. "You not see Halvok because he and his fellows are often out with Jakkar."

"That's right sir," said Halvok. "We're just back from a stint in the south checking the obelisks that way. Got too cold, sir."

"If there are three more like him, I think the rest of us can retire and go home, don't you?" said Rel.

Zhinsky grinned around his apple and shook his head.

"You really do want me to fight him?"

"The big advantage to you, Captain Kressind," said Zhinsky, "is that Halvok here is a very nice man. He will not kill you. I cannot speak the same for the modalmen."

Halvok gave a gleeful look. "Pull your guts right out of your arse while you're still kicking, sir." He let a serving boy powder his hands. He slapped them together, whip-crack loud, sending puffs of chalk outwards. "If you'd like to begin sir?"

Rel took a step forward, then a step back. He rolled his eyes, made up his mind and stepped into the square. He took off his padded jacket and his shirt. "I won't be needing them, I suppose." He felt tiny next to the Torosan.

"You know, they call them godlings. Did you know that? It is because they are so big!" Zhinsky laughed wildly. "No captain," he said, when Rel moved to wave away the boy offering him back his practice sword. "You take that."

"Can I at least have a more suitable weapon?"

Zhinsky cocked his head in query. "You suggest?"

"A lance, a full suit of armour and a battle-hungry dracon? Get me my gun! That would make it fair."

"How about a training club?" Zhinsky twitched a finger. A boy ran to Rel with a single piece of wood fashioned into a shaft three feet long with a smooth, thick head. Rel hefted it.

"That might do."

"Do not worry about hurting Halvok."

"Do you know, major, I wasn't."

Zhinsky clapped his hands twice. "Begin!"

Rel circled the Torosan warily. He had never fought anything so large. They were a rarity in Karsa. The truth of Halvok's size outdid all rumour. Halvok crouched, he swung his arms lightly out and chuckled deeply.

Rel swished the club experimentally. Halvok's legs were long enough to have him over the circle in three bounds. Staying out of reach was not an option.

Rel dove at the giant, drawing out a grasping lunge from him. He sidestepped to the left, then swung the club out in a long loop at Halvok's right knee. He had hoped that Halvok would be slow. He was disappointed. The giant's arm shot out, deflecting the club easily.

"Nice try, sir," said Halvok.

"Thanks," said Rel.

Halvok lunged at him. Rel stepped aside, and knocked the giant hard on the back of the head. He might as well have been tapping stone.

"You will have to try harder than that!" shouted Zhinsky.

Rel breathed through his teeth. He ran at the Torosan. Halvok reached for him. Rel ducked, dropped the club, and grabbed at the Torosan's wrists. Rel swung off them, bringing his feet hard into contact with Halvok's stones.

The air whooshed out of Halvok's lips. His knees buckled inward, and Halvok leaned forward.

"Oooooh," he said.

"Oh! He is a dirty fighter!" shouted Zhinsky. Many of the others training in the room had drifted over to watch. Muted comments were becoming shouts. Wagers were being taken.

Rel scrabbled through Halvok's legs. The giant had one hand clasped at his bruised genitals, but with the other he grabbed at Rel's feet. Rel kicked hard, spraying sand into Halvok's eyes. The giant blinked and shook his head. Rel scrambled to his feet behind Halvok. He turned round, grabbed the giant's belt, and hauled himself up onto his back, kicking off on the Torosan's waistband.

Rel looped one arm around Halvok's neck. The giant lifted his hands over his back, slapping at Rel. At so awkward an angle, the blows lacked their full power. Any harder and his ribs would have shattered, as it was the blows were punishing and drove the wind from his lungs.

With his free hand he unhooked his scabbarded sword from his belt, slid it under the giant's chin. Bracing himself against Halvok's back with his knees, he leaned backward, throttling the Torosan with the sheathed weapon.

Zhinsky leaned forward, rapt.

Halvok grabbed at Rel, half hauling him off his back, but that only increased the pressure at his throat. Giant fingers raked across Rel's ribs and spine. Rel gritted his teeth and held on.

Halvok's face turned purple. His hands moved to the sword, trying to pull it from his neck. Rel would not let go.

"Yield!" he said.

"No-o-o," choked out Halvok.

"Please yield."

Halvok managed to smile. "No sir."

He sank to his knees, the strength going from his arms. He attempted one last throw, trying to flip Rel over his head, but Rel would not be shifted. The Torosan went onto all fours, his chest heaving for breath. His eyes rolled back into his head, and he pitched forward, unconscious. Rel choked him still.

The crowd cheered. Zhinsky held his hands up for silence.

"Very good! Very good! Let us stop now, we do not want to kill him."

"How do I know he is not shamming?" said Rel, but released the giant anyway. He staggered away, leaning with his hands on his knees, breathing hard.

Zhinsky toed the Torosan with his boot. "He is not shamming." He looked at Rel, calculating his strength anew. "He will have a very sore neck when he wakes up. You will have to buy him a beer. It is only right."

"I will."

"He drinks it by the bucket."

"I had anticipated that," panted Rel.

Rel handed his sword back to the arming boy and retrieved his jacket. He winced as he moved. He was going to be bruised all over.

"Well, little merchant boy. I think I stop calling you 'little' now," said the major.

"And the 'merchant boy' part?"

Zhinsky's eyes narrowed. "We see about that. Perhaps when, one day, you beat me."

Zhinsky held up a hand. His sword was brought for him. He swished it through the air. Zhinsky beckoned at Rel. For the second time, the boy returned his sword.

Rel groaned. He never beat Zhinsky.

CHAPTER THIRTY
Trassan and Katriona

A MOST TERRIBLE ACCIDENT
AT VAND SHIPYARD

An accident, yesterday, Homeday 33rd Frozmer, devastated the latest venture of Arkadian Vand, renowned engineer and industrialist, to create the world's first successful ocean-going ship of iron. An investors' tour ended in spectacular disaster when one of the vessel's three glimmer fuelled steam engines suffered catastrophic failure resulting in immediate and terrifying detonation, the report of which was heard as far away as Mogawn-On-Land, over twelve miles from the centre of Karsa City. Your correspondent was present for the calamity, involving more than fifty of Karsa City's wealthiest citizens, chosen by Vand to view the final testing of the revolutionary engine as potential backers for the finalisation of the construction. Fortunately, none of the worthies present were harmed in the explosion;

however, six employees of Arkadian Vand were killed, and several more horribly injured.

Katriona read on. There then followed a description of the *Prince Alfra*, and the preamble to the tour. Trassan's words were quoted. There was conjecture as to the relationship between Trassan and Vand and Vand's daughter. The tone was scurrilous and distasteful in its gloating, thought Katriona. She made a note to change paper.

As was reported by your correspondent in the 27th Leffall edition of this very paper, Arkadian Vand and his protégé Trassan Kressind are constructing the *Prince Alfra* in order to cross the Southern Ocean—with all its perils of ice, and notwithstanding the jeopardisation of the long-standing treaty between the merchants of this nation and the Drowned King—facts that they were withholding from the goodfellows who had put their capital into the project initially in good faith. The public inquiry into the merit of awarding a Licence Undefined to the vessel and its owners, so allowing it free passage across all oceans, continues on, despite the announcement of renowned Maceriyan industrialist and engineer Vardeuche Persin that he intended to race with Goodfellow Vand's enterprise to the Sotherwinter shortly after the revelation of the expedition's intended destination, a purportedly intact Morfaan city crammed with the wonders of bygone ages. Despite the obvious benefit to the national interest of Karsa, there are increasingly loud calls from some that all construction efforts on the *Prince Alfra* be ordered to halt to await the outcome of the inquiry. Questions have been raised as to the safety.

Katriona stopped reading. She looked at page four again. Holdean had failed to hold his tongue. Today was not a good day to be a Kressind.

There was a knock at the door.

"Come in," she said.

"Begging your pardon, goodlady, your eleven o'clock appointment is here."

"Show him in, Hollivar."

"You may go in now," she heard Hollivar say.

A moment later Trassan came in. He shut the door quietly behind him.

"Old Demion's got you working for him, has he?" said Trassan.

"Something like that. Do take a seat, brother. Will you take tea?"

"No thank you," he said. Trassan was wearing his formal engineer's garb. It was exceedingly smart, the buttons and badges of it polished to a bright shine. But he looked haggard and woebegone, and consequently the overall effect was one of shabbiness. He sat down.

"I have been reading the paper."

Trassan picked it up. Fury flickered over his face.

"It's a bit of a fucking coincidence, don't you think?"

"What?"

"Faulty glimmer rods the day of the demonstration. The only reasonable conclusion is that I've been sabotaged."

"Persin," said Katriona, tapping at the man's name in the paper.

"Persin. Probably. Who knows? Could be anyone. Vand doesn't exactly have a lot of friends. And now he's absolutely livid with me. I've got my magister on it, but he insists the glamours on the ship are all intact. It has to be an inside job, but who?" Trassan flung the paper down. "'An engine of my own devising'. My own words accuse me from the page." He took his hat off and rubbed his scalp.

"If you look on page four, brother, you will see that I am also featured."

Trassan picked up the paper again, flipped through. He skimmed the article.

"Holdean Morthrock," said Katriona. "He had been stealing from the company for some time. I had hoped to keep it quiet. I will of course have to have him arrested now."

"It seems we are both in a bit of bother."

"Father will be so pleased."

They smiled shamefacedly.

"Perhaps we can help each other, then. Family should stick together," said Trassan.

"Quite. But how?"

"I want Morthrock to come in with me. The problem with the engine is not a problem with the design. Goodman Banruthen was distraught, let me tell you." Trassan leaned back and plucked a model steam engine from a shelf of many such by the desk. He placed it on the desk and began to fiddle with it. "No, the problem is with the fuel rods. The majority worked as intended. The explosion was caused by two inferior rods, and this despite assurances of quality from Kollis and Son, my contractors."

"A deliberate flaw?"

"I reckon so, sis, but I can't prove it. And it might not have been them, someone else could have got to them or switched the rods. Who knows? Either way, they are worthless as a supplier to me."

"You will be suing them?"

"I *am* suing them. But that does not provide me with a replacement supplier. And I was thinking on that, and it so happens I have a Tyn in my employ, by the name of Gelven. He told me to come to the Mothrocksey Tyn, as their realm is that of iron."

"In conjunction with water, yes," said Katriona.

"He said something about that."

"The fortunes of this mill are built on both," she said. "Oh do sit still, Trassan! You are an inveterate fiddler. You will break it."

"Sorry." Trassan put down the model. "Well then. I have designs, as you will have read," he said bitterly, "that utilise a new form of glimmer rod, one that incorporates iron. It boils water. Your little goblins should be fucking perfect."

"You want me to manufacture it for you," she said. She raised her eyebrows. "Well."

"Are you sure we should not include Demion in this conversation? Shouldn't he be involved from the start? This is important to me. And it will be a big contract. It would be better if I discussed it with him first-hand."

"Men of business will not deal with a woman of business. That is why my husband's name stands prominent over all things. However, dear brother, if you wish to buy our services, it is with me you must negotiate. Not him."

She wondered, was this what her father had felt like? This small avalanche of triumphs as he exercised his power. It was a fine feeling.

"Wait..." Trassan looked about dumbfounded. "This is *your* office sis? You *run* the company?"

"It was the office of Demion's father's chief-of-staff. I have taken it for my own use."

"Now that is something! Congratulations!"

"Thank you."

"I mean it! You always were the smartest. Who'd have thought it would be old Demion who was smart enough to see it, and let you have your head."

"He is not letting me have my head, brother," she said levelly.

"Right. You're not going to take old Morthrock's room? Or Demion's'?"

"Demion's office remains his, when he chooses to come to the mill. I admit that is not often, but still. And to take old Morthrock's place?" she shuddered. "Ghoulish, and presumptuous. But I reiterate, it is me you must deal with. I am in charge."

Trassan watched her carefully. "Be careful, dear sister, that your new power does not go to your head."

"Now we have got that out of the way, let us talk more freely. The inquiry into whether you should be granted a Licence Undefined has not yet concluded."

"This is true."

"This accident will not help your cause."

"Of course not!" He swiped at Katriona's paper. "It's all in there."

"Are you going to the Sotherwinter whether you get it or not?"

Trassan looked shifty. "If I can't trust you, who can I trust? Yes, I am going to the Southern Ocean. That is the primary purpose of the *Prince Alfra*. It is the only vessel that could possibly make the voyage."

"The other ships of iron all sank."

"The riverboats of the Olb work perfectly."

"The ocean is not a river. You are taking a grave risk."

Trassan sighed. "I am, but not how you think. This ship will function. Besides, I do not have time. Persin will get there before me if I am not quick. I can brook no more delay."

"Do you really believe this city still exists?"

"Vand had a seeing. That was in the paper too, back when we were flavour of the month."

"Seeings are unreliable."

"Our magister is reliable."

"I am sure he is. Still, brother—"

"My captain," said Trassan, his voice rising in volume and pitch as he interrupted his sister. "He knows someone who has seen it. A long time ago, and at distance, but this sailor has seen it, and it still stands. Naturally, this was all dismissed as the ravings of a lunatic. The poor fellow had been adrift for quite some time, but we know better. The problem is, that it will not be long before everyone else knows. Time is running out."

"I see. That's all very exciting, Trassan, if it is true. But you have been explicitly told not to go there. The paper says there are calls for you to stop."

"I have not been told to stop." Trassan leaned back. "In any case, the creation of fuel is preparation. And if you choose to manufacture rods to my design, and test them in an engine similar to the one we will use aboard the *Prince Alfra*, then what concern is that of mine? My partners are under no such ban."

"I see."

"Will you do it?

Katriona rearranged the items on her desk, moving the model well out of Trassan's reach before she answered him. "I will consider it. First of all, how are you going to pay for all this?"

"You will not stand me the favour? This could make us all wealthy beyond the dreams of the Old Maceriyans!"

"I cannot afford to perform charitable duty for anyone, let alone family. We have a liquidity problem ourselves. I need money now. Your venture is in some trouble. If I am seen to back a project already under scrutiny then it will make my own investors nervous. Especially with these revelations so kindly provided to the broadsheets by Holdean. I cannot commit to an expensive and dangerous process on the promise of wealth unheard of dreamed up by a mad sailor, and an Ishmalan at that."

The mill's whistles blew, signalling a change of shift. The endless rumble of engines quieted. Doors opened outside, disgorging the workforce. The hubbub of voices penetrated the windows.

"Have you thought of asking father?" she asked. "You were always his favourite."

Trassan grimaced. "That's not true. He tests me heavily."

"That is because you are his favourite. There is no rancour to what I say, brother. I love you dearly. I simply state the truth. He has you in mind for an heir."

"He would never lend me a penny."

"You do not deny it?" she pressed.

"'A man has to make his own way in this life. When I'm dead, you might have my wealth my boy. Not before!'" He mimicked him perfectly. "Now imagine what he might say if he learned the money was passing to you to spend playing industrialist, instead of sitting at home like a good wife."

"I am not playing, Trassan. I am in deadly earnest."

"I don't doubt it, but he would not see it that way, and he'd be furious with both of us."

"More importantly, he would recall the loan." Katriona bit her lip. "Is there no more money to be had from Vand?"

"He is trying to keep his distance," said Trassan. "He is due to make an announcement soon on his work in Maceriya. He poses as an investor and advisor. He won't back the whole project. He is wealthy, but his purse is not bottomless. And he and I have our own disputes."

"Go on."

"He is fond of appropriating my ideas as his own."

Katriona tapped the desk with her outstretched fingers. "A fine mess. How much do you need?"

"To finish? That depends on how much *you* need. But I'd say three hundred thousand thalers. Then there are legal costs, for the inquiry and the ongoing case against Kollis and Son. I should imagine I'll get that back, but it might take years."

"More promises. Castles are not built on promises, Trassan, they need firmer foundations. We do have other family. Have you tried Aunt Cassonaepia?"

"That old troll? No, I hadn't thought to. Do you really think I should?"

"She's rich," said Katriona.

"Uncle Arvell is rich. It is *his* money, the trouble is getting it out of him while she stands watch. She's got her claws into every inch of the poor man."

"I can never truly believe he and father are cousins. Such difference in character. He is weak."

"I'll never get a penny out of them," said Trassan.

"Don't ask her, get it from Arvell."

"That, sister, contradicts what you have just said."

"It does not. Uncle Arvell has one area in his life where he still exerts some will. He will do anything for cousin Ilona. And if you get cousin Ilona to back you, then you will have the way to Uncle Arvell's backing."

Trassan grinned. "You are far too sneaky, sis."

"You are not aware of the half of my cunning," she said archly. "So, assuming you can secure monies from our uncle, then Mothrocksey will do your work. Shall we say one hundred thousand?"

Trassan's mouth hung open. "Are you serious?"

"Deadly. You know it is a fair price."

"It's daylight robbery."

"Manufacturing an experimental, and provenly dangerous, new technology, testing it, shipping it to your shipyard unseen, and keeping it out of the papers? You are asking a lot. It is a good price. I will require the first quarter as a downpayment, the rest over the following sixteen months."

"Twenty months."

"Very well, seeing as you are family. But I want guarantees it will be paid in full whether you return or not." She stood and extended her hand. Trassan took it reluctantly.

"That is cold, sister."

"You have your adventure, brother. I have my own affairs to think of."

Trassan pulled a face. "Very well. A deal. I only do not argue further as I know you far too well," he said. "You know, at your wedding, father told me that your marriage to Demion was the foundation of a great alliance. I imagine this is not what he had in mind."

"Certainly not. But he was right. We shall both of us see this through and emerge stronger because we have worked together."

"And triumph. Such is the Kressind way," said Trassan.

"Gods' blessing to that. Now," she said, "I would tell you to visit my accountants in order to secure a draft contract, but I am afraid I was forced to terminate their employment. The new staff begins next Twinday. I am sure you can wait until then for the paperwork."

"Really, I can't."

"We will start immediately, don't fret brother. If you'll excuse me, I have a lot to be getting on with."

She looked meaningfully at the piles of paper on her desk.

Trassan sighed. "Me too. See you next Twinday then."

"Indeed. And Trassan?"

"Yes?"

"Good luck with the inquiry."

AFTER THREE MONTHS as the head of the Mothrocksey mill, Katriona's office fit her better. A space can be worn in like good clothes, shaping itself to the moods and character of the occupant. So it was with her. She sat behind her desk and no longer felt an imposter. She had changed her manner of clothing, adopting simpler skirts of broader cut with only one petticoat beneath. Her blouses remained stark white, but she had taken to wearing sleeve protectors and a foundryman's apron, while her outer clothes she had made in duller colours that did not show the mill's dirt. She was no longer discomfited by the looks of the male employees of the Morthrocksey Mill, and if they persisted in mocking her, sometimes crudely, behind her back, they also performed whatever task she ordered with more or less complete obedience.

Katriona felt in charge, and was given respect. But her authority, so newly won, was undergoing its first great challenge.

In front of her desk stood Tyn Lydar and two of her deputies. All had their hats off, Lydar and a second female exposing the colourful scarves they wore about their hair. They stared at her with their large brown eyes.

"What do you mean, you will not do it?"

Tyn Lydar was abashed, but insistent. "It is dangerous work, Mistress Kat. The binding of glimmer, iron and silver and magic. Your brother has learned this to his cost. This is of the old ways. He should not take this road."

"That is exactly why he came to us. You are the masters of watered iron among your kind."

"We are, we are. But we do not sell our gifts lightly. The greater gifts cost more in Tyn magic and in Tyn blood than we receive from your kindnesses, begging your pardon, Goodlady Kat. Those are not coins to be spent."

"Surely, this work is covered by the agreement your kind made with Lord Morthrock?"

"Nine hundred years have gone since King Brannon, seven hundred since Master Demion's forefather came to us as lord and master," said Tyn Lydar. "My people, in terrible times, made dealings that we have all regretted. But this industry you ask for was not among them. We will not do it."

Katriona stared at her in displeasure. She laid her hands flat upon the desk, as if she expected to be punished by her schoolmistress. "You are insistent?"

"You can threaten us if you will, but there is no geas upon us to perform this duty," said Lydar's male deputy, Tyn Lorl. "You have no power to make us."

"Have I not?"

"No, mistress," said the other female. Katriona did not know her name. She had a good idea of who the people were who worked in her factories. Fewer in number than the humans, the amount of Tyn remained the same, but the individuals seemed to change, which was impossible.

"Tyn Elly," offered the second Tyn. She smiled kindly, her thick skin crinkling around her eyes. Elly was as old and wrinkled as Tyn Lydar.

"Then let us negotiate," said Katriona.

The Tyn looked at each other.

"Your meaning, Kat?" said Tyn Lydar.

"You know what I mean, Tyn Lydar! You have lived among my kind for too long to profess ignorance of commerce. There must be something you want. Everyone wants something. What I mean is, what payment will you take for the work? You have the ability, and I have the means to pay you. Let us look at this outside of your binding. What do you need? That is my question. Or do you need it in plainer language than even that?"

The Tyn spoke to one another in their own language. Hesitantly at first, then with increasing animation. Kat listened, fascinated. She had never heard so much of their tongue. The Tyn workers on the factory floor used it, but switched always to Karsan when they caught sight of any non-Tyn. She had heard a few phrases several times, a handful of words discernible against the racket of the machines. Their meaning remained mysterious.

In the quiet of her office, she heard it clearly. A bubbling noise, a stream in its bed, interspersed with stony clacks like pebbles knocking one another underwater. Their mouths moved oddly, lips far more mobile than when they spoke Karsarin; pursing far out from their teeth and drawing back, corners stretching for their ears.

They stopped. Katriona regretted the cessation of the sound. There was a mesmeric quality to it, redolent of pleasant summer days in quiet meadows.

"We might do this, Mistress Kat," said Tyn Lydar cautiously.

"You might?"

All three of them nodded solemnly.

"But first we must show you something," said Tyn Lorl.

"What would that be?" She looked from one Tyn to the other. Such was their size that many other humans regarded them only as children, others were terrified of them, believing every scrap of folklore about them to be true. She saw them neither as bogies or children. They were more than both, less than either. Karsa had more settled Tyn than any other of the lands. How had she not noticed these peculiarities of theirs before?

Inattention, she thought. The inattention of the rich.

"We wish to show you where we live," said Tyn Lydar.

Katriona made a sharp high noise of surprise. "Live? If that is all it will take to convince you to do this work, then I will gladly oblige."

"Then we shall go now," said Tyn Lydar.

CHAPTER THIRTY-ONE
Tyn Town

TYN LYDAR LED Katriona through the mill. They crossed over the Morthrocksey's stone cut and headed around the back of the foundries. Their furnaces were cold, and snow wafted softly around them. The other two Tyn peeled away without a word, going back to their jobs. Katriona was left alone with Tyn Lydar.

They turned onto a narrow street around the back of the trio of warehouses. The complex wall came into view at the end of the street, pierced by the railway gate. They passed through the warehouses to the rail yard. There were three platforms. At one a steam engine huffed to itself as the trucks it pulled were unloaded. Piles of iron ore, glimmer sand and coal lined the far side of the tracks in timber stalls.

Tyn Lydar watched the train mournfully, and began to speak. "I remember when there were nothing but meadows here. You could see all the way to the cliff tops, and on stormy days when the Great Tide was high, you could hear the surf pound upon the stone. Up yonder where the cloth mills are there were moors, with thick brown heather and purple flowers and birds that sprang shrieking up, up, up when you came near them. Woods and meadows around the waters of the land. The sea seemed not so far away then, now it is a lifetime's walk. There is only brick, and smoke, and kado, kado, kado, everywhere. This was an island in the river, before your kind straightened the waters and imprisoned them in a jacket of stone. Now what is it? This place. Time was long and the days the same, then your kind came, and everything changed in a blink of an eye. You kado brought your dead with you. We were forced to deal with King Brannon. What else could we do? Fade away or take the iron, that was our choice. We chose iron. We chose form. We chose slavery over dissipation."

They approached a square, windowless building of grey brick. There were no chimneys on it, although like all the mill buildings the many-ridged rooftop was inset with windows on the straighter side of each peak to let light in. This part of the complex seemed ill-kempt. Shattered bits of ore and stone pierced by struggling weeds made the ground uneven. Piles of rubbish, edges fluttering in the breeze, collected themselves into corners. There was a trio of abandoned static engines of an older type, their skeletons bright with rust, gaping holes where useful parts had been scavenged. A second, later sort was by them, this covered over with a massive oilcloth. Perhaps someone had intended to salvage it, or install it elsewhere. Whatever their plans had been, they had been unfulfilled. The oil cloth was torn, the warp and weft visible in the rips where it had rotted through. All over it was greened with the life of small things.

"In summer time thick with grass and flowers, in winter it flooded with silver water. Fish slept there, and Tyn danced on the ice. Now look, river tamed, marshes drained and filled with broken bones of the Earth. Kat will look and Kat will see. We live among your filth." She made an odd mumbling hum in her throat. "This is our home, this building," she admonished Katriona. She had never asked where the Tyn had lived.

A door, bright paint peeling from it, swung open. It was the only opening in the outside of the building Katriona could see. Tyn Lydar led her into a corridor once painted eggshell blue, but now faded and spotted with damp. The floor was wet. Another door opened at the far end. Kat stepped through.

The inside of the building was hollow. A courtyard, lit dimly by the day shining through dirty glass. The walls were full of cell-like accommodation, each one looking out over the courtyard inside. Tyn leaned on railings around the edge, puffing pipes, or simply staring. A few mumbled to themselves, or ground their teeth. Half of them left their positions when they saw Katriona, headed into their quarters, shutting doors quietly behind them.

"They are not happy to see kado here," said Tyn Lydar. "They think I wrong to show you."

Katriona covered her mouth with her hand. Filling most of the courtyard was a stone, tall and proud, a finger of rock that went halfway up to the roof. Its base was at least five yards around. Symbols that were so old and worn they looked grown rather than carved covered its surface.

"This is the home of the Morthrocksey Tyn," said Tyn Lydar. "Our home in freedom for long centuries, our prison for these last nine."

"What... what is that?"

"Our heart stone."

"Do all Tyn clans have such?"

"All have hearts," said Tyn Lydar. "Not all have stones."

"I did not know it was here."

"No one remembers. We show few. We remove the memory from those who see. Some cannot see it, even if we show. This sight is not for everyone." Tyn Lydar took Katriona's hand and pulled her gently into the square. There were few Tyn in the square; most were working, of course. There was a small, dead tree on the other side of the rock, with smooth skin that appeared to lack bark. It had few leaves, all curled and brown and at the top of the crown. Now she came closer, the symbols in the stone had a faint glow to them, a residue of glimmer.

"Is the tree dead?" she asked.

"Yes. And no," said Tyn Lydar. "Is the stone dead? Are you alive? It is there. We are here. Such things as dead or alive do not matter to Tyn like they matter to kado. When your people came to the Earth, we retreated to the islands. But after the bad times you spread. You are vigorous, and bear many young. In time you came here too, our last place. Now it is yours too. This stone and this tree is not for you, it is for us, one of the last of all things that is ours and not yours, nor will it be so. It is a great thing I do by allowing you to see it at all. The men who built this place around the stone forgot. No living kado has seen it for a long time."

"So why are you showing me this?"

"You say it is time to make a new bargain," said Tyn Lydar. "This is not a good place. We want our soil, we want our sun, we want our water back. We cannot leave this place. Even before Brannan. Morthrocksey Tyn are Morthrocksey, and Morthrocksey is the Tyn. We are not fools, it can never be as it was. But it can be better. Better for us. If you give us these things, then we will work harder for you. You have a good heart. I can see it." She reached up her wrinkled hand and rested it lightly below Katriona's breast.

"We could take down the roof, demolish the building... I suppose we could run pipes here from the Morthrocksey..."

"I will show you. This is what we want."

Kat's chest tingled, she blinked. Her eyes itched. Overlaying the desolate scene before her was a brighter place. Water cascaded down from a high silver pipe. The metalwork gleamed. The water fell into a broad pool from which the tree, now a deep and vibrant green, drank with greedy roots. The symbols upon the stone glowed with yellow light. On the tree leaves of silver, bronze and gold rattled in a wind coming in through open skylights. The water was pure, as was the air. Greenery spilled in boxes from the walls. One bank of apartments had been removed. In their stead were tall windows, the tops fashioned of scintillating stained glass. Birds and dracon-birds flitted from branch to branch. And there was laughter. Naked Tyn children, no larger than human infants, splashed in the pool.

"You... You want children?"

"No Morthrocksey Tyn has been born for two hundred years. There are fewer of us every year. Yes, we would have children. Cleanse the river. Bring the river to us, let us be with the river. What was separated by degree can be joined together anew. We understand this modern world, better than you think. You cannot undo what has been done, as much as I wish to roam the moorland of my young days it is gone, buried beneath your Karsa. But you can make us live, as much as we might live. You can free us, as much as we might be free."

Katriona stood on her tiptoes, trying to see what lay beyond the windows. "That is not Karsa City..."

"That is and never can be for you." Tyn Lydar withdrew her hand sharply. As it came away Katriona yelped with pain. The vision faded. Drear reality took its place. With its reestablishment came overwhelming sadness.

"I will see what I can do," she said.

"You will sign legal documents?"

"Yes, yes of course I will."

"You will accept Tyn geas?"

She hesitated at this. Guis's warning about the Tyn came back to her. "I will. When will you make the rods?"

"Not so quickly, Goodlady Kat. There is one more thing you must do. For us to perform this magic for you, you must remove our collars."

Kat's eyes widened. "I cannot!"

"There is no other way."

"Truly?"

Tyn Lydar shook her head. "I would not ask if it were so. To take them off it dangerous for us. I do not want to trick you. But this magic must be worked in the old way."

"Then I will do as you ask, Tyn Lydar, we will remove your collars for the duration of the manufacture. But they must be replaced. You will say that you can vouch for your people, but the ban of King Brannan must be obeyed."

Tyn Lydar nodded, her eyes sad. "So be it," she said. "We will make your rods of iron."

KAT STOOD BY a heavy-wheeled shield, a modern echo of a siege mantlet made of steel. A thin slit glazed with green glass one third of the way down allowed her to watch the Tyn busy about the furnace. She wore a heavy leather apron and leather gauntlets over her clothes. The men of the foundry regarded her sidelong from the corner of their eyes.

She stood up. The gate to the furnace was shut, but the heat was a physical blow. "This is what they asked for?"

"All is prepared as to their instruction, as you asked, Goodlady Katriona," said the foreman. Bal Fret was a heavy man, squat as an ape. He had a broken nose that would honour a pugilist. "I know it's not my place, goodlady, but I can't help but thinking this is a bad idea. If my man was to do this then we wouldn't be doing it this way." He gestured at the simple moulds of packed sand in wooden frames on the floor. "It's not right, very primitive, if you get my meaning." He nervously looked to the Tyn. "You're needing heavy pressures to do this, keep the glimmer from reacting."

"You have never manufactured anything like this before?" she said. The roar of the air pumps to the furnace were growing louder, and the heat intensified. The bricks that made its side radiated an increasingly fierce heat.

"We tried, a few years back, under Horras Morthrock. He was always a one for new techniques, but it didn't work. Damn near blew out the whole of foundry three when it went off. We used a float of molten lead to keep it under weight, three tons of it, and it still wasn't enough. The rods we got were next to useless."

"That is the technique Kollis and Son use."

"Yes, goodlady." Some of the men couldn't get their minds around the idea that a woman would know about such things. Fret was not among them. "But they've got the more experience, patented processes. It's all too dangerous this modern technique. I'd stick with pure glimmer rods. The power yield is lower, and you need a magister, but they ain't too hard to come by."

"My brother was nearly killed by Kollis and Son's bad engineering. Tyn Lydar assures me they have their own methods. They will work."

Fret looked down at the five Tyn waddling around the foundry floor with a mix of fear and dislike. "That they do. But they aren't the methods we should be using."

"I'm not wanting to crack the stone with dropped words, goodlady. But I do agree a little with Goodman Fret here." Ras Tynman jangled his keys. A huge iron hoop, with two hundred tiny keys upon it. The tool and the badge of the Tyn's human overseers. "So, I am not saying I won't be doing as you're asking, but I got to say, are you absolutely sure about this, Goodlady Kat?" Tyn Lydar had started calling her that. The habit was spreading to the rest of the mill. "I seen the Tyn do some marvellous things in my time. But uncollaring them, it goes against all the warnings."

"Have you ever seen a Tyn harm a human?"

"No goodlady," said Ras. "And we Tynmans have been Tynmen for centuries."

"Old tales then," said Katriona.

"I ain't never seen them uncollared more than one or two at a time, neither," said Tynman. "It's dangerous. There's wisdom in old tales, if you look at them right, begging your pardon Goodlady Kat."

"They have given their word. There is nothing more binding upon a Tyn than its own word."

"I've been working with the Tyn for forty years, goodlady," said Tynman. "The geas they place on themselves are mighty odd sometimes, and you are right, they do stick by them. I've never seen one go against a ban put on it that it took on willingly, and when I asked them what'd happen if they were to do that, they go all shuffly and evasive, if you see."

Kat smiled. "I know exactly what you are talking about."

"The job of Tynman has been handed down to me from my family line from lost gods knows when. And I ain't never taken their collars off." He stepped forward, still jangling his keys in his hand.

"No. I expected not."

"It reminds me of something my old dad said once, not long before he died. He said to me one night, when I was just about done with my prenticing to him and Galvan Melsby over at the high farms out past the city. You know what he said to me, my old dad?" Ras reached for the key slot in the iron of Tyn Lydar's collar. "He said, 'If their geas are so mighty strong, why is it we make 'em wear iron collars?'"

The key snapped into the lock. Ras pulled the iron ring away from Tyn Lydar's neck. She shuddered. A half-smile of pleasure crossed her face. She stood taller, drew breath that somehow inflated her.

Her eyes slid open, there was a light in them that raised the hairs on the back of Kat's neck. She gave Katriona a sly look. "Thank you, goodlady."

For a moment, Katriona was sure she had been tricked, and that some terrible peril was imminent. Her heart hammered in her chest. Then Tyn Lydar broke eye contact and called to the foundrymen. "Fill the crucibles!" she shouted. The gates in the walls were opened with long hooked poles held in heavily gloved hands. Bright orange iron roared down chutes, hissing and spitting as it fell into the crucibles, flames sheeting from the flow. They stirred the room with hellish breezes, and Kat ducked behind her shield.

"'Ware!" called Fret.

The gates were sealed. The foundrymen ran to the metal and began raking the skin of impurities from the cooling surface The crucibles were shaped like cauldrons with exceptionally narrow necks, the better to slow the setting of the metal.

"Release the others," said Katriona to Tynman.

"Are you sure?" he said. He fingered his keys, unsure.

"Do it now!" said Katriona. "Before the metal cools."

"Right you are." Tynman went to the collars of the other three Tyn. Like Tyn Lydar, they appeared to physically swell when their collars were removed.

"You should go, Goodlady Kat. This is a tricky job, and no mistake. Things will get uncomfortable. Goodman Fret there wasn't wrong about the pressure, if you do it the kado way. We has our own way of doing this procedure, is all," said Tyn Lydar.

"I have to stay, you understand."

"Then stay behind your shield, Goodlady Kat. You will be safe enough there."

Kat made herself smaller behind the curved steel shield. The layer of glass distorted her view. Through it she saw the four Tyn moving rapidly. A mix of glimmer sand, adulterated with silver iodide, was shovelled into the sand moulds upon the floor. The crucibles were wheeled forward.

The Tyn broke into song. Sudden and powerful, no prelude sounded, no gentle seduction of notes for the senses, they entered the song in the midst of its singing. The force of it was as strong as the wall of heat from the metal. She flinched.

The door banged open. A figure ran through, throwing up his arm across his face against the heat. A foundryman caught his arm and guided him to Katriona's shelter.

"Demion! What are you doing here?"

He was panting, red-faced. "This is still my factory. What the hell is this I hear about uncollared Tyn running loose?"

"They are not running loose!" said Katriona. "They are working their full ability upon a project that will net us a great profit."

"No money is worth this risk."

"That is why you are lousy at making money away from the card table," she said. "You don't agree?"

"No," said Demion Morthrock, dangerously close to anger. "Absolutely not."

"I thought you said that you trusted me, husband?"

"I did, but this... Katriona, this is insane!"

"Maybe it is, but you are too late. Watch."

She made room for him behind the slit, and he bent down to look through it, her hair brushing his face.

The iron, incredibly, flowed slowly into the moulds, arrested by some force of magic. White light shone from each of the six holes in the sand.

Light blazed intensely from the Tyn, subduing the ruddy orange of the molten iron. The sound of a hammer beating iron on an anvil rang out, once, twice, thrice, although there was nothing of the like in the casting room. The ringing took up a steady beat with the song. Huge, glowing figures towered over the Tyn. Their bodies became indistinct shadows within these phantoms of light, their heads and limbs attenuated, until they were reduced to a dark smear, a suggestion of corporeality. The light shone brighter and brighter, swallowing the Tyn entirely, and bleaching out the room. Demion shaded his eyes with his hands, screwed them shut and cried out in pain. The men turned away from the sight, arms over their faces. Ras Tynman reached out for one of the figures, collar in hand, but fell back, overcome by its radiance. Katriona pulled down goggles hurriedly to protect her own eyes. With this additional protection, she could see little. Singing in the bubbling language of the Morthrocksey Tyn cleaved the air, the words trailing streaks of golden light. The pressure in the room greatened, her ears popped, then began to hurt.

"What have you done, Katriona?" demanded Demion. The song and hammering deafened them both. The foundrymen staggered as if hammerstruck. Three fled the room, Tynman lay curled on the floor, his hands clapped over his ears.

A boom, as of a thunderclap at close quarters, or the discharge of a cannon. Katriona fell backwards. Demion caught her clumsily. He too was off balance and they fell tangled together.

She opened her eyes, the singing had stopped. The pressure was dropping noticeably, her ears popped again. She disentangled herself from Demion's limbs, and stood.

The foundrymen cowered against the walls. Four titans of light, brilliant angels, looked down on her with pupilless eyes.

One shining being stepped toward them, holding a pair of tongs that gripped a long, dark bar. A second step, and a third, and he was Tyn Lorl again. He bowed low, holding the iron rod, twice his height, without any apparent difficulty. The rod smoked. Motes of glimmer glowed all over it.

"Goodlady Kat, I present to you the first rod."

"Might I take it?"

Tyn Lorl nodded. "It will be cool enough." There was a wild light in his eyes and a hardness to his face that had been absent while he was collared. But he was eager she be pleased, she saw that, and that lessened the threat she instinctively felt from him.

Kat reached out. She took the rod in her hands. It was hot, the tamed fire inside it making itself felt through the thick leather of her gloves.

She held it up, ran her eyes over it appraisingly. Fret came forward, shaking off the after effects of the Tyn's work.

"What do you think?" she said.

Fret held out his hands. Katriona handed the rod to him. He examined it closely from all angles.

"I'm no expert in this type of metallurgy, goodlady, but it looks perfect." He sighted one eye down the length of it. "Absolutely perfect."

"Stable?"

"If it weren't, what with all that heat and all, it would've blown us all into the afterlife being made like that." He handed it back to Katriona. The silver of the containment matrix was becoming defined, a honeycomb pattern. At the heart of each cell was a single point of starlight. A mote of glimmer, shining with ready power.

"What are you doing, Katriona?" asked Demion.

"It's for my brother," she said. The rod was beautiful. She smiled at the Tyn. For all their wildness, they grinned bashfully.

"Trassan? The ship man?"

"Yes."

"Well. Well I'm glad it went off alright, that's all I can say. And I'm glad it's all done and finished."

Kat lowered the rod. "Finished? Oh no, Demion. This was the test run. He needs one hundred and eighty that are exactly the same as this. They have made six." Fret was inspecting the rest with the Tyn and the foundrymen. Grudging words of respect were being exchanged. "So the process must be repeated thirty times all told."

"Katriona!" Demion said in dismay. "I know we agreed that—"

She placed a rough, leather-clad finger to her lips. He fell silent.

"Before you charge the dracon, dear husband, let me tell you how exactly much he is paying us..."

CHAPTER THIRTY-TWO
The Elder of Alu-mal

REL PACED THE battlements of the Glass Fort, passing a brazier, around which huddled three men. The pocket of warmth around the fire was welcome but brief. Rel entertained the notion of tarrying to force some feeling back into his fingers, but he feared that if he ever stopped he would not get going again. There were a number along the wall. Another would come soon enough.

Everything at the Glass Fort was built to inhuman scale. The ramparts were no exception, wide enough to drive two coaches down side by side. Why the Morfaan had made everything so big, there was a point of contention for the magisters. The last Morfaan were no bigger than men, and their devices and buildings elsewhere were generally sized accordingly. Not at the Glass Fort. A wooden platform had been installed to run alongside the parapet. On this were the men and their braziers and their misery. Rel's feet tocked dutifully along it, each step counting off a half a second. He sank deeper into his fur, although in the face of such cold the benefit it gave was inconsequential. He thanked whichever leftover god might be listening that at least the night was still. Black clouds drifted with sinister purpose over the desert, edged in the Red Moon's glow. The grasslands were a pale block, shocking next to the desert's blackness. In the dark, it was the grassland that appeared lifeless, not the black sands, for over there in the unfathomable distance lights played. Ripples of green lightning that chased each other over the ground. Spirits were the obvious explanation; Rel glumly thought it probably something worse.

Railhead was a cluster of brash artificial lights between, an island of life in a world of the dead. The sounds of the small town reached him in odd bursts: a snatch of song, laughter, shouting, the barking of dogs. Spots of fire and glimmer shone out in the desert, the water stations and guardposts of the railway strung out in the dark. At night they shook off their earthly nature. Isolated between the dark of the sky and the dark of the sands they appeared stars, the dotted belt of a fallen constellation.

The air was exceedingly cold. The steppes were dry. Despite the chill no real snow fell on the desert or steppe. All water was frozen from the sky, its dryness tormented the nose and breath turned instantly to clouds of ice. Rel had let his beard grow, for it took some of the shock from breathing away. He looked dreadful, a mountain man, hairy as a backwoods Tyn.

Looking out over the black sands at night filled him first with melancholy, then with dread. A view that during the day appeared majestic took on an altogether more sinister aspect after dark. At breakfast, one could always tell who had duty watching the wastes the previous night. They were quiet, round-eyed, lost in thoughts they could not or would not articulate. The dreams that followed a night on the wall were black ones. When Rel was upon the battlement, he saw his posting for the punishment it was.

He stopped midway between two braziers and stared outward. None of them were supposed to spend too long by the fires. The heat was comforting but the light made a man blind.

Movement caught at the corner of his eye. He turned instinctively toward it. He saw nothing, and was about to resume his pacing vigil when a light emerged from a fold in the land.

"Light!" he called. "There's a light coming from the north. Bring me glasses!"

Men reacted instantly. Feet thumped on wood. A pair of sentries came to his side and handed him a pair of field glasses. The metal of their rims was painfully cold against his face, and so he held them no longer than he needed to, enough to see that there were three men, one carrying a lantern on a pole. Already riders from the post down at the base of the rampart were heading out to intercept the travellers, their dracons sluggish in the chill. He pulled the glasses from his face. When he put them up again, the light stopped. Dracons circled it. A shouted challenge drifted up. Rel risked the field glasses again. The dracons croaked and screeched. The watch officer dismounted.

"Looks like they are friendly," said Rel.

The light moved to the base of the road to the fort. "They're coming up," he said, handing his glasses back to the soldier. "I'm going down to see what the fuss is about. I'll be sure to let you know what's what, if I am permitted."

"Aye captain," one said. The other of them nodded, his teeth chattering too hard for him to speak.

Rel ran down the wooden stairs laid over the Morfaan originals—so large only the Torosans could use them. The courtyard was full of running people, the alarm triangle rang. "Someone's coming in!" Veremond called as he pelted past. "They're opening the gates!"

"What's the occasion?" Rel called. This was cause for concern, the gates were never opened at night.

"I don't know. I'm going to fetch the major."

Rel walked briskly to the gatehouse. The courtyard was a safe haven from the unrelenting attention of the Black Sands. Illuminated by firebowls on tall stands and lights from the fort's odd slit windows it was an almost human place. But already the gates were drawing back, opening the way for the desert to resume its scrutiny, and Rel's relief was short-lived.

Dracons pranced in, heads tossing, eager to be running. Behind them came two of the garrison on foot. Between them were the three men Rel had seen on the plain. They were flat-faced, leathery, with narrow, down-turned eyes and broad noses. One was much older than the other two. They were not of a type or nation Rel was familiar with. They babbled fretfully in a language no one understood. Rel moved forward and tried to calm them, but they would not be calmed. They grasped his forearms.

"Murthu, murthu, murthu!" one said over and over.

"Murthu? What is that?"

"I don't know!" said the watch lieutenant. "He won't stop saying it!"

"Lucky you, Zhinsky is here, and Zhinsky knows their speech."

Major Mazurek swaggered into the pool of light before the gates.

"What are they saying?" said Rel, trying unsuccessfully to shake the man off.

"Changeling," said Zhinsky.

"A changeling? Like a wolven?" said Rel.

"A man who turns into an angry dog? Pfah!" scoffed Zhinsky. "That is nursery talk. No, this is much worse, mainly because it is real. Now shut up! I am listening. This mountain tongue is hard to follow."

Zhinsky spoke with the three men. They all spoke at once. He held up his hands, and when that did not work he shouted a single word. The men stared at him, blinking in fright. And then they told Zhinsky their story.

Within five minutes, Zhinsky had the colonel out of bed.

REL, ZHINSKY AND Deamaathani stood around the colonel's desk. The office was frigid. Low-ranking soldiers were lighting the stove in the corner, but it was far too small to warm a room of that size.

"There will be a breach," said Estabanado. He was unshaven and still in his nightclothes, a vast, quilted dressing gown wrapped around him. He yawned expansively and poured himself a drink. This time he offered Rel one, giving him also a tumbler each for Zhinsky and Deamaathani. Through numb fingers the glass was treacherously slick. Rel put one hand beneath the tumblers and watched them closely as he handed them out, lest they slip from his grasp.

"Breaches in the wall of obelisks are rare but not unheard of. It is our duty to investigate. I want you to go, captain."

"I will go with him," said Zhinsky. "The village, Alu-mal, is isolated, one of the furthest from other inhabited lands. It will be useful for my government to have me visit."

Estabanado nodded. He had grey bags under his eyes. He was not pleased to be woken at this hour, and not concerned about making it clear. "As you wish. Your facility with the mountain tribe's language will be useful."

"And merchant boy is still green as fresh grass shoots, we don't want him dying!" said Zhinsky. He winked at Rel.

"No. I suppose not. Take a quarter squadron. No more."

"Changelings can be dangerous," said Zhinsky.

"It is all we can spare. If there is a breach, then there might well be other incidents we must attend to closer to home."

Estabanado unrolled a map and weighed it down with a glass weight. "Where is it?"

Zhinsky tapped the map. It was a long way north of the Glass Fort.

A crooked line marked the border between sand and steppe, veering out from the mountains the further one went north or south. Estabanado ran his finger along it. "A lot of ground to cover, but check the obelisks en route. I'll send out other groups to the south in case the breach is there. Magic is infuriatingly unpredictable. What is your opinion, captain-warlock?"

"A shapeshifter," said Deamaathani. "How interesting." He rolled his glass between his hands.

They were a lighter blue than his face, almost as pale along the ridges of his fingers and on his palms as Rel's skin. He looked cold, but he always did. "I have no experience whatsoever with them."

"Do you not study such things at the university?"

"Of course," said Deamaathani. "But three paragraphs in a discredited bestiary does not amount to experience."

"Zhinsky?" said Estabanado.

"I have never seen one," admitted the major. "There are many stories on my side of the mountains, more on this. None of them are good. This is the first I have heard of one in my lifetime. Some dismiss them as legendary."

"Apparently they are not." Estabanado sat down and stared dolefully at the map. "A skinturner."

"We should be careful. On Magister Decatur's scale, they rate a five in terms of relative peril," said Deamaathani.

"There's a scale?" asked Rel.

"Of course," said Deamaathani.

"What does it go up to?"

"Twelve. A rating of twelve being a manifest god of the old powers. So you have an idea of what we might have to face. The remaining gods are lesser creatures. Eliturion and the Duke rate an eight and a seven respectively," he added helpfully.

"That is not encouraging," said Rel. He sipped his brandy. The coldness of the liquid bit him, then the heat of the alcohol hit.

"It is not," agreed Deamaathani. "And the information this rating is based upon is questionable at best. Mathematics are only useful when rigorously questioned, I find. It is best not to accept anything regarding this creature at face value."

"Warlock, can you perform a sending to Perus? An incident of this gravity demands that we inform our superiors," said Estabanado.

"I can, but I will need a day to recover," said Deamaathani. "Sending a message that distance is difficult."

"You may have it. You will depart at first light the day after tomorrow. The villagers may stay here until you return. If it's all a load of dracon's shit they'll answer for wasting my time." He sucked down his brandy and hissed inwardly through his teeth. He looked at the map, towards the west where it ended, then beyond, off the table towards Perus. If the map had continued onward at that scale, Rel reckoned the Maceriyan capital to be somewhere over by the colonel's bookcases.

"If there's one good thing to come out of this," said Estabanado, "it is that they might send us more men."

CHAPTER THIRTY-THREE
A Confluence of Cousins

A LOBSTER, HALF a ham, a half wheel of strong blue cheese. Fruits, steamed vegetables, small dainties expertly baked. These were the dishes set between Trassan and his aunt, Cassonaepia Kressinda-Hamafara.

Vast was the first word that came to Trassan's mind whenever looking at her. Round as a ball, she was a floatstone merchantman vessel plucked from the Lockside and swaddled in organza. Her dress was a size too small for her, parts of her anatomy Trassan really did not wish to see spilled dangerously from it. Her chins were numerous, nose small and upturned as a pygmy sow's. She smiled often but falsely, the expression never reached her eyes. They remained hard and calculating.

"Your father," she was saying, although in actuality Cassonaepia said nothing, but shouted everything at an ear-splitting volume intended to quell dissent to her opinions. These were often erroneous, and just as often outright lies. Cassonaepia did so like to be right about everything. "Your father!" she repeated, belting out the second word with even greater emphasis. "How is he?"

Fat hands plucked at a lobster claw ineffectively. She glared at her footman who hurried over to dismember it. He exhibited signs of nervous exhaustion. All her servants did.

"Oh do stop fussing!" she snapped at the man as he arranged the meat for her. He beat a hasty retreat. "You will like this, Trassan. It was made by Ouseaux, the best chef in the city. Maceriyan, he is. A Perusian, a *Perusian*! Simply the best. I won't have anything else. Absolutely not. The best!"

"That's right dear," said Uncle Arvell.

"Be quiet you silly little man," she snapped. "What's the use with agreeing with me on every matter like that? I can say it for myself."

"My father is very well, aunt. Better than many physics expected."

She puffed up at being called aunt by Trassan. He was the scion of a noble house, and Cassonaepia cared very much for appearances. She wore the name with great pride, like a prince's mantel. She was notorious for mentioning her relationship to Gelbion loudly and often. "There you are, there you *are*!" she said. "Haven't I always said, better to rely on natural healing. Better that than the mutterings of magisters. Bring the dead on you, snip snap! And the physics. They are worse! You cannot trust those quacks, you cannot! Kill you dead as soon as cure a cold. Best avoid it. Didn't I always say that? Didn't I always say? Arvell, Arvell!"

"Yes dear," said her husband. Arvell Kressind-Hamafar was brother to Gelbion, but two more dissimilar men one could not hope to meet. He was as meek as his brother was bellicose. A pale, thin man, insubstantial seeming, as if his wife's cruelty had flattened the spirit out of him in the same manner as a roller flattens steel in a mill, mercilessly and automatically. He smiled nervously, then stopped, then started again, searching his wife's face all the time for guidance as to what he should be doing. He flinched as she scowled at him.

"Yes dear!" she repeated sharply. "See, Trassan, what level of conversation I have to put up with here! Look, I say Arvell, what I have to put up with."

"Yes dear," began Arvell.

"Oh do be silent, you stupid man! Can you not see that Trassan is in the middle of talking. Is that not so?"

Trassan was not, but his aunt never let the truth get in the way of her pronouncements.

"Such a nice boy. Look at him! Working with Arkadian Vand. I often say to the ladies how clever you are, Trassan! How rich you must be. How *rich*! Such prospects, such a *catch*! How goes your wooing?"

"I don't know about wooing," said Trassan. He smiled sheepishly at his cousin Ilona, at the other end of the rectangular table, where she was seated facing her father at the table's head.

"I know! I know! Everyone knows! You are to wed Vand's daughter? A good match. A good match!" she said. Her habit was to shout the second word of these repetitions. Conversation with her was arduous. "I am sure she is slim! And beautiful! Not like me, oh no, so sad. Oh, no more, absolutely not! I was quite the sylph in my earlier days, but even though I eat like a bird my boy, a *bird*, I cannot fit into my bridal gown any longer."

Trassan tried his best to keep his eyes from her plate. Between her barking, the woman had demolished half of the cheese, each knife-full larded onto sweet biscuits. She waited for Trassan to say she was not as large as she insisted. He managed a tactful mumble to that effect.

"You see! Manners my dear! Manners! You would do worse, Ilona, than to find a good, rich man like Trassan."

Ilona gritted her teeth. She was as slim as her mother was fat, as spirited as her father was broken. If she had not been, she would have been driven insane long ago. "Yes mother," she said.

"He's the boss, chop. The boss, *chop*!" Cassonaepia bellowed.

"It has been a long time since we last saw you, Trass," said Ilona. She smiled impishly at him. "Why do you avoid visiting our lovely home?"

"I wouldn't say I avoided it," he said. Wouldn't say, but he did avoid it. Nobody wanted to spend time with Cassonaepia if it could be avoided. "I am terribly busy with the ship. We must be ready to sail in spring."

"I read a book—" began Ilona.

"And of course, we can all believe what we read in those, can't we?" whooped Cassonaepia derisively. "I prefer to put stock in my own eyes. My own eyes!" she bawled. "Isn't that right?"

"Yes, yes it is dear," Arvell agreed meekly.

"Tell me about this book, Ilona," Trassan said, mindful that Cassonaepia was drawing in another huge breath.

"A book of polar exploration, by the Oczerk adventurer Rassanaminul Haik."

"I know the one, I read it myself."

"I hope you have done more preparation than that," Ilona said.

"I am sure he has, dear!" hollered Cassonaepia, annoyed that the centre of conversation had moved from her.

Trassan ignored her. "Yes. Of course."

"You'll be leaving in spring when the ice breaks?"

"That is the plan. The ice does not recede, to the best of current knowledge, until the beginning of summer, but it is a lengthy voyage to the deep south. We intend to arrive as the ice thins, allowing us through. Where it does not part, the engines and prow of the *Prince Alfra* should force a way for us." Trassan warmed to his subject, despite the banging headache his aunt's monologues had given him. He placed one hand flat upon the other, pushing the lower hand down. "Our engines are so powerful, and the weight of the ship so great, that I believe we shall be able to break our way through. Floatstone ships cannot do this. They become snared in the ice and cannot move until it breaks again, or they are carried toward the heart of the Sotherwinter by the gyres of the ice and are trapped there forever."

"Trassan!" Ilona said delightedly. "How ingenious. But did not Rassanaminul have wooden ships? That is the Ocerzerkiyan preference."

Trassan tapped at his plate. "He did. And he lost three of the four. A wooden vessel caught in the ice is crushed into matchsticks by the pressure of it. The ice moves, you see, with tides and storms. It is water after all."

"I have a passing familiarity with hydrodynamics," she said.

Trassan raised an eyebrow.

"Unlike you, cousin, I have little to do other than read. I grow sick of novels."

"Sick! Sick she says! Well, always got her nose in a book this one! She should be out, *out*! Looking for a husband! Waste of time. Books. Yes." Cassonaepia bit noisily into her food. During the space of Trassan and Ilona's exchange, she had eaten half the lobster. Her husband nibbled timidly on his own food. His wife became preoccupied with complaining loudly about the quality of her ham to her footman, so Arvell made an attempt at conversation.

"There is money in this expedition of yours?" he said quietly. Cassonaepia's eyes rose from her food at his temerity to speak without permission, but the footman drew her attention back to the meat. Arvell gave a grateful look to the servant.

"Oh yes!" said Trassan, enormously relieved that Arvell had brought the subject of money up first. "This is a marvellous opportunity. There have been no intact Morfaan cities found anywhere else in the world."

"Oh ho! Oh ho! Here we go, my lad. Who's to know the place isn't a gutted ruin? What then?" hooted Aunt Cassonaepia.

"The others are as they are because they have been looted and pillaged for materials greatly over thousands of years," continued Trassan. He spoke hurriedly, fixing his attention on Arvell in case he retreated back into his shell. "Vand has made a fortune from the items he has found, although Persin has stolen much from him by violating my master's patents. That is Vand's great talent, the rediscovery of the Morfaan's mastery of the physical arts, and reintroducing them, improved naturally, into our modern world. Imagine what he could do with undamaged devices. We will advance the causes of who knows what sciences. The knowledge of the ancients is ours to take!"

"Vand has no money himself?" said Arvell.

"Ridiculous!" huffed Cassonaepia. "The man is richer than King Brannon. King Brannon!"

"Of course," lied Trassan, "and he has invested heavily in it. You are too shrewd for me uncle. You have seen through the purpose of my visit."

"Which is?" asked Cassonaepia.

"Until we have the licence secured to cross the great ocean we are restricted to offering opportunities to a select few. I already have notes of intention from the Westerhalls and the Canderbridges."

"You want to borrow money from me?" said Arvell.

Trassan laughed. "Not borrow, uncle. I thought that you, as family, and knowing of your nose for a good earner, might appreciate the opportunity to share in the wealth my expedition will generate."

A calculating gleam entered Arvell's eyes, a flicker of the man he had once been. "You had an accident, as I recall."

"A small incident. A teething problem, you understand. New technology."

"Quite," said Arvell.

Trassan lowered his voice. "Between you and I, I fear it was sabotage. What does that tell you of our chances, if our rivals in Maceriya, naming no names, attempt to disrupt our efforts by subterfuge?"

"You cannot have my money!" shrieked Cassonaepia. "How dare you!"

"It is not your money," said Arvell quietly. He grew brave. "It is mine. You forget yourself."

"Oh! Oh! And I have done nothing! Nothing at all. That's right, that's right!" Cassonaepia drained her glass. A footman hurried forward to refill it. "You have done all the work, never mind that I sweated and struggled, struggled, I tell you, *struggled* to bring up our ungrateful daughter here while you were off gallivanting with your friends."

Trassan doubted that Arvell had ever been allowed out to do anything so interesting as gallivant.

"Now dear..."

"Stupid man!" The measure of wine, so recently poured, disappeared down Cassonaepia's throat.

Arvell clutched the tablecloth, rucking it. "You embarrass yourself."

"Come, Trassan!" said Ilona, standing with a sudden scrape of wood on marble. "I am sure you would like to see the garden. It has established itself very prettily since you were here last."

"Yes," said Trassan. "That would be lovely."

"Mother, father," said Ilona.

"Aunt, uncle," said he. They got hurriedly down from the table.

Cassonaepia's hooming and hawing boomed around the house as she put Arvell back into his place. Another footman let the door open for them into the night. Someone appeared with furs for them both.

Trassan shuddered as they went out into the garden.

"You'll have to do better than that, cousin, if you are to travel to the frozen wastes of the Sotherwinter."

"It's not the cold that is making me shiver," he said. "It's that beast of a mother of yours."

"She's getting worse. Once upon a time, she could keep a certain appearance of charm, now she acts as she pleases. She has isolated herself, and grows more strident for lack of company to correct her."

"I am sorry for you."

"You have no idea at all, Trassan, so don't you dare feel sorry for me." Her eyes flashed with anger.

"I'm sorry."

"Sorry for feeling sorry. You always were the worst at dealing with other people."

"I don't have Guis or Rel's knack, I suppose. I always felt happier with machines. They don't answer back, and when they make as much racket as your mother, you can turn them off."

She slipped her arm into his. "Come nearer me, I am cold."

They walked around the edge of the garden, keeping to the colonnade that enclosed it. Not true grounds, but a courtyard at the centre of Arvell's townhouse, it was nevertheless artfully laid out. A square of night overhead blazed with stars. The roses were leafless. Frost rimed the grass.

"Come and see the garden. Gods, Ils, couldn't you have come up with something more convincing?"

"Mother won't notice. She is blind as to how others really see her, or what they think. She lacks the ability to judge the feelings of others, that commonality of spirit. Ironic really, as she is immensely paranoid about the way others see her. I think if she had the tiniest bit of empathy, she'd be horrified. Fear is what makes her the way she is. She lacks the insight to see it."

"She will sulk at our absence."

"She will, but she never does for the right reason. She'll assume that I am trying to seduce you, not that we are up to something, or that we are trying to exclude her from our fun." She sighed heavily, her lightness vanished. "She'll sulk anyway, so what is the point in trying to stop it?"

"Are you trying to seduce me?" he asked. She did not answer. He continued in a different vein. "You are at least not like her. It is no wonder that your father is as crushed as he is. I often wonder why he has not left her."

"Love, I suppose."

"How can he love that?"

She pulled his arm so he came closer. "Love is blind, so they say."

"Apparently it is also an idiot."

She smiled. They had made their way around three sides of the cloistered way. They passed wide glass doors; a summer room, lights out, furniture covered in sheets for the winter.

"I find it hard to believe that Arvell is of the same stock as my own father."

"Do you find the same difficult to see in me?"

"Ah, definitely not. You are a Kressind through and through."

She stopped and pushed him against the wall, sliding a knee between his legs to pin him in place. She was no longer taller than him, nor stronger as she once had been. He had a man's strength now, his muscles hardened by his trade. But he could not escape easily.

"You have me at a disadvantage."

"You could just push me away." Her sweet breath washed over him.

"We're not brats any more. Wrestling would be a serious breach of decorum."

"More's the pity." She looked up at him from under her eyelashes and bit her lip. "Perhaps a kiss for your cousin?"

"You *are* trying to seduce me!" Trassan looked pained. He stared off to the side. "Ilona, I'm engaged."

"And not to me. Do you know how upset I was when I heard that? What's wrong with me?" She shoved at his chest.

"We're cousins."

"A bad excuse. You never used to say that when we were little. You said we would be married when we were older."

"Ilona! You can't take a few stolen kisses as a promise of marriage. We were children. They were fancies, experiments. Nothing more than that."

"It was a little more than a kiss, if I recall. And they meant more to me. I've been waiting for you. You made me a promise."

He had, that he could not deny. "I... look, I just fell for someone else. I'm sorry."

She retied the lacings of his collar as she spoke. "Sorry, sorry, always sorry. What is it with you and women, Trassan? Do you even try?"

He shrugged.

"What if I said I can get you that money?"

Trassan was too ashamed to tell Ilona he was hoping that she would open the way for him, and doubly ashamed that it was happening. "Your mother..."

"My mother is an outrageous old witch. I've had it with her. My father is not so stupid as he looks, he's got plenty of money hidden away. He tells her about it from time to time, and she takes it off him, and wastes it on some extravagance or another. Do you know, she has had this house redecorated eighteen times in the last five years? She is destroying his fortune. But he always has one more pot of money hidden somewhere. My father has the spine of a mollusc when it comes to my mother, but if there is one person he will indulge more than her it is me." She stepped back. "There, now you look like a respectable engineer, and not a rake."

He looked down at his collar.

"It does look better," he said.

"I can do it. And I promise to stop teasing you. Really. You know how I am. I've always enjoyed making you squirm a little."

"Like that time at Midfrozmer when you kept dropping hints into the conversation about what exactly we had been doing?"

She made a face of innocence, much like the one she had worn at the occasion Trassan mentioned. "Your father is deaf to innuendo, or I would not have done it."

"A bloody good job too, Ils, or I would have been doing a lot more than squirming when we got home. He would have beaten the crap out of me."

She poked him above his heart. "He would have got the servants to do it."

"It would still have hurt."

"I suppose so. But I can get you the money. And I want to."

"Ils, I can't marry you. I am sorry, but..."

"Shut up. It's not about that. We're still family, even if you bound yourself to some engineer's floozy daughter."

"She's not a floozy."

"Poor you."

"Ilona!"

She smirked at his discomfort. "There is a condition."

"That is?"

She rested both her hands on his chest.

"You have to take me with you."

"Are you mad?"

"I am not mad." She sighed and turned away. "I should be. You've no idea."

"What are you talking about?"

"And you with a sister like Katriona."

"You are losing me here."

"I will make it simple for you cousin. Remember when we played at dragoons and dragons as children?"

"Yes, of course."

"Tell me. What is the principal difference in the game for girls and boys?"

Trassan frowned. "None. You and Katriona wouldn't let there be. We were all dragoons. I remember the one time we tried to get you to be the damsel."

"When we played those games, you did so with the certainty that you could, if you really wanted to, become a dragoon or a knight or a magister. Katriona and I cannot."

"But the world has changed Ilona. You could become a magisterial aide, or a nurse. Or you could—"

"Have you noticed, they are all the roles of assistant, and never the leader?"

"There are women who are not assistants."

"Oh really? Like who?"

"Well," he said, "there's Lucinia of Mogawn. And Katriona. I did meet a very eminent family of lens makers last year, who were led by the most formidable matriarch."

"Exceptions. What do they say about the Hag of Mogawn? I'll give you a hint, it's in the name they've given her. How long do you think it will be before dear cousin Katriona ends up with a similar label, onerous as a millstone to carry, and one that she will never be able to set down? I don't want that, Trassan. Why don't I get to be a dragoon?"

"The world just isn't like that."

"And there you have my point. Well done," she said bitterly. "My mother talks to you about your career, and your prospects. She talks to me about marriage, because that is all there is for me."

"I never became a dragoon either," he said weakly.

"Rel did. Who knows what adventures he is having?"

"Knowing Rel, I am sure he is having a perfectly miserable time."

"But he gets to go! And you, so you are not a dragoon. Did you want to be one?"

"No..."

"So you had a choice?"

"Some..."

"There you are. You instead are the great engineer, building a technological wonder that will fetch back the secrets of the ancients to better the lot of all Karsans! If that is not a hero's role, then what is? Nobody rides dragons any more, Trassan. But heroes remain. The steeds change, that is all. What choice is there for me? To become a wife or a whore."

"Now you're being ridiculous."

"Am I? So, I pursue my own ambitions, and get called, why, a whore, whether I am or not. I bed a man I want to and get found out. What am I? I am a whore! I'd be better off becoming an *actual* whore, because at least then I'd be paid for the insult. I want to be a wife, Trassan," she looked pointedly at him, "but on my own terms. I don't want to be a whore." She smiled. "Well, not all of the time. What I do want is to ride dragons, like the old knights. Fuck what people say I should be.

Yes. Fuck. I've heard you say lots worse, cousin. And are you censured for it? Of course not, because you've got a fucking cock. So you can say what you like." She grabbed for his crotch. She was quick and he fended her off only at the last moment, losing much dignity in the process. "To add injury to the vast insult of my sex, I am forced to remain cooped up in this hellhole with that mad old tyrant until some droopy jawed halfwit with a title pays my mother enough to marry me."

"It's not like that anymore."

"No. 'It's not like that *all the time*, any more.'" She mimicked his voice, ridiculing his mannerisms. "It still is like that quite a lot of the time. You know nothing about it. For you, I will exercise power in one of the few areas open to me, mainly, squeezing a small fortune out of my father. It'll be hard work, but I'll put on a performance that would make one of Guis's actresses look like the rankest amateur."

Trassan paused. "You're sure you can do it?"

"He was half-convinced anyway. There's something sharp lurking underneath the gutless weasel he's become. All I have to do is make him more worried about upsetting me than he is frightened of my mother. You'll see. His desire to earn a good return on his money will do the rest. He has to support my mother somehow. All you have to do is get me away from all this."

"Can't I do something else for you? There are schools... You could go to the Queendom."

"I want to be free where I choose, thank you very much. That's the deal. Take it or leave it."

Trassan mulled it over a while. He held out his hand. "You drive a hard bargain."

"We are all Kressinds."

They shook.

"Now come on. Mother always kicks up such a stink when she thinks people are having fun without her."

"Have you thought about not indulging her?"

"Oh yes. And I have decided it's not worth the trouble not to. Not with my dear old daddy soothing her wounded self-importance and supporting her every lie. She'll be shaking me awake to drunkenly berate me in the small hours already. But that won't happen many more times, because you'll get me out of here. If I do this, and I will, and you even dare to consider leaving without me, I will kick you very hard, right in the balls. So hard, in fact, that you won't be much use to little miss spanner pants at all." She smiled dangerously. "I am sure even you can understand that."

CHAPTER THIRTY-FOUR
Vardeuche Persin

VARDEUCHE PERSIN SAT at his desk eating messily. A jowly man, thick about the waist, his form and his manner of eating suggested that he enjoyed his food. He gobbled impatiently, spilling morsels from his spoon onto the napkin tucked into his collar.

The napkin was richly made, as was his suit of clothes, his furniture, and every other thing. He was not as he first appeared, this gourmand in his rich man's rooms. If someone were to examine him closely, as many courtesans of Perus had had the opportunity, they would find thick muscle beneath the fat, they would feel that his hands were horny with hard work, and that there was always a trace of oil under his fingernails.

Tall windows looked out over the Marmore district of Perus. On a clear day one could see the soaring dome of the Pantheon Maximale, and to the smaller buildings of the Grand House of the Assembly in its shadow where the Assembly of Nations gathered. Over all hung the titanic disc of Godhome, bigger than the city. It had slipped sideways in the sky not long after Res Iapetus evicted its inhabitants and had remained that way ever since. To the east was the canyon of the Foirree and its elegant steel cable bridges, to the west the green expanse and rolling hills of the Royal Park, a wilderness of uncertain depths.

Like Persin, Perus was a study in contradiction. The most beautiful city in the Hundred, it was caked in industrial grime. The most ancient of capitals, it was full of new buildings.

Perus was once known as The City of the Morning, but for two hundred years it had had another name: Umbra, the City of shadow. The sun still blazed its morning glories upon the city from the east, but for the afternoon the sun could not reach the inner districts, its light blocked by the Godhome.

A portion of the rim of Godhome rested daintily upon the highest hill of the Royal Park, the rest leaned over the city like a giant parasol. There were thus two evenings in Umbra, three when the position of the Twin was just so, and for one day every four years there was no daylight at all. A pall of smoke worsened the gloom. White marble had become brown, the carved faces of ancient heroes and the chased-off gods melted by corrosive rain. Only the monumental mausoleum of Res Iapetus had escaped the worse. His statue still gleamed, while the rest lived in shadow. Beauty bore the burden of power, and it had become ugly. Lights burned in the streets all day long.

Persin had his back to all this. Perus was the past. His office, full of models of his achievements in glass cases, was the future. His fingers were occupied with his food, his eyes with the man in front of him.

"Morthrock, you say?" he spoke Karsarin with a strong Maceriyan accent.

"Yes, goodman," said Holdean Morthrock.

"Of the Morthrocksey Mills?"

"Yes, sir." Holdean fingered his hat nervously.

"I know them. Did business with them. Isn't the old man dead, Horras?" Persin tore a lump of bread from a loaf and mopped gravy from his plate.

"These last five years now, sir."

"And his son? He was in charge, was he not?"

"Was, goodman. My cousin has been supplanted by his wife."

"And you are not happy about this turn of events, no?" Persin shoved his plate away, tugged his napkin free and dropped it onto his plate. A servant came forward quietly and removed the tray it was upon.

"No, sir."

"I know this, you know. All of it." Persin dabbed crumbs off his desk with the tip of a finger and popped them into his mouth. "I know also that you were embezzling funds from the factory of your own family." He fixed Holdean with his dark eyes and tutted. "A very big scandal, all over the papers. You have disgraced yourself. And now you have come to me, and offer your services? What kind of man do you think I am that I would consider the employment of someone like you? I, the greatest engineer in the world."

"The woman, Katriona, she is a Kressind. She is supplying the ship of her brother, Trassan Kressind, who works for Arkadian Vand."

"I know of these individuals, naturally," said Persin.

"Any delay to the works there will delay Vand's enterprise."

"Of course." Throughout this discourse, Persin maintained a look of bland disinterest. Holdean sweated.

"You are engaged on a similar enterprise."

"I am." Persin paused. "Are you proposing sabotage, Messire Morthrock?"

Holdean's facial features danced around, unable to find an expression he thought appropriate. "Yes," he said eventually.

"Good!" said Persin, snapping his fingers. "I do hate a man who will not state his intent. How is such a man to be relied upon. Hm? What do you propose?"

Holdean eyed the chair before Persin's desk, but the engineer did not invite him to sit. "If I could make it back into the factory, then I might be able to whip up some sentiment against the Kressind woman. The workers there are not all happy to be taking orders from a woman, and she's showing consideration to the Tyn that the men there will be sure to think unfair. It will not be hard. I did a good job keeping the trade associations out of Morthrocksey. There was a reason for that."

Persin got up, and looked out of the window.

"This city is no stranger to intrigue, Messire Morthrock. The greatest city of the Morfaan lies buried beneath it. For three thousand years it was the capital of the Maceriyan Empire." He pointed out of the window, as if these were self-evident truths written in the sky. "Res Iapetus executed the greatest conspiracy of all not two centuries since, driving out the gods and ushering in this modern age, alas much to the detriment to the beauty of my city."

"Yes, goodman."

Persin swivelled on one heel. He had a long face, well-fleshed, so much so that his skin was stretched by its own weight. It was heavily folded, somewhat lugubrious, a face similar to those of the dwarf hounds of the Maceriyan Altus, whose purpose was the uncovering of delicate mushrooms in the woods. His eyes seemed similarly sad, but there was a flintiness to them. "This is a poor scheme. If you were found out, could I trust upon one such as you to hold your tongue? I do not think so. Might, could—these terms of ambivalence. They are not good enough. One day the energies of the Godhome might run out, or they might not. Wild Tyn could run still in the depths of the park, they might not. I have heard both these stories, messire. Stories that might be true, but I, Vardeuche Persin, have no time for unsubstantiated tales."

"I... I am sorry sir, to have wasted your time."

Persin shook his head. "No, no, no. I did not say that this interview is over. You will go when I dismiss you. I will say if this is a waste of time or not! Do not presume!"

"Yes, goodman."

"You offer your service. What will pay for it, a pretty pile of coins? Your clothes are well made but shabby. Your reputation on the other side of the Neck is in tatters. There is little for you here; none will take you on. Soon the news will have reached Mohacs-Gravo and beyond. The broadsheets enjoy this kind of story."

"She intimated that she would tell no one."

"More fool you for trusting a woman, perhaps? Or is it that your crimes are such the truth will, as your people say, out?"

"I don't know, goodman."

"Or did you further stain your own honour by rejecting a kindness, breaking a simple condition that might have saved your reputation?"

"I will not be humiliated by a woman, a Kressind! The Morthrocks are a proud and ancient family, not... not upstarts! Fishmongers! My ancestors fought alongside King Brannon himself!"

"You are destitute now. You offer me this service for payment, for money?"

Holdean's face twisted. "Revenge! I want that bitch to suffer the way she has made me suffer. All I did was take my due."

"Vengeance is a better motivator. Perhaps we can do business. So tell me again, can you effect what you say, if we can put you back into your place of former employment?"

"I... I believe so sir, I will have to be careful. My face is well known. But given time, I could place agents within—"

"Time we do not have. The Karsans do love their legislation so, but their courts are moving quickly. It will not be long before Trassan Kressind and his master, Vand," he could not help but snarl around the second name, "will have their documentation of passage through the Drowning Sea, and the way will be open to the Southern Ocean. Fortunately for us I have Shrane."

He plucked a small bell from his desk, fussily decorated in the Maceriyan style, and rang it. The doors were opened smoothly by an impeccably dressed footmen. A robed woman came in, the tall staff in her hand lightly tapping on the floor.

"This is my mage, Adamanka Shrane. Now, Medame Shrane, can you change him?"

The woman gripped Holdean's face in cool fingers and turned it this way and that. She was beautiful, but strangely so. She had feline eyes sat very high in her face, sharp cheekbones that rose over flat-planed cheeks. There was a faint ridge between her eyebrows, and an odd sheen to her eyes. She was like no woman he had ever seen in all the variety of the Hundred Kingdoms.

"So his own mother would not know him," she said. Her breath was metallic.

"There you have it, Messire Morthrock. We can, through the agency of Medame's magic here, alter your appearance thoroughly. Do you acquiesce?"

"I..." said Holdean, no longer comfortable with the direction of the meeting.

"This will be no glamour. I shall perform a deep altering. Irreversible." She breathed huskily. Her tongue, he noticed, was uncommonly pink and sharply pointed.

"Will it hurt?"

"Very much."

"Do not scare him away, Shrane!" scolded Persin. She released him and took a step back, to Holdean's relief.

To Morthrock, Persin said, "For the pain, I shall recompense you to the tune of, say, twelve thousand thalers? To be paid upon my satisfaction. Clear?"

Holdean stammered. "I... I... That is—"

"I thought so. Shrane, proceed."

Holdean Morthrock had never seen true magic worked before. His world was full of devices and marvels powered by otherworldly energies, but reality bent by will alone he had never witnessed.

There was no incantation, no incense, candles or anything of that ilk. Shrane breathed deeply through her nose, narrowed her eyes, and stared intently at him.

The next instant he was in indescribable pain. He clutched at his face, trying to swipe away the molten metal he was sure was running over his features. He was dimly aware of Persin shouting for his people, and his hands being wrestled down to his side by strong arms. In the tight grip of two men, he thrashed and howled. The excruciating sensation burned through his skin, taking hold of his skull. He felt the very bones of his face soften and move under invisible influences to a new shape. Pressure squeezed his eyeballs almost to bursting. He howled and begged for mercy. His words bubbled from the lipless hole his mouth had become.

"Hold him tighter!" hissed Shrane.

Something broke in his mind, some tender psychic tissue that connected the image he held of himself internally with his external morphology. He sank to the floor sobbing, pulling the two men after him. The pain receded from his bone, the muscles of his face spasmed as they were tuned to Shrane's design. His skin ceased to writhe, and the heat went from it. It stiffened, hair sprouted unnaturally quickly from his chin and eyebrows. A coarseness crept into his face, his skin rough where before it had been smooth.

"It is done," said Shrane.

The footmen hauled Morthrock up to his feet. His legs shook with the shock of his experience. Tears streamed from eyes that felt pierced by heated needles, but he blinked and could see again.

He pushed the men aside, staggered about the room for a mirror. His sight was subtly different, yellower, the field of vision wider but of lesser height. Persin smiled thinly and pointed behind Holdean.

There was a mirror above a mantelpiece. Holdean walked forward. In the mirror, an unknown man approached him. He wore Holdean's clothes and was of a size and build that matched his own, but the face was entirely different.

Holdean had had aesthetic features; somewhat sickly looking, thin-headed, but handsome in his way. This stranger's head was rounder, his features thicker. Prominent lips surrounded by coarse black beard, a nose above that was squashed and pocked by some disease Holdean had never suffered. The eyebrows were wild and long. He was ugly.

"Is it permanent?" he asked. He reached up to press his new flesh. It yielded like flesh should, was warm as flesh is. The sensations registered as his own.

"It cannot be undone," said Shrane.

"To do great things, a man must make great sacrifices," said Persin. "You will grow accustomed to the change."

"Gods..." he whispered. Only his eyes, the whites pink with broken blood vessels, remained his own.

"You are far from an honest man, Holdean Morthrock, but you are desperate," said Persin, "and that is a far more valuable characteristic in games such as these. Go now and prepare. You leave for Karsa City in the afternoon."

CHAPTER THIRTY-FIVE
The Company of the Dead

"WAKEY TIME! UP up up little merchant boy!" Zhinsky's voice shattered Rel's dreams and propelled him rudely out of sleep. Cold air blew into his room as the major pulled the rags from the slot window. Rel put his arm over his eyes.

"What time is it?"

"We go to Alu-mal. Now."

Rel squinted at the slot in the wall. He groaned and flopped back into his bed. "It's still dark!"

"Commander's condition, we go now, first light. Colonel's orders, merchant boy."

"Bastard."

"Estabanado or me?" said Zhinsky. He was dressed in some robe thing, including headgear from which hung a number of scarves. He wore his ridiculous Khusiak hat, and his goatskin jerkin, to which ensemble he'd added thick wool trousers, these only modestly ballooned. The links of a short-sleeved mail shirt peeked out between the layers. Strapped over his boots were boiled leather greaves, matching vambraces on his arms.

"Both," said Rel. "Ow!" he shouted, as Zhinsky tipped the bed over, depositing him upon the floor.

"We go now, come along! I not wait all day for slug-a-bed Rel!" He laughed uproariously. "This funny phrase! Slug-a-bed. You like?" He stopped laughing abruptly.

"Not particularly, sir."

"I say incorrectly?"

"No," said Rel grumpily. "Your Karsarin is astounding, sir. As good as your Low Maceriyan."

Zhinsky beamed. "Oh, so you just thin of skin."

"Something like that, sir."

"I knew it! Now put these on."

The major threw a bundle of clothes at Rel. They hit him in the face.

"You as bad catch as you are bad at everything, merchant's boy."

"What is this?"

"Sukniar Khusiachka. Khushashian riding clothes. You put on, put your fur on top. You will need them, it is very cold. We go soon! You hurry! Zhinsky not your servant, merchant's boy, rather you are mine! Go fetch your men, six. Bring Veremond, Deamaathani, and four others. You have chosen?"

"Yes, yes. They should be getting ready." He glanced at the window. "If it actually is first light. I told the rest to report to Lieutenant Helaska while we are gone."

"She will like that! They will not!" he laughed again. "Downstairs. Three minutes."

REL CAME OUT into the yard tugging self-consciously at his clothes. They were outlandish, and uncomfortable under his breastplate. The wool pantaloons itched, and the robes rode up under the shoulder strap of his ironlock carbine. Zhinsky was already in the yard of the fort with two dracons. They had Khusiak style saddles with high cantles and pommels, double lance tubes either side. Rel's embarrassment was not helped by Zhinsky doubling over with howls of laughter when he saw Rel. The Khusiak tried to talk, but could not manage it, erupting into giggles each time.

"What's so funny?" snapped Rel. When Zhinsky was behaving like that it was easy to forget he was a major.

"You... you have it on wrong way!" he laughed. Tears ran down his face in such streams he had to flick them away from his moustache beads.

Rel held up his arms. He could not tell front from back.

Zhinsky mastered himself, and came over. "Take your arms from the sleeves. Lift up the top robe. Here, I help. Get this breastplate off! Foolish boy."

Zhinsky span the robe around on Rel's neck, sniggering softly and shaking his head. He giggled even more when he discovered Rel was wearing his uniform jacket under the robes.

"It's cold out here," he protested.

"Yes, this is why I have this." Zhinsky tugged at his goatskin jerkin. "And wool underneath, silk underneath that. Keeps the sweat from your skin. This jacket good for parade, not good for cold steppe nights. Take it all off!" He whistled, sending a boy for the items described. He returned quickly, and Zhinsky helped Rel redress.

"I have never worn one of these before," said Rel, his feelings bruised.

"No, you have not!" He reached behind Rel's neck. "Now, this go here. This here," he said as he arranged the strange nest of scarves around his neck and face.

"Will I be warm enough? Ow!" he said, as Zhinsky pinched him.

"Pathetic girl. Merchant's daughter, not boy. Zhinsky wrong. Yes, yes! You be fine, not too cold. Now, let us put your armour back on over, then fur on that."

He tightened the straps of Rel's breast and backplate while Rel held them against his body.

Zhinsky smoothed his beard, opening his mouth wide as was his habit. "This good quality, thick." He rapped the steel with a knuckle. "But only good when facing men, or guns. Here, you need more. We find you some." He looked Rel up and down critically. He smiled. "Now, you look more like a Khusiak and less like an idiot."

Zhinsky gave more instructions to the fort servants in his guttural language before hurrying off somewhere, leaving Rel with the dracons. One was a pale green, the other a light mauve. They were of a different sub-breed to those he was used to in Karsa, being stockier and heavier in limb and having far more feathers than Karsan dracons. Like those he had ridden before, they possessed the long, spatulate feathers upon their grasping forearms and a crest of four long plumes on the tops of their heads. But whereas the dracons of Karsa were otherwise naked, these were covered all over with downy, hollow spike feathers, leaving only the head, secondary arms and lower legs bare. They preened themselves with their foreclaws and middle limbs as they waited. Neither of them wore muzzles, tail brakes or claw sheaths, and this gave him pause. Never had he ridden one without. The mauve gave him a long, yellow-eyed reptilian stare. Nictating membranes slid back and forth over the eye. Rel backed away a pace.

His men came out of the central stable block leading their own mounts, Veremond first. Five others followed him: the Khusiaks, Zorolotsev and Wiatra—the first tall and bearded, the second short and extravagantly moustachioed—a Karsan from near Stoncastrum named Dramion, then the Correndian, Merreas. Last was an Olberlander whose name no one could pronounce to his satisfaction, so everyone called him Olb. Deamaathani came out of a lesser block and fell in to join them. He nodded at Rel in acknowledgement. All of them had adopted at least some elements of Khushashian riding dress. The odd mismatch of uniforms that characterised the army of the Glass Fort was less pronounced than it ordinarily was. There was a patchwork uniformity to the patrol, excepting Deamaathani, who wore his own outlandish garb in many shades of blue. With it he wore a bronze breastplate, spalders, greaves and vambraces. The warlock rapped his chest with his bare knuckles. "Iron interferes with magic. Bronze serves well."

"Sir," said Veremond. The others greeted him. Wiatra spoke little Low Maceriyan, and Zorolotsev was close-mouthed by inclination. The others spoke quietly to each other as they checked their mounts over.

The servants, a mix of local tribesmen, Khusiaks and fortune hunters from the Hundred, returned in greater number, carrying heavily laden saddlebags and blanket rolls. They dumped them near the dracons before going back for more. An army groom led Deamaathani's mount to him; a handsome, jet black monster that rattled happily when it saw its master. Another brought canteens from the well house slung about his shoulder in threes and fours. Zhinsky came back, carrying additional armour similar to his own. He tossed it to Rel.

Once the supplies were all delivered, Zhinsky dismissed the servants and the soldiers set about loading up their mounts while Rel buckled on the armour. The dracons clicked in annoyance. Zhinsky calmed them with words in his own tongue.

Rel approached his own dracon carefully.

Zhinsky fetched a pair of slender lances from a rack near the hitching post. "So, I finally see you ride today. If you as good at this as you are with your sabre, maybe I only mock you a little. This is Aramaz." He indicated the mauve dracon. "He is named after a famous Khusiak. Very good dracon, I choose him for you myself. Load him. He is waiting you. You do know how to ride, yes?"

"Yes," said Rel. "It's just..." Aramaz cocked his head to one side and let out a series of clicks from its pulsing throat.

"Just what, little rich man?" Zhinsky slotted his lances upright into their holders.

"I've never ridden one without the muzzle and claw sheaths on." He grabbed the reins.

"Pah! They have eaten, why are you so scared?" Zhinsky spat. Rel picked up his saddlebags and slung them over the dracon's thin neck in front of the saddle. Zhinsky tutted impatiently.

Rel was aware that he risked making a fool of himself in front of his men. The other Khusiaks had finished and they in particular were watching him disapprovingly. He loaded Aramaz and mounted as quickly as he could. His mount sidestepped under him, rattling a call of annoyance as he shifted about in the saddle.

"You truly have never ridden a dracon for war? What kind of sauralier are you?" said Zhinsky.

"One whose father paid for his commission. But I can ride, sir."

"Not very well." Zhinsky said dismissively. "So it is. Then I teach you how to do it Khushash way." He put his hands on the pommel of the saddle, one step on the stirrup. "So first, you know the most important part. Stay away from the mouth. This is the biting part. It is dangerous." He hauled himself up. "And the tail. This is dangerous also. But the feet, ah, they are the most deadly." Zhinsky leaned forward over his pommel. His dracon croaked and he scratched the top of its head. "I advise you stay in the middle. Then you will be fine!"

The men laughed. Zhinsky grinned fiercely. In his steppe tribe costume he looked dangerous. A wild man from the edge of the world, fresh from a story.

"Thank you. I know that," said Rel through gritted teeth.

"Very good. Now we are galloping." Zhinsky brought his dracon in a circle around Rel. "You have been at gallop before?"

"Yes!" said Rel in exasperation.

"Very good! We go now."

Whooping in Khushiacki, Zhinsky dug his heels into the side of his dracon. It jutted its head forward, folded in its two upper sets of limbs, and strutted off at a terrific pace. The fort gates retreated into their slots in the wall as he ran at them, and darted through the gap between.

By the time Rel led his men through, Zhinsky was off the switchbacked ramp and heading out onto the plains, waving his hand around his head.

Rel watched him go.

Aramaz looked over its shoulder at him.

"Go on then," he said. "Go!"

The dracon stridulated and pawed at the ground. Rel dug his heels in. "So much for asking nicely. Hyah! Hyah!" he shouted, pricking the reptile's soft underbelly with his spurs.

The dracon lifted its head, roared, and leapt forwards worryingly close to the unbounded edge of the road. Rel signalled for his men to follow before he was too far ahead. He grimaced as the dracon slalomed around the bends and past a wagon crawling up from the plain. He was off the ramp swiftly, scattering pedestrians at the small market by the watchpost, then out over the trackless grasslands of Farside. Wind whistled past Rel's ears. The jerking trot of the dracon became a smooth gallop, its head arrowed forward.

The creature's legs ate up the ground. Rel smiled to himself. This was the first time he had ridden a dracon so freely, and he found it exhilarating. No drillmaster bellowing at him, no walls to arrest his progress, no need to pay heed to formation, men under his command following behind him.

He had a moment of realisation. As tedious as his duties had been in the fort, there was a very real possibility he had been even more bored in Karsa.

He was not bored now, not at that moment, although he was, he added to himself, fucking freezing.

He set his sights on Zhinsky, and followed him unerringly across the hissing grass.

Behind them, the Glass Fort hid itself in the mountains.

ON THE THIRD day northwards from the Glass Fort, Zhinsky reined in his dracon and gestured out over the grass to the desert. His mount tossed its head and chirruped angrily, drawing great gouges in the earth with its claws.

The patrol came to a halt. Zhinsky called Rel to ride up beside him. Rel kept his distance so that the dracons would not fight, but Zhinsky seemed to hold this convention in scant regard, and moved in so close their knees touched. "See!" A dirty finger indicated a black smudge on the horizon.

"What's that?" said Rel, keeping half an eye on his mount. The pair of them nuzzled each other and croaked happily. He was halfway to deciding half of what he had learned about dracons in the 3rd Dragoons was shit, and when he took his eyes from them he was almost comfortable about it.

"Storm of sand. Blow out of Blacksands sometimes onto the steppe." Zhinsky stroked his moustaches down the side of his open mouth with finger and thumb. "Very bad."

"Is it dangerous?" asked Rel. Zhalak gave him that look that suggested he thought Rel an idiot. Rel was growing weary of it.

"A little. The storm might put us off course. But we stay out of the desert, we stay safe. That no problem."

"So what is the problem exactly?"

Zhinsky pursed his lips. He shaded his eyes as he watched the smear grow. "Storm not the problem. What comes with it, that the problem. If the breach is close, then..." He called out to the others. "Storm! We must prepare."

The Khusiak advised Rel to drink as much as he could, explaining that he would not be able to while the sandstorm was on them. Then he showed Rel how to use his Khushashian sukniar to protect his face. The long scarves wrapped loosely around his neck now made sense as Zhalak wound them tightly against his mouth and nose. "Not too tight!" he admonished, wagging his finger, even though it was he doing the wrapping. "Or breathing is too hard." Zhinsky's fingers smelled of dracon and strange spices. He picked up the last scarf. "If it get really bad, wrap this around the eyes. Only if really bad! We call this the oshlepnienie, the, the..." he searched for the word. "The blind! Yes! No, no the blinder."

"Blinker?" said Rel. "Like for dracons?"

"Yes! Yes, this exactly. Blinker. You can see nothing. The thinner veil, this protect eyes in light storm. The blinker is for heavy weather."

"I can barely see with it on," said Rel. Zhinsky was an outline crosshatched by the weave of the cloth.

"You will not see at all with the blinker. You can, if you wish, bring it up so, under the eyes. Leave a small slit to see. But if it is so bad to make you do this, well, should wrap it over face entire. You understand."

Rel nodded. "Can I take it off now?"

"Off? No!" Zhinsky took of his fleece hat, balanced it on the pommel of his saddle and reached for his own scarves. Behind them, the men also prepared. Deamaathani had a leather mask with glass lenses set over his eyes. The others used the scarves, the more experienced helping the less. "Storm looks far, but is moving fast. We have half hour, maybe less. Leave it on until it is over. Do not pull it down. Sand is sharp, kill your eyes."

He had his own scarves done up quickly. "We keep riding. Do not stop! You see anything in the storm, anything at all, do not approach."

"You don't have to tell me twice. I grew up near the sea."

"This not sea. This sand. They come from the sands," said Zorolotsev, riding close.

"The major has never seen the sea." Rare words from Wiatra, and insubordinately dismissive ones at that. "I have. The captain is right, major, it is like the sea."

"Yes! Yes! So Wiatra say, like the sea!" Zhinsky punched Rel companionably in the shoulder. "This place, Farside, similar to the land between sea and shore. The Blacksands are like a big beach place, a place that is two places overlapping, a place in between two places..." He overlaid his hands atop each other then threw them up. "Bah! Braku mina slow. The words, I lack the words."

"Liminal?" said Rel.

Zhinsky laughed. "Ha! Yes. Liminal." His laughter died slowly, not the abrupt cut-off the Khusiak favoured when he was making a point. He looked over his shoulder, wheeled his mount around. The wind was already picking up. The dracon's display feathers stiffened in reaction. The creature sidestepped. "The things of the sands, they come before the storm, they linger after the storm. Not a big problem most days, but if there is a breach big enough for skinturner to get through, we must get away from here. We spend much time talking. Form up! Two by two! Zorolotsev, pair with the captain." He fastened his scarf around his mouth. "Now we ride."

THE WIND CAME first. Then the temperature dropped suddenly. The sky went black, long tendrils of sand chasing the sun away. The storm hit them soon after. Their pace slowed to a crawl. They tried to stay together, but the wind worked hard against their intention, and a gap opened up between the riders. Whirling shrouds of sand hid Zhinsky from Rel. The Khusiak rode with Dramion. They wavered in and out of view, uncertain as a mirage. Rel's dracon plodded on, its forearms drawn up protectively underneath it. The top of its head pointed forward, protective outer eyelids tightly shut, nostrils closed to a slit. Zorolotsev was a vague bulk by his side.

Rel kept his own head down. The swaddling of his sukniar kept much of the sand from his eyes and nostrils, but not enough. It worked its way through the layers of cloth, chafing his skin. It collected in the corners of his eyes, starving them of moisture. Grains found their way under his eyelids, and there was little he could do but blink frantically to dislodge them, wincing as they scratched his cornea. Despite the restrictions on his view, he considered wrapping the thicker cloth of the blinker around his face, trusting to his dracon to carry him out of it.

He looked up. Zhinsky had vanished entirely. He could see nothing before or behind. The grass was hidden by serpents of windblown sand, fine as ash, where patchy snow lay it had turned black. Grass blades whipped about, driven first this way then that. The sun was hidden, its light thin and directionless. There was no way he could tell where the Khusiak had gone.

"Zhinsky!" he shouted. "Zhalak Zhinsky!" The wind tore his voice away.

He looked all around him, yanking on the dracon's reins to bring it in a tight circle. "Zhinsky! Zhinsky!"

The wind made a fluting moan.

"Zhinsky! Zorolotsev!"

"Captain!" replied Zorolotsev. His voice was torn ragged by the wind. He sounded far away.

Rel pulled his scarf down, and regretted it. Sand blasted into his eyes. His view was more obscured than with the scarf. Cursing, he yanked it back up. Sand stuck to the side of his nose and eyelashes. It smelled sharp and bitter, the scent of bad magic.

Ahead, he caught sight of a shape in the whirling dust.

"They are there!" he called. Zorolotsev emerged from the storm and came close. Rel waved at him. "Come on!"

"Captain, nieya!!"

But Rel spurred his way on. The dracon clicked deep in its throat, dug in its feet against the wind.

The shape ahead came and went. Rel could not make it out properly until he was on top of it. It was not Zhinsky, but a man on foot, head down against the wind. He wore a long robe and a hood that was pointed. He was walking toward him.

Rel pulled up twenty yards short of the figure. The wind dropped precipitately. A menacing calm replaced it. The air was hazy with dust. From this sharp fog more figures emerged, walking in single file. A taller shape loomed, and Rel's heart skipped, thinking it to be a modalman or other demon from the wastes. An idol on a pole. That was what it was. Nothing more.

Zhinsky's words came back to him. He thought of the things that roamed the sands of Karsa at night, and his heart raced anew.

These men were not of the living.

He pulled hard at his dracon's reins, urging it back. It was skittish, and croaked. Its head feathers rose in alarm.

Rel wasted a precious second bringing it around. The men were coming closer. They moved slowly, their progress too quick for their pace.

He wheeled about. Zorolotsev was nowhere to be seen; instead the same procession greeted him, coming from the other direction. He looked over his shoulder. The haze there was empty. They were close now.

Rel turned his mount around and around. Every which way he faced, the procession was, their somnolent walk bringing them inexorably upon him.

They were four paces away. He heard a low, droning chant, almost below the range of hearing.

Rel dug his heels into the lizard's side. The dracon shrieked in terror, stepping back and rearing up. He was tipped from the saddle, banging his kidney painfully on the high cantle. He landed hard on the grass. The ground was gritty. Sand had insinuated itself between the blades, the desert swallowing the prairie.

Aramaz ran free.

Rel pushed himself up on his elbow. A circle of hooded figures surrounded him. The patch of sky they framed was black, not the black of the storm, but the utter absence of light. He was terribly cold. The chanting droned higher.

Nearby, someone screamed. The unfettered sounds of terror pouring from a throat. On and on it went. The screams changed pitch, becoming cries of agony.

They stopped.

One of the figures extended its hand towards him. Skeletal fingers cloaked in pale, luminous flesh reached for his face. Rel stared at them, transfixed.

A whooping came from outside the circle. Rel had the impression that it was close by, but it sounded far away, distant. The remembered noises of a dream.

The hooded figure looked behind it. Rel caught the gleam of naked bone beneath its cowl.

His hand reached for his belt unbidden. His fingers slipped under his robes and closed upon the pouch Aarin had given him. He drew it out.

Pain jabbed his arm. White light blinded him. He cried out. Gentle wind kissed his face. Then, the touch of the sun.

He opened his eyes. The figures were gone. The air was still hazy, but the storm had passed. Zhinsky and Zorolotsev were was sat upon their dracons, sabres drawn, amazed. Zhinsky recovered and slid off his mount to come to Rel's side. Zorolotsev turned about and rode around, shouting for the others.

Deamaathani rode up behind them on his strange, slender-legged mount. Yellow witch fire played about his hands, but it was fading, and went out as he reached the others.

"That was a powerful warding. How did you do it?" he said.

Rel held up the pouch.

"Ah," Zhinsky nodded. "A good charm you have there."

"My brother gave it to me."

"He should thank the merchant that sold it. Better, give me his name so that I might thank him and buy my own."

"No merchant," said Rel. "My brother made it."

Zhinsky stood tall. His posture radiated suspicion. "Brother?"

"He is a Guider, a speaker for the Dead."

Zhinsky looked puzzled.

"A death priest, a ghost talker."

Zhinsky passed his hand over his brow and spat. "So, not all spoiled merchant boys."

"I keep telling you, my father is an industrialist."

"He makes things, he sells them. Is the same," Zhinsky sniffed, and sheathed his sabre.

"Are you going to help me up then?" He reached out with his right hand. His left was as numb as if he had held it in iced water.

Zhinsky extended his hand hesitantly. Rel grinned.

"See. Not mocking me now."

"I get over it."

"What was that? I have never seen the like," said Deamaathani.

"Parade of the Dead. Lost souls. I said to you, very bad. Zhinsky said this."

"Bad how?" said Rel.

The major shrugged as if it were a small thing. "They touch you, you follow them forever. Become part of the parade."

"Procession," breathed Rel, unconsciously correcting his superior. He was going to thank Aarin profusely when they returned home.

"Procession, parade. What is the difference?"

Rel frowned. "What?"

"Never mind. You tell me later. And I think the word is company. Yes. The Company of the Dead."

"Interesting," said the warlock. "You have a talent for magic in your family?"

"Not really," lied Rel. "Just Aarin."

"We go to safer places," said Zhinsky. He put his fingers between his lips and whistled. His dracon's head jerked around. Shortly Aramaz materialised from the hazy air. It ran straight for the men and circled them croaking, head feathers twitching. More shapes were coming from the haze.

"See, Aramaz happy to see you." Zhinsky scratched between its flaring nostrils. Rel winced.

"You have to teach me how to do that without losing my hand."

"I cannot," said Zhinsky, "because you are not a Khusiak. Report in! Everyone! Here, now."

The others joined them one by one. Wiatra was not among them.

"Major! Captain!" called the Correndian Merreas. "Trooper Wiatra..." he rode up. His eyes were wide with fear behind his scarf. Dramion appeared, leading Wiatra's mount. "Back there..." Merreas was terrified, unable to speak clearly.

Zhinsky cursed, and remounted his dracon. Rel got onto Aramaz, and followed the major for a hundred yards. Zhinsky stopped, and Rel saw a desiccated corpse, ancient seeming, kneeling in the grass with his arms held upwards to ward something from his face.

It was wearing Wiatra's clothes. Zhinsky clucked his tongue at his dracon and rode away from it without a word. The others rode past it; Merreas cast fearful glances at it.

"What of him?" shouted Rel, lingering by Wiatra. "Should we not report it? Send for the fort Guider?"

Zorolotsev pulled up his dracon and rode back to Rel. He spat onto the ground. "It is too late for his soul captain, " he said. "He walks with the company now."

CHAPTER THIRTY-SIX
Guider Triesko

"Three days, master, I hope it is worth the trip," said Pasquanty. He shivered in the fog.

Aarin frowned at him. "Shut up." He lifted the knocker upon the gate of the monastery and slammed it down twice. The knocker was recognisable as an effigy of the Dead God only through its posture, the crucifixion common to his depiction. The iron had been worn smooth by innumerable hands; arms and legs were indistinguishable from the cross. Hollows hinted at eyes and a mouth around the nub of a nose. The hinge around the pin had become thin as a reed. The plate had long gone, and the feet of the god slammed directly into a dent in the old wood. The wood of the door was grey, eroded into a miniature mountain range of ridges and troughs, the spaces between the planks wide as the gaps between an old man's teeth.

Pasquanty looked uneasily behind him. Between the twins he could see nothing but fog choking the valley. A train whistle howled somewhere within it, impossible to locate.

"This place is too quiet. Dead."

"It is winter," said Aarin. The landscape around the monastery was softened by centuries of tender husbandry, but in the fog they could have been at the ends of the earth.

"It's too old."

Aarin raised his eyebrow at him. "It is not as old as the Black Isle."

"It feels older. Geriatric."

"The monastery has been in constant use since the days of the Maceriyan Empire. And it is home to venerable members of our order. I do believe you are letting your preconceptions bother you, Pasquanty. This is a peaceful place. A reward. In summer it is very pleasant."

"The fog, the hills, soft as old bread. I don't like it. It's like death in life. It reminds me of the... the..." he searched. "The Hethikan afterlife."

"A particularly miserable interpretation of the hereafter."

"I don't know, I think it's probably spot on."

"You really have the wrong vocation, Pasquanty."

The twins shuffled behind them and moaned.

"We need to get fresh servants," said Pasquanty. "These two are rotting. They stink."

"They'll last the winter out."

"You don't have to lead them."

"A privilege of seniority, Pasquanty. Now stop whining."

Aarin hammered on the gate again. It was cold out in the mist, a damp chill that quickens sickness.

"Yes! Yes! We are coming!" said a testy voice muffled by the gates.

The gates creaked back. Two unliving like the twins pulled them wide, shackled to chains attached to the door. The links were as diminished by age as everything else.

A Guider in the sombre black of the contemplative orders looked them up and down. His face was saggy with the weight of years. His hair was white, but his eyebrows remained startling back, giving him the appearance of a disgruntled badger.

"Guider Aarin, isn't it? I recognise the eye." He drew around his own eye with a finger.

"I wrote ahead."

"Yes, yes, we were expecting you." He beckoned them in. "Well do come in, let's not stand about all day."

"Thank you...?"

"Brother Yostion. I am the gatemaster here. The deacon is unavailable, so I'll take you right through. I hope you're not intending to stay here, as we're full."

"We have lodgings in Abledon, down below."

That mollified Yostion a little, and he became less gruff. "Good, good. I can offer you something to eat if you wish."

"Feed my deacon if you would. I would like to speak with Guider Triesko as soon as possible."

"It's for the best, I think. He takes a nap most afternoons and is due it shortly. He's in the garden at the moment."

"In this weather?" said Pasquanty.

Yostion gave him a black look. "The young. No backbone. No wonder the order is falling apart."

"Wait here, Pasquanty. You can go and get some food. We'll be heading back down to Abledon immediately after I've spoken with Triesko. I'll be spending a lot of time here later in my life, if I'm lucky. I don't want to preempt myself."

"Yes, Master Aarin." Pasquanty bowed.

"You know the way?" asked Yostion.

"I do."

"I'll stable your unliving for you, and feed this wretch." Pasquanty scowled.

"I need to take this box from my bearers," said Aarin. Yostion moved aside. Aarin retrieved the small chest carried by the twins. They snuffled and blinked, perturbed by the removal of their burden.

"Now then young man, this way," said Yostion to Pasquanty. "And you, Guider Kressind, do not overstay your visit with Triesko. He tires easily."

"I will not be long."

FOG LAY AS heavily over the monastery as over the landscape outside, thick and cloying as a soaked blanket. Old Guiders and their carers passed as indistinct shapes.

Upon a stone bench beneath a naked tree, Aarin found Triesko swaddled in a coat and fur.

"The triple moon of Longdark approaches, and an old pupil returns! It is a portentous time that you come to me, Aarin Kressind. Woe betide those who seek to trouble those waiting peacefully for death," said Triesko pompously. He continued to stare into the mist at a vista Aarin could not see. Aarin sat down next to him. He put the chest down and sighed with relief; the chest was heavier than it looked and its iron bindings were cold against his bare skin.

"Really? I brought you some brandy." He opened the latches on the chest.

Triesko looked at him from the corner of his eye and smiled broadly. His sanctimonious manner vanished. "Well that puts a different complexion on things. How are you, my boy?"

Aarin made an indifferent face. "Not bad, master."

"And how is your acolyte?"

"He whines half the time, and when he is not whining, he is terrified."

"They are all like that."

"I was not."

"You were more than you remember. Stick by him, he'll see the job done."

"I hope so. The order is not what it was." The shabby fabric of the monastery was enough of a reminder of that. "How are you keeping?"

"The same. I'm old, half-blind, cold, and painfully aware that I will never know the love of a woman again. Other than that, things go pleasantly enough."

"I am glad to hear it."

"I am glad that you are glad. At my age, one is gladdened by the most anodyne of things." He glanced at the chest. "Are you going to open that brandy or not? That may make me a little gladder yet."

Aarin bent to the chest. "There's a few other things in here. A new scarf, a padded jerkin, some of that sausage you used to eat so much of."

"Thank you."

"You're right to thank me. I've never been able to stand the smell."

Triesko chuckled. Aarin took out a bottle and uncorked it with his teeth. There were two small silver cups in the chest. Triesko shook out a gloved hand from under his blanket and took the cup Aarin offered. Aarin poured brandy into Triesko's, then into his own.

"Your health, Guider Aarin."

"And yours, master."

They drank and gasped appreciatively in unison.

"A good drop."

"It's the least I could do."

"Maybe. And what is the least I can do for you?" said Triesko.

"What makes you think I want something?"

"Three days travel from Karsa? Your next visit isn't due until after the winter. Don't be evasive."

Aarin shrugged. "I think I might have overstepped the line."

"You have been consulting with Mother Moude?"

Aarin nodded guiltily. "That and more."

"Of course." Triesko took a nip of brandy.

"You are not surprised?"

"Yes. Why are you surprised by my lack of surprise. You have Mother Moude."

Aarin feared that Triesko might finally have lost his wits to age. "Do you understand what I am saying, I have been using her."

"Everyone who is given Mother Moude uses her! Which is well enough, as only those who are capable of using her are given her. Did you not wonder why she was made yours to guard? It is forbidden, of course, but expected. It is the way of our order."

"I came expecting censure."

Triesko shrugged. "You'll get none from me. You are part of a guardianship, Aarin. Alert minds, trustworthy, given a task they cannot betray because they are not taken into the confidence of what that task is."

"An inner order?" said Aarin.

"No! Nothing so grand. There is no secret inner circle or any of that hierarchical claptrap. Promising young men are chosen, and allowed a certain discretion, that is all. Like I was."

"You used Mother Moude?"

"I did. Many times. And, like you, more besides."

"But it is black necromancy! Forbidden."

"It is."

"I never expected it of you."

"That's why I was chosen." Triesko rasped out a chuckle. It took a lot from him, he leaned forward onto his knees, his breath rattling in his phlegmy lungs. "Aarin, this is the order of death! The world's last priesthood. All of us are engaged in necromancy. I chose you to succeed me because you are one of the few who will use what is given to you properly. Or so I thought. Do not disappoint me, my boy. I want to die thinking I've done one thing right."

"What I have been doing pushes the boundaries of the acceptable."

"By whose terms? The terms of this age? Older times had different terms. The dead answer to those as readily as they do to the rule of the present. It doesn't matter to them. You have overstepped the bounds, Aarin, but you have been allowed to do so."

"There were gods then."

"It is hard to know when you have broken the unwritten rule, Aarin. It is also easy to circumvent. For both those reasons it remains unwritten. We need a little leeway in our work."

"I will not be censured then?"

"I did not say that. If your dabbling became public the Lord Guiders would be forced to act. You'd find yourself ghosting dead sailors mid-battle on the Ocerzerkiyan main without a doubt. But they'll turn a blind eye, Aarin, because you're not a fool, and you are acting from genuine concerns." Triesko paused. "You are acting from genuine concerns?"

"Yes, I believe I am."

"That you are not sure is a good sign." Triesko gripped his knee with a hand gnarled by arthritis. "And what have you uncovered. What is troubling you my boy?"

"The passage of the dead. It is changing. I can feel it. The way the dead go, something is different. Fewer dead need ghosting, but the ones that do... They are more reluctant, more alive, if that makes any sense. I remember my first, they were mumbling shades who faded with peace. Lately they have been unsatisfied. More... vocal."

"It has been noticed by others."

"I cannot understand why. I have consulted with the libraries in Macer Lesser. Guider Kalisthenes of Hethika has passed away, I found. I had been hoping to ask him. There is nothing in the works of our order that suggests this is at all normal."

"No. There would not be."

"Why not? Why is it changing?"

Triesko sighed. "Aarin, not every question has an answer. The world is a very different place to what it was when I was a boy, and would be all but unrecognisable to my great-grandfather."

"But those are the works of men. Men are bound to change. The dead are constant"

"You are correct, it is something greater. Listen to me, my boy. The world we inhabit is not so stable as we think.

Each generation lives in a false bubble of permanence. It is only at times like this, when the fulcrum of change itself moves, that we realise the extent of mutability inherent in all the world. The mages understand this, even as the magisters do not. I cannot fail to see the humour that the greatest change in recorded history is being driven by a doctrine founded on the empirical uncovering of changeless laws which are anything but changeless. Without gods, we have become arrogant.

"Aarin, we are not so mighty as the true mageborn, but you, nor I, would not be able to do what we do without a certain amount of talent. We can perceive this, we who tread the borders of life."

"I wish it were more."

"You have enough for the task ahead of you."

"The dead then, are they perturbed by the altering fabric of our times? The cities, machines, and so forth?"

Triesko sucked in a deep breath of chill air, held it, and blew it out. "It is more fundamental than that. Something is shifting. The modern world owes much to the knowledge of the ancients."

"The Maceriyans?"

"The Morfaan," said Triesko. They sat quietly for a few moments, their clouds of breath moving off to lose themselves in the fog. The day was brightening, individual layers of the mist made themselves apparent. The sun shone through the vapour, a pale yellow circle.

"It was expected that you would come to ask about this. Well done."

"I do not understand."

"Yes you do." Triesko's other hand came out from under his blanket. He handed Aarin a heavy metal medallion, as old and smoothed as the gate knocker. He took Aarin's hand by the wrist in fingers that, though thin, still had strength, and pressed the medallion into his palm. It was warm from Triesko's hand.

Aarin held up the medallion. It was the same as he used in the Guiding ceremony, but far older. There had been an inscription around the edge of the medallion, but it was unreadable. A horned depiction of the Dead God, bearing his twin staffs, danced in the middle.

"The words say, 'He who watches the gate, is watched'," said Triesko.

"What does it mean?"

"What do you think?"

"Death has his eye on us all," hazarded Aarin.

"It also means what with all the fat and useless fourth sons of nobles that make up the majority of our number, we have to be careful who knows what. You are aware of the Monastery of the Final Isle?"

"I am. You are going to tell me that it is not a simple monastery."

"It is not. There again is something that is not widely known. You must go there, Aarin, to one of the gates of death. Consult with the greatest oracle we might access." Triesko gripped Aarin's hand in both his tightly. The wool of his gloves pressed into Aarin's skin.

"Not all the gods were driven away."

"Yes, I know. Everyone knows. There are a number of minor beings who escaped Res Iapetus's wrath, as well as two of the gods themselves."

Triesko shook his head. "There are only two living gods."

"The Dead God was not driven forth?" said Aarin.

Triesko smiled. "You must see for yourself."

"You will say no more?"

"I would, my boy, but I cannot. That is one ban I cannot break."

At that moment, Brother Yostion came over the lawn, hips stiff but stride swift. "You said you would be but a short while!" he complained.

"I am done. I apologise."

"Don't be such an oaf, Yostion. I get precious few visits as it is," snapped Triesko.

Triesko stood stiffly, his blankets and fur falling around his feet. Yostion clucked his displeasure and plucked them up. Aarin embraced his old mentor.

"Good luck, my boy," Triesko whispered into Aarin's ear. "My time is almost done. By the end of the spring I will be gone, following those I have guided into the next world. You and I shall meet no more in this life."

CHAPTER THIRTY-SEVEN

Through Dalszystron

THEY WENT AS swiftly as only dracons might. Muscular, reptilian legs ate up the miles. The desert receded, drawing further and further away from the mountains as the party went north, until it became a black line on the horizon and the spikes of the warding obelisks small as thorns. Eventually the line and the obelisks vanished beyond the sea of grass. A brown haze in the distance became the sole sign of the Black Sands' presence. The steppe began to climb, and the mountains to the west became taller.

They camped every forty miles or so. On the seventh night they stopped early to allow the dracons to hunt. The eighth day they went more slowly, the beasts sated and torpid. Rel felt increasingly at home in the saddle. Zorolotsev showed him how to rig his saddle in the proper Khusiak way—there were marked differences to the saddles of Karsa. All the men were excellent riders, Deamaathani especially, but Rel was feeling less embarrassed of his own abilities.

The land dropped unexpectedly away, sheared by a steep scarp east-west across the steppe. The desert reappeared, coming in a wide bight across the base of the slope, so that their position atop the ridge overlooked sand more than the steppe, both lightened here by thin, icy snow. The grassland widened again to the north, but became hillier and more broken so that the mountains did not rise so abruptly, being fronted by a swathe of foothills absent further south.

The major pulled up his dracon and slid from its back. He gave the call to dismount, and directed his men to stake their mounts away from the slope's brow.

"Keep down," he urged them as they gained the edge. He beckoned to Veremond, who passed him a brass telescope. Zhinsky extended it and set it to his eye. He grunted.

"What do you see?" asked Rel.

"There, about three miles out."

Rel squinted against the brightness of the day. Ripples chased one another over the yellow grasses.

"There," Zhinsky said, directing him to the north east.

A line of black dots moved across the plain, heading from the desert into the mountains. "I see a line of figures," Rel said.

Veremond drew in his breath. "There are no herders this far out at this time of the year."

Zhinsky passed Rel the glass.

Rel brought it up to his eye. The figures blurred, and leapt into close view. Rel gasped. "They are not men."

What he saw walked like men, but they were too tall and too thin. Their bodies were covered in long, feathery hair. Their faces were dark and flat, dominated by wary eyes.

"Some say they are a kind of men." Zhinsky rolled onto his back and looked at the clouds hurrying through the sky. "Or that they were men and are no longer, because they angered a Tyn. Or a sorceress. Or a demon. Take your pick. They were transformed into those half-beasts you see. Whatever they are, we of Khushashia call them Yeven."

Dramion muttered some minor cantrip under his breath. Deamaathani had his own glass out and was watching intently.

"Are they dangerous?" asked Olb.

"Probably not," said the warlock.

"And what would you, native of less uncanny deserts, know of them?" said Zhinsky.

"I know enough," said Deamaathani. "I can feel little malice from them."

"You can do that?" said Rel, surprised.

"When one is engaged in waging war with magic, it is well to know whether or not your opponent bears you ill will. So yes, I can do that."

"They are dangerous," said Zorolotsev. He gestured for the glass. Rel handed it over reluctantly. "There are many legends of them in my village. I come from other side of the mountains, not far from here as the eagle flies. They sometimes come over the mountains and down into the forests in hard winters. Never cross them. They are cruel to those that anger them."

"It does not matter, dangerous, not dangerous," said Zhinsky. "They will avoid us, and we will avoid them. What is of note here, is that they walk directly from the desert, up into the hills, and there the mountain peoples of the Dalszystron live."

"They stay away from people," said Zorolotsev. He spoke rapidly in Khusiacki to Zhinsky, then added in Low Maceriyan, "These are in poor condition. The bull that leads, his fur is matted."

"A sign then," Deamaathani said. He snapped his telescope shut. "I've learned to be wary of signs." He looked at Zhinsky. "It's not them we should be afraid of."

"It is not," said Zhinsky. "It is what they are running from we should be concerned with. They come from there." He pointed. "We make small detour, go look. Now! Up up, my bold warriors."

Zhinsky had them go swiftly down the slope to where the Yeven had come from. Their mounts had not eaten for two days now and so were quicker on their feet, if harder to control, and ran so quickly down the slope Rel feared he would fall from the saddle. The Khushashians and Deamaathani laughed and whooped as they hurtled down to the plain. The others cursed and held on tightly.

Once down, it was a short gallop to the boundary between desert and grass. Zhinsky sent Veremond, Olb and Dramion ahead to the point they judged the Yeven to have emerged from the Black Sands; the rest of the squadron ran along the edge cautiously, stopping every three quarters of a mile to examine the obelisks for damage. Rel had never been this close to the unwebbed desert. The line between sand and steppe was practically a blade-slash. Isolated tussocks of grass deformed the line of the turf here and there, but it was unnervingly close to dead straight.

"This does not look like a natural border," said Rel.

"Who ever said it was? I did not." Zhinsky leaned far forward in his saddle. "The say that the gods made it in ancient days, one side for men, one side for their other children. These obelisks are the border, to keep the bad things out from the lands of men."

"Is it true?"

Zhinsky shrugged, preoccupied by the obelisk they had stopped by. A narrow pyramid twice as high as a man emerging from the turf like a tooth from a gum. It was a dull grey, like iron, although it was free of rust. Four-sided, a symbol on each face at just above head height. "Is a folktale, but there is much truth in folktales. If not for that devil-dog Iapetus, we could ask them, no?" He looked out over the desert. Sinuous loops of sand hissed over the surface. The pale grasses of the steppe rattled back in defiance. "But these things are true, the desert is not a natural place, and there are inhuman things dwell in it, brothers of mankind or not, and the obelisks work. Come! This one is fine."

"It amazes me," said Rel, "that there is one of these, every three quarters of a mile, for three thousand miles."

"I told you before, little merchant boy, this is not Karsa."

Veremond crested a low rise ahead. "Captain!" he shouted. "Major!"

Rel and Zhinsky wheeled their dracons about. Veremond was making his way rapidly down the divide between sand and turf with Olb and Dramion. They met the group halfway.

"The spires, major. You should see. One is down. The Yeven's prints go past it."

Zhinsky gave Rel a foreboding look, and spurred his dracon to a full gallop.

They passed two further obelisks before they reached Zorolotsev, standing guard over a toppled spire. The top part lay half on the desert, half on the grass.

The group reined their dracons in. The lizards clicked and chattered in agitation, raking at the ground with their running claws. Their massive fighting claws twitched. Zhinsky leapt down and crouched by the pylon's broken end. "Merchant boy, you tell me your father is big industrialist. What do you think?"

Rel looked over the edge of the upright portion from the top of his dracon. "Looks like it happened recently. But I can't tell, these things look like they were made last year."

"How did it happen?" asked Merreas quietly. He hunkered into his clothes, and eyed the desert warily.

"It looks broken, but I don't see how." He peered closer. The outside and the inner portion were the same exact shade of dull, silvery grey. "I'm sorry, I really don't know. This stuff doesn't corrode. If there were rust, we could guess when it happened..." Rel reached out to it.

"I would not touch it, if I were you," said Deamaathani. "The spires gather in bad energy. It can cling to them, and discharge unexpectedly."

"You don't want to be a frog, eh captain?" said Dramion. Zhinsky shot him a look that reminded the Karsan who made the jokes in their group.

"Has it been overloaded?" asked Zhinsky.

"It is possible, I suppose," said Deamaathani. "The sigils are intact. But I would have been aware of such a large discharge of energy. And I have never heard of such a thing happening before. Jakkar tells me that they are practically indestructible."

"Could it have been broken, physically. Pushed over?"

Rel checked the sheared surfaces again. "Perhaps. The bottom would have shifted out of true though."

"These things are sunk thirty feet into the ground," said Deamaathani. "They do not shift."

They looked around the base of the spire. The turf was close in to the metal, undisturbed.

"It could have been snapped by force, I suppose," said Rel. "My brother would know."

"And where's your brother?" said Merreas.

"About two thousand five hundred miles away," said Rel.

"Watch your tone with the captain," warned Veremond. Merreas scowled.

"So we're here, in the middle of nowhere, sent to deal with a monster. And now this, broken by something," said Merreas, uncowed by Veremond's rebuke.

"Purposefully, I'd say," said Deamaathani.

"The dead. Is this why we saw them? Is this why Wiatra died?" said Rel.

Zorolotsev made a noise in his chest.

"With this broken the dead are the least of our troubles. This is how the changeling came out of the sands," said Zhinsky.

"And it may not be the only thing to come through," said Deamaathani.

CHAPTER THIRTY-EIGHT
Changeling

ON A BRIGHT but freezing early afternoon they rode into the village of Alu-mal, if such a place were worthy of the term 'village'. A rough collection of hovels made of dry stacked stones and low, turfed roofs. Bones and sun-bleached wood were the rafters. There were few trees in these mountains, and the dark forests of the valleys were haunted by demons, so Zorolotsev said.

Snow lay thick upon the peaks all around the village, but even at the altitude of Alu-mal it was limited to a thin crust, frozen hard. In many places wind had scoured the snow clean away, exposing close-cropped turf of a vibrant green, speckled with goat droppings.

The majority of the huts were in two irregular lines, either side of what Rel generously chose to call a road. Those houses not lining the road were set haphazardly on knolls of stone. They clustered together, half-built into one another. Flimsy ladders led to upper entrances. Many remnants of older dwellings lay further out. Whether they were empty due to depopulation or some cultural practice Rel could not tell.

Dark faced men stared at the troop as they rode in. They were subjects of Khushashia, but they were not Khusiaks. Their skin was a deeper shade than Zhinsky's, almost red. They were short, with narrow brown eyes hooded by folds of skin, and solemn expressions. As different to Zhalak Zhinsky and Zorolotsev as Zhinsky and Zorolotsev were different to Rel. They watched the dracons with faces devoid of curiosity, turning silently on the spot as the troopers rode up the track.

Some of the huts were recently tumbled, stones still scratched white where they had been pushed apart. By these veiled women kneeled. They bowed repeatedly from the waist, beating the frozen ground three times with their fists every time their foreheads touched the ground.

On the slopes around Alu-mal, brown and white goats with clanking bells about their necks watched disinterestedly, their yellow eyes blank as those of the human inhabitants, mouths always working.

Few children hid behind their mother's skirts. There were far more women than children, and they guarded each child in small phalanxes.

"This is where it happened," said Rel. If he had any doubts about the old man's story, they were gone and buried.

"This is where it happened," agreed Zhinsky grimly. They pulled up in the middle of the village. A large slab of rock, almost flat, bordered the road. A shrine of flat stones was stacked at its centre around a crooked pole holding up five lines of triangular flags which snapped in the freezing wind. There was no other sound. Rel looked about uneasily. Zhinsky dismounted and walked toward a hut Rel could not tell apart from the others.

He waited respectfully outside. A small woman pushed aside the goatskin across the door. A few moments later, an incredibly ancient woman emerged. Her face was so heavily lined her eyes were near-invisible in the folds. Her lips had vanished, her mouth a slit in leather. She was bent almost double, but the other villagers touched their breasts when she emerged and bowed. They murmured as they did so; the sudden noise, though quiet, startled Aramaz and Rel patted his neck to soothe him.

The elder leaned on a stick of bone-white wood as crooked as all the other timber in the village, and festooned with fluttering feathers and small bones that clicked.

Zhinsky haltingly exchanged a few words her, then beckoned Rel.

"Captain, with me. The rest of you, stay here."

Rel handed his reins to Merreas and dismounted. He winced at the stiffness of his limbs.

There was room only for Rel, Zhinsky, the woman and her servant in the hut. A low cot took up a good quarter of it, clay cooking pots in neat piles occupied another quarter. Wizened bird and dracon-bird claws hung from the rafters amid bunches of herbs. Sunlight shone in through gaps in the turves of the roof and its smokehole, netting the blue fumes of a low dung fire in shafts of light. The hut smelled of smoke and hard, marginal lives. Rel's eyes watered.

In broken Low Maceriyan, the old woman spoke. "I tell you, I say what happened." She looked at Zhinsky, he nodded.

She settled back, took a deep breath, shut her eyes, and began a chant in her hard-edged tongue, rocking back and forth all the whole. Zhinsky leaned in close to Rel, and whispered a translation close by his ear.

"In the mountains, there was a shepherd. He was young, he was lonely. He watched in the mountains. His flock was scattered, his work was hard. He came to the village at doublemoon for food, for company. But for him there was only the mountain, only the flock. He yearned for a wife. He yearned for a son. But there was none for him, Erdgi the Lame. His flock was scattered, his work was hard."

Zhinsky was concentrating hard on the woman, so hard his accent almost completely disappeared from the Low Maceriyan he rendered the chant into.

"He sat alone upon the mountain. He was young, he was lonely. He asked for the hand of Guhanki. She refused. For him there was only the mountain, only the flock. He yearned for a wife. He yearned for a son. But there was none for him, Erdgi the Lame. His flock was scattered, his work was hard.

"One night he sat, upon the mountain. A voice called from the dark. A woman's voice, soft and sweet. 'You yearn for a wife, you yearn for a son. Let me come to you and give of myself.' Erdgi was frightened, and did not sleep. He stayed on the mountain. His flock was scattered, his work was hard.

"He sat upon the mountain. He was young, he was scared. The voice returned by doublemoon's light. 'I will be yours, you will be mine. Do not be lonely, upon the mountain. Let me warm your bed, let me warm your heart.'

"For nine nights this occurred, as the skies were lit with the gods' green veils. He stayed on the mountain, he listened to the voice. It came with a shadow. Then it came with a shape. On the tenth night he saw her, well-rounded and sleek. 'Let me be yours,' she said. 'You are young, you are lonely, as am I, as am I.'

"Her face was beautiful. More lovely than silver to the miser, more lovely than the baby to the mother. Erdgi's dogs barked and whined. He did not heed them, only his heart, only his loins. Erdgi's soul was caught. He went to her. 'Why should I not?' he said to the night. 'I am young,' he said the mountain. 'I am lonely. My flock is scattered, my work is hard.'

"Into her arms he fell. He found no woman's eyes, no woman's love, Erdgi the lame. He is young no longer, he is alone no longer. He stays not on the mountain. None watch his flock, they are scattered and dead. Erdgi has gone, and his work is slaughter."

The old woman's eyes appeared in the wrinkles of her skin, shiny as beads. She breathed out a ragged breath. Zhinsky's face was hard.

"Changelings," he said to Rel, although he did not take his eyes off the woman. "They come out of the desert in the form of lithe women or beautiful youths. They arouse the lust of the young, and through their lovemaking plant a seed of change within them. If they are caught in time, then that is fine, they are killed and laid to rest. A big shame, but better than what happens if not."

"Not a skinturner," said Rel. The back of his neck prickled. Bannord, Guis's friend, had once told him of Skinturners in the southern forests, at the top of the Sotherwinter, that had kept him awake for a week.

"These are worse. They change you, captain merchant boy. They shift. Their victims stop being men, they stop being women. They become monsters, and then they feast upon the flesh of their kin. This is not a fairy story for little rich boys in comfortable cities, this is real. Old magic, and terrible."

He said some words to the woman. She closed her eyes and nodded gratefully.

"You told her we would kill it."

Zhinsky bowed his head in respect to the elder. "Of course I did, little merchant boy," he said under his breath. "What the fucking hells else do you think was going to happen?"

"Fair enough."

Zhinsky's grin flashed bright in the dimness and he punched Rel on the shoulder. "That is the *right* attitude!"

OUTSIDE THE HUT seemed even colder than before.

"Mount!" said Zhinsky. "We go to fight."

"We just got here," said Merreas.

"Now is the time. We stop, we need to feed the dracons. We feed the dracons, they fight very badly. We will need them to fight, so we go now."

Merreas looked around at the villagers, the fear gripping him showing itself in contempt. "This lot of savages wouldn't have a bread roll to spare anyway. Waste of time, if you ask me. We've lost a good man already. Let's go home."

Zhinsky moved fast. Merreas did not see him coming, and found himself flat on his back with Zhinsky's boot on his chest.

"These people are not my people." He leaned hard on his foot. "But they are my countrymen. Citizens of Khushashia, citizens of the Hundred Kingdoms of

Ruthnia. Citizens you are bound to protect. So, you get up and onto your mount, or I not feed it and let it chase you all the way back to the Glass Fort. I do not like cowards, trooper. Do you understand?"

Merreas nodded. "Yes major," he said breathlessly.

"Good good." Zhinsky removed his foot, held out his hand and hauled Merreas up. At the last moment he yanked Merreas toward him, unbalancing him again. "You start thinking hard, trooper. This will not be an easy battle. It will be easier if you hold your heart and strength, and not lose them. You wish to live?"

"Yes sir."

"Then be brave."

They fitted the sickle-swords to the fighting claws of their dracons. Understanding well what this meant their mounts grew restive. They croaked and called to one another as the men took water from the village well; a spring protected by a conical pile of rocks a little way above the huts and festooned like the shrine with long strings of flags.

Zhinsky asked where Erdgi might be found.

The villagers pointed upwards. The track wound its way through ever-larger crags, past the snowline.

"He is up the mountain," they said. "He is in the old tower."

THE WAY QUICKLY abandoned all pretence at being a track and turned into a goat path—narrow, icy, precipitous and strewn with boulders from the higher slopes. But every now and then paving stones exposed by the rain or by landslips hinted at a grander past.

Rel and Deamaathani rode together, and speculated on the road's origin.

"Morfaan, some other race, creatures from beyond the fences of our world? Who knows? In truth I do not know, nobody does. Nobody probably ever will. This world has buried wonders to fill a million philosophs' life-times. Who cares for such ragged paths and supposedly Tyn-haunted ruins when the artefacts of the Morfaan and Old Maceriyans can be dug from easier soils?" said Deamaathani.

Rel's face became numb from the wind. The day grew old early. It was no later than three of the clock and the sun had already hidden its face behind the mountains. Orange and red snowfields suggested it had not given up day's fight just yet, but they grew more rugose with every second. The Twin was already in the sky, its circle emerging from the dimming day like a ship come out of the fog. Dusk smeared the snow blue and the first stars were out by the time they saw the tower: broken turrets rising over a ridge. They rode through a gap, and came into the glen that housed it. On the far side was the simple fortress, built of drystone courses. Four turrets grouped together into one, giving it the semblance of a stone ants' nest, or a tall tree stump fluted with buttress roots. Two of the turrets had collapsed, their squared-off blocks mingling with scree frozen off the scarps around the glen. Blackness haunted the open interior, darker than any night.

The wind shifted round, blowing from the northeast where the tower was situated. A carrion stench came to them, rank and pungent, even in the deep chill of winter.

Dramion covered his nose. Merreas blanched, his eyes wide in his face. Their mounts caught the smell and grew eager to feast, and hard to handle.

"He will know we are here soon. Dramion, hobble Wiatra's dracon and leave it here, well back. Then everyone spread out!" shouted Zhinsky. "Hit and run, no frontal assault. We attack from all sides at once, it is the only way. Do not get too close!"

Zorolotsev and Rel split right, Deamaathani following. Merreas and Veremond formed up in a wide arrowhead with Zhinsky. Dramion was sent far out to the left, Olb at his side.

"Goad him! Bring him into the centre!" shouted Zhinsky. "Deamaathani, prepare your magic."

Deamaathani tugged off his long gloves with his teeth and stuffed them into his belt. His bronze armour glinted under his robes.

Rel unslung his carbine. He held the reins with one hand, the right gripping the gunstock. He controlled Aramaz with his knees. The creature recognised the shift in guidance, knowing it for a sign of imminent hostility. It dropped into hunting posture, lower to the ground, legs tensed, sickle claws flexing.

Olb leaned back in his saddle. He cupped one mouth to his hand, pointed with the other.

"It's coming! Up there!"

The creature that had been Erdgi the Lame was not in its lair. It came over the brow of the hill, roaring out a challenge.

The creature was ten feet tall, huge across the shoulders, with a thick hide that was dull grey and lustreless. It had two arms like a man, the size of Rel's torso and knotted with muscle. One held a small tree stripped of branches as a club. It was naked, its penis grotesquely large, the pink tip of it peeking from under a dark foreskin. The legs were those like a dracon's or a dog's, knees high and close to the hip, with the ankle held off the ground. On one foot it walked on its toes, of which there were only two, thickly nailed. The other was warty, a club foot twisted sideways, causing it to move with a shuffling gait. A remnant of the lame shepherd boy.

The changeling's head was set low on its shoulders on a short neck. Eyes stared with unreasoning fury from beneath jutting brows. The jaw protruded almost as far, lips drawn back to reveal a broad mouth crammed with yellow teeth. A third eye, irregular and moist as a fried egg, was offset from the centre of its forehead. This part of its face was badly formed, the skull warped and skin slack like a half-melted wax bust. Yellow mucous streamed from this third eye. The ear on the left side of the head was lopsided, and hung low. The left arm was held awkwardly. A large tumescence, hairy and painful looking, could be glimpsed under it.

The changeling's nose twitched at the air. It blinked myopically at the troopers, and roared.

The dracons roared back, dropping their heads and switching them from side to side. Their head feathers stood erect, their scythe claws drew back, blades upon them gleaming with reflected starlight.

The changeling stooped for a rock and sent it hurtling toward Olb and Dramion. Their dracons loped out of way as the boulder exploded into dust and sharp splinters. The creature bellowed and lumbered down the hill after them.

Zhinsky waited for the creature to come into the glen. The changeling chased Olb and Dramion, and

Zhinsky spurred his dracon forward, whooping wildly. Veremond and Merreas came with him, lances couched, pennants rippling loudly.

The creature turned as they came at it. It moved with amazing speed, evading Merreas's lance, and bringing its fist up and down to bludgeon his dracon. With a single blow, the dracon dropped, head crushed, tumbling into a wreck of broken limbs and blood. Merreas was sent flying, landing hard on his shoulder. The changeling advanced on him. Zhinsky's lance bit deep into the creature's arm, Veremond's plunged an instant later into its thigh. Black blood welled up around the weapons. The two troopers released their lances, and rode past, both of the them plucking their second lances from the holders on the saddle behind them. The changeling howled, slapping at its wounds. A raking hand snapped Zhinsky's lance, leaving the point embedded in its flesh. It snatched the other from its thigh as Olb and Dramion wheeled about and came at it. Dramion's lance scored the thing's side, ripping a long, shallow wound along its ribs, the jolt nearly unseating him. Olb missed, and they were past, but the creature turned, and flung Merreas's lance at Olb as if it were a dart. It flew hard and true, bursting through Olb's back and out of his front. The Olberlander flung out his arms and fell sideways. His dracon, uncontrolled and maddened at the scent of blood, turned suddenly, and tore at its dying master.

All of them were galloping now, circling the changeling. It picked up another rock and hurled it hard. The stone split on the rocky ground, a fist-sized chunk nearly taking the legs of Zorolotsev's creature out from under him.

"It's quite a good shot," said Veremond drily.

"This is no good! No good!" shouted Zhinsky.

"It is wounded," said Rel.

"Yes, and no. We have to be quicker!" He pointed at the beast; the long, bloody tear in its side was closing up.

"Why didn't you mention that before!"

"Do you think I fight this kind of thing every day? I only have stories to go on, same as you, captain." He whistled, waving his hand around his head. Deamaathani, Zorolotsev and Dramion streamed into a line.

"Lances!" said Zhinsky. "Drive them deep! Break off the heads if you can!" He turned to Rel. "Now is a very good time to tell me you are a good shot from a moving mount, captain."

"I am."

"Shoot it then. Deamaathani, do you have something for me?"

The warlock nodded. He was staring at a sight they could not see, lips moving silently.

The men broke apart again, their mounts stirred to sudden motion as the changeling charged at them. Zhinsky and Zorolotsev galloped away, looped back and came at the creature from two different direction, confusing the changeling. They crossed, both of them driving their lances into it, front and back. Rel marvelled at their precision and grace. They released their lances at exactly the right moment, giving them maximum penetration without danger of being wrenched from their saddles. The changeling swiped, missing both. Dramion and Rel came in next. Rel waited until he came close, determined not to miss, before pulling the trigger of his ironlock. The hammer pin of the mechanism drove deep into the bullet in the barrel, penetrating the soft silver coating the solid glimmer bullet. In contact directly with iron, the glimmer reacted explosively, driving the bullet out of the barrel. The shot caught the changeling in the neck. It gripped at the wound, but swiped with its club, catching Dramion with a glancing blow that sent him tumbling back over the high cantle. His dracon was enraged, and sprang up at the changeling. It drove its running claws into the creature's side, grabbing on with its long forearms and middle-limbs, and raked repeatedly at the thing with its steel-sheathed murder claws.

Rel snapped open his gun, and slid another silver-jacketed bullet into the breach. He galloped past quickly, coming right under the changeling's left arm. Changeling and dracon grappled with each other. The changeling had dropped its club and was throttling the reptile. The kicks of the dracon's claws became weaker, its cries of rage turning into an awful rasping.

Rel rode up, raised his carbine and aimed for the heart.

The creature lifted the writhing dracon high over its head in both hands, revealing the true nature of the growth in the armpit. A wordlessly screaming human head, eyes rolling like a mad dog's, stared down at him. Its mouth flapped soundlessly open and shut, tongue flapping. Drool ran from its lips but no sound came. The features were boyish. This was Erdgi the Lame.

Rel fired. The bullet slammed home under the chin.

The changeling screamed from both mouths, the human cry of pain by far the most horrible. The creature staggered back, dropping Dramion's dracon. The reptile fell heavily, screeching. It rolled over and tried to struggle up, but its leg was broken and it shrieked and bit at itself in its agony as the changeling fell to its knees, then its hands. Rel wheeled about and reloaded.

Deamaathani got there first. The air shimmered. The smell of magic grew strong, sharp as lightning. Smoke curled from the changeling's head. Incredibly, it was getting to its feet.

Rel fired again as the changeling's inhuman head burst into flame and it began to scream. The fire was no mortal blaze, and burned hotter and brighter than a forge. The howls coming from the changeling turned to bubbling coughs. It fell face forward, rolled from side to side, hands scrabbling at the snow, and was still.

Erdgi's head did not die. It went on shrieking, and shrieking.

Zhinsky rode up, sabre drawn, and stabbed Erdgi's face through the eye. It shuddered, and ceased moving. Zhinsky's sword scraped on bone as he dragged it out.

"Poor bastard. They say some part of them always survives. The mountain folk believe the changelings do it so they can watch them suffer."

"He could not be saved?"

The others rode up: Zorolotsev, Veremond, and Deamaathani. Dramion was holding onto his arm, his face white with pain. Merreas limped over, less badly wounded. They all watched the riderless dracons carefully. Olb's had not done with consuming its former master, and Dramion's was still screaming, repeatedly trying and failing to stand, lashing out at anything that came near. Its fellows clicked and chirruped and watched it intently.

"You think I stab him in the eye if this was so?" said Zhinsky, an undertone of anger in his voice.

"Such a transformation is irreversible," said Deamaathani, exhausted and pale. "It is traumatic to the stuff of the body and the spirit. Not the greatest of the wild wizards could undo this. Not even Res Iapetus himself."

"Your fellow magisters?" asked Rel.

Deamaathani snorted.

"Can he be ghosted at least?" said Veremond.

"He cannot be ghosted," said Zhinsky sorrowfully. He turned away.

The fire around the changeling's head was dying, having consumed the flesh utterly, leaving nothing but grey bone. "Olb dead, Merreas and Dramion wounded. One dracon killed, and the other..." Zhinsky's voice trailed off as he watched it squirm pitifully around, screeching.

"The leg is broken," said Dramion. "It cannot be saved." His lack of emotion hid deep upset.

Rel loaded another bullet, walked up to it and shot it through the head. The report echoed around the glen. When it had died away, the night seemed colder.

"A bad loss. Two men and two dracons dead on this venture, and there was only the one foe. Let us see what can be done for those who lie dead in its lair. Do not let the dracons eat the changeling," he said. "The meat is tainted."

The broch reeked. The smell became unbearable twenty yards out, shit and piss and old blood. Rel knew they would find nothing alive in there the second the stench hit him.

Veremond tossed in a lit torch. Flickering light lit up the interior.

Bones. Flesh. Torn clothing and piles of dung.

"In the stories caves like this are full of treasure," said Merreas.

"There is only death in there," said Deamaathani.

"It killed many," Rel said. "A great many."

"To see such a creature," said Deamaathani. "I did not think they walked in the world still."

"They should not," said Zhinsky. "This is a thing of the black wastes. It should not be in the lands of men, no matter how remote."

"Then why did it come?" said Veremond. "Who destroyed the obelisk?"

"Those are the questions," said Zhinsky.

Some of the corpses were still recognisably human. Bloody bones were jumbled into the mud of the ground.

"These can still be ghosted," said Rel. "They should be."

"They will," said Merreas, a new resolve in his voice. "We will set them out."

"Can Dramion ride?" asked Rel.

Zorolotsev was tending to him close by. He shrugged. "His shoulder was dislocated. I have reset it, but it will hurt."

"Dramion, are you up to riding to the village?"

"Aye sir. Just," said Dramion. He gingerly rotated his arm.

"Take Aramaz. Go for their ghost-talker." Rel looked at the gory mess. "I will get them out."

"We will all do it," said Zhinsky.

The work was grim, and dirty. But necessary. The old woman came in the deeps of the night as they were finishing. The soldiers watched as women wailed and men beat their chests as she coaxed the spirits from the shattered remains and sent them on their way. Most of them were children. Olb's ghost went with them, guarding them as they streaked skywards with never a look to his living comrades.

Rel, Zhinsky and the rest spent the remainder of the night in Alu-mal. The following day, they fed their dracons on a goat donated by the grateful villagers, and set out home to the fort.

CHAPTER THIRTY-NINE
The Road to Mogawn

GUIS STARTED AWAKE with terror in his breast. A fleeting sense of shadowed places where no good could be found, something hunting him through glades of black-limbed trees.

A pounding on the roof brought him to his senses with a start. It took him a moment to gather his wits. The driver pounded again. He pulled the cord that opened the hatch on the front of the carriage. A briny wind blasted through the gap. The fulsome smell of dog it carried could not overpower the tang of the sea.

"I apologise for waking you, Goodfellow Kressind," said the driver, raising his voice over the noise of the carriage and the drays. "We are coming to Mogawn. I have been ordered by the countess to inform all of her visitors when we reach this point so that they can enjoy the approach."

Guis leaned out of the window. Grey marram whipped by him. They were descending a steep road.

"Stop the coach!" he called. Guis had to repeat himself before he was heard. With a cry of "Whoa!

Whoa!" the driver reined in the dogs. They came to a halt. The driver applied the brake.

"Yes, goodfellow," he said. "We can't stay here long. I have to hold the brake. It's mighty steep it is."

Guis hopped out. The road had dug itself down out of the wind into a trench. Prickly littoral grasses scratched his face as he squeezed his way along the coachwork to the front. He bounded up to the driver's seat, somewhat surprising the man by sitting beside him.

"I can't see anything back there, goodman. I may as well respect the countess's wishes."

The driver smiled. "It gets cold this run, this time of year. There's a blanket in the box under the seat. Take it now, goodfellow, and quickly if you would. This brake is murder on my arm!"

Guis dug out the blanket. "Be off then," he said, before he had spread it across his lap.

The coach rumbled on. The spiky grasses streamed by, the wheels ringing off cobbles. Guis caught snatches of marsh ahead, and then the road rose from its entrenchment, and the flats were laid open to view. A green plain riven with glistening creeks. The road descended through a maze of broken hills, cubes of rock clad in the rough grass. If he left this road, Guis doubted he would find it again. The bluff that became the cliffs further down the coast loomed to his left. A sentinel wall. *As far as this*, it said to the ocean, *and no further.*

Fleshy plants and coarse grass carpeted the mud for three or four miles out, before the endless no-man's-land of mud between land and sea spread itself far and wide. The coach rattled on. A causeway met the road where the hills ended, the stones here well laid and in good repair. This ran dead straight between a row of tall iron pillars. Between these hung rusted chains much burdened with marsh oyster and mussel. Out over the marsh then mud the causeway went. It remained level as the mud dropped lower and lower, raising itself on a mole of piled rocks until it was high over the flat.

At the end, some five miles distant, was a tremendous rock of floatstone, hundreds of feet high. It awaited them patient as a toad. The sides were ragged, but atop it were the clean lines of human buildings. They thundered on, picking up speed on the causeway.

"The dogs are tired, but nearly home!" shouted the driver. "They can smell their dinner!"

Guis laughed, pleased with the familiarity of the driver, exhilarated by the whip of the wind, whisking in from the endless, endless foreshore.

Mogawn resolved itself in a series of telling details, coy as a maiden undressing. The great black rocks that anchored it were substantial skerries in their own right. Enormous iron rings lay at rest atop them, chains linking them to Mogawn. These were stupendously sized, each link the size of a carriage. They drooped idly, swags of seaweed hanging from them in long ropes, running into deep, rusty holes in the island. Birds roosted on them in multitudes.

There was a divide in the stone; the bottom two-thirds were sea black, that above tending almost to white. Bright lichens clad the upper part, ending in a perfect line where the black began. All was pocked by the various holes that characterised floatstone, the exposed bubbles that gave it its buoyancy. The ground atop the island was uneven and so vast that a scrubby forest of dwarf sycamore clung to the feet of the castle walls.

The castle was an adornment to this god's ship. Guis saw the great gatehouse and three towers. The keep was set far back, and lost soon to view as the island grew inexorably in front of them.

Pocked cliffs shaded out the westering sun. Mogawn sat in a lake of seawater excavated by the roil of its own turbulence. The scent of the ocean intensified, trapped here between tides, the water was brackish and potent.

The causeway ran on to the base of this mountain of floatstone.

"Where do we enter?" shouted Guis. His ears tingled with the cold.

"Sea gate!" The driver nodded ahead.

The causeway terminated in a wide, circular plaza that intruded into Mogawn's moat. The driver whistled and his dogs drew the carriage around the outside of this construction. Here the mole was at its highest, forty feet and more, and the water around it was dark.

A gate of black wood set into the floatstone at right angles to the causeway creaked upwards. A drawbridge came down as it went up, slamming onto the slick stones of the plaza. Beyond was a tunnel road.

"Hyah!" shouted the driver. The dogs leaped forward, dragging the coach into the passage. They went upwards through the rock in long loops. Where the cavities of the rock had been cut through, they provided natural windows on the approach to the castle. The wind maundered through them plaintively.

They turned a sixth circuit, and emerged beneath grey winter skies again. The castle walls ambushed them, rearing up suddenly. The carriage, the dray team now panting heavily, thundered over a low stone bridge. The gatehouse gate opened, the portcullis behind clattered upwards, and they were within the precincts of Mogawn.

The coach stopped. The dogs collapsed to the flags. Guis beamed, cheeks ruddy with the wind.

The countess came down the steps from her keep, a rich and feminine gown on her body, a warm smile on her face. She bowed ironically.

"Welcome, my lord, to the castle of Mogawn."

"I WANTED TO show you my orrery immediately you arrived, goodfellow," she said, taking him up the steps of her keep. "You must forgive my impatience. I have been waiting some time to share this with someone who I thought might appreciate it. Your bags will be taken to your room. I'll give you a chance to change before dinner."

"I am your guest, countess," he said. "I will go whither you will."

Guis heard the orrery before he saw it, a rhythmic machine noise like that heard outside a mill. The countess led him through the donjon door by the hand.

The orrery took up the whole of the keep's hall. The centre of the device was a dangerous medley of exposed gears. Huge arms swung about the pillar upon which the sun was mounted, scything through the air with enough force to dent a man's skull.

A great bronze globe feathered by stylised rays, occupied the centre. Around it, and around it and around it, wound a grouping of worlds known to every well-educated man. There was the Earth, her familiar continents and seas described in etched brass. There were her two moons, one bright red, the other egg white. Elliptical tracks described their orbits around the Earth, the white about the equator, the red at a forty-five degree angle to the ecliptic plane of the motherworld. About this trio revolved the Twin on an elliptical path. Black and twice the size of the Earth, its own passage through the aether was distorted both by the Earth and the sun. Out it went, then back, then out again. It appeared to be departing on each loop, only to return to perturb the orbits of the moons.

"An unhappy marriage of spheres," she explained. "The other worlds about the sun do not form this odd binary. Their moons rotate about the centre of their mass in peace. Not so the Earth."

She gestured to the five other worlds. Mighty Bolsun swung around the sun in long, unhurried circuits. For every time it went around the sun, the Earth went four. A crowd of moons mobbed it.

Shepherded by Bolsun was the lesser Horaspite, still huge by terrestrial standards. "This world differs to the others in that it spins about a straight axis," commented the countess. "There is no tilt at all, and therefore no summer or winter, or varying nights, but harmony. A perfect world, perhaps. Serene, and peaceful. Not like ours."

"Do men live there?"

"And why not women?" protested the countess. They ducked under the long wooden arm bearing Merrder as it swept over their heads.

"Why not?" said Guis with an apologetic smile. "I will rephrase my question: Do people live there?"

"Who knows?" She shrugged. "I hear that certain magisters have attempted to project themselves hence, but none have yet succeeded. Only the great mages of the past claim to have done so, but their testimonies are untrustworthy. Perhaps magisters will, within our lifetimes, walk in spirit upon the soil of other earths."

She named the other worlds. Between perfect Horaspite wheeled jealous green Merrder, then a collection of moonlets that circled the sun in a ring like dancers. After them came the Earth, then beyond her were the tiny Guuz, and the even smaller Kazzaerok. "Their outlandish names are legacies of their discoveries; both named by Ocerzerkiyans at the heights of their art."

"They have less awkward Karsarin names."

"And I prefer the originals, in honour of the empiricist who found them. They are common across the world. Respect is the bridge by which great minds are joined."

"A quote from Strano?"

She nodded. "The ancients were right about so much, I find. The world today is largely populated by idiots."

Guis laughed aloud, but the countess remained stern. "I am deadly serious," she said.

"What is the purpose of the machine?"

"The Old Maceriyans," she said. "Their civilisation collapsed four thousand years ago. Their writings speak of fire pouring from the Earth. The Morfaan, their reign came to an end twelve thousand years ago, or so it is believed, and they disappeared almost completely sometime after that. What I wish to know is: why? I have constructed this machine to answer that question. The mark of four thousand years is important, Guis. It is the time that the Twin comes closest to our own Earth before receding again. We approach it once again. You notice the Earth tremors upon its near approach, before and around the Great Tides? More often than is usual."

"Perhaps," said Guis. "I had not noticed."

"Well I have. I have documented them, and plotted them. They are more frequent and stronger by the year. I am sure the answer is to be found in the circuits of the spheres. And I would like to know what will kill our feeble efforts at society before it falls. The answer is bound up in the cycles described here. I believe the basic model to be correct, but there are subtleties, permutations that have as yet gone unnoticed."

"You think our time is done? Surely not. We have surpassed the Old Maceriyans. They were wise, but we have built upon their wisdom."

"The Morfaan were our betters in all fields of knowledge, and yet they fell. Our demise is not a possibility, it is an inevitability."

"Then what is the point of knowing?"

"One might as well ask, what is the point of anything?"

A gong sounded. She forced a smile. "Dinner will be served in half an hour. I shall have Mansanio show you to your rooms, where you may change."

CHAPTER FORTY
Tyn and the Darkling

GUIS AND THE Countess sat on opposing couches by the fire, a low table between them. Replete after a fine dinner they drank enriched wines reminiscent of those of Macer Lesser, but of a harsher character. There was something in it other than alcohol.

Guis watched his host, his mind fogged by the wine's odd effects. He was attracted to her, he supposed. She was certainly vivacious, bold, intelligent... But there was that face. He was not sure if he could bear to kiss it. More to the point, he was bothered by what his friends would say if he did. The firelight on Lucinia's features exaggerated her manliness. Her nose was incredible, he thought, a jutting crag. A general's nose, not a goodlady's. He shifted uncomfortably in his seat and glanced away. A man looked back at him from a painting on the wall, the same nose, a glower set around it. The countess looked like her father. He snatched his attention away from the painting, shifting uneasily in his seat. She either did not notice his discomfort, or chose to ignore it, but stared at him unabashed. Flames danced in her eyes, a predatory flicker. He would not have been surprised if she had slunk forward on all fours, as supple and dangerous as a cat.

The illusion shattered when she spoke. Guis blinked drowsily.

"Is the wine getting to you, goodfellow?"

Guis cleared his throat. "A little." A disturbing moment saw the Hag as a hag, and then as her father. Long accustomed to unwelcome images, this nevertheless perturbed him. His affliction was internal, a private show of horrors for his mind's eye. These visions manifested outside.

"It is spiced with a herbal blend. The wine comes from Far Ocerzerkiya. Or rather, if we are to be precise about geography, a far northern realm named Zareiskiya past the borders of the empire.

"I am not familiar with it."

"There are many realms beyond the northern empire. They each have their own names. Realms beyond realms, realms beyond seas, realms beyond this world, even. I find the Hundred disgustingly parochial." She slid off the couch, walked over to a globe imprisoned in transecting wooded circles. She spun the globe with one finger, jabbing down hard. "Here," she said, in invitation to join her.

Guis stayed where he was. "I suppose, Countess Lucinia—"

"Lucinella, please," she said. "We know each other well enough by now."

"Lucinella," said Guis, he smiled lopsidedly. "I suppose it is easier all around to refer to the lands north of the Red Desert as Ocerzerkiya," he said. "That is why."

"Indubitably. But ease is rarely a cognate with correct." She gave him a sympathetic look. "The effects of the wine will change. Drowsiness and suggestibility are the initial symptoms. A sharpening of intellect will follow."

"I may be suffering the indolence of satiation. That was a very fine meal."

"We live far from modern comforts, but I try to maintain standards. One is a countess after all." She affected hauteur.

Guis grinned dopily. His earlier discomfort seemed to seep from his toes and pool around his feet. So convincing was the effect that he had to check he had not accidentally let his water go. He stopped smiling.

"The wine again," she said. "I promise, the coming increase in mental acuity will more than compensate you for the disorientation."

"I find the sensations interesting, and now I know of their cause, no longer unsettling."

"Ah!" she said happily. "A man after my own heart. A quester after new experience."

"If only that were so. I am too timid to chase experience down. On the other hand, I will not turn it away if it comes chasing after me."

"Talk to me then, while we allow digestion to do its work. When you are feeling more awake, I will show you my observatory. You have seen my orrery, the observatory is my second great pride."

"What shall we talk of?"

"Tell me about yourself."

"I would not know where to begin, in any case propriety demands some amount of discretion."

"Fie on propriety! You are a playwright. Is not all that you do a cry for attention?"

Guis sipped his wine. There were bitter herbal notes under the sweetness. "You have me unmasked, goodlady. All writers are but cautious show-offs."

"There you are. Now, tell me about yourself."

"My previous comments notwithstanding, I still do not know what you wish to hear."

"Might I ask you a question then?"

Guis shrugged. "By all means."

"Is it true what they say, that you are mageborn?"

"Simply? Yes."

"And that you almost killed your brother?"

"You are not a shy woman." He set his glass down.

"Have you heard that I am?"

"No. No I have not. Well. Yes, it is true." He settled back.

"And that is why you carry the Lesser Tyn?" She pointed at the creature sleeping curled up on his shoulder.

"In part. The real answer to that is more disturbing."

"Tell me all about it. Please. I am no gossip, but the gossiped about. What you hear will go no further."

"We are alone?"

"Yes."

Guis sighed. "Here is a chance not rarely met."

"How so?"

"I sometimes wish to unburden myself, but shy away," he said warily.

"You are not about to shy here, I hope?"

"I am, and that is why I tell you so in order to prevent it."

"Nothing you tell me can be so terrible."

"You would be surprised."

"I never am," she insisted.

"Very well." Guis leaned forward to pour more wine from the decanter on the table.

"Be careful, it is potent."

"Good," he said. His hands shook. He poured and drank a goodly draught. "I was born a twin."

"Oh?"

"My brother, identical to me, died when I was six."

"Your magic?" she asked breathlessly.

"No! He drowned. A foolish childhood accident, one of those awful things that can occur to anyone, rich or poor. My mother," he waved his hand. "She suffered for it. She bore my brothers as a good wife is expected to." He smiled at the countess to indicate his disapproval of this sort of opinion. "But after my father fell ill from the apoplexy, it proved too much. Her sorrows won out and she became addicted to the Moonflower. She still is, as a matter of fact. She never had a strong mental constitution; as beautiful and fragile as the flowers that succour her."

"How poetic."

"One is a writer. My facility with acts of will began to manifest itself a few years later, when I was nine. Moving objects, minor discharges of lightning when I was angry, that kind of thing. I kept it secret as long as I could. I was as damaged by my twin's loss as my mother was, in my way. You see, I inherited much from her, including her anxieties. I became afraid of the dark. I would not sleep. I was consumed by guilt for my brother's death. That was when my affliction began."

"An affliction?"

"Our ancestors would have thought me tormented by demons. But I was examined by magister and physic both and this was shown not to be the case.

There was nothing uncanny pursuing me, at least not in the beginning. I have an imbalance of the nerves. I am plagued by intrusive images of violence and sex, often combined. A need to forestall my performing these actions—which I hasten to add I have no desire to perform and am indeed repulsed by—forces upon me endless and repetitive rituals. It is a only matter of anxieties let free. But..." he shrugged. Now he was talking openly about it, it did not seem so terrible a thing, and he felt mildly foolish. "Ordinarily, this is a curse upon he who bears it, but no more than that. But, in conjunction with my facility... Well. Magic is a matter of will, and my will is not my own. Left unfettered, the thoughts that plague me repeat, and repeat, and repeat. Now, magisters and wild wizards both must learn to harness this, to bend the world to the shape of their choosing, either with ritual assistance, or by sheer will alone. But to me it comes naturally."

"How intriguing." She leaned forward, fascinated.

"Far from it, because I cannot control my anxiety, my obsessions. And as these tend towards the calamitous..." He sat suddenly up. "The incident you refer to, when I nearly killed my brother Aarin. That was the result of this unfortunate confluence of gift and affliction. I stopped myself just in time. He bears the scar of my insanity, a blinded eye."

He became thoughtful and stared into the fire. "It was then that I was forced to tell. I confessed all, mostly, in floods of tears to my father. What made it all the worse was that he was *pleased* that I had such power. Not troubled that I had maimed my brother. All he could see was the potential for the family's advancement with a magister among its fold. Well, he was disappointed. The magisters judged me too dangerous for the college, and there are precious few masters of the old craft remaining in the world. My will is strong, but my volition not under my control. My mother would not have me sent off to prentice to some madman in a cave, although she endlessly raises the subject of the Magisterial University. My father was forced to pay for the binding of Tyn here to protect me and others from my madness. He disperses any ill effects from my anxieties before they can do real harm. You see, countess, I have the air of a sane man, but I am not. I am dangerous."

Her next question surprised him. "What manner of thoughts do you suffer?"

He turned it over in his mind. Would he tell her of the endless parade of murders, rapes, mutilations, incest, and other vileness that tormented him when he was unsettled? No, he would not. "I will not tell you. I cannot. They are my shame alone."

He was relieved when she let the matter drop.

"My father and I have not seen eye to eye for a long time. I am estranged from my family. And I am glad for it, for without me they are safe."

"You do not wish them harm."

"Of course not! But what I have created does."

The atmosphere prickled, invested with an expectant will. Tyn shifted in his slumber.

Guis's voice dropped. "I said that nothing pursued me to begin with, despite my fears. Alas, those fears bore fruit. All this worry has taken a form. I call it the Darkling. It comes when I am possessed by any of the less noble sentiments. I thought for a time that it was the ghost of my twin. Then I came to realise that my brother would not have begrudged me these years I have had and he has not. He was properly ghosted, in any case. Sadly, my dwelling upon this possibility gave my fears form. The thing is, I am sure, fashioned from guilt and fear that I will suffer his fate, from the happiness that I did not. It is every bad thing I have ever thought. I am, I think, a not entirely pleasant man. I suppose I should be thankful I have this problem, or I would have been a scourge on those around me. I came to realise that the dark thing in the night is not my dead brother, but the living me. This is my true burden." He became grim. "I have worked hard to best it. I decided that if I conquered my anger, then I would conquer the world!" He smiled ironically.

"Is it working?"

"Somewhat. I have less to fear from my other half than I did. I see it now only at moments of extreme emotion."

She fell silent, looked down. "Can I see it?"

"Are you serious?"

"The wine is within you. It will strengthen you. Bring it forth. Let me see."

A suspicion hit Guis. "Did you bring me here for this? Has this been your intention all along?"

"I have shown you my work. Show me yours. Listen to your own words! You talk in this maudlin way, and yet here you are, a man on the brink of success won against the wishes of his father, a man who has bested tragedy. Why should you be afraid of a shadow?" She came to him, spread her skirts and knelt on the floor before him. "I speak in earnest, Guis."

Guis was uneasy, but set his glass down nonetheless. "If you insist. Who am I to deny my hostess her pleasure?"

The countess poured wine into Guis's glass and took it up herself.

"How do you begin?"

"I do not know. I have not attempted to do this before."

"Truly?"

"I have thought to, but not dared. You provoke my courage."

He held his hand out in front of him, and closed his eyes.

How had it come to him in past times? Encouraged by wrath, and envy, and lust, and shame. He put these things aside. He grasped the slippery surface of his will, that treacherous part of his mind that would not do his bidding. Tonight, he would make it obey. The regard of the countess encouraged him. He found her as repulsive as he did attractive. He would be roundly mocked if he bedded her, but he felt himself sliding toward that eventuality anyway. He realised he wanted it, he was letting it happen. He had positioned himself so that it would; a mere relinquishment of agency would see the mechanism of circumstance do its work. By doing so he could convince himself he was absolving himself of responsibility.

And so he let the Darkling happen.

He did not see it come, but the room grew hot and heavy and the countess drew in her breath. "A darkness, gathering in the corner. Does it arrive?"

"Yes," he said. A tremor ran through the core of his being. It twisted, a thing alive, eager to be free. He would not relinquish his grasp. His hand out ahead of him was unneeded. The struggle was within, his heart was a door to places outwith. He groaned, and it was with elation. He was in control.

He dared open his eyes. The Darkling grew in the corner. Shadows rippled around it. The shape came quickly. What was visible of the walls through the murk of its birthing warped. The Darkling tossed its head and shrieked angrily.

Tyn awoke in a fury, and sharply yanked at Guis's hair. "What are you doing? Send it away! It should not be called!"

Guis pulled his hair from the Tyn's grasp. "You see he says I should send it away? He acknowledges I have some influence over it." Triumph swelled his pride.

The Darkling throbbed, its shape distending. Long arms stretched, reaching for the countess and Guis. They curled back, foiled by an invisible barrier.

"Ha!" he shouted excitedly. "See Tyn, I have the measure of it. Look at it squirm!"

"Not enough, master! You call it with intent, and so I have little power over it. Send it away before it is too late!"

The Hag's eyes sparkled. Her wine cup hovered just below her mouth, her lips were parted. Guis bathed in her fascination of him. He held the Darkling, ignoring the sweat pricking his skin.

"Is it oracular? Will it reveal things, the way the dead will to the Guiders. Or the demons of old did to the wild wizards in the days before Res Iapetus?"

"I don't know, I have never tried." He was becoming dizzy. The effort of holding the Darkling was growing.

"Do not talk to it! Do not! Do not!" squealed Tyn. It pawed at Guis's face, scratching him.

"We should listen to him. We have to send it back." He panted the words. This was harder than he had expected.

With an effort that threatened to burst his heart, he attempted to cast it back whence it came. "Begone!" he yelled. "Begone!"

The shadow being wavered. The countess stood.

"You are a magister indeed! Bravo!"

Guis's face twisted. Something was going wrong. The Darkling pushed back. His breath came fast, he unconsciously clawed his outstretched hand. The corner of the room where the Darkling stood darkened, and it grew anew.

"Tyn," he said. "Tyn!"

"*Yeee!* You cannot do it! And now I suffer for your foolishness. Curse the day I was ever made your slave."

The Tyn's eyes flashed bright. It ground its tiny teeth together. The iron collar at its neck spat sparks. Smoked wisped where it contacted Tyn's skin.

"Out! Out! Out!" shrieked the Tyn. Guis redoubled his efforts. The countess remained watching, her interest untainted by fear.

A rending sounded, the grind of stone turning slowly on trapped flesh. The Darkling keened. The air changed density suddenly. Rapidly the Darkling shrank in upon itself, blinding light emanating from its centre. It folded into nothing with a deathly wail. Foul air blew over the countess and Guis, and it was gone.

Tyn pinched Guis's cheek and pulled hard. "Foolish man! Playing with the dark. You could have died, and then what would poor Tyn do?"

Guis shook. "I'm sorry, I'm sorry!"

"Always sorry! Fool!" Tyn tugged at its collar. The thin chain rattled. "Were it not for this I would be gone, and then what would happen? One hundred and one years and a day. I await the day that time is done, so you will suffer as I do!"

Guis flinched. The burn around Tyn's neck was raw and pink.

"I will not do it again."

"Oh, it will happen again," said Tyn, his voice becoming a feline growl. "You master your will, master, and that is a good thing. Maybe you cure your sickness of the mind. But you cannot, will not ever master that," it said, pointing to the corner. "That is a sickness of your soul, and has no healing. Be fearful lest your arrogance bring you low. You have strengthened it. Fool!"

Tyn leaped from his shoulder and scampered along the sofa to where his box lay. He crawled inside, yanked his chain into its slot, and slammed the door.

The countess laid a hand on Guis's. He felt his trembling as she lightly clasped his fingers. Her eyes were alight.

"That was a fine experience! I am going to ask you all about it, you realise. I want to know everything."

"There's not much I can tell," he said. "I am not a magister nor a wild wizard or a practitioner of any sort. I do not know the theory, nor do I know the practice. It is a dangerous parlour trick."

"You would be surprised how much I can glean from limited information." She moved closer. Guis saw an animal hunger in her that quite surpassed her plainness. "But I will leave that for the morning."

Her other hand slipped into his lap. His back stiffened as she worked at his trouser fastenings.

She looked up at him, her eyes asking if she should continue. Her eyes, he decided, were quite beautiful. They regarded each other with the utmost seriousness.

Mansanio shrank deeper into the shadows of the gallery above the fireplace. Unable to tear his eyes away from their kisses, he bit his lip until it bled, his fists shaking.

GUIS HELD THE countess close. Standing with her back to him, it was easy to put what others said about her out of his mind, and he was glad of the warmth of her proximity. But minute by minute, the aftermath of their lust drained away, and he became increasingly awkward about what he had done. She was unaware, and pressed into him languorously. They were in the observatory, looking out from the open shutters over the endless mud. The moons painted their long roads upon it, one pink, one silver. The stars were chips of ice. The Twin stood exactly over the turrets of Mogawn, distant that night.

"You should come back at a time of the Great Tide," she sighed. "The castle rises up, up, like a kneeling giant standing. For a moment, the whole of Mogawn hangs on the face of a cliff of water, and then it is away under us, rolling toward the shore. A sheet of spray shoots skywards, white surf boils up through the cavities in the rock, over the lowest hills..." She made a happy noise. "I love it so. The power of the ocean is incomprehensible. When my father raged at me, I used to go to the gatehouse, to watch the sea burst over the jaws of Mogawn, and I would be glad. The sight made me understand that no matter what a tyrant a man might be, before the fury of the sea he is nothing. Your brother is a brave man."

"Which one?" said Guis.

She slapped his arm playfully. "You know well which! I wish him godspeed over the ocean, but I fear for his chances."

Guis had avoided thinking on Trassan, or Rel. Both of them were in peril. Dwelling overly long on it would conjure forth all manner of horrible fates for them and send him into a frenzy of endless preventative ritual, half-convinced his mere thinking of it would make it happen. He would curse himself for his repetitive touchings and steps, but still perform them, caught between anger and fear.

"I wish I had had siblings. Growing up here was a long and lonely process. You are not the only person with a harsh father. Mine was outraged at the aristocracy's diminished status and his own dwindling fortune. It made him cruel." She craned her neck to look him in the eye. "Everything goes around in cycles, Guis. My mother married outside Karsa to try to preserve her bloodline and keep Mogawn alive. But I shall never become a mother. The Mogawn line will die with me." She said this with such steel that Guis released her. She turned to face him. Her father looked at Guis through her, still angry beyond death. She was so ugly. What was he thinking? She had used him, that was true, but she had opened her heart to him in return. All Guis could think of was what would happen if this dalliance became public.

He was disgusted with himself for thinking this.

He drew away nonetheless when she shivered and held up her arms for a return to embrace.

"It is cold," she said softly.

"It is late," said Guis weakly. "I should retire now. I must return in the morning."

Her face hardened. "I see," she said. The steel returned to her voice. "That is the way it is. I had hoped this would be different, for I hold you in affection. Very well, it is not to be." She looked away to compose herself. "Before you are away to bed, there is one last thing that you must see."

"I am very tired," said Guis dismayed.

"You will see this," said the countess. Her tone brooked no refusal. "You will see it now."

Guis took an involuntary step forward. How his life was, pulled this way and that by things outside his control. His dismay grew.

"Look into the telescope."

He did as he was ordered. The black surface of the Twin greeted him, a pit of hungry shadow. He was glad of the distance between him and it. "It is blurred."

She leaned over him and adjusted something. The image leapt into sharp focus.

"What do you see now?"

"A lighter shade upon the black. Perhaps a cloud?"

"Not a cloud. Wait."

"A flare! I see... fire?"

The countess ran her fingers down his back, he shuddered. Was it pleasure or repulsion? He could no longer tell them apart. "Fire upon the Twin. It grows in ferocity. Soon it will be visible to the naked eye. With each pass it draws closer, and closer, until it will be closer than it has been for four thousand years. Four thousand years ago, the Old Maceriyans fell from grace. Eight thousand years before that, the Morfaan's power was broken, at some point in between the two they disappeared from the Earth but for their sorry ambassadors. I would bet Mogawn itself that it was eight thousand years before the present. Now disagree with me that things are not bound into endless cycles: the turning of the tides, the procession of the spheres, the track of the stars and seasons." She leaned into his ear and whispered rancorously. "Lust, seduction, repulsion, regret, rejection. Over and over again, for all time. I welcome an end to it." She pulled back. "So you see, my machine is not merely the plaything of a lonely woman, despised for her talents, mocked for her appearance. All things are cyclical. And I will prove it before the end."

He cravenly kept his eye to the telescope's eyepiece as she walked away from him. A second flare of bright orange burst on the black face of the Twin.

"Goodnight Guis, I trust you can find your own way back to your room. I will not see you away in the morning."

Only when she was gone did he look up.

CHAPTER FORTY-ONE
The Winter Riots

KATRIONA SAT UP late at home working. Her accounts were open before her, multiple volumes layered on top of each other. Tiredness was a sweet sensation, born from her diligence. Exhaustion won through hard work. She savoured it.

Her books were finally balancing. New procedures were being enacted across the site, and initial results were promising. Soon she could think about bringing more of the factory sheds into use again, and expanding the workforce further.

The sense of satisfaction was sublime. She could see the glory days of Morthrocksey returning.

The Tyn worked hard. One more casting session, and she would have provided her brother with the full complement of fuel rods for the *Prince Alfra*. He had secured the money from their uncle. Everything proceeded smoothly. She thought several times about stopping for the night, but the minutiae of the business was so absorbing she could not tear herself away from it.

For one brief moment, she was happy. A hammering at the front door shattered it.

"Laisa! Get that would you?" she called for her maid. She turned her attention back to the books. Downstairs voices were raised. A clatter of boots on stairs approached her study. The door burst inwards at the hand of Jon Cullen, the head of the factory nightwatch.

"Jon?" she said. "What do you want? Is it the mill?"

Laisa came up behind. "He wouldn't wait, Goodlady Katriona!"

"Is Goodfellow Morthrock here?" Cullen said.

"I told you he ain't!" said the maid.

"Demion is out at cards. If it's the mill, you know to address your concerns to me."

Jon shook his head. "It's the both of you, begging your pardon goodlady, that I was wanting. I'd send for him if I were you. And you better come quick. There's trouble."

A tense ride to the mill through dark streets. They were quickly away from the well-lit boulevards of the new town and into the dark industrial districts, where the mills stood as beacons amid dark formations of terraced housing. The few glimmer lamps buzzed and crackled.

"It started about half an hour ago," said Cullen. "A load of them arrived, pushed their way past my lads. I mean, what were we going to do? These are their friends and relatives, not burglars sneaking in at night."

"How many are there?"

"About three, maybe four hundred."

"That's a third of the workforce!"

"If you include the Tyn it is," he said.

"I most certainly do," said Katriona.

"That might be the issue here, begging your pardon goodlady."

They rounded the corner onto Morthrocksey Lane.

"Res Iapetus's balls," swore Jon. "Things have taken a turn for the worse."

"They've torched one of the factory sheds!" Katriona shouted.

Jon had whipped the dogs all the way, and he whipped them all the harder to the gates. By the time they arrived all four of them foamed at the muzzle and panted heavily. Katriona jumped down and made for the gate. Beyond she could see the outline of the crowd. A single mass with many heads. All the gates were open. A line of nightwatchmen stood their ground in an arc around the main gate, defending an entrance already breached. There was shouting, a man on a box gesticulating, rousing the crowd. In the orange light of the burning shed he appeared demoniac. The crowd was spellbound.

Katriona hurried on. Jon's hand closed around her bicep. "Best be careful, goodlady, the situation is ugly. Let me go first."

The number of men Katriona still called her own was small, and they were armed with nothing but cudgels. From their faces she could see they would not willingly use them on their fellow workers. "We have sent for aid, goodlady, to the watch," said Jon's deputy.

"What have you done?"

"I... I only seek to perform my role, Goodlady Morthrocksa."

"The watch will not come," she said. "The whole factory is here. They will be vastly outnumbered. The watch will not come!"

"I..."

She stepped close to him, pointing behind her. "Do you not see? They will not send the watch, they will send the army!"

The man blanched. Now what had she done? Whatever was about to happen, he would carry the guilt with him forever. She turned, panicked. One of the factory sheds burned, fire licking from its windows. Shouts and the sound of breaking glass came from somewhere far away. The line of workers faced her and her loyal guards, grim faces lit by their lamps and the flames of the burning factory.

"Steady, Goodlady Katriona, he's just doing his job," said Jon.

"And if you did yours this would never have happened! You say you would not harm your friends and relations, but you will see them killed instead. Stop!" she said to the crowd. "What are you doing? It is your own livelihoods you are burning!" She looked at the mill. Smoke poured from a second building. The heat of the shed ablaze seared her front, the cold of the night chilled her back. "What have you done?"

Tears started from her eyes. The crowd ebbed and flowed around a knot of unmoving men about the demagogue. She realised she knew only a few of their names.

"Here she is! Here is the architect of your poverty!" cried the man on the box. She did not know him.

"Is there any here I know and trust and will speak with me?" she said.

The man grinned wolfishly at her.

Another pushed his way out. "Etwen I am, Goodlady Katriona," he said. He carried a stout iron pole as a weapon.

"What is going on here? Why do you riot?"

"What kind of life do you suppose that we have? Toiling here from dawn to dusk, going home to cold houses that cause our children to sicken and die?"

"Why did you not come to me?"

"Why should we? What does a noble lady like you know of the lives of ordinary folk? This dream of yours to make and build, it is built on a foundation of bone and blood. Our bone, our blood!" shouted the demagogue.

Muted calls of "hear hear" came from the crowd.

"Would you have listened?" said Etwen.

"You have to go home. My men, they have called the watch. But they will not come." She paused. "The army will come. Do you not see?"

The crowd quietened.

"Good, because we will show them the hard side of justice, the injustice we have had to suffer our entire lives!" shouted the demagogue.

The cheers grew loud again. The front ranks stepped closer, menacing her. Etwen held up his hand, staying them.

"Why now though, I do not understand? Why let it fester?" she said.

"It is because of them!" cried the demagogue. His finger descended, judgmental as a prophet's. Where he pointed, the crowd parted.

Jeers came from the crowd as Tyns Lydar, Lorl and two others were pushed to the front and forced to their knees.

"Kado love," spat Tyn Lydar. "All of evil." Her scarf had been torn from her. Her face was bloody. The wrists of all were bound behind their backs.

"You offer them special preference, these things that live in our midst," said the demagogue, "while you ignore the woes of your own kind!"

"They are not things!" protested Katriona.

"They are not human," said Etwen, unsure.

"They give the evil eye!" someone from the crowd shouted.

Then another. "They spoil our rations. They steal our work!"

"Aye! And slaves we are and poorly judged, though we work as hard as ye and labour by your sides without complaint, you kado who took our meadows and our..." shouted Tyn Lorl.

A cast stone silenced Tyn Lorl. He collapsed to the cobbles. Katriona ran to his side.

"See! She shows where her loyalty lies!" cried the demagogue. He had stepped off his box and was shoving at his fellows as he exhorted them, approaching a frenzy. "So disconnected are these rich ones that they cannot tell who their own people are!"

"My great-grandfather's father was a simple man, my station is all bought with honest sweat and toil, as yours could also be!" she said.

The crowd laughed. Etwen shook his head. "You know nothing, nothing at all."

"These things talk of slavery, we will show you real slavery!" crowed the demagogue.

Hands reached for her. They raked at her clothes, tearing them.

Etwen was at her side. "Steady with her! Steady!"

"Let me go, let me go!" A great terror gripped her. She was certain she was about to be killed, or worse. "Don't you see? Stop this now, go home or they will kill you all!"

Her arms and legs were tugged mercilessly, but she remained unmolested. The demagogue exhorted his colleagues to stand firm, to not listen.

A horn blared, then another, then another. Shouts came from the gate. Katriona twisted around to see her guards scatter like sheep before wild dogs.

Colonel Alanrys came forward from the smoke blowing across Morthrocksey mainstreet. He wore his dress uniform, darkest red with golden frogging, a bicorn atop his head. Dracon feathers fluttered all along its crest, and he wore a cloak made of the same. He rode upon a silver-grey dracon shod for war. The mouth was unmuzzled. Steel blades covered its sickle claws, its forearms had been fitted with clawed gauntlets. The steel of its weapons clicked on the cobbles as Alanrys trotted to a halt in front of the crowd. Fifty of his men filed through the gates into the wide street, followed by fifty more, their arms and armour bronze in the light of the burning factories. They spread out in a double line, the plumes of their helmets twisted in the heat of the blaze. Their mounts were all as their leader's, decked for battle, not the suppression of civil disobedience.

Alanrys raised an arm. One hundred carbines levelled at the crowd.

"Leave her!" ordered Alanrys. Hammers clicked back on guns.

The rioters backed away, leaving Katriona dishevelled in a shallow semicircle. Alanrys rode up, entirely unconcerned by the mob, his dracon prancing. "Well well well, Katriona Kressinda-Morthrocksa." Alanrys leaned over in his saddle. He ignored the workers. "Here you are, disporting with the lower orders. How very you. You should have married me when you had the chance. You would not have found yourself in such poor company." He surveyed the workers. Makeshift weapons shifted in hands. They had fallen silent, but their demeanour was defiant.

Katriona got to her feet. "Listen to me, Alanrys, stand your men down. It doesn't have to end this way."

"Rioting and the destruction of crown-licensed property are crimes of the highest order!" Bellowed Alanrys. His words were clipped, rich, projected to the very back of the crowd. "You will disperse or I will run you down. I swear this as Lord Defender of Karsa City, appointed by Prince Alfra himself!"

The line of workers bowed backward, uncertain.

"Alanrys! Listen, this is all a misunderstanding. A mistake. I am sure if I were to negotiate with them, to hear their grievances, then this will all be resolved without bloodshed."

Alanrys sniffed. He took in the burning factory, the second whose windows vented smoke prodigiously. "A mistake? A burning mill, a riot, you, a goodlady, manhandled. It is you who are mistaken. This is sedition."

She grabbed at his boot. "Please! If you ever had any feeling for me, do not spill their blood." She glanced over her shoulder, searching out the demagogue. "There are agents at work here. This is not their doing."

He looked down at her contemptuously, and she knew then she had made a mistake in appealing to his better side. "Feeling? I never had any feeling for you, Katriona. I merely wished to have you, and your father's money along with you. As you were unwilling to be had, so I remain poorer than I should. I am not inclined to listen to you." He swept his gaze across the crowd. "Let this scum crawl back to their hovels. They will know their place, or by all the driven gods I will put them in it, and the rest into the hands of the Guiders!" He shoved Katriona away, and rode back to the line of his men. They stared out impassively from under tall helmets. With anguish she understood that had Rel not been sent away, he would be there among them.

"This is your last chance! Return to your homes, or we will have no choice but to remove you by force! Some of you will die! Many of you will die!"

Alanrys's monstrous mount pawed at the ground. Plumes of steam snorted from its nostrils.

"We will not be cowed! We will not live like animals!" shouted the demagogue.

"You bring this upon yourselves," said Alanrys. He drew his sabre and held it high over his head.

"Lances!" he shouted. Three dozen guns were put up. Three dozen lance points dropped. The men of the second rank kept their carbines trained upon the crowd.

"Stand firm!" shouted the demagogue. Murmurs of assent grew in strength. The crowd swelled forward, seeming to grow in size.

Katriona was caught halfway between the crowd and the soldiers. Fifty yards of even ground separated them. If the dragoons charged, it would be slaughter. She turned from one to the other. "Stop! Stop! I will listen to your demands, I swear."

"This night some of us may die!" called the demagogue. "But the world will take notice! We spill our blood in the names of all those who toil for selfish masters! Let the workers of Ruthnia unite! Today is the beginning of revolution!"

"As you wish," said Alanrys.

Etwen's resolve wavered. He lowered his cudgel. "No, wait—" he began.

"Fire!" ordered Alanrys. His arm dropped.

The blast of fifty ironlock carbines discharging simultaneously ripped the night in half. Glimmering trails of blue marked the passage of the bullets across the open ground. Katriona screamed as they found their marks in the crowd, punching men and women off their feet, blasting limbs from bodies, shattering skulls. The slain flew backwards with the force of the impact. The crowd shifted, moaning, a single creature dealt a grievous blow.

"Charge!" shouted Alanrys.

Bugles sounded. Dracons roared and sprang forward. Faced with the reality of its peril, the crowd disintegrated.

The dracons poured past Katriona, snapping and croaking, their riders holding their lances in deadly stillness, targets marked. Pennants she had once thought so bright and bold whickered murderously past her ears, each chasing a foot of sharpened steel.

The dragoons rode headlong into the crowd. Every spear accounted for one life. The impact of the charge bowled over dozens more rioters. Many died under the bladed claws of the dracons. The crowd screamed, a shrill and horrible noise from five hundred throats.

The real slaughter began.

The dragoons unsheathed their sabres, and lay about them. The dracons leapt high, bearing down fleeing men to the ground and ripping them to pieces. Workers scattered in all directions. Some hurled themselves into the filthy trickle of the Morthrocksey. Some ran as hard as they could for the railyards and the wall at the far side of the complex. Others dove into the alleyways between the factory sheds, tugging wildly at locked doors. Another group pushed past the line of dragoons, whose efforts to subdue the crowd had broken them up into small knots of two or three. These ran right at Alanrys's second line.

"Reload!" Alanrys said.

"Goodlady Kat!"

A small hand grabbed her ankle. The dragoons fired. The bullet passed through her, but she was not wholly there, she was a mist, the bullet a breeze.

"Do not open your eyes, Mistress Kat," warned Tyn Lydar. "Do not open your eyes, or you shall never return."

"I am cold."

"This place is not of the Earth." Tyn Lydar's voice was layered, a multiple of voices speaking as one. Like the crowd, one from a multitude. "Do not open your eyes."

Kat did as she was told, keeping her eyes screwed shut, terrified they would flicker open. There was a sense of movement all around her, of presences that watched and waited.

She could still hear the battle, distant, but present. Screams. Gunfire. Isolated now, no longer massed volleys.

Carriage wheels clattered. Dogs bayed. She heard a familiar voice. It kindled warmth in her heart. She started forward. The fingers slipped from around her ankle.

"Goodlady!"

"Demion!" she called.

She followed his voice, flying faster as it grew louder. Demion was shouting, remonstrating with a soldier, not Alanrys. He mustn't. Alanrys was dangerous, Alanrys...

Reality quivered against her, the membranes of being struck like a drum. She was readmitted, stumbling onto the cobbles.

Warmth returned, the fierce heat of burning buildings. The screams were loud once more, but few in number. Dracons croaked rather than roared. Someone was sobbing close by. She looked around her feet. There was no one there. And then there was. Tyn Lydar appeared. Tyn Lorl too, and Tyn Elly. The whites of Tyn Elly's eyes were blood red. The collars of both female Tyn glowed dull orange, the scarves they wore around them gone to ash. The stink of burnt flesh came off them. Tyn Lorl lay upon the ground and did not move.

"Dead," said Tyn Lydar. "Dead, dead, dead." She stared accusingly at Katriona. "One less of those who are too few to begin with."

"Katriona!" called Demion. "I came as quickly as I could." He took her upper arms in his hands. "What happened?"

"The... the workers. A riot. It was the concessions I gave to the Tyn, but I think there was someone..." She pulled away from him. She looked over the fallen. The wounded cradled the dead. There were body parts strewn across the ground, and blood, black slicks of it glinting in the light of her burning factories.

There.

She pulled from Demion's grip, ran to where the demagogue lay fallen. A bullet had taken his shoulder, leaving a bloody mess in its place. The parallel claw-strokes of a dracon had opened his belly. One hand was draped on this wound, fingers in the flow of blood pulsing from it. He lay in a lake of his own fluids. Incredibly, he was still alive. Demion was at her shoulder.

"Kuh... Kuk... Kuh..."

She lifted his head. His blood soaked warmly through her sleeve. "Do not die! Please. Stay with us here. Do not let your spirit go. If you remain, I will do my best to see your demands are met. I did not know, I swear I did not know."

He mouthed something, she leaned in closer.

"Only because you chose not to know." His voice was a breath, barely audible.

Something wriggled against her ear. She jerked back.

The flesh of the man's face writhed as if infested with worms. His head snapped from side to side and he cried out.

"Hold on!" she cried. "Please! Someone help!" But people sat in the gore of their fellows, and none came to her. When she looked back to the man, she gasped with shock.

Holdean Morthrock was in her arms.

"Holdean!" Demion's exclamation was as explosive as a gunshot.

Holdean smiled at Katriona viciously. Blood welled from the corner of his mouth. "You got what you deserved." He coughed. A flood of dark fluid rose from his lips. The bleeding from the claw mark to his chest was easing.

"Why did you do it?" she said. "How?"

He held a palsied finger to his bloody lips, and died.

Katriona turned questioningly to her husband. He stared back at her, uncomprehending. He pulled her to her feet.

Reptilian croaks and rattles broke the eerie calm. The dragoons were returning. Their sergeants and lieutenants barked orders. The reptiles were hard to control with air so heavily laden with blood. A soldier rode past, wrestling with the reins of his dracon. His features contorted with the effort.

One dracon lay dead, scales opened by industrial knives. A soldier limped past, supported by two of his colleagues. One of them stared ahead, face white, mouth hanging open. His eyes were as dead and flat as those of the survivors of the massacre. A trooper on foot fought his mount, attempting to close the muzzling plates of its chamfron. Red jaws snapped at his face.

A woman's wail cut across the street, rising, falling.

Etwen was being led across the square in chains. Two of Alanrys's men had him by the shoulders, their dracons being led by two more behind them.

Etwen stared Katriona dead in the eye. "Our conditions are poor. Giving the Tyn that treatment, it made them angry."

"Hold a moment!" said Demion as the soldiers made to drag him on: "Why was Goodman Holdean agitating you?"

"Holdean?" said Etwen.

"The demagogue," said Katriona.

Etwen looked blank.

"The rabble rouser, man!" said Demion.

"The philosopher? That weren't Goodman Holdean, that were a new man. Only been here a few weeks, but he had big ideas. Made us think we could get something. More fool us." He looked to the floor.

"I promise I will look into it. I will listen to your grievances."

"You won't be listening to his," said Alanrys. "He'll be hung in the morning. Take him away!"

"Please look to my children!" called Etwen as he was dragged off.

"I will," said Katriona.

"How very large-hearted of you," scoffed Alanrys. "Here I am putting down a gross act of civil disobedience for your benefit, and you are offering to tend to their hurts. You should throw them out on the street, or others will follow in his footsteps, mark my words. But you never did know what was good for you Katriona. Perhaps next time we meet, you will learn your lesson properly."

Demion stood straight, chest out. "Look here! I think you better leave. If I see you near my wife or our business again, I will personally see that you are brought up on charges. The name of Morthrock carries weight in powerful circles, Alanrys. My father is owed many favours still. Do not provoke me into calling them in."

Alanrys slapped his gloves into his hand. Both gloves and hands were caked in blood.

"The lapdog barks," he said. "Very well, I shall leave your factory in your hands, courtesy of the 3rd Karsan Dragoons. I expect thanks shall be forthcoming later." He snapped a bow, and went to gather his men.

People ventured in from outside, searching for sons and husbands. Fire engines arrived, four teams from different firehouses. Their firechiefs ignored the carnage around them and began arguing about who would take the job.

"Oh for the love of the departed gods! All of you, put out the godsdamned fire and you'll all be paid!" shouted Demion. "Get on with it or we'll lose more than the two mills!"

He left Katriona for a moment and went to remonstrate with them. By now both factory sheds were fiercely ablaze. An explosion sent a mushroom of fire into the sky. Her heart was as heavy as stone.

Demion returned.

"Alanrys is right," she said. "Father is right. This is what happens when a woman steps outside the bounds of her rightful station." Katriona wept freely. Demion embraced her and she sank into his arms.

"That is not the case, my love. This is what happens when the established order is challenged. The sex of the challenger has nothing to do with it." He cupped her face in his hands. "The truth is, you are brave enough to do it, I am not. We will triumph over this adversity, you will see."

She nodded. She opened her mouth to begin speaking of improvements in the workers' conditions of both races but surprised them both by kissing him passionately and deeply.

He pulled back, astonished. "I..."

"Don't say anything. Please."

He cleared his throat. "We should get you home. I must call in the physics to tend to the wounded, and the Guiders or we will have a second disaster on our hands. So much violent death..."

"I am staying with you," she said.

"Are you sure, my dear?"

She took his hand. "We shall do this together."

CHAPTER FORTY-TWO
The Twin and Mansanio

THE COUNTESS OF Mogawn sat in a high leather armchair in the centre of her orrery. The heavenly spheres clicked overhead, round and round and round, dancing in a wooden sky.

The fires of the Twin were growing in frequency and anger. There was an answer why. Why could she not see it?

Am I to be alone forever?

She chased the thought away angrily. Now was not the time. She stared at the Twin. Was the model correct? While she had sat there, hundreds of years of celestial movements spun by. The gearing was complex. Each model world was designed to follow a path as the real spheres would, changing their cycles gradually in reaction to the proximity of others. This incremental stacking of variables produced complex patterns that she could not have predicted. That was why she had built the machine. She had laid out the pieces of the puzzle and set them in motion, now she watched it for hours, trusting it to solve itself.

The precession of the Earth, perhaps? The subtle wobble of the axis under the influence of the other spheres? Twenty times the Earth went around the bronze sun. A sun cast at her bidding! How droll, she thought rancorously. The Earth shifted slightly in its gimbals. She stared down at the equations scribbled over the papers in her hand. That might make a difference to the weather, the net input of energy from the sun to various quarters of the polar regions would vary. So much heat, it had to go somewhere. But how could that lead to the downfall of two, maybe more, civilisations in the flush of their art? A global shift? She thought no. No evidence. Nothing empiric or magick to suggest something of that scale.

With each accelerated year described by the orbs, the Twin came closer and closer to the Earth. It clunked as the chains propelling it shifted on its gears. Of course the machine was limited but...

Everything was limited. She was limited. How could she hope to hold the dance of the spheres in her mind? Some men respected her for her mind. She had learned early in life that was no substitute for a pretty face. Wealth and beauty were what men craved; succession was what the parents of men craved. These things could meet in happy confluence. Happy for the suitor, and sometimes the bride. Mind rarely came into that. Best to be beautiful and rich. If one were stupid or narrow of vision, so what? If not rich, then the next best thing was to be beautiful and poor. Then it paid to be intelligent. A pretty, clever women could go where she would with a hatful of empty promises and the occasional distasteful compromise, no matter her initial station. Poor, beautiful and stupid was a bad combination, and ended in misery. A man could forgive an intelligent, beautiful woman her own opinions, especially if she added her wealth to his. If ugly, rich and stupid, nobody cared. A prize chased solely for advancement, doomed to an unhappy life, but never alone. Ugly, rich and intelligent? That was no good at all.

The grand irony of it that she wasn't so clever after all. She laughed loudly, resentfully. If she were truly clever, she would have solved the issue of the spheres. Or she would not trouble herself at all with it, but play the genteel idiot, keep her wits to herself. Or was that wisdom? Was it wisdom she lacked? No, she scolded herself, it was neither! To play the fool would be a betrayal of what she was. She was cursed, clever enough to see the world as it was, too limited to do anything about it. Clever enough to know how stupid she and every other human being was.

Her thoughts went around and around her mind as relentlessly as the planets clacked overhead, problems orbiting the irresolvable issue of her face. Her father's face. Where was the justice in the world that she had to look at the man she hated in every mirror?

Her hand rumpled a sheet of paper as it clenched. *Focus! This is not relevant. The worlds. Think! Where is the answer?* She went to the orrery's controls upon the central column, and increased the speed. The glimmer engine within glowed blue white. This was a purely magical device, bound about with expensive spells wrought into silver by magister artisans. No intermediary steam device propelled the orbs, but the power of the glimmer applied directly. It had cost her a small fortune.

Acceleration seized the track of heaven. The orbs proceeded faster and faster. Five minutes, and one hundred revolutions of the sun were made by the Earth and its dark twin. The moons sped along their paths between the louring worlds, fugitives before them both.

Am I pretty?

Stop it. Shallow thinking. Stupid. Unimportant. This. The world, that is a problem worth thinking on, and solvable.

The Twin, the answer is there. So large an object, close enough to touch, dark enough to hide an eternity of nightmares. The fires. The tides. The Twin.

The burnished, blackened bronze of the Twin followed the track she had designed, circling the Earth like a duellist. If she had designed it poorly, she would not know if she were wrong or right, she would not know, she would only see what she thought she should see.

Not like when she looked in the mirror.

Focus. If she were wrong, the orrery would teach her nothing. A reinforcement of preconceptions. Do not become fixated upon it. To solve a problem, look beyond it, not at it. Her face... Was that why Guis rejected her? She smiled ruefully.

Plenty more out there. Plenty more who were attracted by her reputation, by the scandal of it. Plenty who did not care, so long as she were available.

She wanted to be loved. She yearned for it as much as the idea made her laugh. To be trapped with one person for the duration of life. Another face to look at daily and grow sick of.

The Earth and the Twin were the same, opposed, drawn together and pulled apart—she was sure it was a pull now, and not a mutual repulsion as Hool, Toskin and others had it. A firmly discredited idea. Nor was it a building resistance through some theoretical cosmic medium. Why was the air thinner atop a mountain? Why did a weight fall at a constant speed no matter the thickness of the air? She had seen the feather and coin experiments at the Royal Institute last year. The vacuum tube, ingenious.

There was nothing between the worlds.

"The aether is void," she said aloud.

There was something inherent to the celestial bodies that drew them together, the same force, one inherent to all objects, pulled them apart. Nostron was correct. If one could calculate that, she was sure she could calculate the size of the sun. She already suspected it was far more enormous than any other astronomer believed. If only the magisters could penetrate the energy enveloping the world, and leave the confines of this Earth! Perhaps then, they might be useful to her.

She looked to a huge tome balanced atop several smaller. The collected writings of Everian Andor, a mage from before the time of Iapetus. What he said bore out her own work. He had journeyed beyond, so he said. Only a mage could do that. But they lived in an era of magisters, not mages, and she had the power of neither.

All she had was her mind. That would have to do.

So, she thought. A great influence upon this world. The tides, the shakings of the earth, perhaps also the fires upon the Twin, a reciprocal influence. Did that account for the 4,000 year cycle suggested by the historical record? Surely not on its own. The Twin drew near far more frequently than that, superpositions of both moons, sun, Twin and Earth occurred every roughly every 400 years, with a drift of one year per 1,300 years. None so close as the 4,000 year conjunctions, but was it enough of a difference to cause calamity?

She watched the Twin going around and around, coming closer, drawing away, each loop bringing it nearer and nearer. There was a connection.

But there was something missing. Some other factor that she had yet to see. *Look beyond the orrery, look beyond the problem.*

The one thing her father had told her that she valued. *Look beyond the problem.*

She went to Andor's book, shoved the sheafs of paper balanced on it to the floor. She opened it and flicked through the pages. Woodcuts of impossible scenes leapt out. The pages stuck. She licked her finger to turn them more easily and tasted the paper. Must and years as pronounced as any spice.

"Here," she said to herself. The spheres whirring overhead could not hear her. She spoke for her own benefit, to remind herself of her physicality, lest she disappear into her own thoughts.

She read, finger to her lips.

"'Upon the black were tall towers, desert and broken. Dark on dark, unknown until they were upon me and I could not escape their regard. Glassless windows gaped on prospects running with fire. A ceaseless abundance of this vomited from the Twin, as the Three Sisters do in Farthia and Ostria. I witnessed ruination wrought long since, yet felt unwelcoming eyes chase me through over liquid flame. And then I was driven on by my fear, fearing the undeniable call of Andrade to pull me back to Earth before my journey was done, and the city fell behind me.'"

Andrade, guardian of the world's order, a tutelary spirit banished with all the rest by Res Iapetus. An allegory, or an actuality? One never knew with mages.

A consequence of their power, some said a function of it, was that they were nearly all insane. At least when regarded from the confines of the objective consensual reality as experienced by others. But who was to say if the mages were insane, or if they were sane and everyone else mad?

A digression. Ruined cities on the Earth. Why not ruined cities upon the Twin and every other celestial body? Perhaps they also felt the turning wheel of history, the rise and fall and rise again.

Outside the window the brightest stars outshone the glimmer lights of her hall. Maybe something from beyond this system of heavenly baubles? There were those that maintained the stars were suns, and about them turned their own worlds, on and on into an infinity of night. Perhaps it was nothing to do with the familiar worlds at all, but an influence from further away.

In which case, she was entirely wasting her time with this very expensive toy.

Guis. She had expected better of him.

"What the fucking hell does it all matter?" She threw her arms wide and shouted her challenge to the stars outside her windows.

She was no longer sure if she spoke of astronomy or of the more pressing and equally mystifying social dance they were all forced to perform.

The spinning mechanism had no answers for her. The rattle of it suddenly irked her. She shut it off and sank into a battered armchair, placed her thumb and forefinger either side of her all too prominent nose, thinking of nothing, enjoying the pressure of her fingers on the bone.

"Goodlady?" Mansanio spoke timorously. His footsteps were timid; a mouse creeping from its hole.

"Goodlady Lucinia, are you troubled?" He put a hand upon her shoulder.

She placed her own hand upon his. His was warm, hers cold. She squeezed it, smiled and looked up at him. "When have you known me not to be troubled, Mansanio?"

His face brimmed with concern. "Never, goodlady. You should not worry yourself with these questions so much. Live your life easily."

"I do."

He tutted. "Not like that. I mean, to go outside, take the air. Ride your coach along the shore road, find other interests to occupy your fine mind, goodlady."

"I would find problems in all of them, Mansanio. In history, in astronomy, maths, geology."

"I was thinking more of painting or the pressing of flowers."

"I would find problems there too! The matter of true perspective always bothered me, for example. Or perhaps I would occupy myself with the chemical and alchemical synthesis of brighter colours, or with an exploration of the divorcing of form from essence in order to discover the true shapes hidden in all things. Flowers need classifying, sorting. What goes where, why does this grow here, and not there? How do they reproduce, what makes their faces shine? How do they draw sustenance from the ground, do they depend on the sun? What use is there in killing a plant simply to have it? I never saw the sense." She saw his hurt and became gentler. "Mansanio, my dear Mansanio. I am so sorry. You must think me the most diabolical mistress."

"Never, goodlady," he said softly. "You are a wonder to me."

"You a true friend, my rock of permanence in a life of storm-tossed uncertainty." She squeezed his hand again and released it.

He did not remove it from her shoulder as expected. He crouched by her chair.

"Mansanio, why are you quivering so?"

"Goodlady Lucinia, the others, they do not understand you as I do. I have watched you since you were young, so graceless, so isolated, but such a mind! No one else knows you as I know you."

He slipped his other hand around her neck. He licked his lips. His eyes were wide, moon-caught.

"Mansanio," she said warningly, "what are you doing?"

He clutched at her, harder, his embrace turning from one of comfort to something else entirely. He pressed at the back of her neck, pulling her face towards his. She pulled back.

"Stop it!"

Mansanio was past listening. He kissed her cheek and her always furrowed forehead. He breathed hot words of affection into her ear. "I love you, I love you, I have always loved you. Do not be sad."

The countess wrenched Mansanio's arms from about her neck and shot to her feet. Mansanio rose slowly after her, his arms out imploringly. "Goodlady, please."

"Get out now, Mansanio. We will discuss this in the morning."

Mansanio reached for her again. "What is the use? I have told you how I feel. There is nothing for it but to admit how we are bound together, you and I. Be with me. It will be difficult, but you are no stranger to difficulty."

He grabbed her and went to kiss her again. She turned her head, but he grabbed her face and planted his lips on hers. His limp moustache brushed her. She made a moan of disgust as his tongue poked into the corner of her mouth.

"Get off me this instant!" she shoved him back hard.

"My Lucinella, I cannot bear to see you hurt again..."

She slapped him as hard as she could. His head snapped around and he cowered. When he faced her again, blood trickled from his nose, and his cheek was an angry red.

"How I am hurt and by whom is entirely my own affair. How dare you! I am the Countess of Mogawn, a woman of high blood whose claim upon this castle goes back to the time of King Brannon. You are..." She glared at him with outright disgust. "You are a servant and a foreigner! How dare you think that there might be something... Get out! *Get out!* Get out now before I call Aldwyn's boys. As young as they are they will prove more than a match for you. Get out, or I swear by the Drowned King and his sodden horde that I'll have you put over the side of the castle to join him."

"Goodlady, I am, I..." Mansanio grovelled. "I am so sorry, I thought—"

"Whatever you thought, Mansanio, you thought wrong. You will leave as soon as the next low tide uncovers the causeway, and you will never return to Mogawn again."

Mansanio cringed as the countess advanced on him. With a sob, he turned and fled.

Lucinia buried her face in her hands and wept.

CHAPTER FORTY-THREE
Preparations for Departure

"WINTER IS COMING to a close, the ship is almost finished and we still do not have our licence," said Captain Heffi. He looked over a pile of papers at Trassan.

"I thought I was the pessimistic one," said Trassan.

"They are taking an undue amount of time over it, I begin to worry."

"We will have it."

"You speak more from hope than conviction."

"Either way, we need a master of arms still. Do you not want to find one of your own people?"

"Despite what some of them feel, my people make great sailors, and poor warriors. Bring one of your own, someone you can trust."

Trassan drummed his fingers on the desk. They fell into the rhythm of the shipyard outside; the nature of the noise had changed over the last weeks. "As it happens, I have made preliminary enquiries in that direction."

"Wise," said Heffi.

"What? Don't be like that, Heffi. I second-guessed you. I thought the likelihood of you suggesting a Ishmalani armsman pretty remote. You can't have it both ways, telling me that I should find one, but only happy that I have if you have allowed me to choose!"

They were both tired and crotchety, having been at the crew manifest for several hours. Heffi grunted. Neither one way, or the other.

"If you did have a man, he would have been first choice. Do you?"

"No," said Heffi.

"Well then."

"Then who do you have in mind?"

Trassan picked up a piece of paper and squinted at it distractedly.

Heffi cleared his throat.

"What? Oh. I asked my brother Guis. I thought he'd suggest his friend Qurion. He's a good soldier, cocky sod, but handy in a fight."

"Thought?"

"That's the thing. He didn't. He suggested this other fellow, First Lieutenant Bannord."

Trassan waved a crumpled message slip at Heffi as if that might prove something. Heffi declined to take it. "What about your other brother?"

"Which one?"

Heffi groaned. "For the sake of the One! The actual soldier!"

"Rel? I've a lot of brothers. I did think of asking him who to recommend."

"Not asking him himself?"

"Too risky. I don't want to put all the Kressind eggs into one basket. That's not good common-sense, dynastically speaking," he said. Heffi couldn't tell if he were being serious or not. "Besides, he's at the Gates."

"Ouch."

"He was a very naughty boy." Trassan sighed and looked out of the grimy windows. The *Prince Alfra* sat below, slab-sided. Inert. "I'm at that stage, Heffi."

The captain pushed himself back from the table and slumped in the chair. The metallic bang of something dropped rang through the great shed. Distant swearing followed it. But the shipyard was so quiet the sound of Issy snoring in her mansion was the loudest thing in the room. Heffi laced his fingers over his cloth of gold cummerbund, and asked Trassan what he clearly thought was the kind of question that would keep him for some time from more pressing business. "What stage?"

Trassan fiddled with a pen, and addressed his words to it. "Halfway. The ship's nearly finished, we're talking about crew, but why is it at this point in an enterprise I always feel that the damn thing's never going to get done?"

"What do you see there?"

"Little promise of the glorious tomorrows I hope to see. Just an awful lot of iron."

"Well I don't. I don't see that at all."

"What do you see then?"

Heffi puffed out his cheeks. These talks were becoming tiresome. "I see a glorious ship, the finest the world has ever seen. I see fame for me and my family line. I see history in the making. And," he said smiling faintly, "I see an awful lot of money. Have more faith in yourself."

"I do. I'm not my brother Guis. I know it's going to get done. This is alchemy, of a sort. We stand here with our crucible waving our arms and shouting and very shortly we'll know if we'll be successful."

"You fear you will not be?"

"I know I will. Still doesn't change the feeling." He sighed. "I wanted to ask Rel to come, I wish my brothers, at least one, were coming with us. But he's too young. He'd fall into his old patterns around us; he'd lose his initiative. I can't get the best out of him. He needs to find his own way in life. I was going to ask him his advice. But he's too far away, he's too young, he's too inexperienced, and he's on the personal vendetta list of one of the army's rising heroes."

"By extension, you all are."

"I never had any quarrel with Alanrys. Guis and Rel though..."

"You share a name. That is usually enough to guarantee you equal enmity from men like that." Heffi leaned forward and took a peppermint cube from the bowl on the table. "Then what of this Bannord?"

"I've had him checked out. Gold, palms, so forth. Here are his records." Trassan pulled out a card folder from the bottom of a pile.

Heffi smiled and nodded approvingly.

"He's infantry," Trassan went on. "Father's a minor old money, and by that I mean no money. He's a third-rate title and fifteen acres coming his way and nothing else. He's a career soldier, done several anti-piracy tours up north."

Heffi ummed approvingly. "Nautical experience is very necessary."

"And he's been decorated twice for bravery. Killed an Ocerzerkiyan reaver captain himself, apparently. Otherwise it's minor skirmishes in the Olberlands during the last troubles."

"This is better than no skirmishes. Since the treaty of the Hundred there's not been a decent war. Our soldiers don't do enough soldiering."

Trassan nodded. "I couldn't agree more. Track him down, would you? He sounds useful."

"Always wise to stick close to those you know," said Heffi.

"A way of business that has done your kind no hurt."

"That's right. No point denying it."

They went through the list further. There were dozens of names on it. Carpenters, welders, Tynmen, Tyn themselves of various bands, dog grooms, victuallers, mechanics, three archaeologists volunteered from Vand's digs in Ostria, an alchemist and his assistant, a troupe of cooks, besides the endless names of sailors, stokers, glimmermen and all the others required to run a steamship of the *Prince Alfra*'s size.

"For draymaster I have managed to secure the services of Antoninan of Maceriya."

"A good name, but a Maceriyan on board?"

"Persin might be chasing our tails, but Antoninan's no spy. His reputation goes ahead of him. He's an honourable man in that way that only the stiffest Maceriyan can be. And how would he betray us? Barking secret messages?"

"Don't be facetious Heffi, this is serious."

"I am being serious. He has experience of the Sotherwinter, that bit on the mainland, at any rate. He's attempted to find the Southwest route twice."

"With no luck."

"Obviously with no luck! He tells me he doubts it exists, and to go over the frozen sea is too dangerous. His dogs are big and strong, bred from southern stock of the sea peoples. He's been tutored by the Sorskians and the Torosans. There is no one better for this job. He's committed to bringing his best, and that includes Valatrice. He is keen for this, Trass, really, really keen. I got him at a very good price, if it helps."

"Valatrice, Valatrice, I know that name. Why do I know it?"

"Valatrice!" said Heffi. "*The* Valatrice! The hero dog of the south! You know, isolated trading post, terrible sickness, the timely delivery of healing magisters. All that!"

Trassan snapped his fingers. "I remember!"

"Good. We'll need a good set of teams to get us overland once we leave the ship. At best guess it is at least two hundred miles. And I have not got us a good set of teams, Trassan. I have found us the very best. Valatrice is the king of dogs."

"I'm still not sure about it."

Heffi licked his finger and turned a page over. "Ah well, I see. It doesn't matter what you say, he is coming with us. I'm the captain, I have final say."

"I suppose you do."

"He is the best."

"Right."

"Say 'thank you Heffi, you really are a marvel, finding me the finest dog handler and polar expert in all of Ruthnia'."

"Thank you, Heffi, you really can fuck off if you think I'm calling you a marvel. Now, magisters..."

"Right. Tullian Ardovani. He's agreed to come, finally, after making a show of not deciding. A solid reputation, too, once head of the Ember Faculty, blah blah, you know all that of course, seeing as he's been working here for the last twelve months. His interest in the application of fire binding could be useful there."

"He has a little skill in meteoromancy, although he insists it is a hobby and nothing more," added Trassan. "I'm glad he signed on. Still, I can't help but wish for a good old fashioned wizard, you know? Fire and lightning from thin air, breath of the wind gathered in their lungs, all that. Magisters are all well and good, but they take so bloody long to do everything, and half of them like to argue mechanics with me. They're a pain in the arse. Tullian's all right, but there you are."

"A wizard you said?" said Heffi. "Well, well, we might have something here."

"Yes. Have you had any luck? What are you grinning about Heffi?"

"Oh, it is a trifle, nothing more."

"Come on! Spit it out, you old dog."

Heffi slid a contract of employment face down across the desk with his fingertips. Trassan plucked it up and read the name at the bottom, a signature rendered in huge loops and whorls.

He lowered the paper. "No! Really? Fuck me. You've outdone yourself this time."

"I have, haven't I?" said the Ishmalan with a chuckle. "His ancestor might not have got rid of my god, but he did a fine number on the rest."

Trassan read the name again. "Well, well. Vols fucking Iapetus. Great-great-grandson of the goddriver himself. Ha! Perhaps things are looking up after all."

"Yes, well." Heffi eyed the pile of paperwork meaningfully, his good cheer leaving him. "There's a little more to be done yet, Trassan."

Trassan sighed. "Let's get back to it, then."

* * *

TWIN WEIGHTS PRESSED hard on Vols Iapetus long before he got to the city. The weight of iron, and the weight of souls. By the time he was passing through the awkward patchwork of factories, mills and soot-stained fields that made up the ragged edges of Karsa City, hammers rang hard against the inside of his skull. The pain was made worse as the coach bounced hard on potholed roads. Not one of the ways through this nowhere land seemed to be in good repair. The villages grew drabber, bloated with poor quality housing and looming mills whose chimneys sent long banners of glimmer-tainted smoke into the sky.

The scrubby spaces between villages grew briefer, the fields broken increasingly into factory workers' allotments before disappearing altogether. Iapetus would not dare eat a vegetable grown there, raised as they were in the muck of industrial by-products.

The road improved abruptly as they passed onto the new turnpike, but his headache worsened. The presences of so many minds, each working unknowingly upon the underlying fabric of the world, wore at him. He feared to lose a firm impression of who he was, and that led to more fear.

Lucky then that his gifts were so erratic.

As they came from the upper vales, richer houses began to line the road. His coach clattered over tram tracks set into the road. The rich smell of melting bitumen blew into his carriage at these better districts, as road teams covered sets in smooth tar and grit. It was the first sign he saw of Alfra's modernisation programme. It would be far from the last.

They came down off the higher lands, down into the drainage basin of the Lemio. Here the little streams and brooks of the highlands gathered together all of a sudden, and the river appeared as if from nowhere. The roads clung to the edges of stone spurs, the hills were low but their slopes steep nonetheless and crammed with houses built high. There should have been a view into the heart of Karsa from there, but the air was thick with smoke. The sky above was clear and the day was cold, so the fumes were trapped as a poisonous broil in the Lemio's wide valley. The Twin was in the sky, pale grey in the sun.

Unconsciously, Vols took a deep breath as his coach plunged into the fume. Thick as a fog bank, it engulfed him without preamble. From clean air to filthy in an eyeblink. The smell of burning flooded his coach. A smoky evening fell. He felt the passage of spent glimmer overhead, carried on currents in the air made clear to him by their cargo of magic. A throbbing troubled the rear of his head. Every time the rims of his coach wheels rang from tram lines, it was a hot spear to the heart, two-pronged and murderous.

The coach climbed again, and with a parting billow the smokes opened.

They mounted a steep incline, heading up and into the Spires and their warrens of strange mansions. Fantastical follies of carved stone and brick told of money. They were streaked with dirty rain marks thick with soot just the same.

The carriage reached the highest point of the ridge. For a few seconds, Vols Iapetus looked into both the Lemio and Var valleys, the sprawling industrial heart of all Ruthnia and its one hundred fractious lands. Grey-brown fog boiled in the hollows of the rivers, flowing toward the sea. This he saw distantly, a glittering line on a flat horizon many leagues away. Between him and it lay the unconquerable marches of mud.

Then down, into the catchment of the Var, and back into the diabolical smoke again.

In the Varside centre huge buildings loomed that he did not remember from his last visit. Already confused by the smog, he lost his bearing completely. His dogs had been running for a half day, and their breath was phlegmy with effort and the filthy miasma. Vols had little extraordinary care for his dogs, but he wished the journey over so that they might rest and be away from foulness.

Street sounds were muffled, noises that were close sounded far, those that were far sounded close, all switched about by the smog. Pervasive always was the drone of human endeavour. Picked apart, it could be broken into its constituents: traffic rumble and mill noise, the hum of multitudinous conversations. But loudest of all was the clashing of hammers, ringing against stone. By the decree of Prince Alfra, the city had acquired a new heartbeat, and it was hell upon Vols Iapetus's nerves.

He settled miserably into his seat. Once, his had been a luxurious coach, but its heyday was past. The velvet covering the interior was threadbare and peeling, bleached yellow where the sun shone upon it. On the side, in flaking gold leaf, were the letters 'RI'. Those initials had meant something once. He remembered from his youth that, even then, people would have looked up in quiet awe as it passed, or shouted in anger, if brave enough. Whether they loved or loathed him, every person in Ruthnia had known Res Iapetus, the goddriver, he who banished the slavemasters of mankind from the mortal sphere forever.

Now none spared it a second glance.

The sorry vehicle was an apt metaphor for Vols Iapetus's entire life. A shabby thing, clinging to the faded glory of an distant past. All he had was his name, and like the monogram upon the coach, it was a shabby, threadbare thing. He was thin and unimposing, myopic, and bald but for a tuft over each ear and one at the top centre of his head. What hair there was was coppery, as was the scruffy goatee he wore. In conversation he was halting, and too slow with his rejoinders to excel either in argument or in matches of wit. He often berated himself when, an hour or so after conversation, the perfect thing came to him to say. His appearance was one of weakness, not power. The name gave him a taste of that, but only a taste.

He sneezed. The return indrawing of breath brought a peppery, burning flavour to the back of his throat that made him cough and splutter.

"Nearly there, goodmage!" cried out his coachman.

Sure enough, not five more minutes passed before he found himself deposited by the side of stone docks a bare decade old, full of oily water. He climbed down from the coach with his battered carpet bag, and placed his top hat on his head. Vols' footman jumped from the back of the coach and made himself busy taking down his master's bags; a trunk Vols had thought looked suitably nautical when he had bought it, but now worried looked like a silly affectation, and two suitcases.

"Sorry about the weather, master," said the driver. "The smogs are bad and getting worse, but they are not found often on days other than these. Cold, and still. A bit of wind off the ocean will blast it all away."

"Thank you, Gerrymion," said Vols. His voice was high, somewhat lispy thanks to his prominent incisors. While at school, he had encouraged his classmates to name him 'Red Fox'. They chose 'Red Rabbit' instead. It had stuck.

He tossed a purse up to his man. "Stay a night in the city if you wish before heading back, although I ask that you find somewhere of cleaner air for the sake of the poor hounds."

Gerrymion, whose face was wrapped twice about and tightly in a thick scarf, nodded in agreement. "Aye master."

"Now," said Vols, to both the footman and the driver. "You all have your instructions. I will direct a sending to Goodwife Meb if I require collecting. Make sure she rests after taking it! I do worry for her. Tell her not to exert herself in my place. Any enchantments requested or that fail can wait, please do make that very clear to her. She tries to do too much."

"That I will, master," said Gerrymion.

"Where should I put your bags, master?" asked his footman.

"Put them by the door." Vols pointed to the entrance to the shipyard, big as a pair of castle gates. "Have some of Kressind's men deal with it. Then get yourselves out of this fog."

"Like the hellgods themselves are breathing all over us master, if your illustrious ancestry had not driven them all away."

"Just like that, Gerrymion," said Vols wearily. "You and the rest take care, keep Holywend well for me.

With luck and fortune I will return home in no more than eighteen months."

"I'll be here and waiting. If you says, then that's what'll be."

"The future is not for me to see, Gerrymion," said Vols. "It is not for anyone."

"Right you are, master. Is that it, master?"

Vols looked glumly about the city. He clutched his carpet bag tighter. "Yes, yes it is, I suppose."

"Don't much like the look of it."

"The ship probably looks better. You may go in and see it, if you wish."

"No thank you master, it's not for me," said Gerrymion.

"Then goodbye, Gerrymion."

"Gods' speed, master."

Gerrymion clambered down from the carriage and went to a small dock officer's box by the quayside. They could only see it at all because it was painted a bright white. Yellow lamplight shone from its windows, blurring its outline into the fog.

Why, wondered Vols, as he walked to the hideous, high-sided shed looming over the docks, did people still persist in using such turns of phrase as "Gods' speed". There were no gods. There had been no gods for two hundred years, not what any right-thinking man would think of as gods, at any rate.

Although, he reflected angrily, if it had been down to him and not his great-grandfather, they would all be overrun by the bloody divine bastards. Of that there was no doubt.

He rapped on the door with his cane, and presently was admitted by a man who was expecting him, and greeted him with many smiles.

The high door rolled shut. The building, wrought of stout girders and crinkled sheets of metal, must have been three hundred feet high from footing to roof; a boxy crane hanging from rails rolled overhead, a cargo net full of bulging sacks descending toward the unseen deck.

The city had been noisy, but deadened. Inside the shed the sound of industry threatened to break Vols' head open like a hammer hitting an egg. Scaffolding, mainly it appeared to his untrained eye to facilitate access for painters, climbed up the side of the ship. Three-quarters of the craft was painted white and black, the rest was the dull grey of uncoated metal.

He dropped his carpet bag and stared up at the ship. His neck arced back to an uncomfortable angle before his gaze reached the gunwales high above. Never in his entire life had he been in the presence of so much cold, magic-killing iron. The sheer presence of it was almost more than he could bear. The taste of rust crawled down the back of his nose.

"If you'll wait here, master, I will fetch foreman Tyn Gelven," said the man. "There is another magister here at the moment, perhaps it would be pleasant for you to become acquainted? I am sure they might break their tour so that you may join them."

Vols gave the man a long stare by way of reply. He coughed uncomfortably into his hand.

"I will be right back sir."

"Master Vols Iapetus?"

Vols followed the voice toward the floor. A male greater Tyn, one of the water clans he thought, looked back.

"Hello? My friend! Are you alright?" A man in the robes of a magister stood behind the Tyn. He appeared pained but cheerful.

"So much iron," Vols croaked. The taste of it made him cover his mouth.

"Aye, it is difficult. You'll get used to it," said the Tyn. "And there's shielded quarters aboard for those as are sensitive to it."

He held out his hand. Vols took it limply. He felt the jolt of the Tyn's etheric presence. The handshake of the magister was similarly charged, although less powerful.

"Tullian Ardovani," the magister introduced himself with a bow. He had pale brown skin and a clipped accent, something of a song to it. Cullosantan, or Vols was a Tyn himself. "I find it a little too much myself," said the magister. "But I cannot depart! I have been here many times, but I have never seen it so close to completion. Such vision to apprehend. I must see it all. It is a fascinating machine, with much resourceful application of the magisterial engineering arts. So impressive!"

Vols ran his eye over the ship again. "It is not finished?"

"No, goodmage, but it shall be soon, mark my words," said the Tyn.

Vols would rather take the word of a dog over a Tyn.

"Stocking of the vessel is well underway," said the magister. "Do you have more bags? Is there anything more I can do? Forgive me, master Tyn, I have been here only a day and yet I feel comfortable. I do not mean to overstep the bounds of my position."

"No harm done, Goodmagister Ardovani. All hands on deck, as I am sure you will grow used to hearing."

"You have been to sea before?" asked Vols. His soul felt leaden, his skin clammy. His stomach churned. He leaned on his cane.

"No, goodmage, have you? We Tyn are not great voyagers."

Shifty little bastard, thought Vols. Never trust a Tyn! His mother had said over and over again.

"And there have been no sea trials, no testing? I was told we are to depart in a month."

"Everything has been tested. Sea trials are due to begin next week. Goodfellow Kressind has been assured of a positive outcome in his pursuit of a licence. All in the national interest," said the magister.

"Whose nation?" said Vols suspiciously.

"I am afraid there was little else we could do," said Tyn Gelven. "But we will be prepared once the time comes."

Vols nodded dumbly. "I... I am afraid I feel a little faint. Could you perhaps find me a glass of water?"

Gelven called for water. It was swiftly brought.

"My dear fellow! You do appear ill." said Ardovani. "Perhaps I should take you to our lodgings? Until the vessel is ready to set sail, we are lodging at the Blue Dracon. It is well situated for our kind, on the edge of the docks. Water is on three sides. The clientele can be a little rowdy, but the positioning lessens the strain of being around quite so many people."

"And so much iron," said the Tyn. In spite of his own nature, the Tyn appeared unaffected by it.

"We are not of a kind, you and I," said Vols. He intended to speak haughtily, but it came out as a feeble croak. "I am the scion of the house of Iapetus. You are a magister."

"He is mageborn, as are you," said the Tyn. "All of us here feel the weight of this ship, beautiful though he is."

"Of a lesser quality," insisted Iapetus. "Magisters are not mages."

"Some could be, but I could not. You are correct, goodmage. This vessel is a greater problem for you than I. The might of the individual dictates the effect of iron." Ardovani bowed. "I bear you no ill will. The relations between our orders are testy, ours need not be. Perhaps over the course of our coming acquaintance I can convince you of the beauty of rational magic, for industry is a magic of itself, and the efforts of such as I only help to gild it, as this ship demonstrates so finely."

"Will is the master of reason, not vice versa," said Vols. He winced inwardly at the weakness of his voice.

"Another article of faith to debate. But we shall leave all that for later. We will have plenty of time to talk. I see you must rest."

"Will we now," said Vols, who had no intention of society with either Tyn or magisters.

"Oh yes," said Ardovani pleasantly. "We are to bunk together, as the sailors say."

Vols's made a quizzical face.

"We are sharing quarters, you and I," said Ardovani. "With the Tyn."

CHAPTER FORTY-FOUR
Winter is Over

"TUVACS! TUVACS! GET up, you lazy little prick!"

The door rattled to Julion's pounding. The flimsy frame of the building shook, the canvas of the roof rippled.

Tuvacs yawned and opened his eyes.

"Get up! We're late."

Suala stirred next to him. She smiled sleepily and reached for him. Tuvacs pushed her hand off. "I've got to go," Tuvacs said. Five months at Gate Town and he had gained a good grasp of her language.

"Get a move on!"

"Will you cut that out?" he shouted, switching to Karsarin. "You'll have the door off the hinges!"

"If that gets you up quicker, so be it," said Julion. But the pounding stopped, and he retreated away from the door, his footsteps crunching on ice.

Tuvacs hauled himself out of bed. He was warm under his coverlet and blankets beside Suala. Outside the bed the cold made him wince. He dressed quickly.

The residual heat of last night's fire radiated from the small stove at the back of the tent. Here his clothes were arranged around it so they at least were passably warm. He pulled them on quickly over flesh already goosebumped. Undertrousers, thick overtrousers, two layers of socks, a linen tunic, over that a woollen and then a fleece coat with the hair turned inwards. He felt as big as a cow under all the clothes, but he'd freeze without them.

He emerged under a sky so clear his eyes watered at the sight of the stars.

Gate Town and Railhead in winter were half the size they were in summer. Miners and railworkers from the Black Sands came off the desert to wait out the snow in better climes. Many of them went home for the winter. Enough stayed to make it worthwhile for the likes of Boskovin to remain. It had been a good time for Tuvacs, and a stable one for Boskovin's trade. His mobile saloon miraculously found a semi-permanent place on a siding close to the centre of town. Firebowls and a canvas roof on poles had made it bearable to sit outside, even as breath froze into beards. Boskovin's aggressive pricing strategies helped business be brisk, if not exactly profitable.

"About bloody time!" said Julion. "Have fun last night?" he leered.

"None of your business. Thanks for the gentle wake up."

"You are getting later."

"I was working until four this morning. What were you doing?"

"None of your fucking business." Julion had grown a beard. All of them had, it being nigh on impossible to find water hot enough to shave with, and it kept the wind from their faces. Tuvacs' was a poor, wispy effort. Julion mocked him for it daily.

"Boskovin wants the dogs fed. He's got another shipment of brandy and whisky coming on the three o'clock."

"I know, Julion."

"Good for you, you little smartarse. You'll be wanting to come down and look over the boxcar, we're moving out today, back to Railhead."

That did surprise Tuvacs.

"Yeah, you heard right. Near Mine is reopening. There's talk of the rail crews going back out to begin the spur out to the Deephollow deposit. Can't you see?" He nodded to the sky. A pure blue line gathered over the mountains, morning preparing to storm the walls. "It's getting warmer. No snow clouds over the mountains for a week. That's the way it is out here. When that happens, you can be sure as sure no more is coming. Get out from the mountain shadow, you'll see the first green shoots in the plain. Real pretty it is," he said sarcastically. Julion was not a man for the glories of the natural world.

"In Mohacs-Gravo, winter is not over for another month."

"Yeah, well you're not in Mohacs-Gravo now, are you?" Julion was delighted to know something that Tuvacs did not, and was not about to let the opportunity to enjoy his ignorance go by. "Further north here, eh, you little shit."

He clapped Tuvacs on the back, a rough action that was half shove.

"You've got half an hour. We've a lot to do. Boskovin wants us out at the railhead on the first train before the crew arrive. Get the best spot. Kiss your little girlfriend goodbye. Winter is officially over. It's time to get back to work properly."

A day of work was what Julion promised, and he delivered. Tuvacs spent his time hacking ice from the box car's wheels. By noon, the sun shone and water trickled from icicles on the bottom of the car that had lasted the winter out. That done, Tuvacs and Julion went to feed the dogs. They yipped and howled when they saw the two men, Rusanina greeted them with dignity, nuzzling Tuvacs affectionately, and giving Julion a cold, dismissive stare.

"She doesn't like you," said Tuvacs. "They smell bad. Are they alright?"

"They'll sort themselves out. The filth will come out when they moult." Julion yanked a fistful of fur from the flank of one dog. Its head snapped round and it showed its teeth.

"See? It's coming out already."

"Be a bit more careful with them and they might like you more."

"Shut up, you," said Julion. He threw handfuls of offal mixed with grain on the floor. The dogs snarled and scrapped with one another for the food. All except Rusanina and her consorts. She waited for a bucket to be placed before her, and her mates waited until she had finished eating before taking what was left.

"It's been a frustrating winter for them," said Julion. "Dogs like this are bred to snow, and we've had them doing nothing. We'll soon have you back at it my lovelies, don't worry."

Rusanina curled her lip at him.

"Not very talkative today, are you?" said Tuvacs.

"No," said Rusanina, and bent to her meal.

"It hurts them," said Julion. "Dog throats were never made to make men's sounds. Magic meddling with the right order of things."

"Seems normal enough to me," said Tuvacs. His Karsarin had also improved over the winter, and only a trace of his Mohacin accent remained.

"That's because you don't know everything, no matter what Boskovin says."

Rusanina butted Julion, nearly dropping him in the icy mud.

"Oi!" he said.

"They still like me better," said Tuvacs.

"Don't get cocky," said Julion.

A train whistle blasted in the far distance. Tuvacs stood on his tiptoes. Far to the south, threads of white and black hung on the air.

"Oh for fuck's sake, the fucking train's fucking early!" said Julion. "We better get our lunch now, because Boskovin's going to want us to meet the bloody thing. The man's a slave driver when he gets the wind behind him."

They worked hard for the rest of the day.

AFTER THE CHILL day, the warmth of Tuvacs' tent home was welcome, but the warmth of Suala was more so. They briefly made love, and lay a long time entwined under the heaped furs of their bed.

"I am going to miss winter," said Tuvacs.

Suala stroked his face. "Why? It is cold and dark. Now is the time for new things to grow. It is a fine time of the year."

"It has been too cold to do much of anything all winter except work and hide in bed screwing," he said. He coloured saying the word. Profanity had never come easily to him. Suala's language was liberally peppered with such expressions.

She gave him a playful slap, then drew him close.

"There will be other winters."

"Not soon enough." He nuzzled her and breathed deep her scent. Sweat, woodsmoke and woman. "Why don't you come with me?"

"You know why. The rail camp is not safe. Too many men, too few women. I have to stay here. My grandmother will return from our village, we start work again. Many new workers will arrive soon."

"How far is your village?"

"It is not far, and it is not close."

She was maddeningly evasive about her home. He had never had more of an answer to his questions about it than that.

"You could come with me. Your grandmother is too old to work surely. Let her rest. Come with me. I will keep you safe. I spend all my time in the boxcar, it's not like I'm out at the rail head laying rails ten hours a day."

"My grandmother does what she must. She has a gift, and must use it."

"Can't she use it at home?"

"No." She drew his hand down onto her belly. "And it is not only me who must keep safe."

She pressed his hand onto her belly below her navel. The skin there was smooth, pleasingly rounded, soft and warm.

His eyes widened as he realised what she was telling him. "No!"

She bit her lip, fearful for his reaction, but her eyes glowed. "Now is the time for new things to grow."

"I..."

"You are not pleased?"

"I, why, I... Of course I am pleased." He sat up suddenly, lifting the covers from their bodies. Cold air slipped between them, prickling their flesh. She drew them back down. "I am young to be a father, seventeen, I think. Perhaps eighteen. No more than that."

"Older than some, not young for my people."

"And what will they say?" He turned back to her. "What will they do to you?"

Disappointment at his reaction deadened her smile. She shrugged. "Nothing. What wrong is there in two people falling in love and making a child? Is this a problem in your land?"

He rubbed his face. "Sometimes. Not always. It's complicated. In some of the Hundred it is a big problem. In others not."

"It is a strange world you are from, Tuvaco."

He smiled broadly at her, dropped back down to one elbow. "I want to show you it all. And him."

He gently brushed his fingers against her stomach.

"You are happy?"

"How could I not be? I love you." She smiled in relief and put her arms around his neck.

"It might be a her."

"That it might be," he said. "I must get Boskovin to write to Lavinia to tell her she will be an aunt." He felt a sudden pang of guilt. His sister was well, so he was told, but she was far away and alone.

Suala's kisses pushed his concern for his sister away. Five minutes later he had forgotten it altogether.

CHAPTER FORTY-FIVE

Out to Sea

"HANG ON! HANG on!" shouted Trassan, belting his dressing gown about his waist. The knocker banged hard again. He came off the stairs into the hallway, gasping as his feet hit freezing tiles. He made it to the door, opened it a crack. He closed it again, and undid the security chains before opening it wide.

Garten was upon the step, dressed in his uniform of office.

"Can I come in then? It's perishing out here."

"What the hells do you want at this time in the morning?" Trassan looked up and down the street. The sky was still dark, glimmer lamps burned. The street, wide and lined with fine townhouses, had upon it only those whose work took them about in the early hours: grocers, coal merchants, collectors of the pure taking advantage of the lull in the traffic, rag and bone men and the like. "And what the hells time is it anyway?"

"Five of the clock."

"What?"

"I thought you would probably want this."

Garten held out an envelope. A heavy seal of purple wax with four ribbons closed the back.

Trassan blinked and took it. "The licence?"

"What else? Now can I come in? I could have gone home to bed, but I know how important this is. The least you could do is give me a mug of tea."

Trassan cracked open the envelope and skimmed the contents. "Yes, yes, come in, come in!" He waved his brother through the door and shut it behind them. "My apologies, brother, but my maid is away on some family errand or other. Something to do with her mother, I forget."

"You should get more."

"I don't like big households, makes it hard to think, all that racket," said Trassan.

They went downstairs into the kitchen. Garten sat at the table, laying his hat and gloves upon its scrubbed surface. Trassan lit a candle and fussed about reviving the stove. He unbanked the embers, dropped kindling upon it, and had a merry blaze going in short order. He arrayed lumps of coal around it, and shut the door. He removed the covering hotplate from the top and placed a kettle of water in its place, its bottom exposed directly to the fire.

"You'll have to wait ten minutes for the coal to catch," Trassan said.

"You were always going to get the licence."

"Yes."

"And I'm sorry I could not simply give it to you. You know... Procedure."

"Procedure. What do I need to do?" said Trassan.

"Sign the chit at the bottom of the final sheet, and the licence. Give the chit to me, keep the licence."

"That simple?"

"Not everything in my work is complicated."

Trassan hunted out a pen and inkpot. He made to sign quickly, but Garten caught his wrist.

"Before you do, there is something I should tell you." Trassan paused. Garten released him. "You are getting this licence at this time in the morning because it has been hurried through. News came from Perus yesterday that the High Legate's sickness has taken a turn for the worst. He has become erratic. It looks like he will be removed."

"You can't just wait for him to die?"

"That was the idea, but no. These are dangerous times. Shortly I will be away to Perus with Duke Abing, after months of waiting. The Assembly of Nations of the Hundred is already gathering. Consequently, the inquiry into this licence has been sped on. Prince Alfra is keen that you beat the Maceriyans to the Sotherwinter continent."

"And? What does all this mean apart from the fact that I've been kept waiting for fucking ever by purple bloody ribbons?" He flapped the ribbons on the envelope at his brother.

"We have adhered to the conditions of our agreement with the Sunken Realm as best we can. But we are pushing it, Trass. Between you and me, I do not think that this licence will appease the king under the water."

Trassan laid his pen down. "So, I sail away into danger, having waited on tenterhooks for the whole winter, just so the big hats up in the Three Houses can let me die with a clear conscience?"

"It's not quite like that?"

"The fuck it's not!"

"There is more to this than you, brother," said Garten, his demeanour hardening. "Provoke the Sunken Realm, and we are at war. As we have followed the letter of our treaty, that will not happen."

"But my safety is not guaranteed."

"No. Come on, you knew this. You built your ship to cross the Drowning Sea in the face of his majesty's objections. You would have gone, treaty or not. This way, you can do so without plunging the entire nation into danger with the king of the drowned dead."

Trassan looked at the document. "All that, for this. I was hoping that the wait would bring me some advantage."

"I'm sorry. That's the way it has to be. I have worked very hard on your behalf brother, just for this."

Trassan took up his pen. He stared at the sheet a moment before signing. He blew on the ink to dry it, then tore off the chit and handed it to his brother. Garten folded it once, and tucked it into his inside pocket. He held out his hand. Trassan took it, and they shook.

"Are we square?"

Trassan nodded. "Not worth falling out over."

Garten flashed a quick smile. "I've not heard our old expression for a long time."

"That's because we've not had anything to fall out over for years."

"I suppose not."

Trassan's eyes narrowed and he held his brother's hand tightly. "We came close this time, Garten. Very close."

* * *

THE END OF the shed had been dismantled. The *Prince Alfra's* prow pointed at a tall opening ablaze with sunlight. Men waited tensely about the dockside and ship, hands at ropes and windlasses. From the wheelhouse, Captain Heffi looked onto the foredeck, his command crew ready. A brass band stood beneath the window. Bunting hung in bright swags from the five masts.

On the roof of the ship's superstructure, Trassan gripped the rail. Behind him were Veridy, Arkadian Vand, his father, Garten, Aarin, Tyn Gelven, and many others. His attention was only for the vessel, not even Ilona, glaring at him from her father's side, could distract him. A hundred men looked to him expectantly. Total silence in a shed where for nigh on two years there had been nothing but ceaseless industry. For the first time since the shed's erection, wind blew within. He could hear the murmur of crowds out on the dockside; the cries of seagulls. Everything retreated, until there was only he and his ship. A fierce, overwhelming pride took him. His flesh tingled at the thought of what he was about to do.

He stood tall and raised a hand. Two hundred pairs of eyes followed him. "All clear!" he shouted.

"All clear!" came an answering voice from the deck.

"All clear!" came a third from the dockside. A bell rang frantically. Before the prow of the ship, huge windlasses were turned by teams of dockers, dragging sluice gates up toothed tracks.

With a spurt that became a swift flow, the waters of the dock flooded the drydock. By the gates the fall whipped up a scummy foam. Toward the far end the flood's fury was spent feebly against stone walls, and it swirled with oily rainbows.

For five minutes the water poured in, the initial waterfall rush choked off as the level reached the gates and the inflow became a bubbling upon the surface. The water rose black and sinister and choked with trash. Men waited by winches to take the strain on the ropes and chains of the ship.

A tremor ran through the hull; a whisper of excitement from the people. Trassan held the rails tightly. Here was the moment of truth. A long, metallic groan sounded from the *Prince Alfra* as it lifted. Seamen and dockers erupted into noisy activity as they worked to keep the ship from banging into the sides.

The ship groaned and rose higher and higher. Dockmen payed out their ropes. The ship shifted slightly to the right. Dock chiefs bellowed orders, chains rattled, and the drift was arrested. Another bell rang. At the bow the gates to the wider docks opened. Shouts came back the length of the ship, one man to another.

"The gates are open!"

Heffi's First Officer, Volozeranetz, stepped up to Trassan. "Goodfellow, I report the gates are open," he said formally, "we may depart."

Trassan turned around and nodded to Arkadian Vand. The engineer bent to a speaking tube at his side and spoke into it.

"Captain Heffira-nereaz-Hellishul vovo Balisatervo Chai Tse-ban, take us out."

Moments later, the ship shuddered. White steam leaked from its three funnels. Blue glimmerlight glowed from the top of each. With a ferocious churning, the paddlewheels either side of the ship spun, biting into the water. The ship's horn hooted, a long and mournful sound. A loud cheer from outside answered. The brass band struck up a stirring air. Slowly, the *Prince Alfra* emerged from its drydock into the greater docks of Karsa City. A bright spring day greeted them. A stiff breeze kept the fumes of industry at bay, and the sun was bright and warm.

Every side of the dock was lined with people, thousands of people. They stood by the water twelve deep, hung from every window around the basin. They lined the hill above. They cheered again as the *Prince Alfra's* full length emerged from its housing. The ship answered with a two-note hoot of its whistles, scaring up a screeching storm of seagulls.

The great ship filled the basin one end to the other, but Captain Heffi's steersman had it turn smoothly, its paddlewheels churning in opposite directions until the prow pointed out on the canal; that would take them to the main Lemio-Var shipway then on to the locks. Puffing clouds of brilliant white shot with blue light, the *Prince Alfra* made its way slowly along the waterway. This too was lined with people. Music played everywhere, each source attempting to outdo the other. A wall of noise louder than the loudest day of the ship's construction pushed the iron ship all the way to the Slot.

At the head of the first lock, on a specially built platform, Prince Alfra himself and the royal family looked on. The lockmaster left his offices to take the toll himself in a ceremony of ridiculous complexity. Then the first gate opened, and the ship cruised into the uppermost dock. At the top of that watery stair, Trassan felt like a king. All of Lockside Karsa was below him, houses clinging to the walls of the locks and high wharfs, a flotilla assembled below upon the muddy ocean to greet them. The iron ship was the largest vessel ever to descend the locks, and even these mighty works appeared modest in comparison.

Twenty minutes each lock took, and the crowd never stopped cheering. Only when they reached Lock Five, where Lowhouses marked the last permanently dry part of the city docks, did the noise abate a little.

The tide was in, an inundation of the middle sort. Bottomquay was covered and they did not have to descend the last three locks, but exited instead from Lock Four directly. The vessel proceeded with care past the tower marking the position of the submerged locks. Ships of wood and floatstone crowded them, some large craft in their own right, but the *Prince Alfra* dwarfed them all. A narrow corridor of muddy water was their way free. Once past the impediments of ship and submerged lock, steam came quicker from the funnels and the great ship surged forward, leaving its suitors behind.

The *Prince Alfra* performed a long loop about Slotbay. From the clifftops of Growling Point the guns of the battery popped a rippling salute. Captain Heffi came up to the top deck. Beaming as he performed complicated bows to Trassan and Arkadian Vand, he pronounced, "Goodfellows, I have the pleasure to inform you that we are now at sea. All three engines are operating at peak efficiency, Goodfellow Kressind, Goodengineer Vand."

Trassan caught Katriona's eye. She leaned into her husband and smiled at him broadly.

All aboard the ship cheered, drowning out the band still playing on the main deck.

Vand gripped Trassan's elbow hard. "Well done, young man," he said into Trassan's ear. "Now the hard work begins. Two weeks' sea trials, no more. You are to depart on the Twentieth of Little."

"We should be leaving this week." Trassan tensed at Vand's contact. Relations between them had been difficult since the accident. Vand had dismissed the incident, but Trassan held the elder engineer responsible, and had become wary of his pride.

"Patience, Trassan. A week won't matter. It might be better for us."

"It's better for Persin. We'll lose our advantage."

Vand grinned ferally. "He'll never beat this ship, Trassan. Persin is not due to leave for ten days. Imagine the look on his face when you steam right past him. Two weeks, my boy. Two weeks."

CHAPTER FORTY-SIX
Modalmen

"Ho, HO! DOWN down, lay it down!" sang the workgang. "Ho, ho! Hammer swing, slam it in!" A row of hammers fell as one onto rail spikes, beating them into wooden sleepers and cinching the rails tight. A gaugeman checked the width. Already, four more lengths had been set out ahead, reading for spiking. To the sides of the track iron web weavers worked, laying out three offset rows of iron pegs joined by wires in a diamond mesh pattern. The railway was progressing along a stony ridge that ran for seven or eight miles. On one side was a dry valley, on the other a series of broken hillocks, too uneven for rails. In those places beyond the wire web nothing moved but dust. But on the ridge life held sway; a desert empty for millennia was filled with human activity.

Tuvacs and Julion walked their cart up the line. The four dogs pulling it did so with their heads down, tails and ears low. A gentle breeze blew from the south, ruffling the dogs' fur around their harnesses and bringing the threat of returning winter.

"This lot are bored stupid," said Julion, nodding at the dogs.

"So am I," said Tuvacs.

Julion stopped the cart. Tuvacs went round the back, hauled off a tall tin water pail and dumped it onto the rocky ground by the railway. The track stood proud of the ridge on ballast hacked from the desert rocks and ground in a steam crusher back at camp. Only in a few places was such an extravagant amount of stone expended in levelling the ground, mostly the sleepers were laid straight onto the flattened sand, but here terrain was uneven, and required greater care. Work was slow.

"My head is killing me," said Julion.

The gangmaster was a cheerful man of mixed Farthian and Hethikan extraction, straight-nosed and dark-skinned. He overheard them and shouted back, "Lot of glimmer in these parts, that'll be it. Gives a mean headache, but it'll make us all rich, once we get this stretch laid!"

"Not you," muttered Julion. "And not I either, selling water. What by the gods does Boskovin think he's doing?"

Tuvacs leaned against the stationary cart and put his hands under his armpits to warm them. Longdark was gone, the first week of Little well underway and the sun came a little earlier and a little stronger every morning. But it was still cold. Julion had to smash the ice on the water pitcher before doling it out. Dirty snow, grubbied by blown sand, patched the rolling landscape.

The air had a desert's clarity, and Tuvacs could see for miles. A brilliant glare shone off a field of glassed desert to the north cast, but it could be endured for a time, and Tuvacs scanned the wide horizons. He frowned, and took a step forward.

"Hey," said Tuvacs. "Look over there."

"What is it?" said Julion.

"Something in the sky, a dust cloud."

"Can't see anything."

"It's past that glass field."

"Too bright to see," said Julion dismissively.

The gangmaster joined them and looked where Tuvacs pointed for a moment. "A dust storm. They're not unusual this time of the year. When they get up, they can be a real bitch. Not as bad as the Sisters back home, as I say. Best ignore it. It don't belch fire."

"I know what a dust storm is. If it's a dust storm," asked Tuvacs, "why is it moving against the wind?"

The gangmaster spat into the sand. "Beats me. My job is laying the rails. Yours is delivering water as per my contract with your master. Meteoromancy is beyond the pair of us." He grinned with a set of perfect teeth. "We'll leave the weather forecasting to the magisters."

"Cock," muttered Julion as he walked off. "On, Rusanina." She yawned, exposing a long pink cavern of a mouth. A short yip had the dogs pulling again. They stopped twenty yards on. Tuvacs pulled another tall container of water from the cart, dumped it on the ground, broke the ice, moved on. They outpaced the track gang, then those laying the sleepers, heading on to where other work crews topped barrowfulls of pulverised rock into heaps and raked them out. Past that were red rags tied to sticks laid out by surveyors. Engineers watched critically, levelling the gravel or calling for more. Further on still, others prepared the railbed as the railway's six guards watched the desert nervously.

All the while, Tuvacs' eyes returned again and again to the banner of dust against the sky, the thick column at its head was moving toward them. He looked at the guards, counted them for the hundredth time. Six did not seem enough out here, not by a long measure.

NIGHT FOLLOWED DAY in the usual order, quickly at that time of year. The days had yet to equal the duration of the night.

Dark was when Tuvacs did most of his work. In his boxcar, the side down, selling liquor and the occasional finer beverage at a healthy—Boskovin's word, he preferred 'obscene'—mark up to the rail workers.

At morning's second bell, as per their agreement with the rail company, he stopped serving, and closed the shutters in the face of many drunken protests. He left it twenty minutes, until after the most determined drinker had stopped hammering upon the wood, to go outside and douse the fires in their bowls and encourage the remaining men to go home in case they pass out and freeze to death. Even in summer, desert nights were cold, and they were a long way from summer.

Tuvacs was packing up the boxcar when Boskovin came to see him.

"Hello, hello my boy!" Boskovin climbed aboard. A solitary paraffin lamp lit Tuvacs' work space. All the lights outside were off, and consequently Boskovin's sagging patrician features were cast in a web of shadow. On a man who was more imposing, it might have been sinister. Or on a man who was less drunk. As it was, Boskovin had the appearance of a drunken pantomime devil comically trying to act sober. "Is business good?"

he took a swig from a bottle in one hand, black in the low light.

"Not bad boss," said Tuvacs. "The rail workers are drinking double. And they're happy to pay for it. This place has them on edge."

"It's the glimmer!" said Boskovin, absurdly portentous. "Out here. Very disturbing. It's the whispers you see. I find this helps." He sloshed the wine around in the bottle.

"I find it doesn't. I don't hear anything, just the headache." He nodded at the bottle. "That makes it worse."

"You're lucky! They are there, all around, if only you listen carefully enough..." His head jerked from side to side, a flicker of fear on his face. He rallied himself with obvious effort. "Still, it warms you. Would you like to share it with me? It is from my personal supply. Good wine gives no headache." He moved closer. Tuvacs finished placing his last bottles into a rack built into the wall and pulled across the thin steel cover. The chances of a break-in were unsurprisingly high. He padlocked it in place.

"Clever to think of that," said Boskovin. He took another gulp of wine. His breath was sour, his cheeks red. "A clever boy, an exceptional boy. I was lucky to find you." An expression settled upon Boskovin's face that Tuvacs did not like.

"Thank you." Tuvacs took up his rubbish pail and waited for Boskovin to move to one side. He did, eventually. He kept his stare fixed upon Tuvacs.

"A very, very clever boy."

Tuvacs hoiked the bucket out to the camp midden, past the last tent, and tipped it out. A faint line of light played over the Twin's black surface. Tuvacs blinked, and frowned, focusing more intently. The second world was so large its motion was clearly visible as it rushed for the horizon. Seeing nothing untoward, he dismissed the light as his imagination.

When he went back, Boskovin was still in the boxcar.

Tuvacs went through the last few motions of closing up the saloon. Money he dumped into a large leather purse, tied the drawstring and handed it to Boskovin. A minor earth tremor shook the boxcar on its temporary siding. Bottles clinked. When it finished, Tuvacs checked the brake. Dogs barked in the disturbance, falling quiet one by one.

"Brake's still tight," he said.

"Yes," said Boskovin. He took a step towards Tuvacs. His breath came heavy. The coins in the sack chinked as he placed them onto the counter.

Boskovin touched the nape of Tuvacs neck tenderly, fingers slid around it, and he gripped it, a gentle version of the avuncular clasp he used when making a point or a joke. Only this was not so avuncular.

Another hand came at Tuvacs' waist. His eyes fixed upon the boy's, Boskovin grasped Tuvacs' belt, pulling the tongue free of loops and buckle. Tuvacs' trousers loosened. Tuvacs put his own hand over the belt to stop it being drawn free.

"Please, Boskovin."

Boskovin's hand pushed its way into his trousers, cold fingers wriggling into the thatch of hair there.

"This is not for me," said Tuvacs. "I am not interested in men that way."

Boskovin looked down. Slowly his gaze slid up Tuvacs' body, settling upon his face. He pursed his lips in amusement. "This little soldier here says otherwise. I believe he stands to attention." Boskovin chuckled, a soft purring laugh. Stale wine wafted up Tuvacs' nostrils. "We won't do anything you don't want to."

"I don't want any of it." Tuvacs was angry, partly because of his sex's reaction to the touch. He seized the man's hand and pulled it firmly from his trousers. "Like I said, I am not interested."

"I won't think anything less of you. Give it a try, boy. We can stop any time you want."

Tuvacs pulled away and turned around. Boskovin's hands gripped either end of Tuvacs' unfastened belt, trapping him.

"Just like I could have stopped at any time when I went into the Drum. Like I could have turned and walked away before I paid your fee," Boskovin continued. "Like I could have left your sister to fend for herself."

"No man owns me."

"No, no, no, dear boy. I don't own you." Boskovin let go of one end of Tuvacs' belt and tugged it free of the loops. "But then, perhaps I do."

"No." Tuvacs gripped Boskovin's hand, hard now. He had laboured since he was small. Six months of hard work in Farside and a decent diet had seen his strength flourish. Boskovin drew in a sharp breath in pain. "This goes no further. I have a girl. I am to be a father."

Boskovin's face changed, from lusty to threatening to sad, a drunken gurning that revolted Tuvacs.

"Tuvacs, you do not know what regard I hold you in," Boskovin wheedled.

"I can guess. Now let me pass. I will not let you force me. I will stop you. Don't think to threaten me with my contract. There is no law out here."

Boskovin's face fell at the suggestion that he would force Tuvacs. An understanding that this was not a game but a genuine rejection pierced the fug of wine. "My boy, I, I, I am sorry." He backed up, bumping into the whiskey cabinet and making the bottles clink. "I am not that kind of man. I would never dream of it. I..."

Tuvacs released Boskovin's hand. "Don't worry about it. Good night, boss." He pushed past quickly, before the wine could reassert its influence over his master, and jumped down from the boxcar.

Tuvacs crossed the camp with as much dignity as he could summon. His legs trembled and had to be forced on.

In his haste he had left his coat behind. He had his belt in one hand, but did not think to stop to replace it. He walked mechanically onwards, holding his trousers up. The night chilled him, but he could not go back. In his need for space he headed away from the boxcar and went straight for the edge of the camp. The tents of the workers and their framed canvas barracks were all at the centre, gathered around the silver engine at its platform. An isolated, gruff command from a gang boss disturbed the night, ordering a straggler to bed. The silver engine coughed a loud cloud of steam. Total silence was coming, creeping into the camp, sleep in its wake.

The men's quarters gave way to storage tents and stacks of rails and lumber. By these stores the camp blacksmith sat alone outside his odd cart-cum-tent, lit redly by the light of the portable forge inside. His eyes followed Tuvacs as he walked past, but he said nothing.

Past the last stack of supplies, he emerged into a circle of empty ground. The pressure of the glimmer-rich sands beyond gripped his head. Still he found it favourable to the confines of the camp, and struggled up a low dune to the north. The ground was soft atop, and the weavers of the web had set their peg and wire patterns up there for the ease of it. He stepped up to it, and after a moment's thought went over the first line. Rags of cloud choked off the light of the moons and stars, leaving only the Twin. Far larger than Tuvacs had ever seen it before, even though more than half of it had now sunk past the limits of the Earth. He watched a while, seeking the odd light he had seen before, but it did not come again.

The pounding in his head grew worse. That strange draw he had felt in Railhead returned to him, encouraged by his memory of it that day he had met Suala. He took a step forward. There was only one wire between him and the desert. Witchlight played out there, whisking over faraway dunes. This was not the involuntary draw he had felt before, but alloyed with a reckless impulse all of his own, and he was compelled to obey.

"Hey Tuvacs! Tuvacs, man! What the hells has got into you? Best stop right there."

Tuvacs was grabbed. Julion had him, his face creased with worry.

"Step over that and they'll never see you again. Are you insane?"

Tuvacs shivered.

"Where's your coat? What's happened to you?"

He glanced down at Tuvacs' belt brushing against his leg.

"Ah right. No. Let me guess. Boskovin. He was on the wine earlier tonight, never a good sign. Did he put the moves on you?"

"Yes."

"Shit." Julion ran his hand over his hair. The moons fought their way free of the clouds, lighting Julion's face in their combined pinkish glow. "Did he hurt you?"

"No, I don't think he could. He's not capable and I would not let him."

Julion nodded with relief. "That's something. He's a good man but lonely. Lonely men are desperate. Drunk lonely ones the worst. Puts a demon into a man's cock that can't always be silenced."

"I'm alright. Just a bit shook up. I've had that happen to me a couple of times before. But when I turned him down he backed off. He was ashamed of himself, I told him not to be."

"You *are* a pretty boy."

"In the gleaner clans, they didn't always ask. Tuparrillio—my foster father—he taught me how to fight them off, for me and my sister's sake."

"You have a sister? You don't talk about her."

"I had to leave her behind, so I don't like to."

Julion looked out over the desert, his lips twisted. "I hope you didn't hurt his feelings too much, he'll be really fucking sheepish come the morning."

"Are you and him...?"

"Me? Ha!" Julion smiled widely at the idea. "No! I mean, I don't care. He and I have had our tumbles in the past. In tastes I'm like the blueskins. Man, woman, doesn't make any difference to me. There's pleasure in all flesh. I don't hold old Mather in any special kind of affection. But I do owe him. I hate to see him get hurt."

"You don't respect him much."

"There's not much to respect! Look, he's been good to me. He and I have been running together for a

good number of years. But I get annoyed with him..."
Reluctance halted him.

"What?"

"He's the world's worst businessman!" Julion said.
"There's a fucking fortune to be made out here. Finding
glimmer, supplying tools, timber for the sleepers,
finding crews to lay the rails, supplying the miners
with food. And iron! Iron! Do you know how much
iron they get through here? The residual glimmer in
the sand corrodes it, needs replacing *constantly*. And
what has he got us doing? Flogging booze at night."

"It makes a profit," said Tuvacs.

"Oh aye, it's a tidy income, sure enough, if you're a
grocer. It's not the fortune he was counting on. This
is my third adventure with him, the man's hopeless.
From the look on your face you're surprised by this,
but think about it. We turn up here to sell tools, see
the market is in mass supply, he makes noises about
it, but he's already looking at buying boxcars to sell
hooch from. He buys a full team of dogs, that's not
including the small fortune he dropped on Rusanina
and her lovers, and starts talking about selling them
within days of arriving. And then, because it would
make sense, mind, he doesn't sell them. Do you know
how much a Sorkosian team leader costs?"

Tuvacs shook his head.

"There's probably only two hundred, say two
hundred and fifty of them in the entire Hundred.
Maybe that'll give you an idea. So, anyways, full team
of dogs, and a fucking talking princess of the dogs no
less, what's he do with them? Has us dragging them
about, selling water for pennies. He doesn't rent them
out in winter, he doesn't use them for the long range

supply runs he intended. And we've still got to feed the fuckers."

"I didn't realise. He seemed... Well, he seemed like—"

"He knew what he was doing? Yeah. He takes a lot of people in. His bluster is convincing, his energy carries him through the first stages. He's had plenty of experience of travel, and does have some good ideas, but he just has too many at once. Do you know what I mean? He never knows which to pursue. Any one of the things he had in mind here might have worked. Hells, selling booze is kind of working. None of us is starving, are we? But it's just like Ocerzerkiya all over again. He has his idea, puts it into play, gets distracted and never sees the damn thing through to the end. Fortunes promised never appear, while the money he gets from his family disappears."

"He's a decent man, and he has been good to me—"

"Apart from tonight."

"A misunderstanding," said Tuvacs. "I said he was embarrassed. Maybe I looked like I was interested."

"Maybe, but put enough wine in him and he's ready to try whether they do or not. Why do you think he's out here, man of means like that? The Boskovins are not a poor family, major merchants they are."

"Why is he here?"

"Because his family want him out of sight, out of mind. He's embarrassed? No my friend, he is an *embarrassment*. This kind of thing," he gestured at Tuvacs' crotch, "not the done thing in Karsa, oh no. We're not Amarands, so they say. Well, fuck them. Boskovin is a decent man, and worth looking out for, because that man has a big heart, indiscretions aside. But I will tell you this without any shade of dogshit to it, not a one of us will ever get rich off him or his schemes, no matter what he says."

"What did he do for you?"

"It's a long story," said Julion. "And it makes me look like a prick, but if you come back down to the camp with me, maybe I'll tell you."

Tuvacs made no move. He faced the desert.

"Do you see the lights, out over the dunes there?"

"Yes. Everybody does."

"What about the lights on the Twin?"

Julion looked perplexed. "No light there, my friend. Listen, this isn't my first time out east. It's best not to look into the desert. I'm not surprised you're seeing things, it's easy to see stuff that's not there. I'm pretty sure every bastard in camp has probably said that to you."

"They have. If that's so, what're you doing up here?"

"Same as you, needed some space. Went to see the dogs. Rusanina gave me her 'piss off' look, so I came up here. There's something about it, isn't there? Alluring, that's the posh word." He shivered. "I could do with a drink before bed, it's fucking colder than Frozma's tits out here. Care to join me?"

Tuvacs nodded.

Julion held out an arm, showing that Tuvacs should go first. It was the very last thing he ever did.

He jerked. Shock forced his eyes wide. A black wave of blood welled over his lips. He grabbed at Tuvacs' shirt, dragging Tuvacs down. Lying by the dying man, Tuvacs saw the gory head of a dart protruding from his chest, a long shaft fletched with black feathers emerged from his back, quivering in time to his dying heartbeat. Three shakes, each harder than the last, then Julion sighed, and his glassy eyes stared heavenward.

A tremendous lowing shattered the silence. Dogs in the camp began howling and barking madly.

The air rippled and cracked, a twist in the shape of the world, and a huge shape materialised from nowhere. A giant possessed of too many limbs, jet black skin scored with bright, swirling, luminescent patterns in pale golds, greens and pink. A head as large as a cart swung over Tuvacs, six legs pawed at the ground. Tuvacs rolled to the side, under the web. The creature reared up over him, and he saw a rider. The thing on the back was as black-skinned as his mount and decorated in the same patterns of light, hard to distinguish from the creature it road. Eight feet tall, four arms, a blocky head. Yellow eyes burned down at him without seeing. The riding beast set its rear four limbs into the ground and pawed at the air with the fore pair, showing four-toed feet, and then it was away, trampling the ironweb to shreds. The night bulged, and more of the creatures followed, leaping from shimmers in the air. Screams broke out in the camp. Gunshots snapped sharply.

Tuvacs crawled to see into the camp. The huge riders were among his people, smashing men down with oversized clubs, their mounts bursting through shacks and tents. Blue streaks from glimmer bullets crisscrossed the night. He saw a monster fall from its saddle, shot through the head. But very few of the people below had firearms, and all of the guards had drunk their fill that night at his boxcar.

"Modalmen," he whispered.

Dogs snarled and barked. They leapt at the creatures in defence of their masters, but the great drays were as puppies to the raiders. Canine yelps intermingled with men's screams. Tuvacs shrank back into the sand, lying flat. He did not know what to do, or where to go. The shouts of the giants were terrible, a musical roaring as harsh as thunder. There were perhaps a dozen of them, far fewer than the men below, but they were ogres amid children.

With his heart in his mouth, he backed away. His foot snagged on the ruined iron web. It flexed under his foot. On the other side was only sand, grey and black and blood-dark in the moons' light.

A modalman tossed a flaming ball into the boxcar. Glass shattered, and it was burning. Tents ignited, one by one. Fire was everywhere, the modalmen rode round and around, their giant mounts stamping the camp to flinders. Their destruction done, they corralled the workers below, flinging nets and lariats, snaring men as if they were livestock. A man was snatched up carelessly by a rider. He squealed shrilly as his arm broke in the monster's massive fist. The modalman shouted and discarded the worker, driving his spear through his ruined prize.

Showing his back was an invitation to die like Julion, a dart through his heart. Staying even worse.

Tuvacs backed away, stepped over the web, and fled.

In the silence of the Black Sands the screams quietened, but never died. Frantic looks back showed a pillar of light and smoke scarring the dark.

Tuvacs ran. Panting came from behind him, the gallop of feet thumping into sand. Tuvacs gritted his teeth and ran faster than he ever had in his life. The cold air scorched his lungs; sand slid treacherously around his feet. The sanctuary of a dune was ahead.

Something barged into him from behind, knocking him face first into the sand. He spat grit from his mouth. A heavy paw pressed down between his shoulder blades.

"Stop! Stop, Tuvacs. Why run? Is I, Rusanina."

Tuvacs rolled over, and let out a noise halfway between a sob and a laugh.

"You get on back. I carry."

"I will hurt you," said Tuvacs.

"Sit near front. I be fine for short time. If not, no matter. We die if we stay."

"Run! Leave me here."

"Then you die. Get onto my back!" she swallowed between each faltering word. This was the most Tuvacs had ever heard her speak.

He grabbed a handful of fur and clambered gracelessly onto her back. He had never ridden anything before. The ground was a worrying distance away.

"Sit still!" she growled.

Wetness soaked his leg. He felt with his hand, bringing it back before his eyes. It was dark with blood.

"You're bleeding," he said.

"I run. I run, or we die."

She broke into a gallop from a standing start, sand spraying from her feet. The firelight of the burning camp retreated behind them. Howls and screaming chased them across the sand.

Rusanina crested the dune and cantered down the other side and made for a gap between two rounded crags half-swallowed by the desert.

From the corner of Tuvacs' eye, he saw movement so swift he had no time to call out.

A heavy body slammed into Tuvacs' side knocking him from the dog's back. He caught a flash of moonlight on teeth. Rusanina snarled savagely. He struck sand with his head. Bright points of light shattered his vision into a falling mosaic, and he felt himself tumbling upwards and away.

CHAPTER FORTY-SEVEN
The Ship Sets Sail

ON THE 23RD of Little, the *Prince Alfra* departed the docks of Karsa City, and set a course southwest.

A small crowd came out to see the ship cast off amid the pelting rain. A Major Tide had taken the sea almost as far as the Bottomhouse Quay, and from there muted cheers and the music of a soaked band competed with the drumming of the raindrops.

Greasy brown water heaved with a queasy swell, troubling the iron ship not at all, but sending those vessels attendant upon it bobbing up and down. Under an awning by the dockside sundry Kressinds and investors marked the occasion with the opening of sparkling Correadan wine. Trassan looked up to them. Arkadian Vand gave him a nod. Veridy by his side wept daintily into a handkerchief. His mother and father were absent, as was Guis, but Garten was present in his official capacity as Admiralty representative. Cassonaepia and Arvell were among the family party. He was extremely relieved that Ilona was nowhere to be seen. There was, of course, no way he could have fulfilled his promise to her. Guilty at his relief, he nevertheless preferred a little guilt to confronting the effects of his own cowardice.

"So your great adventure begins," said Aarin to his brother. Rain dripped from the peak of his hood.

The whistles of the *Prince Alfra* let out a long, sorrowful blast.

"You are welcome to come with me all the way, brother," said Trassan.

"Only as far as the Final Isle."

Trassan nodded distractedly. The wheels of the ship excited the water, pulling it from the wharf. Glimmer steam whipped around the vessel. When the prow pointed seawards, Captain Heffi had the screw engage and the ship accelerated, rapidly outpacing those few vessels that chose to trail it. Within twenty minutes the last of them had been left behind. The Lockside, the Slot, and all of Karsa City were reduced to a collection of grey blocks on the shore. Half an hour after that, the rain hid the whole great metropolis. Only the cliffs remained visible, a black band that shrank above their wake.

To the southwest they went, passing the small space of open sea by Karsa City and into the teeming isles and islets of Karsa. Over five thousand, so it was reckoned, from the very smallest to islands the size of counties. In the towns and villages of these places, people gathered to watch the marvel of the age steam by. Not all were aware of the iron ship's existence. More than one fishing smack made out of the *Prince Alfra*'s way as if pursued by the very largest of anguillons.

The tides were high for days, and they were able to take the most direct routes. The further south they went, the meaner the towns became, the rockier the islands, the poorer the people, until dry land shattered into a loose groupings of skerries and sea rocks. Atop some of these were the towers and hamlets of foreshoremen, those who made their living from the mudflats when the tide was at its lowest. All were fortified and hung with iron wards and silver charms. It was not unknown for the Drowned King's men to come this far inland.

The towers became rarer. They passed the last on the 29th, a ruin scorched by recent fires. The run of Major Tides was done by then; the ruin stood on a black mountain whose summit was fringed with terrestrial grasses, the bulk of it was sea-stained stone dotted with hardy, semi-aquatic flora. The ship steamed through a canyon fringed with seaweed whose deeper parts the sea never relinquished. All eyes were on the dripping cliff tops around the ship. But they saw no sign of men nor of other threat.

The canyon widened. The sea proper opened before them, the true ocean. The seabed there was forever drowned. No tide of any magnitude would reveal it. Turbulence in the water betrayed the presence of anguillons, these abyssal giants come to the edge of the land to feed. One raised its head, and stared with cold eyes the size of cartwheels at the ship, gills pulsing behind its monstrous jaw. No matter how mighty, no anguillon could do aught against the *Prince Alfra*. The eel slipped back under the water into its own kingdom.

Fairer weather took hold; cloudy, dismal, but with no rain or wind. The ship performed beyond expectations. Free of the risk of rocks and shoals, they increased speed, cleaving the waters swiftly and left the isles behind them, all bar the last.

These things were remarked upon favourably, if with little celebration. The minds of all aboard were fixed on the future; to three days away, perhaps four, when the *Prince Alfra* would dare the Drowning Sea and its dread king.

Aarin, troubled by the errand he was tasked with and not wishing to be under the feet of others, took to spending his time at the ship's prow. He made his way there in the mornings, and stayed there most of the day. Ahead and to all sides was nothing but the dark blue sea, wrinkled with waves capped with lines of blown spume. The ship was too large to be affected as much as a floatstone ship by the swell, but the roll of it as it plunged up and down each wave had been too much for Pasquanty. Discovering himself to be a poor sailor, he passed the day moaning in his bunk.

One day, when Karsa's last islets were a memory forgotten somewhere over the horizon, Vols Iapetus joined him.

"I have seen you here every day," he said. "I trust I am not intruding, Guider."

Aarin endeavoured to be polite, but not welcoming, because he desired no company. "Not at all," he said. Vols' costume was not one Aarin associated with a true mage. He wore an expensively tailored, if threadbare, morning suit, grey gloves, a silk bicorn. He carried a cane, not a staff.

"Might I?" said Iapetus. He pointed his cane at the shelter Aarin stood beneath, a waxed tarpaulin suspended from the ship's rigging.

Aarin's nod was barely perceptible in his hood. Iapetus was grateful, and came to stand next to him.

"A good idea," he said, looking up at the tarpaulin, "what with the weather we've been having."

"A gift from the sailors."

"That's kind."

"They are disturbed by my presence, I am a reminder of death. It is ill fortune to bring a Guider on a ship. All who die at sea that do not belong to the One God of the Ishmalani belong to the Drowned King. That is the treaty. This keeps me out of their way and out of their thoughts."

"Ah," said Iapetus awkwardly. He blinked owlishly at the stinging spray. "Do you place us at risk, Guider?"

"I have an errand at the Final Isle. My order has a monastery there. I have the appropriate credentials." He let the amulet given him by Guider Triesko flash in his hand momentarily. "If there is a risk, it is from my brother's audacity."

"He is audacious, isn't he?" said the mage. He had a peculiarly high voice, a slight build. Aarin had imagined the seed of Res Iapetus to grow mightier trees. "How do you find all this?" Vols tapped the deck lightly with his cane.

"My brother has built a fine ship, quite a marvel. I had not expected it to be so large."

"Indeed not, but I was more interested in how you found the presence of so much iron. It took me a few weeks to learn how to bear it. You joined us the day we set sail, and have had no time to acclimatise yourself. You Guiders are mageborn also. Does it not make you ill?"

"I see, goodmage." He took his hands from his sleeves. Clearly, he was not going to be rid of Iapetus easily. "I have enough sensitivity to perform my function as a Guider. My brother though—not Trassan, he has the talent of an iron bar, but Guis—he is true mageborn." He tapped the rim of his eye socket below the white of his blind eye.

"An accident? I am sorry," said Vols. "It takes us time to find our feet. Tragedy dogs our childhoods." His brow creased. "But I do not recall a Kressind among my colleagues. There are few of us now, we know each other's business to a tedious degree. I suppose he became a magister?"

"No. He is a playwright."

"An unusual choice for a mageborn."

"He never did find his feet, that is why. His mind is damaged, a problem of the nerves. He is prone to fits of anxiety."

Understanding crossed Vols' face. "Obsessive?"

"Yes."

"A bad character trait in a mage. Or a good one."

"He does not see it as so."

"All we mages who remain are close to insane. The division between convincing oneself that something is entirely the case when it isn't, and exerting enough will upon the stuff of creation around you so that reality itself is convinced to change to your desired vision is razor sharp. It cuts, and requires a keen sense of balance. To fall to the wrong side at any time leads to insanity on the one hand, or disaster on the other." He raised a hand and waggled it. "Lunacy and destruction are never far from the acts of the mage. To be truly great one has to be utterly sure of who one is, where one is, to make the cloak of reality ripple to one's design."

"That sounds the antithesis of madness."

"On the contrary. To appreciate the riddle of existence, and maintain one's identity in the face of it requires an arrogance tantamount to lunacy. One has to be mad, from a certain point of view."

Aarin examined the small man carefully. "You do not seem terribly mad yourself, Goodmage Iapetus."

"That is why I am not among the great," said the mage apologetically. "I have the name and the legacy it grants, but little talent of my own. I am much too sane."

"I am sure it outstrips mine a thousandfold."

"I do not mean false modesty," Vols replied. "Nor to belittle your ability. But when one has the Goddriver as an ancestor, one has little hope of living up to the name."

"Very true. What is your purpose here then?"

"I am not entirely useless. And I need the money."

Vols' words could have been the complaints of one who believes themselves short-changed by life, but he spoke with such frankness that Aarin found himself warming to him.

"Do you like it out here, on the ocean?" said Aarin.

"I love all wild places. All mages do. My own home is very remote. In cities magic of the will doesn't work so well, there is too much iron, there are too many people. From the least aware dullard to the greatest mage, all of us exert our will upon the world to a degree. Mages have to fight a torrent of desires; it ever was a swim upstream, and grows worse the more the population grows. Never tell Ardovani, but our days are done. This is the age of the magister. Stable magic bound to devices, without active will of its own, or employed through precise ritual. That is the future. We mages are a relic. In the remote wildernesses of Stonscire I can pretend it is as it always has been."

"Arkadian Vand believes magic has been tamed."

"Oh, oh!" said Iapetus cheerily. "I never said that. No no no! Magic has lost too much of its mystique, I believe. The effects of cities has led to a certain sureness... People are careless in cities. Away in the villages, in the mountains, in the fields and woods where man's will is not always paramount, people are more careful in what they say and do. Many old traditions die, but they were practiced for a reason. People see ghostings, they see the new glimmer devices, they believe magic to be something inert and useful, like a lump of coal—aside from a certain grubbiness, unthreatening until the fire within is kindled. They forget the wildness of magic. It and the beings it succours are treated with a dangerous lack of seriousness."

Aarin thought on his own concerns, the change in the ghosts. But for all his talk on the matter, Vols Iapetus made no mention of this. His opinions were those of a man who mourns the past, not of one who fears for the future.

"It is the same for the Guiders," Aarin said carefully. "In the city, people begin to forget the need for guidance to the beyond. And so our income falls, our college is half empty. The Dead God's quarter lessens in ability. In the countryside they remember, but even there..."

"This age brings much benefit to us all," said Vols. "But not everything it discards is worthless. Man is attempting to sidestep the riddle of life through rationality. The beginning of this was the banishment of the gods. For if one can master the gods, no task seems too great. You see, my great-grandfather brought about the beginning of the end for his own kind. The grand irony I believe is that the world cannot be mastered. Life is its own answer, it does not need solving, man is not necessary to it. I fear a correction may be overdue."

Aarin tucked his chin deeper into his hood, chilled by the foreboding that Iapetus was right.

CHAPTER FORTY-EIGHT
In Pursuit of the Modalmen

REL LEANED ON the pommel of his saddle. Aramaz stepped from foot to foot and let out a long croak.

"Hush now," said Rel.

Wreckage was strewn all over the desert. Canvas from wrecked tents cracked in the wind. Lines and cables thrummed and moaned. No human voice was heard. The camp's exact location was discernible only by the thickening density of shattered wood and iron. At the very centre the pioneer engine, a stout machine plated with silver, lay on its side. Bodies lay tangled with the wrecks of their homes, pale but otherwise untouched by death's decay.

"I don't see enough bodies, sir." Dramion sniffed harshly, a ripping snort, and hawked up a gobbet of phlegm.

Veremond coughed in polite disapproval at Dramion's manners. Merreas rode round the perimeter, dracon strutting. Their mounts were tense, eager to feed. Their heads strayed constantly in the direction of the carrion, necessitating constant correction from their riders.

Zorolotsev had dismounted, and led his dracon on a long rein as he walked on foot by the wrecked rail tracks, intent on the ground.

"Five days ago?" said Rel.

"An educated guess, captain," said Veremond. "The last messenger came in to the supply station three days before that. Another was due four days ago."

"Deamaathani, can you wave your hands a bit and get me a more accurate answer?"

"Please, Rel, don't be so facile about my art."

"Can you?"

"No. Too much raw glimmer. Attempting a reading out here would be an enormous waste of time."

"Zorolotsev! Get away from the engine!" shouted Rel. The Khusiak looked up, glanced at the locomotive and backed away.

Three trucks were on the tracks, one burned out. The fourth's wheels were off the rails. The fifth, that closest to the engine, had been smashed in half. The silver engine had been toppled by a force they could all too readily imagine. The ticks and pings of metal unevenly heated by its ruptured glimmer assembly were audible where the three officers and Dramion sat on their mounts.

"Stay away from that," Rel told his men. "There's no telling if it'll go up."

"It hasn't yet, captain," said Dramion.

"That's no guarantee. Stay away from it. I didn't learn much from my father, but I did learn when to stay clear."

"What the hells happened here?" said Dramion. "Why did they attack? There's not been a modalman raid in three years."

"Two years, eight months," corrected Veremond.

"Fine, fine," said Dramion irritably. "When was the last at this scale?"

"None of us were here for the last, we're not fit to judge the scale," said Veremond.

"Can we not find a dead man to ask? There are always a few lost ghosts after something like this, especially out here," said Dramion.

"Do you know how to speak to them?" said Veremond.

"No."

"Well then."

"What about Deamaathani?" Dramion continued sourly.

"I can't do it," said the warlock. "You need some talent to be a dead speaker, but not too much. I'd be as likely to shred the poor bastards into smoke as get anything useful out of them."

"He's just too good," said Dramion sarcastically. "It's why he's so bloody useless."

"Something like that," said Deamaathani.

"Watch your tongue," said Veremond, but his heart wasn't in it.

"I don't sense the dead," Deamaathani continued. "They have all departed."

"We're lucky then," said Veremond.

Rel pulled a face and looked around the camp once more. "This was inevitable. We're pushing deeper into the desert. We were bound to upset the modalman at some point."

"It's not a certainty," said Deamaathani. "No one knows where they dwell. This bit of desert looks much like all the others. They've not hit the railway for years. How can we avoid offending them if we do not know what causes offence?"

Merreas rode down from the ridgeline. He wore no hat and his extremities were pink from the cold. "The iron web has been ripped up, same as the track back that way and up ahead."

"Any sign of movement?"

"No sir," said Merreas.

"Keep looking. Dramion, get up there with him. It'll be dark in a few hours. I don't want ambushing."

"That is what they did here," said Veremond. "Only one dead." He nodded to the corpse of the modalman, large as a beached whale in the middle of it all. There was no sign of its mount. "Six men armed with guns, and that is all they managed."

Rel rode over to the inhumanly sized corpse. In death its skin was dark grey, deep spiral scars over two thirds of its body. Its four arms were curled about it, embracing itself. The hairless head was a pulp. Aramaz recoiled from it and paced back, exhibiting no desire to eat it.

"Gun got this one," he said.

"It's the only way to kill them," said Deamaathani. "I wouldn't want to fence with one of these."

"Why did they do it?" said Rel. "They left nearly all the supplies, they didn't do it for valuables. That engine is four-tenths silver."

"Slaves. Meat," said Deamaathani. "The dogs are all gone as well as the workers."

Zorolotsev came to them. "Captain, where they come from, I not know," he said. "Modalmen tracks are very easy to see. They start outside the ironweb from all sides, nothing to show from where."

"How many?"

"Difficult to say, lots of tracks cross each other. More than six, less than twelve."

"Which way did they go?" asked Rel.

Zorolotsev pointed. "That way. Northeast. Two lines, mounted, driving captives between them."

Rel wheeled Aramaz about, away from the modalman corpse "We will follow the trail, see what we can do."

"Is that such a good idea?" said Deamaathani.

"Have you got a better one? We have to scout their forces before reporting back to the fort."

"Very carefully," said Deamaathani.

"Am I ever anything but? Some of the workers might have survived."

The dragoons gathered together at the ridge top. There, in the tangle of the broken iron web, they found a set of footprints peeling away from the tracks of the modalmen and their captives, the prints of a dray dog running with it.

"An escapee," said Rel. He looked up the line of the tracks. They crossed over a flat run of desert before going up over a low dune.

"No," said Zorolotsev. "This is from before." He pointed at the ground. "These tracks of the raiders go over this one."

"They probably got him too, and his dog," said Veremond.

"Only one way to find out," said Rel. He spurred his dracon. The others came behind him. The tracks became confused halfway to the dune. Zorolotsev halted his dracon. "Here, the tracks join." Prints of man and dog were intermingled. "He got on the dog. See? Dog tracks deeper, no sign of human feet."

They continued on down the line of tracks. They went up and over the dune, and headed out toward a space between two low crags some three hundred yards ahead.

"Fine place for an ambush," said Rel.

"Yes," said Zorolotsev pointing at a patch of brightness. "The dog. Hyah!" he spurred his dracon ahead of the others.

Half-hidden between the crags was the body of a dog, its fur a contrast to the flat black of the sand. Rel galloped up to Zorolotsev, Dramion and Merreas with him. Veremond and Deamaathani fanned out either side, riding up to the tops of the rocks.

"Dead dog," said Dramion. Zorolotsev was by its side.

"You idiot, that's a Sorkosian leader," said Rel. "Someone get me some water!"

"What is he on about? It's just a dog," said Dramion.

"It's a talking dog, you twat," said Merreas.

"Too late captain, it is dead," said Zorolotsev.

"Who had one of them out here? It must have been worth a fortune," said Merreas.

"Ain't worth nothing now," said Dramion.

"There are only a couple," said Veremond. "This one looks like the one that belonged to that Karsan merchant. Baskovan or something."

"That's not a Karsan name," said Rel.

"Karsarin's not my strongpoint. Could have been Buskovin."

"Boskovin?"

"Aye, that's it. Still doesn't sound very Karsan to me."

"It's not, not originally, it's Farthian, but the family has been in Karsa for years. The Boskovin clan are quite well-to-do," said Rel. "Merchants, the lot of them. I wonder what one of them was doing all the way out here?"

"Well-to-do! Get him," said Dramion.

"You speak Maceriyan like a duke, captain," said Merreas.

"I had a duchess for my wet nurse, you oik. Veremond, go with Merreas back to the fort. Let them know what happened. Tell them the state of the track, let them know that the engine might be salvageable. The track bed is still sound. Make sure Estabanado listens to my recommendation, the workers need proper protection. It's happened once, it'll happen again. Get Zhinsky to put the case for more men, and soldiers from the garrison, not hirelings. It's time we got ourselves out of that fort."

"What about the waystations?" said Veremond.

"Stop and warn them all. No, order fourteen through seventeen back to the fort, that takes us down to the Deep Cut spur. Leave it staffed, but see if you can get some men sent back to guard it."

"Aye," said Veremond. The two men dipped their heads, and spurred their dracons into fast bobbing trots. The dracon's legs kicked up clods of damp sand as they raced westwards. In minutes they were gone from sight.

"What about the rest of us, sir?" asked Dramion.

"We'll get on with searching the camp for survivors. I want to be done before we lose the light."

"Tonight?" said Zorolotsev.

"We'll camp. Not too close to this charnel pit. Deamaathani, can you salvage enough of the web to ward us?"

"Of course."

"And tomorrow?" said Dramion. "What do we do tomorrow?"

"Tomorrow we follow the trail. They won't have got far, not with men on foot. Nothing outpaces a dracon."

"But the desert..." said Dramion disbelievingly. "You can't be ordering us out into that..."

"We've got a magister-mage with us, or did you forget? No one else has any chance of finding these poor bastards. Or are you suggesting we leave them to their undoubtedly terrible fate?"

"No, sir," mumbled Dramion.

THE NIGHT LASTED long. Strange noises troubled them all, bubbling cries that came drifting on the wind. Wet snufflings skirted the light of their fire, but when Deamaathani flung back his blankets and conjured a blaze, nothing could be seen. The sounds returned as soon as Deamaathani's witchfire dimmed. Their minds always on what lurked in the darkness, none but Zorolotsev slept soundly. They welcomed the sun gladly.

The attackers had come from nowhere, as far as they could tell, but were unable to repeat the trick. The tracks ran true, straight as the railway through the desert of changing character. Needles of worn sandstone, red as the dawn, grew from the black sands. Small and widely spaced at first, they became denser until they were as tall and numerous as trees in a forest.

Zorolotsev stopped often to refer to the sun, noting his observations carefully in a book. The tracks carried on their course to the northeast, heading always deeper into the desert and away from the railway. They changed heading only once, turning suddenly directly north.

Noon was well past when Zorolotsev held up his hand and put his fingers to his lips. The desert was deathly quiet, no living thing moved, the wind was a dying breath. Over the thump of his heart Rel heard nothing.

"Wait here," said Zorolotsev.

Rel nodded. Zorolotsev rode on, his dracon dodging between the pinnacles of rock. Five minutes went by, then ten. Then fifteen.

Rel was close to ordering the rest forward to find Zorolotsev when the Khusiak returned. His face was grim.

"Captain," he said. "You had better see this."

ZOROLOTSEV TOOK THEM to a place where the pinnacles grew closer, merging to become a cliff face. There he had them dismount. They left Dramion below minding the dracons, and climbed up a treacherous slope. Zorolotsev held his finger to his lip then motioned for them to go forward on their bellies.

The looked down into a large depression in the desert, surrounded by walls of rock, a crater like one of Three Sisters, only far larger. Three miles or more across, and every scrap of space was occupied by modalmen.

"By all the driven gods," whispered Rel. "How many are there?"

Skin tents the height of towers dotted the camp. Cages barred with bones held human captives in abject misery, bloody piles of offal near them indicating their fate. Huge corrals contained enormous six-limbed animals saddled for riding. And everywhere went modalmen, armed and gigantic, a camp of monsters fit to despoil any nation of the Earth.

"Over two thousand," said Zorolotsev. "And there is that." On the far side of the camp was a stone stockade, studded with spikes whittled from long bones.

Rel made to get his glass, but the Khusiak shook his head. "Reflections give us away," he said.

"What is in there?"

"Wait."

A scaly crest flashed over the wall. A head lifted high, like those of their dracons but immeasurably larger. The creature shook out the frills around its jaw and horns, showing a long neck bound about with chains of bronze, then sank once more from view.

"A dragon?" said Rel. "A *dragon?*"

"We can do nothing for the prisoners," said Deamaathani. "To go down there is suicide."

Rel spoke quickly. "We have to go. Now. Get back to the fort, get a message back to the west that there's an army of modalmen out here. If this lot fall upon Railhead we'll lose it in an instant. They'll invest the fort, it'll be a disaster."

"Yes, captain," said Zorolotsev.

"They might be big," said Rel. "But I'd like to see them shrug off a cannonade."

They slid away undetected, mounted their dracons and rode fast from the forest of stone.

CHAPTER FORTY-NINE
The King of the Drowned

"Ware! Ware! Flotsam ahead!" Fog muffled the lookout's voice, stealing the power of his words. The ship's bell tolled, two rings. The bow of the boat was invisible, the deck fading out into white blankness halfway down the length of the ship.

"I can't see a damn thing," Trassan growled. "Isn't there something you can do about this, Tullian? Wish the fog away."

"Regrettably not, goodfellow," said Ardovani. "Meteoromancy is but a hobby, and this is no normal fog. Perhaps Mage Iapetus might?"

"I've not seen him all damn day."

"Be quiet now goodfellows," said Captain Heffi quietly. "My men—*your* men— know what they are doing."

Steersman Tolpoleznaen stared into the mist, still with concentration. His hands alone moved, making minor adjustments to the ship's wheel, sending the vessel gracefully round the mat of wreckage. Heffi's other men stood ready, ears straining.

A thin shout came back from the prow. "Ten degrees starboard!" Another voice repeated it. A sailor stationed at the door spoke into the wheelhouse.

"Ten degrees starboard."

Tolpoleznaen was already turning the wheel, hands shifting quickly on the pins.

"Should we not turn with the paddlewheels?" said Trassan. He spoke under his breath, mindful of disturbing the crew.

"No we shouldn't," said Heffi tersely. "The tiller is enough. We go slowly under the screw. The less disturbance we make to the water the better. With luck and the guidance of the one, we will cross the Drowning Sea without so much as a whiff of the dead. Now with sincerely meant respect, goodfellow, shut up."

Shouting came from the invisible prow, loud and frightened. Other voices relayed it, more than those given the task.

"The king! The Drowned King!"

"Fuck it, Heffi, you spoke too soon. Ardovani, come with me."

"I will join you momentarily, goodfellow," he said, and headed for the steps at the back of the wheelhouse that led below.

Trassan rushed from the wheelhouse, pushing past the sailor at the door. A commotion was breaking out on deck.

Heffi followed Trassan out into the fog, stopping at the railing to the balcony round the wheelhouse while Trassan took the stairs to the main deck three at a time.

"Where the hells do you think you're going? Wait for the damned emissary!"

"What if there isn't one? Get Bannord, Iapetus and my brother up here!"

"Trassan!" yelled Heffi. "Let us handle this!"

Trassan ignored him.

The ship's bells rang, calling everyone to arms. Bannord was already on deck, the ship's twenty marines behind him, all armed to the teeth. They each carried a fusil, a pistol and a heavy falchion. They wore jerkins of thick anguillon leather, and half-sets of plate—spalders, vambraces, open faced helmets and a light breastplate.

"He's showed up then?" said Bannord, falling in next to Trassan. His men jogged behind them.

"Looks like it."

"What are your plans?" Bannord grinned. Trassan got the impression Bannord was enjoying himself.

"Spread out, keep a look out. Don't fire until I say."

"Sounds good to me." Bannord slowed. "Fan out! Firing positions!" Trassan had allowed Bannord to choose his own men, and he seemed to know his work. They needed little direction. They took their positions, rested their fusils and aimed out across the water. The third and second mates went about the ship followed by two sailors carrying sword chests, distributing weapons among the ratings.

The crew was experienced, and prepared quickly. The activity of their preparation had been a welcome break to the eerie silence of the sea fog, but it ceased and the quiet enveloped the *Prince Alfra* again.

They reached the prow. Trassan slipped over, slamming painfully onto the slick wood. He limped hurriedly to the front of the ship. Freezing water droplets coated his skin and clothes.

The lookout had a ironlock pistol in his hand. "Goodfellow," he said. "Below."

Twenty yards out, the sea fizzed and heaved, a spout bubbling ten feet ten feet high. Waves slapped against the ship's hull. Trassan looked down to see bodies in the water, dozens of them. Their flesh was the bloated, fish-white of the drowned. Dead eyes stared back at him. Pallid hands pawed at the sides of the ship.

"My congratulations, goodfellow," the sailor said. "If this were a floatstone ship, they'd be up over the side and among us already."

"Aye," said Bannord. "That'll buy us a bit of time."

"You're not optimistic."

"A realist, my friend. The Drowned King is a slippery fucker. No pun intended," said Bannord.

The water burst outward. A giant emerged from the ocean, water streaming from its face. A crown of broken wooden spars and shattered floatstone crowned him. A hundred drowned bodies made up the face, packed together so that their slimy flesh formed one mass, but individual limbs, heads and gleaming bone could be discerned. Long, rank kelp made hair and bearded his lips and chin. Up and up the giant rose, revealing shoulders comprised of many dead men. His chest was a pair of whale carcasses, furred white with rotting blubber, hagfish hanging from their ragged skin so they resembled exposed, diseased lungs. The hull of a wooden Ocerzerkiyan corsair made up part of its belly. Its arms were huge, biceps comprised of dead seamen, pulling as if still at the oars as they flexed, tendons were anguillons, muscles tight knots of fish skeletons. Hands unfurled, each finger the corpse of a drowned man.

The giant ceased to rise when it was half clear of the water, its legs and lower belly still hidden by the sea. Water poured from cracks in its composite flesh, fish and juvenile anguillons slipping back into the sea. Putrid air wafted over the deck, the briny sweet stench of waterlogged meat.

Aarin joined his brother and Bannord, Iapetus timid behind him. Ardovani came a moment later, carrying a magister's weapon, a large gun of copper and brass, set with diamond down the length of the barrel, yet lacking a hole in its muzzle.

"Go and tell Heffi to get the engines ready," said Trassan to a rating. The man fled astern, grateful to be free of the horror unfolding at the prow.

"The King of the Drowned," said Aarin. "Every unghosted ever lost at sea, made one."

This hideous patchwork of a thousand stolen lives towered over the *Prince Alfra*. The eyes, when they opened, only they proved to be the king's own.

Eyelids made of stolen arms parted. A cold, green light shone from within. Four corpses made his lips. These flexed, parting to show a mouth full of stacked skulls arranged to resemble teeth.

"You trespass in the realm of the drowned," said the king. A foetid wind blew his words over the ship. "You break the treaty between the Undersea Kingdom and the Kingdom of the Isles."

"Not so!" shouted Trassan, fighting to keep the tremor of fear from his voice. "I have here a right of passage signed by Prince Alfra of Karsa himself."

He held it up in a shaking hand. In the swell below, more dead pressed themselves against the ship, beating ineffectually against its unbreakable hull.

"And you, priest of the dead, your kind is forbidden crossing of our domain."

"I have the sigil of the Dead God," said Aarin. "I invoke my right to cross to the Final Isle." The iron medallion flashed in his palm, with the other he scattered silver into the water. "My offering."

The Drowned King reached out a vile hand. The dead men of his fingers unfurled, reaching for the paper with their own rotting digits. The one serving as the king's forefinger snatched the paper, and lifted it to empty eye sockets. The corpse dropped the document, and was withdrawn into a fist. The arm lifted back.

"Permission is not granted. We were not consulted."

"The paper is in order," said Trassan.

"We were not consulted. The agreement is void. By ancient treaty, the priest's badge and silver buys his passage, your paper does not buy yours. You cannot pass. Your ship is ours. Your lives are ours." The water surged before the king, bearing moaning dead halfway up the side of the *Prince Alfra* before sucking them away.

"Stand ready!" shouted Bannord.

"Heffi!" called Trassan. "Get us out of here."

The Drowned King surveyed the ship. "Time marches on. The art of the living increases. Your ship is mighty, your weapons grow deadlier. But our armies are legion."

"You cannot stop me," said Trassan. "Let us pass."

"Wrong. We will not allow it."

The king drew back his arm, and swung it at the deck. The gestalt limb smashed through rigging and shattered spars. Sailors screamed as they were hit by falling wreckage.

"He cannot hurt the hull," said Trassan.

"I do not think that is his intention," said Aarin.

Like a fishing boat's net opening, the arm split, sending corpses skidding all across the deck.

"Holy mother fucking hordes of lost gods!" said Bannord. "Open fire!"

His men wasted no time, the sailors were only slightly behind. Guns banged and glimmer bullets hissed in the fog.

"Brother!" cried Aarin. The king aimed a second fist at the prow. The arm broke over the railings. Dead men rained into the sea at either side, but well over a dozen sprawled about the foredeck, knocking Trassan and Iapetus to the planking. The dead haltingly got to their feet, teeth gnashing. Rusty swords and knives were plucked from belts by decayed fingers.

One of the Drowned King's subjects rose over Trassan. Aarin unflinchingly clapped his hand to the thing's head, whispering words only meant to be spoken at the ghosting. A feeble shade warbled its way upwards, and the corpse collapsed.

"I can't do that for all of them!" shouted Aarin over the report of gunfire.

"What do I do?" yelled Trassan.

"Put father's fencing lessons to practice! Draw your bloody sword, you fool!"

Trassan snapped out of his shock and did as Aarin said.

Battle raged all across the ship. Ladders of corpses hung over the side of the boat, allowing those dead in the water to clamber upwards. With a booming hoot of the whistle, the engines engaged, paddlewheels slicing soft bodies into soup. The ship leapt forward, but they were already close to being overrun. The Drowned King laughed at their attempts to flee and toppled forward, his great head and shoulders bursting apart amidships, reinforcing the rotting boarding party as the ship pulled away.

Ardovani's weapon made a deafening noise. A wide beam of golden energy burst from the end of the gun, scything down a half dozen of the unliving. Bannord hacked the head from a drowned sailor wrestling with Iapetus and hauled the slime-covered mage to his feet.

Trassan hacked and shoved at the unliving. Together with Bannord and Aarin's efforts, they created a small circle in the unliving. Weapons rang, guns fired, sailors and marines cursed and swore, but the dead were eerily silent.

"Do something!" screamed Trassan at Iapetus.

"I... I... can't," said the mage.

Aarin grabbed another dead man, laying him to rest with a hurried whisper. "Now is not the time for a crisis of confidence!"

"I..."

Ardovani let off another shot with his weapon, cooking rotting meat. He shouldered it and grabbed Iapetus.

"You don't have to do it." Ardovani glanced at Aarin.

"I... I suppose not," said Iapetus.

"Help the Guider! Now then!" said Ardovani. "Keep them back from the mage!"

The circle pressed smaller and smaller. Bannord's gun barked one last time and he threw it down, pulling out his sword. He swore as he cleaved at the dead, the steel sticking. With a boot to the chest of his opponent, he tugged it free.

"It is like hacking at clay!"

Trassan stabbed again and again at a dead man, but his sabre had little effect until he shoved the corpse back and gained space to split its skull.

Iapetus stood totally still, his eyes closed.

"What the hells is he doing?" he shouted.

"Working!" called Ardovani. He fired again, but the gun was wrestled from his arms. Trassan looked down in horror; the sundered limbs of the dead were flopping across the deck, scrabbling for his feet.

All of a sudden, Aarin's voice became deafeningly loud. His whispered guiding amplified a hundredfold, cutting through battle and fog alike. A silver ring of magical energy emanated from him, boiling the fog off in burst of multi-coloured steam. Where it struck the dead, they dropped instantly to the deck.

With a terrific howl, the trapped spirits of two hundred drowned men went skyward. Trassan felt his own soul lift, desperate to be free. A dark sky roared into being over him, alive with green lightning and seething faces. With energy born of terrible panic, he fought to keep hold of his flesh, and the vision vanished. Not all the living were so lucky, their ghosts racing into the afterlife with the Drowned King's slaves.

The bodies fell as one, leaving the crew reeling. They clutched at their chests and heads, some weeping at the glimpse of the afterlife each and every one had experienced.

Trassan leaned against the foremast, bile in his mouth. He spat. Aarin had collapsed on the deck. Ardovani attended to him. Bannord was gathering his men, checking their wounds. Sailors stood in disbelief. Ishmalani knelt in the mulch of flesh and blood, kissed the icons about their necks, and pressed their heads to the deck in thanks heedless of the filth.

The *Prince Alfra* steamed ahead at full speed, exhaust from the stacks sending the chill mist awhirl.

The fog ahead thinned. The sun appeared, wan but growing brighter.

A furious cry pierced the fogbank, but the ship was swifter than the king's wrath, and presently the sounds of more natural seas returned.

Vols Iapetus sat on the deck, his suit besmirched with unspeakable filth.

"I didn't know I had it in me," he said, and fainted dead away.

CHAPTER FIFTY
The Darkling Triumphant

IT HAD BEEN a long winter, and Guis was glad it was over. He arrived back in Karsa two weeks after his brother had departed. He could have been there, he supposed, but had made his excuses, unwilling to face a difficult farewell, his mother, or anything else to do with his family.

For many days the sky had been clean and blue, free for a time of pollution from the foundries, and his mood had improved. The sunlight had a lucid quality lacking at other times of the year. Bright and clear, it sparkled upon windows and water droplets, fragmented into discreet rainbows. After so long in the dark, Guis's eyes were refreshed. He saw the sunshine as a newborn might, or a prisoner long kept from the day; as a glorious thing, notable in itself. Soon enough he would come to forget its miraculousness, the light of the sun would diminish in glory to mere illumination. At best it would warm him, at worst it would irritate eyes tired by late nights and endless penwork. But for now it brought prickles of joy to his face. He rolled up his sleeves to feel it more, disdainful of the disapproving expressions of others. With great disregard for convention he hooked his finger into his coat collar and swung it over his shoulder.

"Let the others sweat and suffer, eh Tyn?"

"Yes master," said Tyn grouchily. Its long nose quivered as it sniffed the air. Their reflections warped and danced alongside them as they walked along a row of grand shop windows.

"You can't fool me, Tyn," said Guis. "This weather raises your spirits as much as it does mine."

"I think of the forest, and I lament, master," it said.

"Yes, well. Let's enjoy the rising sap and budding leaves here, eh? Let me buy you something. There's a seller there with apples."

"Last year's," sniffed Tyn. "Wrinkly." But he did not spurn his when Guis bought one for each of them. The stallholder looked at Tyn warily.

"Yes, goodman?" said Guis.

"Nothing, goodfellow," said the stallholder, and took Guis' money.

Guis wandered the streets aimlessly, strolling first down the Grand Parade and then into those new boulevards on the north side of the Var that lead from it. They walked most of the morning in this manner, Guis simply thankful at being out of doors after so long cooped up. He thought of Trassan, and Aarin, who had apparently gone with him for reasons of his own. There wasn't a paper in Karsa that had not run with the *Prince Alfra's* sailing. Thankfully, the fuss was dying down, and the endlessly debated subject of the High Legate's failing mind returned to the front pages. When the ship was mentioned, talk was of the expedition's likelihood of success; whether Trassan was a hero or risked provoking war with the Drowned King, if he would disappear forever or return with wonders that would enrich the nation.

Guis had no doubt his brother would come back. Trassan rarely set himself a goal he did not think he could achieve.

He followed the Lemio until it was swallowed by the docks, then onto the bank of the shipway as far as the top of the cataracts a half mile from the locks, where the overspill from the network of water in the city sluiced out to the sea, one nominally the Lemio, the other the Var. The river hissed down twenty-seven stepped weirs in the direction of Lockside where the water not stolen by the factories, houses, lock mechanisms, canals or funiculars ran down the spillway to spread its dirty load upon the mud of the foreshore. He found a patch of sunshine and stopped a while to watch the gleaners on the topmost weir fish detritus from the stream with long poles. The river sparkled, making of it an agreeable scene, and leaving Guis with a hankering to paint.

"A fine day," he said. He looked about. "Time for lunch, I think. Not here. Too expensive." He headed off into what Prince Alfra's improvements had left of the Lemio stew. Grand buildings of shining white stone gave out suddenly to brick tenements and uneven cobbled streets. He turned south, and headed toward a chop house he knew that way, cutting through a stinking alleyway. Overflowing waste tuns stood in a line either side of the back door of a tenement. A windowless wall rose up on the other side, so faceless and tall its bricks seemed to go on forever.

It was here that he was accosted.

A man stepped into his path. Guis's hand went straight for his smallsword.

"Get out of my way," he said. "Don't even think about laying a hand on me. I am armed, prepared, and well-instructed in the arts of defence."

The man cast his hood back, revealing a filthy face. Rattails of greasy hair tickled the underside of a chin half-heartedly colonised by a beard.

"Those are belligerent words for a playwright."

Guis leaned forward in surprise. "Mansanio?"

Mansanio sneered at him. "You remember do you?"

"What are you doing here? What on Earth happened to you?"

"You happened to me, you filthy Kressind bastard."

"How dare you address—"

"Save your protests. I am done with taking orders from the likes of you, *goodfellow*."

"You left the countess's service?"

There was a feverish look in Mansanio's eye. "Thanks to you."

"How is that my business? What did I do?"

"Only what every other bastard has ever done. Fucked the woman I love, played with her heart and crushed it, while I had to watch. I go to comfort her and this is my reward!" He held up his arms, revealing tattered finery beneath a filthy cloak. "But I will not take it, no, goodfellow. No longer will I bend my knee to worthless scum like you."

He gave a curt nod over Guis's shoulder.

Guis had his sword halfway out of his sheath when a blackjack slugged him behind the ear. He staggered into the rubbish barrels, upsetting a swarm of early spring flies.

"Hold him!" snarled Mansanio. Two ruffians clamped hard, unforgiving hands about his biceps and yanked his arms behind his back. His sword was withdrawn and cast down the alley.

"You won't get away with this."

"Like your father will care. I listened intently to what you had to say to poor Lucinella, before you broke her heart and turned her against me."

Guis kicked. His heels slipped on the filth coating the cobbles, and he nearly dragged the men holding him down.

"He's a lively one!" said one.

"Keep a hold of him!" Mansanio snarled. He strode over and kicked Guis hard in the ribs, once, then twice. Mansanio reached behind Guis's neck.

Guis' blood ran cold as he realised what Mansanio intended.

"Leave him be!"

"Where are you, little fiend?" muttered Mansanio. He scrabbled at the back of Guis's neck, then drew back with a curse as Tyn sank needle-like teeth into the webbing of flesh between his thumb and forefinger. "Bastard!" he said, and grabbed at the chain about Guis's neck. Tyn sprang from Guis's shoulder, but his jump was cut short. Tyn's leg was tangled and he screamed as Mansanio yanked at the chain, breaking his ankle. Another ferocious tug parted the links. Mansanio had the struggling Tyn in his hands. Tyn squirmed, but Mansanio had a firm hold, and would not relent.

"What has he done to you? Your quarrel is with me! Set him free if you do anything at all."

"Nothing," said Mansanio. "He has done nothing at all."

"Master!" squealed Tyn.

A savage expression descended over Mansanio's face, and he squeezed. Tyn's eyes bulged, little hands clutched at Mansanio's thumb helplessly. There was a wet crack. His head lolled.

"That it?" asked one of Mansanio's thugs.

"Yes, that's it." He cast the corpse of Tyn into a barrel and wiped a thin smear of blood from his hands on his dirty cloak. "No one's getting murdered. Not in the normal sense, anyway." He gave a nasty smile. "Enjoy the day while it lasts, Kressind."

Guis's arms were released. He started to get back up, but a heavy blow sent him sprawling. A kick to his solar plexus had him writhing on the floor, his breath driven from him.

Laughter echoed up from the end of the alley.

He gulped until he could breathe again.

"Tyn!" he said. "Tyn."

GUIS BLUNDERED ONTO the shipway walk clutching the broken corpse. The world tilted under his feet. He span dizzily on the spot, searching the crowd for help. The street grew remote, as if he observed from some place half out of kilter with the mortal world. Every face he saw held the trace of a sneer. Every smile hid a rebuke meant. His breath came short and did not refresh his organs. His throat tightened, his chest was constricted. He fumbled hopelessly at the buttons of his costume, and could not open them.

He stumbled to his knees. Blood rushed in his ears. He retched, bringing nothing up but despair. People recoiled from the bloodied Tyn in his hand. Someone helped him up.

"What happened to you? Have you been attacked? Someone call the watch!" The man's voice came from far away.

"Help me..." Saying it brought the realisation that no one could. He shoved the stranger aside and dove into a sidestreet. A hue and cry set up behind him, dogs were barking. The bell of a watch wagon rang from nearby.

He looked about. Every shadow held peril. He moaned in terror as a formless hand groped from a drain. Panicked, he ran deep into the stew.

The cries diminished. He looked about, hunted. There was nobody there. Soot-specked washing hung from lines overhead. A boy in a flat cap passed across the mouth of the street, sparing him a single, dismissive glance. Tyn still held ahead of him, Guis set off again.

Something grabbed at his foot, sending him sprawling. Tyn's body flew from his hand and skidded across the cobbles.

He rolled over onto his back. The sky was a thin blue line trapped by the street, far overhead. The colour leached from it. Sound deadened. Darkness crowded in on him from all sides. He scrabbled backwards on his elbows, bloodying them. He tried so hard not to think of the Darkling. But the harder he tried, the more it intruded into his thoughts, until it dominated them utterly.

The street darkened, a patch of it taking on utmost blackness. The Darkling stepped through, and it was shadow no more.

It wore his face, it wore his clothes. It was like him in every respect, save that his eyes were the purest black, and held no reflection. Matt orbs that swallowed all light. It smiled horribly, lips stretched far further than they should.

The Darkling reached out a hand toward Guis with taloned fingers.

Guis screamed, shut his eyes and pressed himself back into the stone. The Darkling's fingers extended impossibly, growing long and attenuate, until the digits touched upon his face. Fore and middle finger slipped into his eyesockets, the three others caressing his cheeks. A chill so severe that it exceeded all pain speared through his body.

Guis's scream grew higher and reedier, passing beyond the register of human hearing as his body passed beyond the register of human sight. The Guis on the floor flattened, thinned, and vanished as mist will beneath a strong sun.

The Darkling shut his black eyes, and breathed deep of the air of the world. His face was alight with pleasure.

"There he is! That's him!"

Footsteps clattered up behind him. A hand gently touched his back.

"Is there anything wrong, goodfellow? What happened to you?"

The Darkling opened his eyes, and the blackness of them vanished. He smiled oddly. "Why, constable," he said. "There is nothing wrong. Nothing wrong at all. Thank you for your concern."

"I am going to have to make a report, goodfellow."

"There is no need."

"What's that?" the constable pointed his nightstick at the dead Tyn.

The darkling shrugged. "I have no idea. A Tyn is it? I understand some people keep them as pets." He gave a heartless chuckle. "The very idea."

"There were screams..."

"I heard nothing." The Darkling looked down the street, then back at the watchman. "Now, if you do not mind, I have things I need to be doing."

"Wait! Goodfellow! What is your name?"

The Darkling stared at the man until he stepped back.

"My name is Guis Kressind, the playwright," it said. "Perhaps you have seen my plays?"

CHAPTER FIFTY-ONE
At the Final Isle

THE *PRINCE ALFRA* rode the waves at anchor, three miles out from the Final Isle. The tide was at a middling height, and the island's extensive platform of wave-cut rock was exposed. The pavement ended in a steep slope, not quite a cliff, but an exposed reef edge, sharp with shells and cruel stone. At the bottom the sea surged fitfully, foaming circles that spread angrily upon the deeps.

One clear stretch led from the reef, smooth as a scar. Along this water road an eight-oared long boat of wood, now swift, now slow on the currents.

The *Prince Alfra*'s whistle blew, and a rope ladder was flung over the side, a sailor hurrying down it before the bottom had finished banging against the hull. Aarin waited at its top, Pasquanty with him, Mother Moude's chest on the deck between them. The deacon's seasickness ailed him yet, and his face was pale and green.

Trassan stood with his brother, watching the boat coming toward them. It cleared the deep sound, coming into the ocean swell that hid and revealed it. With each appearance coming closer, black-robed Guiders of Aarin's order bent at the oars. A rowing drum broke through the rushing of the surf on the rock. Once free, it became louder, stroke by stroke.

"I don't know what to say, Aarin," said Trassan. "Somehow, it was easier to say goodbye to everyone in Karsa."

"You were busy, they were many. This is a more intimate business."

The brothers grinned, and clasped one another in a tight embrace.

"Stay well, brother."

"And you, Trassan."

The rowing boat was coming along side. A painter was flung to the man at the bottom of the ladder, who scampered up to the deck and secured the rope to a bollard. Aarin swung one leg over the edge, and mounted the ladder. Hanging from the railing of the boat, he addressed his brother. "I wish you all the world's luck in your venture. I am afraid that you may need it."

"Maybe. If I'm lucky, the Drowned King will be the worst I have to face."

"If only that could be true. Be careful."

"When I'm done I'll stop by and pick you up," said Trassan. "I'll be sure to tell you all about it."

"I hope to be away some time before that, brother."

Trassan's smile faded into seriousness. "Goodbye, Guider Kressind."

"Goodbye, engineer."

The chest was lowered carefully overboard. Once it had been stowed on the long boat, Aarin descended the ladder toward the steel grey sea. At the bottom hands grasped his legs and guided them into the boat. Pasquanty followed, his desire to feel dry land beneath him bettering his terror of the water.

THE LEADER OF the rowers spoke, a quiet voice from the depths of his cowl. No hint of his face showed in the shadows. "Guider Kressind."

"I am he," said Aarin. "And my deacon, Pasquanty."

The hooded man sat motionless a moment, then spoke for the second and final time. "To shore then." The rowers grasped their oars and heaved against the surging swell, sending the boat skimming quickly over the water. Aarin turned from the *Prince Alfra* to watch the jagged slopes of the Final Isle grow over them.

The boat came to a slender jetty of blocks cut from the sharp black stone of the Island, one of five set at different levels in the rock. The boat bumped the stone, one of the rowers sprang ashore and secured the painter. Aarin and Pasquanty disembarked, Aarin overseeing the unloading of Mother Moude. They were shown to the base of a steep, switchback stair cut into the rock at the end of the jetty. The steps were clogged with weed and hollowed by the sea, in whose cups and cavities shore creatures waited for the tide.

At the summit, the wide, level plain of eroded stone awaited them, holed as floatstone, more rockpool than rock. A single path of cut stone went dead straight to shingled shores and a solitary mount of bright grass; that small piece of the Final Isle that remained permanently above the waves. A grim, windowless building crowned it.

Aarin turned back to take one last look at his brother's engine. From the top of the steps the iron ship was toy-like, an improbable lump of metal floating on an endless sea whose vastness threatened to swallow it without trace.

As if sensing Aarin's eyes upon it, the *Prince Alfra* sounded its horn. From its deck a lonely figure waved, hand held high. Perhaps it was Trassan, but Aarin could not be sure. He waved in return. White steam huffed from the funnels, lit underneath as blue as the hidden skies. The ship's paddlewheels turned once, twice, then quickly. With gathering speed, the iron ship turned to the south.

Aarin did not stay to watch it sail away. His own task was at hand, upon the Final Isle.

The cowled Guiders stepped aside, and he set his foot upon the path.

"Come, Pasquanty," he said.

NOTES ON THE
HUNDRED KINGDOMS

THERE ARE NEITHER One Hundred Kingdoms in the continent of Ruthnia, nor are they all kingdoms. Instead, the collection of Principalities, Duchies, Counties, City States, one Queendom and a number of actual Kingdoms make a total of ninety-five. That is thirty-nine major states, the forty-nine minor territories of the Olberlands and the seven free cities and statelets of the so-called Herring States, which occupy the mainland coast of the Sea of Karsa.

This territorial division is, it has to be noted, only one way of reckoning the numbers of the Hundred. Another is by the right or the custom of each country to send a representative to the Assembly of Nations in Perus. Farthia, for example, is one country divided into four semi-independent provinces, each of which has their own representative in the Grand House. Some states ordinarily send no representative, such as Kuzaki, which although nominally independent and having the right to do so, has such a tiny population it is administered mainly by Khushashia. Khushashia is sometimes divided into three separate entities by cartographers (near, north and Farside), and has in the past provided two representatives. To confuse matters, parts of Khushashia, such as northern Farside and The Black Sands, over which it claims suzerainty, lie outside the customarily agreed bounds of the Hundred. Whereas Maceriya, the most powerful of the Hundred, boasts three representatives, but could technically only be divided into two actual parts; the city of Perus, and the rest, the third representative being a holdover from its dim imperial past.

The Morfaan, long absent from the Earth in any numbers, also have two representatives present at the assembly, and so the hidden kingdom of their remaining few people is sometimes reckoned among the Hundred.

Many of the political entities in the Hundred are the fractured remnants of older empires. The Old Maceriyans ruled much of the west thousands of years past, and the people of Maceriya, Marceny, and Macer Lesser—as well as some other peoples—still self-identify as 'Maceriyan', even though their governments are often at loggerheads. Mohaci likewise dominated the southeast, although in much more recent times. There are provinces within both Mohaci and Maceriya that constantly lobby for their own independence, and they too are sometimes counted as individuals. Not only these imperial rumps states could be further broken down, but Toros is a federation of tribes, Suveren of principalities... And so it goes on.

Therefore, numerous manners of subdivision of the Hundred are possible, and numbers of the Hundred Kingdoms (or Hundred Lands, as some prefer) can be calculated at anything between eighty-three and one hundred and fourteen.

On the Geography of Ruthnia

THE EARTH IS circled by two moons and shares a common orbital point with its sister planet, most commonly named 'the Twin' in the Hundred's many tongues. The influence of these heavenly bodies upon the sea are responsible for the large variation in and complex nature of the tidal levels described in this book. The tidal range of the sea around Karsa's islands can be in the order of hundreds of feet, making for a very broad swathe of littoral that does not belong fully to either the land or the ocean. The sea can retreat tens of miles in places, while the rivers of Ruthnia are subject to tidal flow for most of their often considerable length. The Great River Olb is tidal all the way to Mohacs-Gravo, a distance of some one and a half thousand miles. In light of this, the map provided of the Hundred shows the water level at the highest or Great Tides. A map which showed the lowest tides would look considerably different. As those lands are in the main useless to the inhabitants of the Hundred, only areas that are always free of inundation are depicted.

Additionally, the Earth is much troubled by seismic upheaval. The geography of Ruthnia tends to upland, its rivers follow major faultlines. Actual mountain ranges are found only along the northern coasts, southern peninsulas, and the east, where the Appins fence off the hundred from the Black Sands. However, much of the rest of the continent is dominated by high plateau or rugged hill country that can be traversed only with difficulty. Even the plains of Khushashia and Maceriya are many hundreds of feet above sea level, and these are cleft by the Great River Olb and its many tributaries.

The extreme tidal nature of world's oceans dictates that sea travel is also not undertaken lightly, much of the coast is not particularly navigable, and so many lands of the Hundred have, at different times in their past, undergone periods of isolation.

The continent of Ruthnia occupies part of the southern hemisphere. North takes one towards the equator, south towards the pole.

On the Languages and Peoples of Ruthnia

THERE IS NO single common source of origin for the languages spoken within the Hundred, nor for the people that speak them. Since the sudden population of the continent in prehistory there has been much admixture of tongues, and the dominant languages of certain periods, most notably Maceriyan, have evolved into distinct language families of their own. These can exhibit marked differences to one another, having absorbed features from various original populations, but they share a common root nonetheless.

The other tongues are startlingly diverse, and despite large numbers of loanwords, principally from Maceriyan (high and low), they remain very different. This diversity of speech within the Hundred has been largely preserved by the difficult geography of the continent.

Six main languages are in wide use across the Hundred today:

High Maceriyan – The language of the ancient Old Maceriyans, much influenced by the Morfaan. In this era it is primarily a language of learned discourse and high government, but is falling out of fashion.

Low Maceriyan – The modern language of Maceriya and Macer Lesser is the lingua franca of the Hundred, and used across the length and breadth of the continent, excepting the southeast.

Hethikan – The ancient language of the far north, another language of learning, also falling out of use.

Khusiacki – The sheer size of Khushashia means that Khusiacki is spoken in many places. The languages around it form a rare continuum and are mostly mutually intelligible with one another.

Mohacin – Used for over five hundred years as the administrative language of the Mohacin Imperium, it is this rather than Maceriyan that is used both as the lingua franca and language of learning in the southeast.

Karsarin – Owing to the rapid industrialisation of Karsa a century ago, and the export of expertise and huge amount of trade this engendered, Karsarin is increasingly heard in the mercantile hubs of the Hundred and beyond.

All languages have been rendered into English where spoken by individuals who can comprehend them. I have taken the liberty of altering the writing style slightly when Maceriyan is being spoken. Similarly, the retention of the likes of 'Kressind/Kressinda' is intended to indicate the highly inflected nature of Karsarin.

Khusiacki is the most often heard language spoken by one person but not understood by another. For this I have chosen a modified Slavic, although the true language little resembles it.

Similarly the names have been adapted. Zhinsky's true name is not alone in being virtually impossible to transliterate into a Latin alphabet, and is similarly difficult to pronounce. Some names are close to the original, others have been invented for ease of rendition and to heighten regional contrasts that might not be obvious to speakers of English. You must therefore lay the blame for any inconsistency or error at my door, should you come across either.

As 'the Earth' is what the inhabitants of Ruthnia call their homeworld, that is what I have chosen to call it. There are other, high-speech words for it, but as we do not wander around calling our Earth 'Terra' (and indeed, Terra is only 'Earth' in Latin), neither do they do the equivalent. No confusion is intended; this is not our world.

On the Correct form of Address

IN KARSA, ONE addresses those of a high social rank as "Goodfellow" or "Goodlady" and those of a lower to you as "Goodman" or "Goodwife" for married women and those over thirty, and "Goodmaid" for unmarried women under thirty. The addition of "Good" to a person's occupation, ie "Goodmage", "Goodengineer" is suitable when dealing with someone who is of equal or slightly higher status than oneself, but whose profession or standing demands a higher level of respect. "Goodlady" and "Goodfellow" should always be used when dealing with the nobility.

Similar conventions exist across The Hundred, although the titles differ, and in some places there are numerous levels of degree and associated titles. For the sake of simplicity, I have stuck with the Karsan standard throughout.

On Dragons and Draconics

THERE ARE A number of varieties of what might be called 'draconic' creatures in Ruthnia, ie six-limbed, reptilian creatures, ranging from sparrow-sized up to an animal similar to our mythical dragon. In a few remote areas of the Hundred this clade of creatures dominates, in most they are increasingly rare. Only a few have been successfully domesticated by humanity and so prosper alongside them. Chief among these is the riding dragon or 'dracon', a medium, bipedal animal with a large fore pair of grasping limbs and a lesser middle pair. There are several sub-breeds of dracon, mainly distinguished by their size, colouring and the amount of feathers they bear.

Too dangerous for day-to-day use, dracons are employed exclusively by the armed forces in more civilised realms, although in wilder places they are utilised as a common riding beast. As the dracon is the draconic creature most commonly encountered by people in the Hundred, in Karsarin and Maceriyan, the term 'dracon' has come to be applied to all draconics excepting dragonlings and the dragons themselves.

Of course, the use of the word dracon in this English text is my conceit, intended to convey a sense of the beast in question.

Of the Tyn

WHO THE TYN are and where they come from are topics much speculated upon by the philosophs of the Hundred.

There are many, many kinds of Tyn, but the most noticeable divide is between the Lesser and the Greater Tyn. Lesser Tyn vary widely in individual appearance but tend to be between ten centimetres and (rarely) a metre in height. The majority of the 'Wild Tyn', meaning those that are innately dangerous or are antagonistic to humanity, are of this sort. The Greater Tyn are larger, and though they lack humanity's homogeneity, their numerous clans and tribal groupings are far more easily reconcilable as stemming from the same stock. The vast majority of Greater Tyn dwell in Karsa. There are scattered populations—rumoured and genuine—of Lesser Tyn throughout the Hundred. In Karsa only do either sort dwell side by side with humans, albeit in circumstances little better than slavery.

ACKNOWLEDGEMENTS

THERE ARE AUTHORS who insist the only way to tell a truthful story is to mine one's own life for incident, and ruthlessly. I have shied away from this practice, fearing, I think, to reveal too much of my inner self, and not wishing to embarrass those I know.

For *The Iron Ship*, however, I decided to abandon this stand. Therefore, this story that you hold in your hands is the most personal I have written.

I come from a large family very much like the Kressinds. The characters of the brothers are drawn to degree from those of my own siblings. All of them are talented, capable, and ambitious people. Some are closer to their real-world counterparts than others, but these are not intended to be accurate portraits. I've borrowed characteristics, melted them down, and recast them as new people. No matter how talented a writer, it is virtually impossible to truthfully capture an entire person, with all their contradictions, flaws and qualities, on the page. Even if people stayed forever the same—and they don't—so much of what we believe to be true about anybody, even ourselves, is also mutable, and always subjective.

So don't worry, boys, these people aren't you. Even had I intended it, they couldn't possibly be so.

Primarily they are not the same because of their upbringing. Our father and mother are the opposites of the Kressinds. Our father is good-natured rather than bitter, our mother is strong rather than weak. Both offer us valuable guidance and support instead of pressure. Our father, like Gelbion Kressind, suffers a disabling illness. However, my own father's reaction to his misfortune is utterly at odds with Kressind senior's. Although his life has been much altered by his condition, our dad has borne his with a fortitude and good humour that I find deeply inspiring.

It goes without saying that we all love you very much, mum and dad. But sometimes it should be said.

What I have tried to capture accurately is the deep affection between my siblings and I. Part of my intention with this novel was to explore a family that was as close as mine, but who had been raised in very different circumstances. I'm glad to see that they stuck together.

Another personal element here is Guis Kressind's 'ailment of the nerves'. In our world he would be diagnosed with obsessive compulsive disorder. I suffered from this condition for twenty years, during which time it affected me severely. Although I was able maintain the appearance of sanity—until, of course, I couldn't—it dominated my life.

I am extremely lucky that I recovered more or less completely. Guis's story is, to an extent, an exploration of my experiences. Although in his fictional world the consequences are of a far higher order, the fear is the same and all too real. If you are afflicted by this pernicious and debilitating betrayal of the self, take heart, it is possible to get better.

Thanks are also due to the brilliant team at Solaris who have encouraged and praised me, and most importantly of all, like my writing enough to give me a chance. To Jon Oliver in particular, I owe the warmest gratitude.

PAUL KEARNEY'S
THE MONARCHIES OF GOD

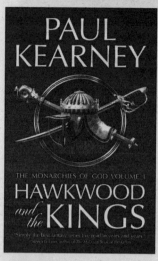

VOLUME ONE

HAWKWOOD AND THE KINGS

ISBN: (UK) 978 1 906735 70 8 • £8.99
ISBN: (US) 978 1 906735 71 5 • $9.99

For Richard Hawkwood and his crew, a desperate venture to carry refugees to the uncharted land across the Great Western Ocean offers the only chance of escape from the Inceptines' pyres.

In the East, Lofantyr, Abeleyn and Mark – three of the five Ramusian Kings – have defied the cruel pontiff's purge and must fight to hold their thrones through excommunication, intrigue and civil war.

In the quiet monastery city of Charibon, two humble monks make a discovery that will change the whole world...

"One of the best fantasy works in ages."
– SFX

VOLUME TWO

CENTURY OF THE SOLDIER

ISBN: (UK) 978 1 907519 08 6 • £8.99
ISBN: (US) 978 1 907519 09 3 • $9.99

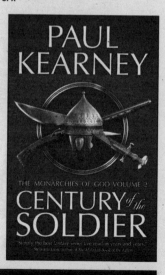

Hebrion's young King Abeleyn lies in a coma, his capital in ruins and his former lover conniving for the throne. Corfe Cear-Inaf is given a ragtag command of savages and sent on a mission he cannot hope to succeed. Richard Hawkwood finally returns to the Monarchies of God, bearing news of a wild new continent.

In the West the Himerian Church is extending its reach, while in the East the fortress of Ormann Dyke stands ready to fall to the Merduk horde. These are terrible times, and call for extraordinary people...

"Simply the best fantasy series I've read in years and years."

– Steven Erikson, author of the
Malazan Book of the Fallen

ROWENA CORY DANIELLS

BESIEGED

EXILE

SANCTUARY

The FALL *of* FAIR ISLE

BROKEN VOWS • DARK DREAMS • DESPERATE ALLIANCES

'Well-drawn characters, a ruthless streak to the
plotting, weighty themes... pleasingly complex.'
SFX on *Besieged*

It has been six hundred years since Imoshen the First, Causare of the T'En, brought her beleaguered people across the seas to Fair Isle. The magical folk mixed with the natives, bringing culture and sophistication, and made the island one of the wealthiest, most powerful nations in the known world.

But all glory is temporary. The Ghebites, savage barbarians from the warm north, have rolled over the mainland, conquering all in their path, and now they have taken Fair Isle. Imoshen, namesake of the first Empress and the last pure-blooded T'En woman, is all that survives of that great heritage. Now, just seventeen years of age, she must offer herself to the Ghebite General, Tulkhan, and do what she can to ensure her survival, and that of her people.

One other T'En survives: Reothe, Imoshen's betrothed, newly returned from adventuring on the high seas. As the T'En warrior foments rebellion against Tulkhan in secret, Imoshen must choose, both as a woman and as a leader, between a past now lost and an uncertain futureε

This volume collects *Broken Vows*, *Dark Dreams* and *Desperate Alliances* for the first time.

GAIL Z. MARTIN'S
THE CHRONICLES OF THE NECROMANCER

BOOK THREE
DARK HAVEN

ISBN: (UK) 978 1 84416 708 1 • £7.99
ISBN: (US) 978 1 84416 598 8 • $7.99

The kingdom of Margolan lies in ruin. Martris Drayke, the new king, must rebuild his country in the aftermath of battle, while a new war looms on the horizon. Meanwhile Jonmarc Vahanian is now the Lord of Dark Haven, and there is defiance from the vampires of the *Vayash Moru* at the prospect of a mortal leader.

But can he earn their trust, and at what cost?

"A fast-paced tale laced with plenty of action."

– SF Site

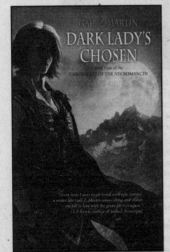

BOOK FOUR
DARK LADY'S CHOSEN

ISBN: (UK) 978 1 84416 830 9 • £7.99
ISBN: (US) 978 1 84416 831 6 • $7.99

Treachery and blood magic threaten King Martris Drayke's hold on the throne he risked everything to win. As the battle against a traitor lord comes to its final days, war, plague and betrayal bring Margolan to the brink of destruction. Civil war looms in Isencroft. And in Dark Haven, Lord Jonmarc Vahanian has bargained his soul for vengeance as he leads the *vayash moru* against a dangerous rogue who would usher in a future drenched in blood.

"Just when you think you know where things are heading, Martin pulls another ace from her sleeve."

– A. J. Hartley, author of The Mask of Atraeus

JAMES MAXEY

GREATSHADOW

BOOK ONE of the DRAGON APOCALYPSE

The warrior woman known as Infidel is legendary for her superhuman strength and skin tough as chain mail. She's made few friends during her career as a sword-for-hire, and many powerful enemies. Following the death of her closest companion, Infidel finds herself weary of life as a mercenary and sets her eyes on one final prize that will allow her to live out the rest of her days in luxury, the priceless treasure trove of Greatshadow.

Greatshadow is the primal dragon of fire. His malign intelligence spies upon mankind through every flickering candle, patiently waiting to devour victims careless with even the smallest flame. The Church of the Book has assembled a team of twelve battle-hardened adventurers to slay the dragon once and for all. But tensions run high between the leaders of the quest who view the mission as a holy duty and the super-powered mercenaries who add power to their ranks, who dream only of Greatshadow's vast wealth. If the warriors fail to slay the beast, will they doom mankind to death by fire?

"Maxey's newest novel plunges us into one of the most extravagantly fantastical worlds I've ever seen... this one is worth reading right now."
— Orson Scott Card

WWW.SOLARISBOOKS.COM

Follow us on Twitter @solarisbooks

BOOK ONE OF THE CURSED KINGDOMS TRILOGY

THE
SENTINEL
MAGE
EMILY GEE

"An addictive story."
SFX Magazine on Thief With No Shadow

In a distant corner of the Seven Kingdoms, an ancient curse festers and grows, consuming everything in its path. Only one man can break it: Harkeld of Osgaard, a prince with mage's blood in his veins. But Prince Harkeld has a bounty on his head - and assassins at his heels.

Innis is a gifted shapeshifter. Now she must do the forbidden: become a man. She must stand at Prince Harkeld's side as his armsman, protecting and deceiving him. But the deserts of Masse are more dangerous than the assassins hunting the prince. The curse has woken deadly creatures, and the magic Prince Harkeld loathes may be the only thing standing between him and death.

"Dark and compelling...
Emily Gee is a storyteller to watch!"
— *New York Times* Best-Selling Author Nalini Singh